Z RESURRECTED

RESURRECTED

DANA FREDSTI
TOM LEVEEN
JOE MCKINNEY
ERIC A. SHELMAN
MARK TUFO
T.M. WILLIAMS

Cover Design: Jason Vollario

Half-Light Publishing
ISBN-13: 978-0692556160 (Custom)
ISBN-10: 0692556168
BISAC: Fiction / Anthologies

"I don't think anyone wants to cuddle with a zombie."
- Norman Reedus

INTRODUCTION

There are anthologies and then there are resurrected zombie anthologies. The only thing deadlier than a zombie are the one's that keep coming back from the dead… again.

CONTENTS

PINKY SWEAR

By Dana Fredsti

www.danafredsti.com

*B*alancing on the rickety stepladder inside George's Zoo Deli and Market, Luke peered out the top of the window above the store's front doors. He'd left a piece of wood unsecured at one end so he and his three fellow survivors could lift it and check outside to see if the coast was clear.

So far, it hadn't been. He knew that even before he'd climbed up to check. You'd have to be deaf not to hear the low, insistent moans and the sounds of shuffling feet moving slowly down the sidewalk and streets outside the store.

Zombies... walkers... whatever you wanted to call them. They were reanimated corpses with a big appetite for human flesh.

And wasn't that fucked up?

"Are they gone?"

Jenna peered up at Luke, brown eyes wide and hopeful. He had to bite back the impulse to snap something snarky like "Yeah, and like all the moaning and shit you hear is just people on their way to the zoo to check out the lemurs."

But he didn't. Because not only would it be a lousy thing to say, but if Jenna didn't wallop him for it, Phil would. Either way, it would hurt.

So Luke curbed his irritation and kept his reply to a simple, "No."

Jenna gave a little hitching sob, doing her best to swallow the noise before it came out. Phil, her uncle, and the owner of George's Zoo, put an arm around her.

"Hey, you hear the one about the dyslexic devil worshipper?"

Jenna shook her head. Phil had an apparently endless supply of jokes, good and bad, and had been pulling them out at random in an attempt to cheer her up.

"He sold his soul to Santa."

Jenna tried to laugh, but all that came out was another weird little choked off sob.

"It's okay," Phil said quietly. "We'll get out of this. At least we have a safe place to stay, right? And we have plenty of food. How many places you think have a generator? Not a lot. We're okay for a while."

Jenna nodded, surreptitiously wiping her eyes before tears fell.

Luke saw Jenna brush away tears and felt even shittier for his earlier impulse to snap at her. She could handle the toughest customers George's Zoo had to offer and he knew she didn't want anyone to see her cry. She'd seen her father die and

15

come back, several of their regular customers torn to pieces ... but she still managed to hold things together enough to help them board up the place. She deserved some patience.

As if on cue, rotting hands slapped against the front doors, demanding entrance. Jenna and Phil looked at each other. They knew who it was.

Aaron had just stopped by George's to visit his daughter and brother, have a cup of coffee and a sandwich, and shoot the breeze with some of the regular customers. They'd been talking outside when one of the local homeless guys, Sod -- short for 'skeevy old dude' -- had shuffled up.

A meth-head, Sod was always trying to sell staff and customers old baseball cards or toys or whatever he'd picked out of a dumpster. With the rotting teeth and walking cadaver appearance of a long-term tweaker, Sod generally looked like shit, but he'd looked even worse than usual this time. The whites of his eyes had gone all yellow with streaks of red, breath rattling like marbles in a can, smelling as rancid as a sour milk and shit cocktail. Then he'd gone into convulsions, dropping to the ground as black fluid and blood streamed out of his mouth, nose and eyes.

Aaron had barely finished dialing 911 when Sod had died... and then woken back up to take a bite out of Aaron's right calf. Aaron had screamed and collapsed on the ground with pain and shock. Sod took advantage of thisand ripped a hunk out of Aaron's neck and then turned his attentions to Sean and Jim, two other George's regulars unlucky enough to be there.

By the time Phil grabbed a crowbar from the back of the store and cracked Sod's skull with one powerful swing, his brother was dead on the pavement with Jenna screaming over his prone body. Sean and Jim were bleeding from bite wounds and more fucked up dead things like Sod were lurching and crawling towards the entrance to George's Zoo. Phil had dragged his niece back into the store and slammed the doors shut, but not before they both saw Aaron's eyes open and watched him fall on Sean and Jim before they could run.

The hands slapped again, plaintive moans filtering through the locked doors.

Dylan, the part-time counter help, looked up from his men's magazine. Normally clean-cut except for a wild mop of dark hair, Dylan hadn't washed or used deodorant in days. He grinned, a piece of lettuce stuck between his front teeth. "Guess your dad's here for dinner, Jenna."

Jenna gave Dylan a stricken look and ran into the depths of the store, vanishing behind plastic crates and stacks of wine boxes. Dylan smiled and went back to his magazine.

Luke took a step towards Dylan, fists clenched, but Phil stopped him with a hand on one shoulder. "No point," he said. Luke knew he was right, but still...

Dylan had gotten ahold of his mom on her cell phone the first night ... and heard the sounds of her being ripped to pieces along with his brother. Something in

Dylan's mind had fractured, turning the formerly sweet kid who'd have punched himself in the face before hurting Jenna, into a borderline nut job in the space of two days.

Luke's fists slowly unclenched. "I'll go check on Jenna."

Phil nodded. "Yeah. I'd appreciate that. Maybe check the door into the garage too, make sure it's still okay."

"Right."

Luke checked the back door first. It led into the garage of the apartment building next door and above the store. They'd pushed the large trash, recycle and compost bins in front of it, piling up crates as well to keep those things from pushing it open if they figured out there was food on the other side. Luckily it opened inwards. If it'd opened towards the garage, Luke doubted a few plastic bins would keep the zombies out. Everything was still in place, though, and so far as far as Luke could tell, the garage wasn't a popular zombie hangout.

He went to check on Jenna next, finding her at the back of the store in what they jokingly called 'the atrium.' The size of a small elevator, the space was enclosed on all four sides with a four foot by four foot sliding glass window leading in and out of it. The walls ended two stories up and the top was open to the sky other than a wide meshed screen. They'd stuck a couple of folding chairs, an upside down crate serving as a little table.

Luke pushed aside the plastic to find Jenna seated on one of the chairs, staring up at the rapidly fading light. "You okay?" he asked, sitting down across from her. He remembered to breathe through his mouth. The smell filtering down from outside was foul.

"I know he can't help it," she said. "But it still sucks."

"Dylan, he doesn't..." Luke searched for the right words to excuse the inexcusable. He couldn't find any.

Jenna gave a sad smile. "Yeah."

The sudden sound of footsteps on the roof had them both on their feet in an instant. Luke stood so abruptly that his chair tipped over backwards with a painfully loud clatter.

If some of those things had gotten up there, maybe from the three-story apartment that butted up against the store, man, they would be so screwed.

"Hey! You guys dead or alive down there?"

Jenna and Luke looked up to see a guy dressed in what could only be described as informal SWAT gear crouched down on one side of the atrium ledge. He looked as carefree as someone out for an afternoon stroll. Luke eyed him warily. What the hell was this dude doing on the roof?

The stranger grinned. "Well, you're not jumping up and down trying to eat me, so I'll guess alive. How many of you are there?"

"Who wants to know?" Luke knew he sounded truculent, but this guy could *be — and probably was — a total nut job. Who knew what he might do?*

"Name's JT," the guy said cheerfully.

Luke and Jenna exchanged glances. Jenna gave a slight nod.

"There's four of us," she said.

"Why are you on the roof?" Luke had to know.

JT – if that was his name – shrugged. "Easiest way to move around outside and stay alive. There's a shit ton of zombies out here, and more headed this way."

Jenna blanched. "More of them?"

JT's grin faded.

"Sorry. That's my bad. I'm leading them away from my team."

"Well, that's just great," Luke snapped. "Thanks a hell of a lot."

"The police are going to be sending rescue teams, right?" Jenna looked at the stranger with huge hopeful eyes.

He shook his head. "They're in the same sinking boat with everyone else. Shit's really hit the fan big time. This stuff's gone global."

Jenna gave a choked sob. Luke almost echoed it, his heart dropping into his Doc Martens.

JT frowned. "Look. I might be able to help, but you'll have to wait at least a few days, maybe longer. Trust me when I say this is one of those 'the good of the many outweighs the good of the few' situations."

"Why should we trust you at all?" Luke wasn't ready to cut any slack.

"Because I'm one of the good guys. So are the people I'm working with. Mostly." Then, "You guys have enough food to hold out for a while?"

"We'll be okay for a few days," Luke said, purposefully vague just in case this guy was scouting for potential caches of food and supplies. "But we'll need to get out of here soon."

"I'll do my best." JT stood up, flexing his knees as if warming up for a run, and turned to leave.

"Hey!"

He stopped, and turned back, looking down at Jenna, who stared up at him with fierce hope. "Promise you'll come back."

JT nodded slowly, as if considering something.

"Okay. Yeah. I can't say when, but I swear I will do my best to come back." He turned to leave, then stopped again. "Unless I'm dead. And then you probably wouldn't want me to anyway, right?"

More moans rose, the sound muffled by the fog. JT looked out over the roof.

"I gotta go meet my team. But first I'll see if I can get some of these dead-heads away from your front door." He flashed his carefree grin and then bounded away with a war whoop that must have been audible for blocks.

"Wow." Jenna's expression could only be described as hero-worship.

"Don't get your hopes up, Jenna," Luke cautioned. "Even if he's on the level, the odds of him staying alive out there? Not good."

Jenna didn't answer. She was too busy staring up at the foggy sky like a kid waiting for Santa to come down the chimney.

Luke didn't believe in Santa Claus either.

*   *   *

"Tell me again why we're doing this?"

I looked at JT, who sat across from me. He wore his trademark red paisley bandana by way of a hat and a blue tank top that said *"I flexed and the sleeves fell off"* on the front.

Typical JT.

What was atypical of my hyper, free-running pal, however, was the focus with which he studied the San Francisco city map spread out on the cafeteria table between us. He held a highlighter in one hand, using it to mark a path from USCF – our current location -- to the southwest tip of the city, out by the zoo.

"Because I made a promise."

I snorted. "What, did you, like pinky swear or something? Because I've made promises before and unless you pinky swear, I don't think they count."

"I don't do pinky swears," he said. "The size of my pinky is enough to intimidate normal men and women." Before I could deliver another retort, he continued, "In my world, a verbal promise is the same as a signed contract. If you don't want to help, I'll go by myself. Not like I haven't parkoured the shit out of this city before, right?"

I nodded. "Fair enough. But here's another question for you. How do you expect to get them back here?"

JT shrugged. "Not sure yet. But better to try than let them starve to death where they are, right?"

"What about asking for help?"

"I did. I asked you."

I rolled my eyes. "I meant, like, asking Colonel Paxton. Like, helicopter borrowing type help. It's not like helping rescue survivors isn't part of our mission statement, right?"

JT cocked his head to one side and considered my words. "Well," he said, "I didn't think about asking Scary-Ass mo-fo Paxton 'cause I kind of assumed he'd say no."

I raised an eyebrow. "I have to say, I'm kinda surprised at this unexpected jellyfish backbone of yours. I mean, for someone who's not afraid of barreling through streets and up walls onto roofs like a monkey on angel dust while in the middle of a full on zombie apocalypse, you're pretty much being a wuss when it comes to Paxton."

JT regarded me unapologetically over the map. "Did I mention 'scary ass mo-fo?'"

He had a point. Paxton was, as far as I could tell, an honorable man, but when it came to ethics, he was definitely a "needs of the many outweighs the needs of the few" type person. I'm more Kirk than Spock on this issue, so it's not surprising we'd butted heads when Lil and I had gone rogue, so to speak, to rescue Lil's cats without permission. We'd brought back valuable Intel along with two overweight felines, but Paxton had threatened to have us locked up if we did anything like it again and I had no doubt he'd been totally serious.

Which meant if I wanted to help JT – and I really did because I had to do something that made a difference to someone, somewhere, or I'd go crazy – I needed to talk to Paxton.

Damn.

I heaved a sigh. "You want me to talk to Dad for you?"

"Would you? He's always liked you best."

"Fine," I grumbled. "But you're coming with me. And I need more coffee first."

" " "

JT gave a slight mental sigh of relief when Ashley left the table to get a cup of java to go. He liked Ashley. The girl was smoking hot and a veritable zombie-killing machine, but her level of sarcasm sometimes made his look normal and reasonable. Not an easy thing to do. And since they'd returned from San Diego, she'd been worse than usual.

One of the reasons he'd asked Ash to help him was because she'd seemed… well… lost ever since Lil's Mom had turned up. Looking after Lil had been the one thing Ashley could hold onto after the search for Gabriel had ended with a possible cure for the Walker's, … and Gabriel's death. Not even a Sophie's Choice type thing either. Just a real fucktard stepping in to make the world a shittier place by taking out one of the good guys for no other reason than vengeance. JT wished the guy was still alive so he could kill him, even though Ash had done the job herself.

At any rate, he was pretty sure her current ratcheted 'goes to eleven' level was an emotional buffer to keep from being hurt by anything else. He also sensed that trying to talk to her about it would be pointless. No, the girl needed a good old-fashioned

20

rescue mission: to get out there, save a few people, and kick some zombie ass.

Zombies. They'd gone from the ginger-haired stepchild of the pop cultural monster world, to the belles of the Horror Ball, to the probable end of the human race. And didn't that just suck? Unless, of course, Professor Fraser, Dr. Arkin and her associate Dr. "Crazypants" Albert could perfect that vaccine they were working on.

According to Ash, there was at least a decent chance they could whip something into shape that would bolster people's resistance to the zombie virus. JT wouldn't mind that, although he'd prefer the full on immunity plus enhanced senses and abilities that wild cards like Ash had.

"Ready?" Ash returned, a to-go coffee cup in each hand. "Black, right?" She plunked one down in front of him. The kind of thoughtful gesture he hadn't seen from her in a while.

JT gave himself a little mental pat on the back. Yup, a good old-fashioned rescue mission was just what the doctor ordered.

* * *

"You're asking for a helicopter to fly you across San Francisco on the off chance these people are still alive, and then bring them back here to take up our resources?"

JT and I sat near Colonel Paxton and Simon in the first floor briefing room, Paxton at his usual place of power at the head of the large conference table. JT had the map of San Francisco spread out in front of them.

"Yessir, that's about it."

I could tell JT wanted to punch Colonel Paxton in the chops even though he kept a big smile on his face. Or maybe I was just projecting my own violent urges here. I definitely wanted to hit him.

"Isn't our job to find survivors and see that they get to a secure facility?" I stared at Colonel Paxton coolly, then added, "Or is that just something we're telling the surviving media for good press?"

Yeah, if there was a Geiger counter for sarcasm, it'd be doing that clicking shit right off the charts. I didn't care.

Paxton matched my cool look and lowered the temperature to arctic. "Yes, Miss Parker, that's part of our mission."

Unfazed by the polar chill, I leaned in and said, "Then let us do this."

"Point of fact, Miss Parker," Paxton replied, "is that one of our helicopters is currently being utilized for just those purposes across the

21

bay in Marin, and the other is ferrying supplies from our base at Big Red. There won't be one available until tomorrow morning."

I turned to JT. "So we make our way there on foot, see if your peeps are still alive, and then call for extraction."

"Works for me."

Simone frowned.

"JT, you do realize Ash and the rest of the wild cards have enhanced night vision. So what might be easy for them could be a fatal stumbling block for you."

"I've got great night vision," JT said with a shrug. "And I know San Francisco. Part of the challenge – and the fun of free running - is practicing in all types of weather, night and day. No offense, Ash, but I can run circles around you when it comes to getting from Point A to Point Z."

I couldn't argue with him.

"Professor Fraser, may I have a word with you?" Paxton walked out of the room without waiting for a reply. Simone gave me an apologetic glance before following him out.

"Guess he doesn't want us to hear whatever he has to say."

"They couldn't just whisper on the other side of the room?" JT started tapping his foot impatiently.

I pointed at one of my ears. "Wild card hearing, remember?"

Whatever Paxton had to discuss with Simone, it didn't take very long, maybe five minutes. That was a good thing 'cause JT didn't do waiting very well and he was likely to start climbing the walls. Literally.

Simone and Paxton sat back down at the table, Simone taking the seat closest to mine.

"We haven't set you out on any of the rescue missions because we thought it was too soon after… well, after what happened at Point Cabrillo."

I bristled visibly. Simone put a hand on my arm and looked at me apologetically.

"Ashley, you went through so very much. We wanted you to have a chance to heal, both physically and emotionally, before asking you to go back out into the field. I realize now that perhaps this wasn't the best decision for you. I'm sorry."

Talk about taking the wind out of my self-righteous sails.

Paxton turned to JT.

"What route are you proposing to take, son?"

JT swiveled the highlighted map towards Paxton.

22

"Under normal circumstances," he said, "the quickest route from here would be a straight shot down Kirkham to Sunset, then up Sunset to Sloat, then Sloat to 44th."

"Good thinking," Paxton said neutrally.

"Yeah," said JT, "but given the shit ton of people who live in the inner and outer Sunset and who are probably now zombies, I'm thinking the open space reserve in back of UCSF here might be a safer bet. We might run into a few zoms, sure, but not as many. Then we hook up with Crestmont Drive above the reservoir, and then cut across Laguna Honda to the chichi neighborhood above West Portal." He flashed a grin at me. "I can never remember the name. Anyway, from there, we hit Stern Grove from beginning to end, and take our chances on the best route the rest of the way."

Paxton nodded slowly. "Not bad, son. Not bad at all."

"I figure I can run any distraction needed to keep the zoms off Ash." JT grinned at me. "Up to and including twerking."

I groaned, remembering JT's impromptu twerk-a-thon on a roof when Nathan Tony and I needed some time to raid a Walgreen's and make our way to a rendezvous point.

Oh well, it had worked, right?

"Very well. "Colonel Paxton sat down. "You'll take radios and contact us when you've arrived, and let us know how many survivors we'll be extracting. We'll send at least one sharpshooter to help clear out an area for landing and keep the dead at bay while you board the helicopter."

Simone cleared her throat. We all looked at her.

"Ashley," she said, "you shouldn't be alone on the ground if JT goes bounding off into the ramparts. Both Colonel Paxton and I would feel more comfortable if you took one other wild card with you as well," he said.

"Fine by me," I shrugged. "Which one?"

"Well, Gentry and--" Simone smoothed her perfectly coifed blond hair in an almost unconscious gesture. "--Nathan went with the helicopter to Redwood Grove," Simone said, stumbling almost unperceptively over the name of her sort of kind of boyfriend's name. I say 'sort of kind of' 'cause they were still working through past history and hadn't figured their present shit out yet.

"Nathan has a lot of ordinance at his compound," Simone continued. "Colonel Paxton thought it would be best to bring it here."

I grinned. I'd been at Nathan's compound with the rest of my team before we defended Big Red against a zombie swarm and I'd seen his gunroom. To say his weapons collection was a survivalist's wet dream didn't do it justice. He'd been loaded for bear. Big honking prehistoric cave bears. And possibly T-Rexes too.

"Okay." I weighed our options. "So that leaves Lil and Tony. And it can't be Lil. We'll be right by the zoo. Last thing we need is her haring off to feed the animals."

"Or let them out of their cages," Simone said.

"I think someone already did that," JT said. "I'm pretty sure I saw lions in the parking lot last time I was over there."

I groaned. "Great. So lions and tigers and zombies, oh my?"

"Possibly. "

"Okay fine. Tony it is."

JT looked uncomfortable.

"Um, he kind of took a bad fall yesterday when I was showing him some parkour moves. His wrist is kinda fubar at the moment."

"And he was going to tell me this when?" Simone raised an eyebrow, once again making me wonder if there was a Vulcan in the woodshed of her family tree.

"I think he was waiting for it to heal on its own."

Simone heaved a beleaguered sigh. "I'll go take a look at it when we're finished here."

"I feel obliged to point out," I pointed out, "that this pretty much leaves us with me and JT."

Colonel Paxton raised an eyebrow. "Aren't you forgetting someone?"

*   *   *

"So why are we doing this?" Griff sauntered next to Ashley as they walked with JT down the corridor of the sleeping quarters towards the elevator.

"Because JT made a promise to some cute young thing." Ash flashed JT a wicked grin. "I believe they pinky swore."

JT shot Ash a look. "While yes, the young lady in question was undeniably cute, I like to think I'd have promised regardless."

"Fair enough," Griff said with a lazy shrug.

All three wore the modified SWAT type gear of joined Kevlar armor covering black BDUs, long sleeved shirts and portable radios. Ash and Griff had firearms and hand weapons. Other than a lightly loaded backpack and a long coil of rope slung crosswise around his shoulder and waist, JT went empty handed. His ability to stay above and away from the zoms was his best defense. He had also made his own modifications in clothing to allow him the freedom of movement needed for parkour, including shoes with more traction and give than Ash and Griff's lace-up black boots.

Griff also wore an undeniably smug expression. He reminded JT of a cat. And while JT liked cats as a general rule, Griff had the more irritating characteristics that cat haters accused all felines of possessing, including a bad habit of biting the hand that fed him.

If he had any loyalty or attachment, though, even JT could see that it was for Ashley. Griff had saved her life twice in San Diego, lying about it the second time to protect her. He hadn't done the same favor for the rest of the wild cards, but then again, he'd found Lil after she'd run off to the San Diego Zoo, all because he'd promised Ash that he would.

Griff might not lift a finger to help anyone else, but at least Ash would have reliable backup. And JT would happily take care of his own safety. So maybe he wasn't the worst person to include on this little expedition.

JT also found it interesting that the two looked so much alike, with vivid green eyes, dark brown hair, and strong, angular features. Kind of like if Jamie and Cersei Lannister had been brunette instead of blond. And if Cersei saved lives instead of taking them.

Oh well, not the best comparison but what the fuck. It'd do, pig. It'd do.

They reached the elevator, taking it to the top floor, where they went through a deceptively bland lobby to the super secret elevator in and out of the DZN Laboratory facility. They rode it up to a glass-enclosed walkway that linked the Center for Regenerative Medicine and one of the medical buildings at UCSF.

Griff started to hit the button that would summon yet another elevator that led to loading docks and a parking lot at ground level, but JT held up one hand.

"Not that way."

Griff visibly bristled. JT didn't give a shit. This was his party, his charter.

"Why not?" Ash asked. "I mean, what other choice to we have?"

JT pointed over the loading docks to the locked steel gates, all that kept a metric shit ton of zombies from swarming over the drive and loading docks below.

"No way to get out the gates without attracting too much attention."

Ash nodded. "Or getting eaten."

"That too."

Griff folded his arms. "Which way then, smart man?"

JT flashed his manic grin. "I hope neither of you is afraid of heights."

Ash looked at him warily. "I prefer to think of it as a sensible respect. Why?"

JT's grin got even wider. "Don't worry. It'll be fun!"

* * *

Clinging to a strut on the far side of the Center for Regenerative Medicine — what was essentially a glass and metal enclosed platform -- I made my way slowly towards the ground below, concentrating on looking in every direction but down.

This was not my idea of fun. Eating gelato on a hot summer is fun. Watching bad movies with good friends and lots of alcohol is fun. Hell, even thwacking the heads of zombies could be considered a good time. But climbing down a network of metal supports from forty feet above the ground?

So not fun. Maybe even anti-fun.

Then again, if I fell and died, at least I wouldn't hurt so much any more.

JT and Griff were already waiting for me in the shadow of pine and eucalyptus trees in the nature reserve, hidden from sight of the zombies clustered around the gates. A few stumbled aimlessly up the drive in our general direction, but obviously weren't aware of the potential meal lurking in the woods.

My foot slipped on the cold metal and I barely stifled a gasp as I slid down a foot or so much faster than planned, my sheathed katana and tanto smacking against one of the struts with a loud clang. Between the swords, my M4 and my Ruger, I made more noise than a nest of rattlesnakes.

Shit.

Stopping my all too rapid descent by grabbing for a vertical piece of metal. My hand did not thank me for having to suddenly bear all my body weight, even for a few seconds. The edge of the strut dug into my palm and it hurt, even with the leather padding on my glove.

Crap crappity crap!

Okay, fine, I wasn't ready to die yet. On the other hand, I would *so* kill JT if I didn't end up in an Ashley shaped splat. Of course, maybe I'd get lucky and land on him.

A plaintive moan told me my misstep had blown our cover. I'd better move it. I could practically feel JT's barely contained impatience to move.

Tough shit, Monkey Boy.

I inched down the trusses and supports, reliving my years as the nerd on the playground at recess.

Five feet from the bottom, the vertical supports ended. I knew it wasn't all that far, but it took a hefty dose of 'nut up or shut up' for me

26

to dangle by hands and let myself drop the rest of the way. I was even almost grateful for Griff's supporting hands on my thighs as I let go. At least until one hand lingered overly long on my butt as I landed.

I stepped away, glaring at him.

"My hand slipped." He didn't even try for an innocent look.

I smacked him in the ribs hard enough to elicit a satisfying 'oof.'

"So did my elbow."

I pushed past him and followed JT deeper into the trees. I heard a chuckle as Griff followed us.

*   *   *

"Ugh. It stinks in here."

Jenna wrinkled her nose and shot a pointed look in Dylan's direction. He flipped her off, but otherwise ignored her. His dark hair had more mats and tangles than a Persian cat with a grooming aversion, and he hadn't washed in days, not even a mop up with paper towels and hand soap in the small bathroom. None of them were exactly poster children for good hygiene – they'd been stuck in the same clothes for eight days now -- but wet wipes and deodorant helped.

Luke's sandy blond hair and formerly neatly trimmed mustache and beard had gotten scruffy, and Jenna had taken to wearing her mane of curly, dark brown hair in a tight braid to keep the oil off her skin. Phil, with his bald pate, was lucky. A splash of water and a quick swipe with a razor, and he cleaned up nicely.

Dylan refused to try. His facial hair grew in irregular patterns. He looked worse than Sod had on a bad day. Contestants at the tail end of season of Survivor were cleaner than he was. He'd laid claim to a corner of the store by the deli, making a nest out of now nearly two week-old newspapers, and spent the days thumbing through men's magazines.

Even worse than Dylan's funk, though, was the smell of rotting meat. Most of it had been fresh when things had gone south, but once the generator had gone out, it had turned quickly. Stuffing the rotten food into plastic trash bags helped a little bit, but the odor still permeated the store. Putting the bags outside or into the garage wasn't an option.

They'd opened the garage door once so Luke could dump out the bucket they'd started using for a toilet after the water stopped working. There'd been one lone zombie, what had once been a little boy in Sponge Bob Square Pants footie pajamas. Luke had spotted it and hastily shut the door, but it had already started hobbling across the cement floor towards him, smearing blood from one partially devoured foot in its wake. Its plaintive moans were enough to call in friends and now zombies clawed and pounded at both doors day and night. Opening either one would be suicide.

So they were stuck with the stench.

Still, Dylan wasn't helping.

"How 'bout a beer?" Phil held out a six-pack of craft brew IPA, wiggling it enticingly in front of Jenna and Luke.

"Right on," Luke said with the first enthusiasm he'd shown in days.

Jenna looked at her uncle in surprise. He'd been pretty strict about rationing the alcoholic beverages ever since Dylan had drunk two bottles of Jägermeister on an empty stomach, and puked up all over the bathroom.

Phil caught his niece's look and shrugged.

"Figured we could use a break, y'know?"

Jenna nodded. "Yeah, we can. If you don't mind, though, I'm gonna go for some wine instead."

"Hey, look at you, Miss Classypants." Phil reached out and chucked her under the chin. Jenna gave a half-hearted swipe at his hand.

Dylan emitted a loud and juicy belch, apropos of nothing. The other three ignored him.

"Hey," Phil said. "How do you kill a circus?"

"Go for the juggler," Jenna said tiredly. She'd laughed the first three times her uncle had tossed this one out, but she didn't think she had any more laughter in her.

"Guess I've already told that one, huh."

Jenna looked up at Phil's defeated tone. She threw her arms around him in a sudden, fierce hug.

"You keep telling the jokes, okay? Just let me get me a corkscrew and pour some wine first."

* * *

The ululating of the pesky zombies who'd tried to follow us from Medical Center Drive had faded away as we moved further into the nature preserve, the fog and trees blanketing the sound and hopefully masking the noise of our movement.

There were several well traveled trails on Mt Sutro, but the nearest to us, the Historic Trail (and whatever made it historic was a mystery to me) wasn't the most direct route through the woods.

"Still," I argued when JT pointed this out, "Isn't it faster to take a cleared path than try and find our way through the trees and hope we stay on course? I mean, unless you brought a compass and a machete…"

JT nodded. "Good point."

You had to love JT's lack of investment in being right. It almost made up for his more super-sized ego when it came to his mad parkour skills. I wasn't sure he was entirely sane, but I trusted him to have my back as long as he paid attention and didn't get all *"squirrel!"*, distracted by the next best surface to scale.

We moved as quickly as possible along the sometimes-muddy trail. Dense fog shrouded the trees above us and random tendrils wove their way through the branches. And even if there hadn't been fog, the streetlights had gone out several nights before and nighttime in San Francisco had taken on a whole new level of dark.

The sound of water dripping on the needle and leaf carpeted forest floor seemed unnaturally loud. The pungent odor of eucalyptus almost masked the now ever-present sweet and sour smell of rotting flesh. An entire city filled with putrefying corpses on the hoof. There wasn't enough Febreeze in the world to cover it up.

I had to give JT credit – I know he could move a lot faster than the pace he currently set, but he seemed to be making an effort to slow it down so Griff and I could keep up with him without huffing and puffing like out-of-shape ninjas.

Okay, *I* felt like an out of shape ninja. Griff moved quietly and gracefully, while JT was like the lovechild between a ninja and Tigger on steroids.

The trail angled sharply upwards, mud and pine needles making for treacherous footing. Even JT was finding it a bit tricky, and I was pretty sure he had mountain goat in his genetic makeup.

Griff stopped ahead of me and I barreled into him before I could catch myself. The collision barely moved him. The man was all lean, solid muscle. He smelled like cinnamon and chocolate, and I tried not to wonder if it was his natural scent or if he'd discovered an aftershave guaranteed to attract most women.

Good thing I was immune.

Mostly.

No, I was over bad boys. Without trust between two people, forget it. After what happened in San Diego, Griff would have to walk a few thousand miles to get me to trust him. It wasn't just about me. It was also about my friends, the people who'd been as much my family as my parents. He'd let them go down without so much as blinking, and that was a deal killer.

Still … Griff smelled good. I'd just try and look at him as a giant sachet against the ever-present stench of necrosis.

JT also had paused ahead, one hand held high in a universal "stop" gesture. He pointed further up the trail where it crested at a high point. Several figures milled about aimlessly, heads canted to one side and arms hanging down at their sides with a limpness that screamed 'walking dead.'

We crept as silently as possible through the bushes lining the trail and into the trees beyond, resuming our climb while remaining as parallel to our original path as possible. After a hundred feet or so, we came to a clearing where someone had pitched a small pup tent, perfect for a romantic campout for two.

The blood-spattered ground in front of the tent's mouth and a pungent "we're dead in here" stink told us all we needed to know about how this particular camping expedition ended.

JT slipped past the tent as silently as ever, Griff right on his heels and just as quiet. Leave it to me to step right on a branch with a loud crack that broke the fog-shrouded stillness of the night.

I froze as a muffled moan sounded from the tent.

Shit.

I *so* didn't want to see what was inside there, but I needed to take care of it before the zombies on the trail answered the moaning dinner bell and came looking for us. I drew my katana from its back sheathe and used the tip to flip open the right flap of the tent opening, peering cautiously inside.

You wouldn't think one layer of canvas could do much to mask bad smells, but the increased stench of gross that poured out of that little tent nearly knocked me on my ass. I held onto my supper by sheer force of will and cautiously peered inside.

Ugh.

What had once been two young men, both clad in rainbow T-shirts and flannel pajama bottoms, looked up at me from a nest of gore stained blankets and pillows. One of them was missing large chunks of flesh and his right arm, while the other was mostly intact except for a bite on one muscular bicep. Both sported matching silver bands on their wedding fingers.

What a shitty way to end a long-awaited honeymoon.

Both zombies reached for me with grasping hands and open mouths. I shoved the business end of my katana through both of their brains, one after the other.

"Ash, you okay?" JT peered at me through the tent flaps.

"As okay as it's possible to be under these particular circumstances."

I backed out of the tent, letting the flap fall back to cover the sad remains inside.

JT put a hand on my shoulder. "Have I thanked you yet for coming with me? You didn't have to do this."

"Yeah, I kind of did. If we can bring anyone home alive out of this… it'll be worth it."

"Unless we all die," Griff said with a derisive snort. "Then I'm not so sure your math adds up."

"Shut up," I growled. "No one forced you to come along."

"Actually Paxton and your professor made it very clear that room and board at the beautiful DZN hotel come at a price."

I opened my mouth to deliver a scathing retort, but Griff held up a hand and continued, "But that's not why I tagged along."

I rolled my eyes. "You think you're gonna get laid because of this. Is that it?"

Griff rounded on me, his expression fierce enough to make me take a step backwards.

Okay, a half step. I refused to let him intimidate me.

"It would be nice," he said softly, "but that's not why I tagged along either."

Before either of us had a chance to say anything else, the sound of unsteady footsteps shuffling through the undergrowth in our direction reminded us that we needed to get our asses in gear.

* * *

JT shook his head as he made his way swiftly through the woods, the steep uphill slope as easy as a flat sidewalk as far as he was concerned.

How could Ash be so savvy in some areas and so clueless in others?

As much as JT didn't want to trust Mister Too Sexy for His Swat Gear, he was pretty sure Griff agreed to this little expedition to make sure Ashley made it back alive. Sure, maybe he just wanted to get laid. Unless JT's intuition was totally off, however, he thought Griff actually cared about her.

At least as much as someone like Griff could care about anyone or anything.

Either Mt. Sutro hadn't been a very popular spot or most zombies didn't recognize it as a place that was once very important to them, because they reached the hill above Crestwood Drive and Forest Hill without further incident.

The street below looked quiet as well, but in a bad way, like the aftermath of battle in a war zone. Bits and pieces of former residents were smeared in bloody swaths across lawns and pavement, and the all too familiar tangle of partially smashed vehicles blocked streets and sidewalks alike. JT couldn't remember seeing a street free of crashed metal since the day the authorities had recommended people evacuate the city.

That had really not gone well.

If JT hadn't sensibly abandoned his car and made his way on foot, he'd most likely be trying to eat people too. He wondered if his free-running skills would have translated into life as a zombie. Probably not.

"Which way?"

Ash had reached the crest and now stood next to him, Griff a few paces behind. She kept her voice down, casting cautious glances at the landscape below as Griff joined them.

JT pointed towards the reservoir. Normally a peaceful pool of blue, it was now a barely visible blot of inky blackness in the nighttime fog.

"That way. "

"You really do have good night vision," Ash remarked.

"He's practically a wild card," Griff said in bored tones.

"Very true," JT agreed cheerfully. "Imagine the ass I could kick if it turned out I had disease-ridden, necrosis imbued super powers. Yours, for instance."

Griff snorted. "Not on a bad day, Spider Man."

"You both should be able to hear the sound of my eyes rolling," Ash said. "Can we get going now?"

* * * *

Taking a page from *Shaun of the Dead*, we took a shortcut over some fences and through a few backyards to get to the path around the reservoir and avoid as many surface streets as possible. Being a wild card may have improved my overall physical abilities, but climbing fences gracefully was not and probably never would be in my skill set. I watched JT bound over fences with the gravity-defying ease of a circus acrobat, while Griff scaled them more conventionally but no less effortlessly.

I hated them both.

We reached the path after one real rat bastard of a cement wall. It had concertina wire stretched illegally out along the top, and if it hadn't been for JT's warning, I'd have gotten a face full of ouch when I hoisted myself up. I shoved the razor sharp stuff away with one gloved hand, clearing enough space to pull myself up onto my knees. Not a comfortable position.

"You want a hand with that?" Griff crouched like a large cat on top of the wall a foot or so away. JT was already a short distance down the path, scouting ahead.

"Thanks," I said shortly. Accepting help from Griff did not come easily, but this could turn into a literal case of cutting off my nose to spite my face and I didn't have time to let pride make me stupid.

Griff helped me shove the rest of the wire off onto the ground below, where it bounced like a deadly slinky and tumbled off into a tangle of blackberry bushes. He leapt easily onto the dirt path a good six feet down, landing with flexed knees and a self-satisfied smirk. I took my time and swung my legs over the edge first to minimize the drop.

Did I mention I'm not a fan of heights?

Griff and I hurried along the path, catching up with JT at a point close to the edge of the water. The place stunk and one glance at the corpse-choked reservoir told me why. Some of the waterlogged bodies floated face down, while others moved sluggishly through the reeds lining the edge of the man-made lake.

So much for the quality of San Francisco tap water.

"Why the hell are they all in here?" JT said with a puzzled frown.

"Maybe it seemed like the only option." I shook my head sadly. "Maybe some of them were infected and didn't realize what they were doing."

Something grabbed my right foot. I looked down to see a female zombie suffering from the worst case of water retention ever clutching at my boot with fingers so bloated that the tips were peeling backwards, like sausages splitting their casings. It crawled on its stomach through the mud and reeds, lower half still submerged in the water.

Ugh!

Thwork. Katana blade, in and out.

The sausage fingers relaxed as the thing collapsed face first in the mud.

"Does this ever get less gross?" I said to no one in particular as we moved on along the path.

JT shook his head. "Considering that the bodies will continue to putrefy as time goes by, I seriously doubt it."

Ugh.

We reached the end of the path at the base of the reservoir.

"So I figure if we head across that neighborhood—" JT pointed west. "—that it'll be relatively clear."

"Why is that?" Griff asked.

JT pulled out the map. "Look." He pointed at the neighborhood in question, and a bunch of streets that wound upwards in a terraced series of half circles and dead ends.

Griff shrugged. "And?"

"It's pricey, it's in the hills, and the houses are likely to be single family homes instead of multiple households full of several generations of Cantonese immigrants."

Griff looked like he wanted to argue, but couldn't.

"Once we hit 19th Avenue, the zombie population is gonna increase, I guarantee it," JT continued. "Figured we might as well cut ourselves a break until then.

"I concur with my colleague," I said. He was right. The fewer people who'd lived there, the fewer potential zombies there'd be to slow us down.

We only needed to get across the river of steel that was Laguna Honda.

A favorite route of San Francisco commuters, it was now a sea of cars and bodies, impassable unless on foot. And even then, given the number of living corpses staggering through the tightly packed wreckage, it wouldn't be a walk in the park.

Griff took his M4 out of its sling.

"How about I clear our path?"

"What about the noise?"

"If they see us, they'll moan. If I shoot them, they may hear the gunfire, but at least some of them won't be able to follow us. And the ones that do…"

JT grinned. "We'll go for Operation Distraction and clear those out."

"Just a mini op, though," I said. "We should stick together as much as possible until we cross 19th. Then we'll probably need your crazy twerking skills."

Griff snorted. I couldn't blame him.

"Fair enough," JT said. "I'll make just enough ruckus to give you two a clear shot across Laguna Honda, and then do the stealth ninja routine and meet up with you."

"How will you find us?"

"Those of us who travel the skies have the benefit of a birds eye view."

"Was that supposed to sound wise?" I asked. "Because it was seriously bad fortune cookie time."

"You wound me deeply."

"Uh huh." I nodded at Griff. "Feel free to clear us that path."

Griff's aim was good. Very good. Almost up to par with Gentry,

34

if not on the same level as the late Gunsy Twins, our team's snipers who were killed in San Diego.

I wished I hadn't thought of them, since Griff had been at least partially responsible for that, even if just by inaction. I glared at him.

He noticed my glare. "What?"

I took a deep breath and said nothing.

"Just shoot, okay?"

"Whatever."

I rolled my eyes at that. Oh well, at least he didn't do the "W" with his fingers. I turned to JT. "Ready for Mini Operation Distraction?"

JT grinned. "See you on the other side of this mess."

With that he bounded out from the path onto the sidewalk and dashed down towards Laguna Honda, whooping and hollering with the suicidal enthusiasm of a War Boy bound for Valhalla.

Griff and I watched as he bounced off a chain-link fence and re-bounded onto the roof of a supersized SUV; the kind of vehicle that had no business driving around in a city like San Francisco. No sooner did his feet hit the top than hands reached out of the open passenger window, grasping in vain as JT spring -boarded onto the car next to it, an ancient VW Beetle.

The zombies shambling in between the stalled cars turned in JT's direction, following the sound of his passage and leaving a relatively clear path for Griff and me provided we avoided the grasping hands of the zombies trapped in the vehicles.

Griff looked at me. "Ready?"

"Let's get it over with."

We dashed off the path into the undergrowth and onto the side-walk, following more sedately in JT's path over and in between the cars. Hands reached out and grabbed at us as we dodged in and out of the cars. I hacked them off at the wrists as necessary without looking into the cars. I didn't want to see the faces that went with those hands.

Most of the zombies not trapped within the crushed metal fol-lowed JT's commotion, leaving Griff and me to make it across Laguna Honda without incident. Insofar as it's possible to qualify being clutched at by undead hands as 'without incident.'

Griff and I dashed uphill into the neighborhood and stopped in the shelter of a carport a couple of blocks up the street to give JT a chance to catch up with us.

"Looks like Spider Man was right about zombie demographics in this particular neighborhood," Griff commented as several minutes went by without any undead activity.

"Of course I'm right."

I'd like to say Griff screamed like a girl when JT suddenly appeared next to him, hanging upside down from the carport roof like a maniacal bat, but it was more of a strangled cat noise. Whatever, it brought a smile to my face.

JT swung his body up in a half arc, spread out his arms and sprung off from the roof, landing on the concrete drive as lightly as a dancer.

"Shall we?"

*   *   *

Forest Hill was made up of curving, dipping, hill-circling streets, with enough whimsy in the architecture to rival a fairy tale. English hunting lodges faced Dutch cottages, and French palaces with marble pillars adjacent to edifices rivaling Collinwood from *Dark Shadows*. The entire effect was an idyllic picturesque neighborhood for its residents and a confusing labyrinth of one-way streets and dead ends for motorists.

I tried not to look at the random gory tableaus that bespoke of recent tragedies. I'd seen enough blood, viscera and body parts over the last month to last me this lifetime and a few reincarnated ones as well. Still, it was impossible not to notice things like a picture window in a faux French farmhouse broken in from the outside, blood still staining the jagged shards, and not imagine the fate of the residents. Or a stroller lying on one side, the formerly cream colored interior now—

No.

I turned my gaze resolutely away from that little nightmare and kept moving.

Keeping an eye out for the dead, our little trio took advantage of the connecting stairs, making our way cautiously but quickly downward towards West Portal, another relatively ritzy neighborhood.

"Lot of old school San Franciscans in West Portal," JT informed us as he leapt back and forth from the ledges on either side of the stairway. I could tell he was trying to slow himself down to keep pace with Griff and me. "These stairs, by the way," he added, "are one of the lesser known stairway walks in the city."

"I'll cross it off my bucket list," Griff muttered, stepping over a bloodstained Thomas the Tank engine toy on one of the stair landings.

Dogs howled in the hills above us, the sound augmented by the unmistakable yipping of coyotes. It was a good thing Lil wasn't with us or we'd have a rag tag army of stray animals trailing us the entire way.

Undeterred by the canine racket, cats slinked through the yards adjacent to the stairs, most of them looking well fed.

"There must be a lot of rats around here," I commented as a particularly fat tabby strolled in front of us, hopping the fence into a large backyard. I peeked into the yard, where a good dozen felines lolled.

"How do you know they're eating rats?" Griff shot me a challenging look over one shoulder as he trotted down the stairs.

"What else would they be eat—"

Ewww…

They're eating rats." I glared at Griff. "That's my story and I'm sticking to it."

We reached the bottom of the last stairway, a couple of streets away from Taravel, one of the main drags stretching between West Portal and the beach. A quick glance in either direction showed a few zombies, but still nothing to worry about.

Worry set in when we reached Taravel.

*　　*　　*

"Jeez fuckin' louise, they're everywhere."

Taravel was shambling with zombies. A very good example of how neighborhood demographics could change one block to the next. Griff and I hunkered down on either side of JT behind an Escalade. JT had the map spread out again.

"Hmm." JT looked at the zombies with a clinical eye. "Time for another episode of JT Saves the Day."

I stifled a laugh with one hand. Griff didn't bother covering his snort. It kind of blended in with the zombie ambiance anyway.

"Fine," I whispered. "What's the plan? Where do we meet you?"

"We are here." JT pointed at the map. "Here's Stern Grove. Haul ass across 19th Avenue and then turn hard left at either 20th or 21st, whichever looks better. And by 'better', I mean zombie free."

"No shit," Griff muttered.

"I have to second Griff's 'no shit,'" I said. "I mean, no offense, but we're not exactly new at this."

"Ah. No, you're not." JT folded the map. "Sorry. Since I'm relatively new at this, I suspect I'm projecting."

I grinned. "No shit."

"There's a lake at the west end of the park," JT continued, "and

37

a little picnic area right before it. I'll see you there. Then we'll probably have to rinse and repeat to get to the store 'cause I have a feeling it's only gonna get more crowded the closer we get to the zoo."

He folded up the map and tucked it into his knapsack, pulling out a bottle of water. He drained half the bottle and handed it to me. I took a swallow and passed it to Griff, who drained it and set the empty bottle on the sidewalk.

I guess recycling wasn't exactly an option.

"Time to rock the Kasbah."

With that, JT rocketed to his feet and took off eastbound on Taraval, using abandoned cars and zombies alike as launching pads, and making no effort to travel quietly. He paused on top of an Escalade and executed a quick jig, resulting in a metal denting cacophony and a decent *Lord of the Dance* imitation.

Damn, that boy can move.

All zombies within hearing distance slowly turned towards the source of noisy Riverdancing, weaving clumsily in and out of the cars, coming out of driveways and up the sidewalks as JT sprinted off, leading them away from Griff and me.

Griff and I waited until the coast was more or less clear, un-hunkered ourselves and moved cautiously westward, dispatching the zombies that drifted into our path like calm, homicidal robots. I used my katana and tanto, depending on whether a decapitation or a *schlorp* through the eye socket would work better. Griff stuck to his M4, wielding the stock of the weapon with deadly effect, the strength behind the blows more than enough to crush zombie skulls.

By the time we reached 19th Avenue, the sight of crushed skulls, smashed cars, body parts and puddles of gore ceased to register beyond obstacles we needed to circumnavigate. Mangled toddlers, limbless teens, shredded bodies of all shapes, sizes and nationalities, they all blurred together in one gory stew, the only difference being whether nor not they moved.

Other than choosing where to place my blades I didn't look at them. I didn't want to discern nationality, gender or age. Especially age. The little ones still managed to pierce what was left of my broken heart.

* * *

JT looked down from the roof of the West Portal Muni tunnel, noting with satisfaction how many zombies he'd managed to lure away playing his version of the Pied

Piper.

And wasn't that a grim story. What happened to all those kids anyway? Did they go to some fantasyland where they're stay forever young and eat candy all the time or did they end up as food for all those rats?

Oh well, not his problem. What was his problem was backtracking west without this bunch following, which meant some fancy footwork and mega stealth mode. Shouldn't be a problem, right?

He didn't want to head back in the direction he'd come because while Ash and Griff were all sorts of bad-ass, they couldn't move nearly as fast on the ground as he could up above, and the whole point of this exercise had been to clear away some undead meat so they had a chance to put some space between them and the hungry throng.

He scanned the surrounded area. At first glance, West Portal Avenue was a no go, so thickly packed with zombies he doubted he'd get too far even with his unique ability to crowd surf.

He supposed he could hop over the buildings on Ulloa leading to Claremont, but that was heading further east and he didn't want to get any further off course than he already was.

No, he'd have to risk heading west briefly and then hope to lose his faithful followers with some stealthy rooftop hopping. Or he could stay where he was for a while longer, sing a song or two and insure his teammates had a chance to hoof it to Stern Grove. But if he waited too long, he'd have a hell of time getting anywhere. Too bad the trains weren't running because—

His gaze sharpened, resting on a series of stalled Muni trains heading out of and into the tunnels on West Portal Boulevard. It looked like they'd been running in both directions when the shit hit the fan. Mostly two cars, but even one rare three car M line stretched out down the street.

The trains were at least 10 feet high so he would be well out of reach of all but zombie basketball players. Even better, there was a train located conveniently beneath the roof of the station, an easy jump for anyone, let alone him.

No one had ever accused him of false modesty.

JT reckoned he could travel south along the tops for several blocks. It would be easier to ninja his way into the neighborhood away from the business district and lose the zoms. The wind had even kicked up, dissipating enough fog to reveal a bloated full moon, which in turn illuminated his path nicely.

He gauged the distance and then jumped, landing on the roof of the train in his best improbable superhero three-point landing, one hand down, feet wide apart in a crouch, one hand on the ground in front of him, the other outstretched behind him. His badass glare was lost on his audience, but dammit, what a wasted photo-op.

Ah well, to business.

"See you later, my peoples!"

With that, he took off at a run down the top of the first train. When he ran out of that train, he bridged the gap to the next on with a graceful leap worthy of Gene Kelly in his prime. He didn't bother with the picturesque landing this time; just let the momentum carry him down another car length, then another, ducking and weaving around the guide wires.

He was about to run out of train again, but this time there wasn't another one conveniently in front of him. There was, however, one that had been heading into the tunnel in the opposite direction, only a scant six or so feet across the tracks. Zombies jammed the space in between, hands reaching upwards for the tasty treat out of reach.

JT grinned. He could do this. But first, a little running start would be good. He went back half a car, flexed his knees once, then twice, and went for it, pushing off with his left foot against the edge of the train to get the full momentum behind the jump.

He sailed through the air, laughing as rotting fingers reached for his soaring body. He felt something brush the bottom of his feet right before they landed on the adjacent train. It wasn't more than a feather touch, but it was enough to throw him off his game just enough that he started, falling just a little short of his goal. His rear foot hit air instead of metal and he felt his body start to drop backwards. Throwing himself forward, JT grabbed onto a raised outcropping on the roof, landing heavily on his front knee hard enough to make him wince.

But he was safe for the moment.

Damn. That was too damn close for comfort.

JT didn't exactly experience fear, but he felt something close to it. He flipped over onto his back and lay there for a moment, staring up at the moon.

"Let's be more careful, shall we?" he told himself quietly. "You get bit and it's one big game over. Unless you beat the odds and become a wild card, and let's face it. You've already won the awesome lotto so that's probably not gonna happen. Wouldn't be fair."

He listened to the relaxing sounds of hungry zombies for a few minutes longer, then got resolutely to his feet. His right knee kinda hurt. Okay, it throbbed. But he was pretty sure it was just a bruise. And if it wasn't, he'd deal with it later. His body hadn't let him down to date; he wouldn't let it start now.

* * *

"Ow! Motherfucker…"

I uttered both words in a quiet but heartfelt whisper. The hillside path Griff and I took into Stern Grove crumbled beneath my feet when I'd stepped too close to the edge and I'd landed on a pile of broken branches. I'd landed there after a very ungraceful toboggan ride on my ass. Stupid crumbling path.

Griff bounded down the slope to my side. "Anything broken?" he asked quietly.

The sounds of unsteady footsteps up above and breaking branches in the trees told us we weren't alone.

Great.

Was it too much to ask for even a short break from all the carnage, even if it was just five minutes? Just a nice walk in the park under the full moon with... well, with Griff.

Okay, scratch that.

I let him help me to my feet, wincing at various aches and pains. Luckily none of them were debilitating. Getting injured at this stage of the game would be a bad thing indeed.

At least I'd managed to hold on to both my blades during my undignified decent. That was something. I sheathed the tanto, tired of carrying both.

We continued through the trees, the temperature down in the little mini canyon we were now in a good ten degrees cooler than it had been in the streets. It felt good after all the chopping and hacking and thrusting.

What would feel even better was a hot shower. Both Griff and I were splattered liberally with blood and other things I didn't want to think about. Normally one would have to wade through a slaughterhouse to achieve this level of gore saturation.

The narrow tree-lined path opened up into a large grassy area, with an open-air stage on the left and terraced cement seating on the right. A half dozen or so zoms in various stages of freshly dead to uber gooey staggered aimlessly across the lawn. Griff and I moved silently along the back of the seating area, doing our best to stay out of sight.

We made it to a parking lot, only partially filled with vehicles. A curving drive leading out of the park was blocked by an overturned van, the passenger sliding door partially open, an unmoving, half-eaten body slumped partway through as if the person had tried to climb out.

The other cars in the lot looked empty with the exception of an old Nissan hatchback, the interior of the windows smeared with blood. It held two bodies, a woman and a little girl. The woman was dead. The little girl... not so much. It clutched one of the woman's hands, one of the fingers in its mouth as if nursing on a pacifier.

41

Ugh ugh ugh!

My brain would explode if I saw one more horrible thing.

I heard growling and turned to see a good dozen dogs of various breeds and sizes worrying on the corpse of a young woman, lying under a sign that read "Dog Play Area." She'd been wearing baggy pants and a tank top when she died and had a number of dog leashes looped diagonally around her shoulder and torso like a punk rock baldric. All I could think was she might not have minded ending up as food for her charges.

To my surprise, my head did not explode.

One of the dogs, a largish black lab, looked up and growled, muzzle dripping with gore.

"Keep moving," Griff murmured.

I didn't argue.

We made a wide berth around the feeding dogs and continued toward the lake, which lay on the other side of the wide open grassy play area.

The fog had completely blown away and the light of the full moon made visibility a snap. The down side, however, were the gusts of wind increasing in strength. Branches in the eucalyptus trees all around us creaked ominously.

Even more troubling was the thought that the copter might not be able to come get us if the wind picked up too much more. I had no idea how many miles per hour the gusts had to be before flying a copter was a no go, but the way the branches were thrashing around, I worried we were getting close to the limit.

Griff and I hugged the edge of the park as a handful of zombies wandered across the grass. A loud crack signaled a falling branch on the other side of the dog play area and a little old lady zombie dragging a leash with an empty collar turned and stumbled towards the sound.

The dirt path intersected with an asphalt walkway leading past a chain-link fence lined with trees that bisected the field.

"There." Griff pointed towards a little building with carousel animals painted on the wall. I saw a tiger, a giraffe, a unicorn, and a seal balancing a ball on its nose.

We picked up our pace and jogged over to it, ducking around the corner before any of the zoms wandering forlornly through the area could spot us.

There were cement picnic tables and a large grill on the other side, and more painted animals decorating the walls. A sign reading Pine Lake Day Camp was duct-taped to a pillar.

42

I could see the edge of Pine Lake no more than 20 feet away. We'd made it to the rendezvous area and, wonder of wonders, no zoms. A little rest would be nice while we waited for JT. But first...

I turned to Griff. "I need to use the bathroom."

"Do you always announce it?"

I glared at him.

"Only when I need someone to stand guard so I don't get bushwhacked by a zombie clown."

"A zombie..." Griff trailed off, shaking his head. "Never mind. I'll stand guard."

Other than a clogged toilet, there were no nasty surprises in the girl's bathroom. The faucet didn't work, but there was standing water in the sink so I dipped my hands quickly in and out and shook them dry. No way I was wiping them on my viscera spattered clothing. I didn't bother looking in the mirror. I didn't want to know what I looked like and I didn't particularly care.

As I rejoined Griff outside, my radio went off in a burst of muffled static.

Quickly unhooking it from my belt, I hit the receive button.

"Hey Ash." I recognized JT's cheerful voice even with the fuzzy sound quality. "We have a little bit of a problem."

* * *

"So let me get this straight," Griff said as we moved rapidly past the lake towards the end of the park. "All the zoms Monkey Boy led away in the first place are now following him this way?"

"Yup." I looked longingly back at the picnic area, my plans for a rest shot to hell by JT's news. "He hurt his knee so he's moving slower than usual, and a few of them stuck on his trail, and you know how that goes."

Griff nodded. "Like a big pack of carnivorous lemmings."

"Stinky carnivorous lemmings," I amended. "At any rate, he thinks he can stay ahead of them, but not far enough to give us a decent lead time if we wait for him here. He said he'd catch up to us at--" I paused, waiting for my short-term memory to kick in. "—at Wawona and 43rd, a block from the store."

The path rose up as we passed the end of the lake.

"So much for Operation JT Saves the Day," Griff muttered, striding ahead of me.

43

"Save the snide shit," I snapped as quietly as I could. "He's done a good job of distracting them so far."

"And we've done a pretty good job on our own so far."

"It's called teamwork for a reason." I sped up my on pace to keep up with him. "But then you're not exactly a team player, are you?

Griff stopped in his tracks and I smacked into him for the second time.

"Being used as a human lab rat doesn't engender much team spirit, he said softly. I did what I did in San Diego to save you. I couldn't save everyone.

"You didn't try, though, did you?"

"No."

I shook my head in disgust and started brush by him, but he grabbed my arm.

"If I had tried, we'd all be dead. You, me, the rest of your team." He paused, then added, "You've said it yourself, Ash. You can't save the world."

"Maybe not," I replied, hating him for being right. "But I'm going to do my best."

With that, I pushed past him, practically running the rest of the way up the hill, wishing I could outrun my memories as easily.

* * *

Clipping the radio back on his belt, JT resumed his journey, leaping gracefully from one roof to the next on a row of attached houses. He found if he ignored the pain, he could move at about three quarters his normal speed. Not bad for lesser mortals, but pretty shitty for him, especially under these circumstances. He really should stop and wrap the knee, but that would use up precious minutes he needed to keep ahead of his adoring fans.

So he kept moving, albeit with slightly more caution than usual.

He'd ditched the Muni trains at 15th where the number of zoms had thinned out just enough for him to cut across West Portal into the residential part of the neighborhood. Unfortunately a few diehard zombies – and yes, he did laugh at his own bad pun, thank you very much – stuck on his trail like the persistent posse in Butch Cassidy and the Sundance Kid.

"Who are those guys?" he muttered, annoyed.

He decided to abandon his plan to slip through Stern Grove and stick to the rooftops. Even if he couldn't shake them, they couldn't catch him. And he'd be able to catch up to Ash and Griff that much sooner.

"I am totally a leaf in the wind," he said to himself as he prepared to take a five-foot drop to a balcony. "Watch me soar, yo!"

He hit the balcony, only wincing slightly when his knee complained at the impact, and then swung over the wrought iron railing to the shed roof below. From there he bounded onto the hood of a Prius in the driveway and car-hopped across the street to the next row of houses.

He had this by the ass… as long as he didn't fall on his.

* * *

Griff and I made it to Wawona and 43rd, ducking behind cars, fences, and sometimes in and out of side and back yards to avoid the ever increasing number of zombies. We put down the ones that got directly in our path, but otherwise tried to stay out of sight.

The houses were all dark. Some had broken windows and front doors ominously open. Others were boarded up from the inside. Every now and again I'd see movement inside, and once I thought I saw the flicker of what could be candlelight coming from an upstairs window, but there was no time to investigate.

And despite my brave words to Griff, I knew I couldn't save everyone.

By the time we reached 43rd Avenue, early morning light started to streak the sky. Normally I loved watching the sunrise, but this morning it didn't illuminate anything I wanted to see.

43rd Avenue ended at Sloat, like a small tributary opening up into a much larger river. The intersection was clogged with cars, including a pile-up involving an over-sized Ram truck, a Comcast van, and a bright yellow Humvee.

Who the hell thought owning a Humvee in San Francisco was a good idea?

The pile-up was nasty. The van had flipped on its side, and the truck and Humvee angled into it, front ends smashed to form a sort of inverted "V." The moonlight clearly illuminated blood and body parts both in and under the vehicles involved. It did, however, also, give Griff and me a relatively safe place to hide behind so we could get close to and take a look at Sloat Avenue and see what we were going to be dealing with to get to the entrance of George's Zoo.

Crap. This is bad.

I didn't voice the thought out loud because aside from the now ever-present demolition derby automotive aftermath, Sloat was crawling with zombies. Not quite swarm sized, but enough to make traveling the short block to our destination tricky at best, suicidal at worst.

45

And holy shit, was that really a lion strolling through the cars across the street in one of the auxiliary zoo parking lots?

Griff nudged me and pointed. "Lion," he whispered.

Yup, it really was a lion. Or lioness, rather.

The zombies seemed to be ignoring her. I wondered if it had eaten enough of their undead comrades that they steered clear out of some survival instinct or if lions just didn't taste good to zombies. Either way, our odds of being tasty to both zombie and lion were pretty high, which made this trip even more interesting, in that whole "May you live in interesting times" Chinese curse kind of way.

Peering over the Comcast van, which had flipped onto its side, I looked west down Sloat to the next corner, and spotted the yellow and black George's Zoo sign with a gorilla sipping a cup of coffee. Just like JT had described.

One block away. Just one lousy block. It might as well have been a mile.

We couldn't scale walls with the greatest of ease like JT, our own Flying Walenda, and even more to the point, where were we supposed to land a helicopter in this mess? And even if there'd been a clear spot to land, we'd be swarmed by opportunistic zombies before we made it to the copter. As if to emphasize the fucked uppedness of the situation, a gust of wind blew through the streets, picking up trash and swirling it into the air before depositing it at my feet.

"How the hell are we gonna get out of here?" I said as much to myself as to Griff.

"They'll have to hover and let down a ladder," Griff replied. We both spoke in undertones.

"Can they do that if it's windy?"

"It's not that windy."

Another gust howled down the streets, the sound as eerie as the moans of the zombies.

"It'll be fine," Griff assured me.

A low whistle sounded behind us. Griff and I swiveled around to see JT crouching on the roof of the house on the corner of Sloat and 43rd. He waved. I wiggled my fingers in response. Griff didn't bother.

Eschewing his usual flamboyance, JT climbed quietly down from the house he perched on by way of a trellis covered with bougainvillea, nimbly avoiding the thorny vines. He then ran over to us, body bent over to stay out of sight. I noticed he was favoring his left leg. Not a lot, but it was still worrisome.

46

"Hey there," I said as JT squeezed into the space between the three smashed vehicles. I handed him a bottle of water from my backpack.

"Hey there yourself," he said, taking the water and draining the bottle in one long draught.

"Now what?" I asked.

"I'll go up top. You and Mister Sexy Pants use the front door."

"If your people are still in there," Griff said, rather admirably ignoring JT's insult, "they'll have it barricaded. And if we go hammering on it, why the hell would they let us in?"

"Simple," JT said with a shrug. "I'll drop down from above and let them know we're here to save the day."

"Good plan, Mighty Mouse," Griff said. "But we need some sort of signal to let us know it's worth our time to run the risk. If they're dead, no one's gonna be letting us in and then we're dead too."

"It's not rocket science," JT said dismissively. "If they're dead, I'll let you in."

"It may not be rocket science, but it's not that simple." I couldn't believe I was defending Griff, but he was right. "If they're dead, they might be zombies. If they're zombies, you'll have to hightail it out of there before they bite you, because if they bite you, *you'll* be dead. And if you have to hightail it out of there, that leaves me and Griff stuck outside attracting all sorts of attention."

JT thought it over. "Good points. So you two hide out here and I'll go check inside the store. If they're alive, I'll play decoy and use my luscious ass to tempt the crowds away from the front of the store. If they're dead, we can use the rope I brought to get you two up on the roof to wait for extraction."

"It's great plan," Griff said, "but there's only one problem."

He jerked his head to one side.

What looked like an entire platoon of zombies was lurching its way across the street and up 43rd towards us. The time for hunkering down was past. We needed to get inside George's Zoo or some other shelter, pronto.

I looked at JT. "We're kinda screwed if we don't move now."

Griff pointed towards the door of the second house closest to Sloat. The entryway's iron gate was ajar. "In there. It'll buy us some time. We can get out through the backyard if Spiderman can draw this bunch away."

"How will we know if it's safe to hit the front of George's?"

47

JT tapped his radio. "Just be ready to move fast."

"You gonna be okay on that knee?"

"Please," JT said. "Take more than this to slow me down."

With that he took off again, leaping from the roof of the Humvee to an SUV parked in the driveway, to the second story window box. From there he shimmied the rest of the way up using the rain gutter like a native scaling a coconut tree.

Meanwhile the zombies heading towards us on 43rd were a scant ten feet away, more than close enough to see details I didn't want to see. Griff grabbed my arm and pulled me to my feet. The two of us scrambled away from our barricade-soon-to-be-deathtrap and ran for the entryway, slamming the gate behind us just as the frontrunner of the mini-swarm reached the driveway.

* * *

JT stood on top of the roof and smiled.

"I'm on top of the world, ma!" His voice rang out across the rooftops and to the throngs of rotting cannibals below. They looked up at the sound and immediately started shuffling towards the house, arms stretching up towards him. He felt like Bono in a U2 video, doing his messiah imitation.

Now what?

Hmmm.

"How about some music, maestro? Don't mind if I do."

JT cleared his throat and burst out into Music of the Night, *one of his favorite numbers from* Phantom of the Opera. *The acoustics weren't the best, but good enough to attract the attention of even more of adoring crowd below. If it wasn't his imagination, he believed he saw the gang that had followed him from West Portal shuffling towards him from a block away.*

That should give Ash and Mister some breathing space.

And in the meantime, he'd suss out the situation at George's Zoo.

He hoped they were still okay. The pretty gal with the big eyes still haunted him. He'd made her a promise, and JT was not one to renege on his word.

Inspired, he switched over to Brown Eyed Girl *and bounded over the rooftop to his destination.*

* * *

If Griff or I had hoped for some downtime waiting for JT's signal, we were doomed to disappointment.

The stench of rotting flesh was, if anything, worse inside the two-story house, probably because there were a shitload of zombies

48

inside, all trying to jam into a room off the downstairs hallway, moaning hungrily. The ones in the rear pawed at those in front, too distracted by whatever was in that room to notice Griff and me right away.

Giving each other an 'oh shit' look, Griff and I raced up a staircase right off the front door. The stairs were tacky with semi-dried blood, the soles of our boots making little ripping sounds with each step.

Upstairs was slightly better in that all of the corpses were in bits and pieces, and none of them were moving.

And how fucked up was it that this was now my definition of 'better?'

The living room looked like an abattoir, the formerly cream colored walls splashed with reddish-brown. The kitchen wasn't much better. Someone had gone to town on a zombie with a cast iron skillet. The zombie, once a little old Chinese grandma, flopped over in a corner like a zombie Raggedy Ann doll, and bits of brain and bone splinters spattered the black and white tiled floor.

There were three other rooms upstairs: a bathroom and two bedrooms. All three doors were standing wide open and the rooms appeared empty. I pointed to the bedroom further from the stairs with a west view window, and padded in silently, Griff on my heels. He shut the door behind us with a barely audible 'click.'

The room was filled with bow-bedecked anime felines from the bedspread to the wallpaper and curtains.

"Well, hello kitty." Griff looked around with a sneer.

"Don't be an asshole," I said. "I'm sure this room belonged to a little kid, okay?"

He pointed wordlessly to a glass with dentures in it on the pink and white bedside table.

"I hate you," I muttered, and went over to the window, pushing the pink and white curtains apart and raising the window to let in some not-so-fresh air.

* * *

"So when we get out of here," Luke said, "what's the first thing you're gonna do?"

He, Jenna and Phil sat on overturned crates near the front of the store eating cold Pop Tarts and dry cereal. Dylan lay next to the front counter sleeping, a pile of airplane sized rum bottles scattered around his prone body.

Phil took a bite of a frosted strawberry Pop Tart, swallowing before answering Luke's question. "You mean after a hot shower? Go play eighteen holes at Pebble Beach."

Luke nodded appreciatively. "Nice. I'm gonna take a few weeks and go to Hawaii, do some snorkeling and get shitfaced on Mai Tais."

"You can totally do that here," Jenna pointed out between handfuls of Frosted Flakes. "Why go to Hawaii?"

"Dude," Luke said. "Hawaii." He took a bite of his own Pop Tart, washing it down with a swallow of warm cream soda. "What about you, J?"

Jenna gave a wistful smile. "Take my new Mustang out for a drive on the freeway. You know the only place I drove it aside from home off the lot is here, right? Everything went to hell that day."

Luke shook his head in sympathy. "Dude, that totally sucks."

Dylan gave an unexpected cackle. "Like there's gonna be anywhere to drive it even if you get out f here," he said, eyes still shut, that weird-ass smile he now always wore plastered on his face like some sort of a half-assed Joker. "Which you won't."

"Shut up, Dylan." Jenna glared at him.

Dylan kept grinning. "Yeah, just imagine all those rotting pus-bags touching your car, bits of skin sticking to the handles, pus on the paintjob, that black shit all over the windshield--"

"Shut the fuck up! "

Jenna threw her box of cereal across the aisle. It bounced off Dylan's head, frosted flakes scattering onto his prone body. He gave a little whoop of amusement and stuffed a handful of the cereal into his mouth.

"Yup, that sweet ride of yours is gonna be totally fucked up by the time we get out of here. Ain't no detail shop in the world gonna get that shit off of it."

Jenna grabbed a can of soup from the shelf next to her and pitched it with uncanny accuracy. It smacked Dylan square in the chest, wiping the grin off his face.

"Hey," he said, looking genuinely offended.

"Hey, your fucking self!"

Dylan stumbled to his feet just as Jenna threw another can of soup. This one clipped his elbow and he gave a howl of pain that was cut short when another can smacked him square on the nose.

50

Luke had to admire her aim.

Blood spouted from Dylan's nostrils and he lurched to his feet.

"I'm gonna pay you back for that," he promised, taking a threatening step forward.

Then he took two stumbling steps backwards as Phil stood up, twice as wide and just as tall as Dylan.

"You threatening my niece?" Phil's tone was deceptively mild as he walked up to his employee.

Luke stayed by Jenna, who already had another can in her hand, ready to hurl.

"She threw a fucking soup can at me," Dylan protested. "Three of them."

"I said, are you threatening my niece? Because if you are—" Phil closed the gap between them with a speed that belied his size. "--I swear I'll toss you out to those things without thinking twice." He poked Dylan in the chest. "You dig?" Poke.

Even though they were the same height, Phil towered over Dylan, who had shrunk back against the counter, blood dripping freely from his nose.

"She made me bleed!"

"Yeah well, you deserved it for being an asshole," Jenna shot back.

"Bitch!"

Phil reached out and grabbed Dylan's shirtfront. "You wanna take that back or do I toss you out the back door?"

Dylan's reply, whatever it would have been, was cut off by a voice from the back of the store.

"Hey, what does a guy have to do to get a ham on rye here?"

Jenna whirled round, ready to throw the soup can in her hand when she saw who stood at the entrance to the atrium.

"Spiderman!"

Jenna ran over and threw her arms around the newcomer without hesitation. He gave a pleased grin and gave her a one armed hug.

Phil let go of Dylan's shirt. Dylan slumped back against the counter.

"Holy shit, you actually came back," Luke said, staring at 'Spiderman' in disbelief.

"I promised, didn't I?"

"Who the hell are you?" Phil folded his arms. Luke could tell he didn't like the way Jenna was looking at this young dude, all oozing hero worship and shit.

The kid strode over to Phil and held out one hand. "Name's JT. But I kinda like Spiderman. I'm here with my team to get you out of here."

Phil stared down at the kid's hand as if it was a cockroach. "And why should I trust you?"

The kid shrugged. "Maybe you should ask yourself why you shouldn't trust me."

Phil turned to Luke. "This the guy you and Jenna told me about?"

Luke nodded. "Yeah. He promised he'd be back. I thought he was full of shit."

Jenna frowned. "I told you he'd come back." She smiled shyly at JT. "I knew you would."

"Aw," JT said with an embarrassed grin, "Now you've gone and made me blush."

Jenna giggled, a sound Phil hadn't heard in the last ten days. He was torn between delight that his niece could still laugh and distrust at this kid walking in and acting like he was the messiah or something.

"So where's this team of yours?" Phil knew he sounded aggressive. He didn't give a shit. "And just where is this magical safe place you're gonna take us?" Phil wasn't quite ready to trust this cocky little SOB yet. He might be on the level or he might be someone looking to steal supplies or worse, screw with Jenna.

JT seemed unfazed by Phil's questions. "My team is waiting for me to let 'em know when it's safe to come to the front door. We're holed up with a bunch of secret government agent types at UCSF at an equally secret laboratory facility where they're working on a cure for this shit. Oh," he added. "There's also hot water and showers."

Luke stepped forward. "Um, as much as I'd personally kill for a hot shower and a shave, the front door is kind of boarded up." He pointed towards the two-by-fours nailed down across the entrance.

JT eyeballed it. "Okay, yeah, I see your point. Is there another entrance?"

"What about how you got in?" Jenna asked.

JT shrugged modestly. "I have skills beyond those of mortal men."

Luke snorted. "Okay, Tony Stark."

JT flashed him a broad smile. "I'm not nearly as much of an asshole."

"Yeah, well, we'll be the judge of that," Phil said.

"As you wish." JT cast a quick look around. "So you're saying it's either the front door or the roof?"

Jenna pointed towards the back where a few plastic garbage bins were wedged in between the wall and a door. The sound of wet meat slapping against metal was clearly audible. "That door leads into the apartment garage, but those things have been trying to get in for days now."

JT nodded. "Okay. Can you get the boards off the front door?"

"Sure," Phil replied. "But if anything happens and we get stuck here, we'll be pretty much screwed. So tell me why we should take those boards off."

"If we can take the boards off," JT said, "my team will be here in minutes. We can help you all climb up to the roof, we'll have a genuine 'get to the choppah' moment and get the hell out of here. Sound good?"

52

This last was to Jenna, who nodded vehemently.

"How the hell are we gonna get up to the roof?"

"For thems that can't shimmy up the pipes the way I can, we have this." JT pulled his knapsack off his back and pulled out a coil of rope. "And we'll have two very strong people to help haul you up."

Phil and Luke exchanged a brief look.

"Luke," Phil said, "Get the crowbar."

JT smiled broadly. "I'll radio my peeps."

*   *   *

The curtains billowed in the wind as I looked out into the backyard. It was zombie free, but the drop down into the cement backyard was at least ten feet. The risk of a sprained or broken ankle was very real.

"We can't go out the front door, and there's no way to get out the back on the ground floor without killing a buttload of zoms."

Griff smirked. "May I inquire how many zombies constitute a buttload? "

"However many are downstairs." I chose to ignore his sarcasm. "I wonder what they're after in that room."

"Something living, most likely," Griff said with a shrug. He pulled the sheets off the bed. We can use these to go out the window, just like proper escaped convicts.

"Shit." I shook my head. "We have to go see if someone's still alive down there.

"Are you crazy?" Griff grabbed my shoulders. "We're immune to infection. We're not immune to getting ripped to pieces and eaten."

I smacked his hands away. "If there's someone alive down there, how do you expect me to leave them?"

"Same way you've walked past dozens of houses that probably had survivors in them. You just keep walking."

Before I could deliver a scathing reply, my radio squawked. Glaring at Griff, I took it off my belt.

"Ash here. "

"Hey doll, it's your hero. You ready to rock and roll?"

"You got survivors?"

"Roger that. Four." JT paused. "Although one of them is kind of loony tunes."

Kind of par for the course, I thought sadly. One of the people we'd rescued had been so terrified and crazy that she'd killed one of our team without realizing what she'd done.

"We're unboarding the front door of George's now," JT continued. "I'm heading up top for a quick jaunt down the block for an 'everyone look at me' moment. I love that part. Give it five minutes or so and then head over."

"It may take a little longer than that. We might have a survivor here as well."

"Actually," Griff said, "we may not have five minutes."

"What's that?" JT had good hearing for someone who wasn't a wild card.

"Hang on a sec." I turned to Griff, now looking out a partially cracked bedroom door. "What the hell are you talking about?"

*Whoever may or may not have been alive downstairs?" He shook his head. "They're definitely dead now."

"How do you know?"

"Because all those zombies who were clamoring to get at them are now heading our way."

I heard slow but relentless footsteps mounting the stairs.

Griff slammed the door shut. There was no lock. And it opened inward.

"Shit."

"Deep shit," Griff agreed.

"JT," I said into the radio, "Do your best, but we just ran out of time. We're headed your way now."

I hit the off switch and shoved the radio back on my belt.

Without saying another word, Griff and I both took a side of a heavy wooden dresser painted an unfortunate Pepto Bismol pink, and muscled it in front of the door. Hands pounding on the door echoed the thump the dresser made when we dropped it on the carpeted floor.

It didn't take long for the dresser to start edging towards us as the door slowly opened under the combined weight of lots of determined zombies.

"Here."

I ran over to the heavy wooden-framed twin bed. Griff joined me and we dragged it over as a bulwark against the dresser.

Griff held up the Hello Kitty sheets.

I nodded, punching the screen out of the window with my fist while Griff quickly tied the fitted and flat sheets together lengthwise, yanking hard on the knots to make sure they'd hold our weight.

He looked around for something to use as an anchor.

"Tie it to the bedpost." I suggested.

He raised an eyebrow. "You or the sheets?"

I narrowed my eyes. "Don't ruin the moment."

Griff smirked and tied one end of our sheet rope to the bedpost closest to the window. He gave a hard yank. The bed moved just a little bit. Hopefully it would stay in place long enough to let us hightail it out of there before the zombies broke through the door.

Griff tossed the sheet rope out of the window. "You first."

I didn't argue. I just grabbed the sheet and rappelled down the side of the house into the backyard. I landed in front of a large window

As soon as I touched ground, Griff practically leapt out the window, hand over handing it down next to me in record time.

"They're in," he said.

The downstairs glass window burst outwards.

"And they're out."

We took off to the other side of the backyard, which dead-ended in a rotting wooden fence, the boards warped and gone green in some places.

"Mine," I said. Pivoting on one leg, I slammed a sidekick into a particularly rotted-looking section of old redwood. It shattered most cooperatively so I kicked the slat next to it, making a gap large enough for us to squeeze through.

"Nice," Griff said with an appreciative look.

We emerged into the backyard of the house that straddled both 43rd and Sloat, a short chain link fence the only thing between us and a buttload of zombies.

And possibly a lioness.

This did not look good.

"What do you think?" Griff crouched down next to me in the corner of the yard, M4 in hand. "Do we wait for Monkey Boy to do his magic or just go for it?"

Zombies from the house we'd just vacated were hammering at the fence, not quite smart enough to squeeze through the gap we'd created. Some of the zoms wandering down Sloat had noticed us and were slamming against the chain-link fence, bringing more of them over to see what the fuss was all about.

"I think if we wait any longer," I said, "we're totally screwed."

"If they don't have the door open, we're screwed too."

I nodded. "Yup. But I'd rather move and take my chances than wait here."

Griff reached out and gave my hand a squeeze. "If we don't make it ... I'm really sorry I didn't a chance to get you into—"

I held up my free had. "Don't spoil the moment, okay?"

He grinned. "Deal."

"Is that..." I heard singing. "Is that yodeling?"

"High on a hill was a lonely goatherd
Lay ee odl lay ee odl lay hee hoo..."

Yup, it totally was.

The zombies following us from the house next door broke through the redwood at the same time the zombies on Sloat trampled down a section of the chain link fence.

I unslung my M4. No need for stealth any more.

"Let's rock!"

* * *

JT stood on the roof a few doors down from George's on 44ᵗʰ. His knee hurt like hell, but his vocal chords were feeling no pain.

His yodel rivaled Julie Andrews' as far as volume and perfect pitch, and got the attention of the zombies below. Not all of them, but enough to hopefully give Ash and Griff a good chance to make it to the entrance of the store.

It also felt great to let rip with some show tunes without being told to shut up.

* * *

Griff and I opened fire at the same time, Griff focusing on the ones following us from next door while I took on the newbies from Sloat.

I wasn't the best shot in the world, but at this range it was hard to miss, provided I didn't panic. It helped that a number of the zoms were evidently *Sound of Music* fans and followed the sound of JT's voice down the block and around the corner.

"We're good back here.

I risked a quick look and saw that Griff had created a nice little barricade of dead zombies in the breach they'd made in the fence. Other zoms pushed against the unmoving rotted flesh of their fallen comrades, but it would take them a little while to make it through.

Both Griff and I renewed our attentions to the ones on Sloat, clearing out enough of them to create some space on the sidewalk.

"Now?" Griff looked at me.

I switched out the M4 for my katana. Running and aiming and firing at the same time? I'd be lucky if I didn't hit my own foot. Then I nodded.

"Now."

* * *

Luke and Jenna stood sentry at the front doors. Phil waited right behind them, crowbar in hand, and ready to smash in the skulls of anyone without a pulse. The wooden boards were now piled in the aisle, revealing the metal theft prevention grills on the inside of each door.

They could hear JT singing, the sound carrying down the atrium. Jenna cocked her head to one side.

"What the hell is he singing?" she asked.

Phil shook his head in disbelief. "You've never seen Sound of Music?"

Before Jenna could answer, gunshots echoed outside and fists pounded on the front door.

Luke and Jenna started to open it, but Phil held up a hand.

"Who is it? "

"We're JT's friends," a female voice yelled. "Please open the fucking door!"

Jenna and Luke wrenched the doors open.

A man and a woman clutching a rifle and a Japanese sword, respectively, practically fell inside, undead hands reaching for them.

The man turned around and fired his weapon into the skull of a zombie in a zoo uniform while the woman thrust the point of her sword into the eye socket of a former surfer in a wetsuit. The ex zoo employee tumbled backwards onto the sidewalk while the surfer collapsed, falling facedown, its front half in the store.

"Seriously?"

Rolling her eyes, the woman shoved the surfer out the door with one foot even as more zombies lurched towards the store's entrance. Luke and Jenna slammed the doors and twisted the locks. Zombies piled up against it, splatting open palms on the outside. The metal grills on the inside shook, but held firm.

The woman turned to face them, face and body covered in blood and viscera. Luke tried not to flinch at the smell, which was even worse than Dylan and the rotten food.

"I'm Ash, and this is Griff." She nodded towards the guy, equally drenched in gore. "Let's get out of here, shall we?"

* * *

I looked at the worn, filthy trio before me. A youngish blond guy with a surprisingly neat beard and mustache. A young woman with a sweet face wearing a wary expression, curly dark hair trying its best to escape a single braid. A big guy in his early 40s maybe, bald, wearing a blue apron over his shirt and shorts.

"I'm Phil," the big guy said. "This is my niece Jenna."

Looking at Jenna, JT's determination to keep his promise made even more sense. Not that I thought he was shallow enough to only want to save cute young women, but...

...it couldn't have hurt.

Of course, the way the girl was staring at Griff, even under the layers of yuck, didn't auger well if JT had hopes in her direction. The big guy, Phil, noticed it too and gave Griff total stink-eye.

The blond guy stuck his hand out. "I'm Luke."

I shook my head. "We're covered in infectious fluids," I said. "We're immune. You're probably not."

He withdrew his hand hastily.

I paused. "JT said there was four of you."

"Yeah," the girl said. "Dylan. He's—"

She looked around and frowned. "He was here a minute ago"

Phil shook his head in disgust. "Probably sulking in the bath-room."

* * *

Fuck them," Dylan muttered.

No one noticed as he crept towards the back of the store, taking care to move as quietly as possible. He didn't want to leave George's Zoo any more. Sure, he'd have loved to have gotten out during those first few days, but now?

What did he have left out in the real world? His mom and his brother were gone. There was no future. No place for Jenna to drive her stupid car. No colleges, no jobs, nothing. Just a lot of rotting pus-bags that wanted to eat him.

No, he wasn't going to leave. And neither would the rest of them. He'd told Jenna he'd pay her back. And he would.

He began stealthily moving the garbage and recycle bins away from the back door.

* * *

I radioed JT.

"You can stop yodeling," I said. "We're in."

JT gave a last yodel, then said, "Cool. Heading back. I'll drop the rope down. Jenna can show you where. We can pull everyone up on the roof and wait for the copter."

"Roger that."

"And a whiskey tango foxtrot to you."

"Just call for the copter, okay, smartass?"

"Roger that."

He signed off before I could call him a smartass.

I turned back to the trio of survivors and Griff.

"Jenna, can you show me how JT got in and out of here?"

Jenna nodded eagerly and pointed towards an open sliding glass window, a faint shaft of sunlight shining down behind it. "The atrium."

I peeked through the window up at the open sky at the top of four walls. I noted the pipe running down one of the walls. Child's play for JT to scale, but not so easy for the rest of us.

I heard a holler and looked up as a thick rope tumbled down along the side of one wall, the end tied in a makeshift noose. I looked up to see JT waving from the roof.

"Ready Betty?" he called down.

"You have no idea," I yelled back.

I stuck my head back inside. "Okay, gang, let's move it."

*　*　*

He had to push the door hard. The weight of so many hungry zombies on the other side did a good job of keeping the door shut. Once Dylan got it cracked open an inch, however, mangled fingers clutched the doorframe and others reached in for the fresh meat waiting for them.

Dylan laughed with glee. This would show Phil he couldn't be pushed around. See how he liked zombies in his precious store. And see how Jenna liked—

A still meaty hand with a gold band sunken into one putrefying finger reached through the gap, grabbed a handful of Dylan's hair, and yanked hard. Dylan's outraged scream cut off as teeth sank into his neck.

*　*　*

Someone screamed from deep in the store, the cutting off abruptly into a gurgle.

Shitsnacks.

I clambered back into the store, blades out.

"Shit. Dylan!"

The young blond guy, Luke, ran in the direction of the scream before anyone could stop him. He reappeared almost immediately, eyes wide, nostrils flaring like a panicked horse as several zombies staggered after him.

"Jesus, they're coming in the back!"

Griff immediately moved towards the commotion, pushing Luke out of the way and swinging the stock of his M4 to connect with skulls with the efficiency of a wind-up mechanical zombie slayer.

I grabbed Jenna's arm and hustled her into the atrium, shoving Luke after her.

Phil didn't need any urging to follow them.

I looked past Griff down to the end of the aisle where zombies bunched up in the bottleneck a partially open door and two large trash bins. The body of a young man sprawled on ground, several zombies chowing down on his cooling flesh. The zombies on the other side of the door pushed past one at a time, stepping unheedingly on the corpse and their fellow zombies, stumbling towards us.

Griff coolly dispatched each one as it made it past the blockage.

"We need to get out of here now," I said urgently. "JT's gonna need help pulling everyone up."

Smashing one more zombie in the head, Griff followed me into the atrium, sliding the window shut behind us and latching it. For all the good that would do. I figured once enough zoms started pounding on it the glass would hold maybe five minutes. If we were lucky.

"You first," Griff said, holding the noose end of the rope out to me.

I shook my head. "No. You'll get up there much faster than I will and then you can help pull the rest of us out."

Griff started to argue, then realized I was right. Without wasting any more time, he used the rope to climb up the wall, tossing it back down after he'd hoisted himself over the top onto the roof.

The first zombie, a young man with bushy brown hair, reached the atrium window. It slapped its hands against the glass, smearing it with fluids. Jenna blanched when she saw its face.

"Dylan," she whispered.

Phil stepped in front of the window and blocked her view.

"Get her out of here," he told me.

I helped Jenna step into the noose. "Hold on tight," I advised. She did, shutting her eyes as JT and Griff hoisted her quickly up to safety. Luke followed suit as more zombies joined Dylan at the window, moaning and pounding on the glass.

"You next," I said to Phil when they'd tossed the rope back down.

Phil looked at the rope and then at me, shaking his head.

"I got news for you, hon. Gonna take more than those skinny ass guys to pull me up."

"Griff is stronger than he looks," I assured him. "So am I, for that matter."

"So you go first," he said.

I opened my mouth to argue, but the sound of breaking glass stopped the words in my mouth.

"Dammit, go!"

"Uncle Phil," Jenna yelled, "Get your ass up here!"

I went to work with my blades, hacking, slashing and thrusting with all the finesse of a Cuisinart on crack, doing my best to keep the zombies from climbing through.

One of them --the one that used to be Dylan -- reached in and grabbed my belt, pulling me towards the opening. Another managed to grasp my left forearm, preventing me from using my tanto. I tried to get a good angle with my katana, but the blade was too long. Teeth sank into my gloved hand as my face and neck were pulled closer to reeking, open mouths and jagged shards of glass.

Strong arms encircled my body from behind, yanking me backwards away from the waiting mouths. The one zombie lost its grip on my forearm, but the Dylan zombie kept hold of my belt, sliding through the window, face and arms slicing open along the broken glass. I shoved the point of my tanto in one of its ears until it slumped down, limp fingers sliding down my legs.

Ewww.

Other zombies began squeezing through the window, heedless of the damage the glass did to their skin.

Phil and I looked at each other. Without a word, he shoved the rope in my hand, picked me up, and heaved. Holding on for dear life, I practically flew up the three stories as Griff and JT pulled me up and onto the rooftop.

"Hey Jenna," Phil called up as zombies converged on him. "What did one zombie say to the other zombie when they were eating a comedian? This tastes funny."

Jenna looked down and started screaming her uncle's name.

Phil yelled when the first zombie bit him. Griff took careful aim and made sure he wouldn't feel the next bite.

* * *

Ash and Griff were both stretched out full length on the rooftop, using their knapsacks as pillows as they waited for the helicopter to arrive. Luke leaned against a chimney, eyes shut while Jenna sat off by herself, staring numbly into the distance.

JT felt oddly hollow. He'd done his best, but had only managed to keep half of his promise. He felt responsible for how things had played out. He should have seen how far gone the one kid had been, somehow stopped him from opening that door.

Now he knew how Ash felt.

He went over and sat next to Jenna.

"I'm sorry about your uncle," he said simply.

She didn't say anything. After a few minutes of silence, he patted her awkwardly on the shoulder and got up, leaving her to grieve in peace for the time being. He crossed to the side of the roof overlooking the ocean and heaved an unaccustomedly heavy sigh, watching gulls fly over the white-capped waves.

"You did your best, you know."

He turned to find Ash standing next to him.

"Feels like I could have done more."

"You can't save the world." She was quiet for a moment, then added, "I should know."

"But you still tried."

Ash looked at him. "So did you."

He nodded slowly. "I guess that'll have to be enough."

PANIC

By Tom Leveen

based on characters appearing
in the novel SICK

http://www.tomleveen.com

Tuesday, November 12
Phoenix Metro High School
Phoenix, Arizona

5:04 p.m.

U*m*—

My name is Laura Fitzgerald, I'm seventeen . . . and I really, really want to be eighteen someday.

I don't know what's going on, exactly. It feels like the world is ending out there. I'm scared, and there's no one else in here but me. This is Cody's phone, not mine. I guess you know that. Whoever you are. Whoever finds this, I mean.

If Cody's mom or dad hears this, I'm sorry about Cody, I did everything I could. I swear.

God . . .

I don't know . . . I don't know how long I can stay in here. I don't have any food or water. But they're still out there, I can hear them. Sometimes I hear someone scream out there.

Um . . .

Honestly? I'm kind of surprised I can even talk right now, usually I'd be curled up in a little ball somewhere. That's what I really want to do. But I can't. They'll get me if I do.

Oh, God. God.

No. Okay. Stop. Breathe. I can do this. I can do it.

Uh—

I just, I thought I should explain everything, because maybe it will help? I don't know. I don't know if anyone will ever find this . . . but, um . . .

Okay.

This is what happened.

Tuesday, November 12
1:50 pm

"This is my worst nightmare," I told Mackenzie Murphy as I forced one step after another toward the gymnasium. Around us, hundreds of other students pushed and shoved and yelled and cussed. It felt like being in human soup, drenched in clammy sweat and the breath of thousands of other high school students.

I don't do well in crowds. Phoenix Metro High School grew exponentially a few years ago when another school closed down. There are way, way too many of us. Definitely way too many for me.

Kenzie smiled and tugged my pony tail. I yelped, and Kenzie laughed. "Don't worry, you've got a bratty-little-sister-type friend going with you to keep you all distracted."

Despite how my arms and legs shook under my hoodie and jeans, I managed to smile back at her. Kenzie's brother Brian had broken up with me a few weeks ago, but Kenzie didn't act all weird about it, thank God. She kind of *was* like a little sister to me, even though she wasn't that much younger.

I forced myself to take as deep a breath as I could. It wasn't easy. I wanted a pill. All I had to do was reach into my bag and grab my bottle of clonazepam and in twenty minutes or so, I'd be able to handle all the noise and shoving and shouting, mostly because I'd be a half-asleep zombie.

But I didn't do it. I didn't take one. I didn't want to *have* to anymore. It was something I'd been working on for a while.

"I can't believe Brian didn't come with us," I said to Kenzie as people jostled into us. Each anonymous touch made my stomach clench.

Kenzie grabbed my arm and pulled us out of the worst of the foot traffic. I appreciated it. It made it easier to breathe. Our classroom buildings are all open, not enclosed; not indoors. That meant we had to deal with whatever the weather happened to be. Today, it was nice outside, sunshiny and a little cool but not cold. It wouldn't get cold until December, or even January. We never got snow, and it only rained maybe a dozen times per school year. The roofs and awnings over the sidewalks

69

were mostly for providing shade.

I think the open hallways helped me deal with my panic disorder and agoraphobia. I could usually handle being in classrooms, but gatherings any larger than that made me feel like I'd been put into a coffin and pushed out to sea like Danae in the Greek myth—enclosed and muffled in darkness, lolling out into an endless rollercoaster ocean, sick to my stomach and utterly trapped.

It wasn't the greatest way to spend each day.

"Fuck Brian," Kenzie said, sincerely but without any real hatred. She loved her brother a lot. "He's being an ass-bag."

"But gosh, how do you *really* feel, Kenzie?"

"He is!" Kenzie kept me moving toward the gym, but an angle, out of the bulk of the foot traffic. "You are awesome and so totally good for him, and one day, he'll figure that out."

"Yeah, we'll see."

I drew in another breath. It came back out like a stutter.

"Hey," Kenzie said, as we reached the doors to the gym. "You got this. And if you don't, we'll mosey. I'll go with you to Nurse Garrett or whatever. Okay?"

"Thanks. But, no. I can do it. I can do this."

Kenzie lowered her voice. "Have you taken anything?"

She and our friends knew I carried a couple bottles with me in my bag at all times. Klonopin and Paxil. The Pax I took twice a day, but the Klonopin I took as needed. I usually needed one a day. Sometimes two. That had been normal up until a few weeks ago. I'd started a lower dosage of Paxil, and been avoiding the Klonopin as best I could. But no one besides my doctor and my parents knew that yet, not even Kenzie or Brian. Maybe it was stupid, but it was a fight I wanted to take on myself.

I stopped walking and pulled away from the gym doors. Kenzie came along without protest. Someone behind us said, "Look out, bitch!"

The outburst certainly did not help calm my nerves. Phoenix Metro High School isn't the friendliest place on Earth.

"Listen, I need to tell you something," I said as the bell signaling the start of seventh hour went off.

"Totally," Kenzie said, her eyes serious.

"It's just that... I haven't been taking all my pills all the time."

Kenzie's eyebrows rose. "Yeah?"

"I've been backing off them. Slowly. Lower dosages and stuff. So this whole pep rally thing, it's kind of an experiment, you know? Like, if I can sit through this, then maybe... I don't know."

"Okay. What can I do?"

"Nothing, just…. I just wanted you to know, so in case something really bad happens to me—"

"Do whatever you have to. I'll be there. Does Brian know?"

"Not yet. That's what I wanted to talk to him about tonight."

Brian and I had crossed paths earlier that morning, before he and his friends Chad and Jack ditched fourth hour. When I'd told Brian I wanted to talk to him, I think, or maybe *want* to think, that he looked happy about it. Or at least intrigued. We'd stayed friends since we broke up, because we hung out with a lot of the same people, like Cammy and her boyfriend Hollis. Them, Kenzie, Chad, Jack—we hung out a lot at lunch and things like that. They were my best friends. When Brian said he thought we needed a break, I'd had a pretty epic meltdown afterward, worried that all my friends would stop talking to me. It turned out to be the opposite. Honestly, while I know we were all still friends, I think they were angry with him about the breakup.

I'd be lying if I said that didn't make me a *little* pleased.

Kenzie's surprised expression changed to suspicion. "Okay, Laura? It's really cool that you're willing to try going to this dumb pep rally thing, and I'm happy for you. That's awesome you've been able to back off the meds. But you're not doing it for Brian, are you? Because, seriously? Don't."

"No, not *for* him. It's more like—I don't know. He kind of had a point. I should be able to go to a movie, you know? I should be able to go out to eat with him, or with anyone, not just stay home all night. That's all. But no, I'm not doing it for him."

"Okay," Kenzie said. "That's good."

A security guard shouted at us to either get into the gym for the pep rally or get to class. Kenzie and I hurried into the gym. The doors closed behind us.

I sucked in a breath the instant we passed through the lobby and my Vans touched the hardwood floor. The gym, decked out in our red and white school colors, overflowed with students. The band had already started playing on the visitor's side of the bleachers, while the cheerleaders did routines on the floor. The football team lounged around at the opposite end of the gym, waiting for a cue to run out and be introduced to the crowd as if we didn't go to class with the athletes every single day.

"What do you want to do?" Kenzie said over the noise as I froze in place. The noise assaulted me, and I could feel the walls closing in. I felt like a rat in a maze.

Our friend Cammy became head cheerleader this year, and she executed perfect backflips across the basketball court. At the end of her flips, she saw me cowering against the wall. She couldn't wave, because it would be like breaking character, but she smiled big and sent me a wink.

That helped. Cammy is the opposite of everything I am. I wished sometimes I could be more like her.

"I'm okay," I said, half truthfully. "I'm okay."

I stepped toward the stairs leading up the collapsible aluminum bleachers. Kenzie and I found seats at the very top, near all the depressed smokers who always seemed to congregate together. They were harmless, though, compared to some of the other students.

"All right," Kenzie said, making sure I had the aisle seat in case I needed to run. "See? Not so bad. You got this."

I nodded, but couldn't respond. I had to focus hard on my breathing. Panic attacks usually feel like heart attacks, except panic won't actually kill you—it just feels like it. Already my chest felt constricted, but I'd been practicing some breathing and meditation techniques. I focused on them now: *Breathe in one two three four, breathe out five six seven eight . . .*

I was jealous of every single person in the gym. Many were bored, a few seemed genuinely excited, not counting the cheerleaders and dancers. They were so lucky, and they didn't even realize it. To them, it was just *ho-hum, another day of school, at least I get to get out of math this period.* For me, it was anything but. It was *everything.*

Kenzie put a hand on my knee, her crimson nail polish glaring beneath the high florescent lights. Into my ear, she whispered, "You're shaking."

I rubbed my arms, pretending like I was cold, even though I didn't have to do that with Kenzie.

"Chilly," I lied. And my friend Kenzie nodded. It's hard to describe how much I appreciated that.

Then the gym exploded. So did my heart.

1:56 p.m.

It started with someone screaming a cuss word from among the group of football players. Everyone looked.

From the direction of the locker rooms, a guy came barreling toward the football team on his hands and knees, like an ape. Even over the band and the general chaos, I could hear him *growling*.

The team turned toward him just as the guy leaped. It seemed inhuman, like no person should have been able to jump that high from that hunched of a position. The guy tackled one of the football players, taking him to the ground.

People started screaming. I stood up, legs quaking, wanting to head straight down the stairs and out of this gym and out of this school and *home*, please, God, just let me go *home*. . . .

The hunched-over guy grabbed the player's arm in his hands, and bit him. The football player on the ground shouted and started punching the guy in the head, but it had no effect. Even from as far away as I stood, I could see blood flying across the basketball court, staining the wood. I could see the football player's face go from surprised to angry to being in serious pain.

The team went to work. They dogpiled the two of them as security and teachers rushed to the scene. Everyone in the gym was on their feet now, some cheering, a few wincing, but all watching. We'd been transported to the Roman Empire, become spectators in the arena.

On the court, the fight slowly got contained. Someone got on the gymnasium PA system and said, "All right, everyone sit down, it's over, sit down please . . . it's under control, please sit down, everyone."

Most of us did. I didn't. I couldn't. My feet had melted and become stuck to the aluminum bleachers, my arms cramped straight down and motionless.

Our school resource officer, Doug Shepherd, had the attacker face-down on the court and in handcuffs. Officer Doug bled from his hands, and the guy flailed like a fish out of water. The football team congregated at the end of the gym again, several of them holding wounds on their arms or faces.

The crazy guy had done a whole lot of damage in not very much time at all.

Kenzie summed it up best: "Holy *shit!*"

"Yeah," said a kid sitting next to her. It was one of the smokers dressed head-to-foot in black—jeans, jacket, shoes, cap. He looked as spooked as I felt. Either he was naturally pale, or else the fight had drained the blood from his face. He seemed young, maybe a freshman.

Kenzie took my hand. "Laura? You okay?"

I closed my mouth as a janitor came out and began pouring bleach on the floor where blood had spilled and pooled. Officer Doug wrestled the crazy guy out of the gym somehow while we all watched. Then someone started applauding, and pretty soon the whole gym was cheering and clapping. I wanted to think it was for Officer Doug, but wondered if it was for the fight. For the blood.

Somehow, I managed to sit down. "Yeah," I told Kenzie. "I'm... no, I'm not okay. But I'll make it."

I forced myself back to my deep breathing practice while teachers got the gym under control. Several football players left the gym with a couple of coaches, headed back into the locker rooms, I assumed to get bandaged up.

I took my phone out and tapped Brian's name. I sent him a text: *Big-time fight at rally. Not feeling real good but I am here!!!*

On the one hand, maybe I shouldn't have even bothered touching base. On the other, I needed him to know I could sit at a pep rally without going catatonic. Technically, that remained to be seen, but still. It felt right to point out something scary had happened and I'd survived.

Kenzie leaned over as I typed, and smiled. "Yeah, that's it. Shove it in his face."

Something resembling a laugh coughed out of me, and I set the phone down beside me. I might need to dial 911 before the pep rally was over, the way things were going.

"I never seen anything like that," the kid next to Kenzie said, and wiped his face. I could smell the cigarette smoke on his clothes. "Man, fuck this place."

Kenzie gave him an understanding grin. I found myself nodding. I wasn't a big fan of this place, either.

"I'm sorry my brother's such a tool," Kenzie said as things settled back down and Cammy got the cheerleaders arranged on the sidelines.

She seemed to be giving them a little pep rally of her own, getting them to focus.

"It's not your fault," I said. "I get it. I wouldn't want to hang out with me, either."

"Oh, he wants to hang out with you," Kenzie said, grinning a grin far too sly for her age. "He wants to do a lot more than hang out with you."

I poked her leg, which made her cackle.

The band started playing again, and Cammy guided her cheerleaders back onto the floor, well away from the area the janitor marked off with orange cones and yellow Wet Floor triangles. I thought I could smell the bleach he used on the blood.

Cammy got on the PA microphone. "Whew, okay! How's everybody doing?"

The students roared back. I guess they were doing great. I guess seeing people bleed was exciting for them.

"That was really crazy," Cammy went on. "But you know what? We're cool now! Yeah! Let's hear it for Officer Doug!"

Cheers. I shrank in on myself, rolling my shoulders forward. Kenzie put a hand on my back.

"Now let's focus on the positive, all right? Let's talk about how our team's gonna smash the Sabercats!"

Oddly, I think Cammy managed to change the overall feeling in the gym right then. I don't know how, but it felt to me like the excitement turned to actual school spirit. Or maybe the difference between smashing Sabercats and the team smashing the crazy guy just wasn't all the big. As long as someone was getting smashed, our student body was all for it.

Cammy began announcing the team by name. The guys would come forward one at a time, jogging to the center of the court, slapping hands with the guys who'd already been called. They looked even more cocky than normal, probably still pumped from beating up one guy.

"Spirit Week," Kenzie grumbled, shaking her head. "It's Tuesday for God's sake. Why are we even doing this?"

"We're not in class," I said. "So that's something. I think they're trying to make us happier to be here."

Kenzie snorted, looking more like a worldly college student than a sixteen-year-old sophomore. The truth is, this fight we'd just seen wasn't unusual in and of itself. I didn't think people normally got bitten in school fights, and I didn't think a single person could usually draw so much blood from so many other people. But an on-campus brawl wasn't

75

unheard of by any means. We had one once a month, I'd guess. Once, there'd been a riot. Windows broken and everything.

Needless to say, I hadn't handled *that* day very well, and I hadn't even seen it in person. I'd been shaking under the American flag in my history class, the lights off, as Principal Winsor announced a lockdown.

A tall white fence surrounded the entire campus, supposedly to keep us safe. What it did instead was make the school feel like a prison. Brian and his friends knew how to jump the fence, which freaked me out because the ends were tapered to points, and I worried they'd impale themselves one of these days. We used to have an open campus for lunch, but they closed it a few years ago. So, combine all that with adding twice as many students than the school was built for, many of whom had to get up extra early in the morning to bus in from an entirely other side of town, and it was no wonder tempers flared.

Not exactly the kind of place for a girl with my particular mental baggage.

Still—here I was, and while I definitely didn't feel at ease, I hadn't bolted for the doors, either. Thanks to Cammy's cheering, a sort of positive energy began building in the gym. As I let my gaze drift across the bleachers opposite ours, I spotted our friend Jack standing near the bottom bench, doing some kind of hip-pumping dance and making a selfie-style duck-face with his lips. Typical Jack. Not everyone saw the humor in it, but I kind of did. He caught me watching him, gave me a surprised wave, and proceeded to pantomime about a dozen sexual positions, only half of which I've ever even heard of. I tapped Kenzie and pointed Jack out. She saw him and cracked up.

So when my phone vibrated the bench under me and I saw Brian had texted me back, I think I even managed a smile. With the fight over, and practicing my deep breathing, Jack's antics, and now Brian returning my message... I almost felt *good*.

"Hey," I said to Kenzie, loudly over the drums and horns and shouting. "Look."

I showed her my screen. Kenzie grinned. "See? He's not a complete idiot. Still an idiot, but, you know. Not *completely*."

I laughed. I couldn't remember the last time I actually laughed while at school.

Turns out it didn't matter, because then I screamed.

I wasn't the only one.

2:51 p.m.

At first, I assumed it was a joke. Maybe some kind of belated Halloween thing, but Halloween was two weeks ago. Then I thought maybe it was some kind of school spirit skit. That didn't work either. My last hope was a senior prank.

It wasn't. It wasn't any of those things.

Less than an hour ago, one crazy student tried taking on members of the football team. Those athletes had been led away toward the locker room. Now they'd come back.

And they all acted just like the crazy guy had.

One moment, Cammy's leading the cheerleaders in a spirited chant that's starting to catch on in the stands. Then the doors to the locker rooms flew open and the football players who'd been hurt in the fight sprinted toward their teammates, the cheerleaders, kids sitting on the lowest benches . . . anyone they could reach.

The cheerleader closest to the lead player didn't even see him coming. He ran full speed, hunched over, and smashed her to the ground. He buried his face against her throat before anyone else could even move. Suddenly the athlete pulled his head back for a second—and in that second, we all saw everything our nightmares were made of.

Bright blood washed his face. A patch of skin from the cheerleader's neck hung from his teeth. Even over the noise of the band still playing and other cheerleaders still chanting, I heard a nauseating gurgle coming from the cheerleader's mouth as blood sprayed out of her. She grasped for the wound, as if trying to scoop the fluid back into place, her sneakered feet thumping helplessly against the court floor. The athlete lunged back in again and...

...and I am almost certain that he began to chew on her throat.

"What the—" Kenzie said, and stood.

In the amount of time it took her to say it, the other enraged players raced onto the court, attacking anyone within reach. One of them grabbed some boy in the first row of bleachers across from us, and yanked him off his feet. The football player gripped the boy's arm in both hands and bit down. He tore skin and muscle away from the bone as if the boy's limb was a raw drumstick.

My stomach lurched so hard it brought me to my feet.

"*Jee-zus!*" the smoker kid beside Kenzie squealed. He stood up, too.

All of us were on our feet by then, screams piercing through the voices of the cheerleaders who didn't yet realize something had gone hellishly wrong.

Pills, I thought. *Need my pills, need to have a pill or two or ten, oh God please just let this stop now—*

Cammy caught on faster than some of the others. She started shoving her cheer team toward the exit, shouting, "Get out of here! Go, go! Run!"

Her directive acted like a light switch, empowering everyone in the gym to bolt for the exits. Everyone not being attacked, I mean. By then, there were a dozen or more people bleeding from wounds. All the wounds were the same, it seemed—arms and necks. One cheerleader sat on the floor, trying to pull herself backward on her hands while one of the possessed athletes gnawed on her shin.

And for me, things got quiet.

Muffled. I knew where I was, and saw but didn't understand what was happening around me. All my muscles loosened and went slack. My heart went from stuttering at a hundred miles an hour to an impossibly slow thunk behind my ribs, barely enough to pump my blood.

Blood—

So much of it now on the floor. Spraying through the air. Like a war.

Over the chaos, I thought I heard someone talking over the school PA system. Principal Winsor maybe. I only made out a few words: "Faculty—students are—remain—for the—period—lockdown—"

I felt Kenzie grabbing me, shoving, trying to get me to move. I couldn't. My fight-or-flight responses failed completely and chose instead to make me just stand there, motionless, maybe hoping the monsters in the gym wouldn't notice me at all.

My hand began to shake. No—vibrate. I raised it to my eyes and saw that I'd accidentally tapped Brian's contact button while his message was still on my screen.

When a recording kicked in reciting his number back to me—sending the call to voicemail—something inside me twitched and my panic came back in full force.

"We gotta *go!*" Kenzie screamed.

The smoker kid beside her shouted "Fuck this!" and ploughed past both of us, trying to scramble down into the exodus below. Everyone in the gym had flooded toward the exit leading out to the breezeway, the main sidewalk that split the campus in half from north to south. But the stampede resulted in a human traffic jam. It also allowed the bloodstained football players to pick off anyone being kept from the doors. One by one, they'd leap and drag to the ground anyone pressed up against the tide of humanity trying to squash through the double doors. It looked like trying to use a funnel the wrong way around.

"Here, take . . ." I said, and pushed my phone toward Kenzie as my brain spun on a merry-go-round, trying to find a safe way to get out of here.

I barely heard her talking behind me as we both took quiet steps down the bleachers, keeping our backs to the wall. I still wore my backpack over both shoulders, so I pulled it off and carried it in one hand while trying to unzip the front pocket with the other. If I could just get to my pills—

One of them saw us.

I stopped in place and Kenzie banged into me as the football player, mouth ringed with crimson matching the red school color of his jersey, came scrambling over the bleachers toward us. His eyes gleamed yellow and his mouth and arms seemed swollen as he slobbered and growled his way up the bleachers.

He did not stalk us, did not try to pin us in place by how he moved his body. I only know that in retrospect—in the moment, all I knew was this big guy was coming at us and wouldn't stop for anything. And I know *that* much because I said it: "Stop."

Just said it. Didn't scream, didn't throw up my hands to ward him off. Just, "Stop."

It didn't work.

The athlete dribbled thick strands of saliva and blood from his mouth. It swung back and forth as he leaped at us.

My body took over. I used the only weapon I had.

I'd taken my pink backpack off and held it by the loop while I'd tried to find my pill bottles. As the athlete came at us, I swung the bag as hard as I could at his face. The bag connected, my heavy English textbook thunking him solidly enough to disorient him for a one heartbeat's worth of time.

"*Go!*" Kenzie screamed at me.

And I went. We both did, sliding more than running down the bleacher steps to the floor. By then, much of the traffic jam had cleared as kids ran the opposite direction, toward the locker rooms or else climbing and dodging up and down the bleachers, pursued by guys who trained to do things like run up and down steps for an hour at football practice.

Kenzie and I pushed toward the doors. A few people were still jammed up between the doorframes. I looked back into the gym, trying frantically to comprehend the carnage.

In that moment, I didn't think I'd ever sleep again.

The gymnasium floor was half covered with bodies. Some of them didn't move, lying in thick puddles of their own blood that poured out of ragged throat wounds. Many rolled around, coating their clothes in the fluid of others, screaming or moaning, holding arms or legs. One kid howled, "*Mommy! Mommy!*" as his forearms spilled red. The crazed athletes continued their hunt, knocking people over and attacking their throats or arms.

Something else I didn't realize until later: They weren't working as a team. Each guy initiated his own attack. Every so often, one would stop and sniff at a dead or dying student, growl, and move on. They didn't stalk, didn't select victims. It wasn't as if they targeted smaller kids, younger kids, black kids, white kids, brown kids, boys, girls… just whoever was closest. They used no athletic moves, like juking or faking, the way I saw football players do when my Dad watched NFL games. They just charged, like animals, unstoppable, no pausing to stop or consider or listen to pleas.

What *was* this?

I don't know how long I stood there before Kenzie pulled me by the sleeve. I stumbled after her, thinking, *My pills, my bottles, in my bag, my bag, need my bag…*

Outside was no better than inside. People ran screaming down the open-air hallway, headed toward the performing arts department that anchored the south end of campus just like the gym anchored it north. In between those two points, the two-story A, B, C, and D buildings were emptying, students and teachers alike scurrying like insects into and out of doors as they tried to make sense of the chaos. Those buildings sat like gargantuan rectangular cinder blocks on either side of the breezeway, with a staircase tethering each one in the center. The staircases overflowed now with escaping students, like fans at a concert trying to rush the stage.

"Laura!" Kenzie gasped as we came to a stop in the middle of the breezeway. "We gotta get outta here, the—the parking lot, maybe—"

Then she was gone. Fleeing students bashed into us, knocking Kenzie one direction and me another. I hit the concrete on my elbows with a shriek, realizing only vaguely that the soft material of my hoodie probably saved my bones from splintering at the impact.

I shouted for Kenzie as she was half-carried down the sidewalk by students trying to escape. I lost sight of her maroon shirt a moment later, buried amongst hundreds of other people.

"*Help!*" someone cried. "Help me, please!"

I turned my head. Lying on the ground no more than a car length away, a girl younger than Kenzie gripped her ankle. She wasn't bleeding though. I guessed she'd been hurt in the mad stampede from the gym, trampled by the running, panicked boots and sandals and sneakers of a hundred high school students.

Our eyes met. Hers were brown. They were also wide with terror.

"Please," she said—maybe whispered, though how I could've heard a whisper over the insanity going on around us, I don't know.

"Help me," she went on. "I can't walk. *Please.*"

I pulled myself to my feet and stood still, staring at her. I mean—I'd *heard* her. I'd heard her perfectly clear. I even saw that her expression shifted as I stood up, as if thinking I'd risen specifically to come over and help her.

Except I didn't.

All the shouts and screams climbed into my ears like fire ants, stinging and poisoning me. I lifted my hands to my ears and squeezed my arms as tightly to myself as I could. Yet even as I did this, I gave the campus a lighthouse scan, right to left, and saw nothing but blood and dust and the dead or dying.

I had no concept of how long it had been since the football players came tearing out of the locker room. Maybe a minute, maybe an hour, maybe a year. But however long it had been, they'd decimated what looked like a quarter of our school's population.

I turned back to the girl. She had a hand raised toward me, expecting me to help her up. I stood there and stared at it.

For me, there are many kinds of panic. There are the attacks that raise my heart rate to terrifying speeds; I start babbling and shaking, and feel like I'm going to puke non-stop for the next week and a half. Then there are the attacks that go way past scared, and deep into paralysis.

When that happens, it's almost a relief. My heart almost stops. My skin tingles, then numbs. I can't hear anything. It's what I imagine a stroke must feel like, staring at some blank point in space, unable to move, to talk, to think. It's acceptance, in a way. A fundamental shut-down of all my systems as my body and mind prepare to give in to whatever fate

81

I'm doomed for. It's the worst kind of attack, and also kind of the best, because there is no fear exactly—just a mantra, a chant, telling me *You're going to die now. You're going to die now. You're going to die now.*

The girl's expression shifted again. I'm almost eighteen, and in the past seventeen years, I'd never seen a human being give me or anyone else a look of such utter shock and disgust. She looked at me like I'd just admitted to murdering her family, friends, and pets.

I lowered my hands.

No, I told myself. *No, don't let this beat you, dammit, don't let it. Help her, help her now—*

I swear to God I thought those things. I did.

But then she was gone and it was too late. A blur of red slid into her with a teeth-rattling crash, followed by an almost cartoonish puff of dust as she smashed out of my line of sight and out of my periphery. It was like I was a movie camera and she'd been knocked out of frame.

When I turned to look for her, I wished I hadn't. What I saw there—what I saw the guy who'd smashed into her *do* to her—

His mouth opened wide, wider than should have been possible, I think. His hands seemed covered in some kind of yellowish scales, and with one of them, he yanked her chin backward, exposing her throat. He rammed his teeth into her neck, shook his head like a dog with a toy, then pulled away, taking flesh with him.

I could have fit a fist in the hole he left behind. The girl issued a burbling, choking sound as blood spewed out of her. The guy spit pieces of her flesh out of his mouth, then dug into the hole with his fingers, yanking pieces from inside her throat, bringing them to his nose, sniffing, then discarding the bits he didn't like . . .

Or feeding himself the bits that he did.

She died quickly. Her head fell to one side, brown eyes fixed on mine. I think I was the last thing she ever saw: the girl who stood and let her die.

Something inside me shuddered, and I felt the paralysis start to creep in again. I might have stood there until one of the athletes came for me, except right then, my brain finally did something useful for once: It pointed out that I was still alive, but wouldn't be for much longer unless I found somewhere to hide, fast.

I'll never know or understand why none of the players tackled me in those moments while I stood uselessly on the covered sidewalk. Probably it was dumb luck. There were plenty of other people around, plenty of targets to choose from. I honestly believe it was all a matter of chance.

"Run," I said out loud, and finally, my feet became unglued and I took off for the C buildings, which were closest to me. There was too much anarchy happening further down the breezeway, past the B and A buildings, and admin and cafeteria beyond.

Past that was the performing arts department, where Brian and his best friend Chad were supposed to be this period. I wondered where they were. If they were—

Impulsively or instinctively, I don't know which, I raced for the nearest set of stairs to go up to the second floor of the west C building. The stairs were empty now. I didn't want to be on the first floor, not on the ground with these insane killers. On my way, I saw the smoker kid dressed in black who'd been sitting next to Kenzie. He stood pushing on a door to one of the first-floor classrooms, screaming to be let in.

It wasn't happening. I reached for his arm as I ran past.

"This way!" I said, and pulled him along behind me—maybe to make up for what I'd just done, or not done, for the girl with the broken ankle, the girl I'd watched get torn apart.

I must have sounded like I had a plan, because the kid came willingly. We bolted up the stairs and around a single switchback, toward the nearest classroom door as one of the mutated athletes roared and gave chase behind us.

Me and the kid both screamed as the athlete propelled himself up the stairs on his hands and feet, bellowing with each step as if in agony, his face contorting. And his face—the skin seemed to be melting somehow, falling down from his skull... *my God.*

We reached the door, which opened readily; the classroom was empty, the lights on. We leaped inside and shut the door. I flipped off the lights while the kid backed away from me, holding his left arm to his chest. I felt around the doorknob to throw the lock, realizing only then that the classroom doors had to be locked from the inside or outside with a key; there was no way to lock the door without one. Funny, the little details you don't notice even after three and half years.

"Shit," I whispered.

"What do we—?" the kid started, but I waved at him to shut up, pressing my ear to the door.

I could hear the athlete bellowing wordlessly, but not right outside the door. I thought he was most likely still on the stairs, possibly on the broad landing where the staircase switched back on itself. I could also still hear screaming outside, but further away.

After another minute, the groans of the athlete faded, and I heard nothing immediately beyond the door. I realized then that I was also listening for sirens, but not hearing any.

I slid my way up the door, keeping my body pressed against it, and searched for my phone. Nowhere. Dammit, Kenzie had it last.

"I think we're okay," I whispered to the kid.

He nodded and licked his lips, then winced.

"What's wrong?" I said.

"My arm." He walked over to me, pulling up his long black sleeve. "One of those fuckers bit me. Look."

I did. The kid had a chunk of his skin missing, and the wound still dripped blood. But it wasn't deep, and it was on the top of his arm, not near a vein.

"Keep pressure on it," I said, sounding for all the world like I knew what the hell I was talking about, which I didn't.

He nodded and wrapped his right hand around the wound again.

"What's your name?" I said.

"Cody. You?"

"Laura."

"What the hell is going on out there?"

I shook my head. Tried to form words. Couldn't. Shook my head again.

Then I looked at the clock.

2:54 p.m.

"We should put something in front of the door," I said.

Cody nodded. I tried shoving the teacher's desk, but it wouldn't budge. Together, lifting and dragging, the two of us managed to move it in front of the door. I glanced up at the windows. In these buildings, the only windows were narrow and set high in the wall by the ceiling—plenty to allow natural light in, but not allowing anyone to look out of. God forbid we get distracted or daydream.

I hopped onto the desk and stood on tiptoe, using my fingers to pull myself up one more inch. This wasn't the best vantage point in the world; I could only see a sliver of the ground past the second-floor railing, and maybe ten yards up and down the sidewalk outside this classroom. The only really helpful thing was I could see the stairs plainly, and at that moment, they were empty.

"It's clear," I said, feeling like a weak parody of an action movie hero. I climbed down and sat on the desk, elbows locked beside me, taking deep breaths.

"Man," Cody said, and that was all for a little while. Then he said, "We need to call the cops."

I got up and went to a tan phone embedded in the wall. It had probably been installed when the school was built. I picked up and immediately tried 911, but didn't get so much as a dial tone or busy signal. I tried the zero button. Same result.

By the time I'd hung up, Cody had a cell phone out and up to his ear. I watched nervously, waiting.

Cody shook his head. "Nothing."

"Who did you try?"

"My mom. I'll try my dad."

"No, 911 first."

"Oh, yeah, huh? Good call. What're you, a senior?"

I guess he was making a joke. Sadly, I couldn't laugh. But then Cody didn't look like he expected me to.

He dialed the number and turned on his speaker. The line seemed to ring for way too long a time. Then a click sounded, and I involuntarily took a step closer.

We are currently experiencing a high volume of emergency calls. Please hang up and try your call again.

"Whoa," Cody said. "That's not good."

I didn't bother to reply. He was right.

"Damn," Cody muttered, setting his phone down on a desk and gripping his arm again.

"How is it?"

"Hurts. God *damn*. What kinda pussy bites someone? Er—sorry. I don't mean that, I mean, like... chickenshit. He was a chickenshit."

"It's okay." I didn't think either term fit for the type of person who could do what I'd seen done in the past ten minutes.

"What's the matter with them?" Cody said.

"I don't know. But they were hurt. Something's wrong with their faces. And skin."

"Maybe they're sick," Cody said.

"Yeah, maybe." My gaze dropped to his phone. "Hey, is your internet working?"

Cody started pacing, holding his arm tight to his chest. "Try it."

I picked up his phone and sat down in a student desk. He had the same phone I did. I opened the browser, then hesitated, not sure where to even start. I tried a local news site first.

We'd made the news. Not Phoenix Metro High School, but the entire *city*.

Several hospitals in town had been quarantined. Every available law enforcement officer had been called into duty, and were already stretched thin. Two fires raged in downtown high-rises, though they couldn't be connected directly—yet—to what was going on in the rest of the city.

And what was going on amounted to panic. The news sites told people to stay home, or to go indoors right away, lock doors and windows, and not let anyone in because 911 was overwhelmed and police couldn't necessarily respond quickly. This announcement had apparently then led to isolated looting, but the looters hadn't gotten very far because they were "allegedly" being attacked by "concerned citizens" on the street.

I didn't think they were concerned citizens at all. Concerned citizens didn't usually bite people.

I swiped the browser closed. "Can I check your socials?"

Cody nodded, his face masked in pain.

His networking sites were more helpful, and much worse. People were already uploading videos and photos of attacks. They looked pretty much like what I'd seen in the gym. The most recent posts began sharing one common thread. It almost became a meme all on its own.

Don't get bit!

I gave Cody a clandestine look as the individual pieces of today's events started clicking into place. The news sites seemed reticent to leap to conclusions, and that was fine, that wasn't their job. Social media and citizen journalism, on the other hand, notoriously leaped to conclusions. But this time, the conclusions seemed pretty consistent: I was sitting in a barricaded classroom with a kid who would eventually become one of the raving maniacs who'd bitten him in the first place.

My trusty old fear came flooding back into my system. I tried to order it back.

No, I thought. *Stop. Think. You're alive, you're not hurt. If you want to stay that way, you have to STOP and THINK.*

"How's your arm?"

"I told you, it hurts," Cody snapped. "Jesus."

"We should clean it out. Sterilize it."

"How you plan on doing that?"

"I'm not sure. Just saying."

Cody rolled his eyes. "What'd you find out online?"

"Um—not much, still looking. Give me another minute."

I'm not a good liar, but Cody didn't come try to look at his screen. I kept searching, trying to find something to help me. Most of what I found were instructions on how to clean out and bandage bite wounds.

Tapping onto a website, the page wouldn't load. I tried again. Nothing. So I tried another. Then another. And realized as I waited and tapped and waited and tapped that things were definitely going from bad to worse.

We'd lost the web.

Heart beating more quickly now, I tried my mom's number. No connection. Hers was the only one I had memorized, but I had a feeling it didn't matter what number I tried.

Cody stopped pacing suddenly, and twisted his shoulders back and forth as if trying to crack his spine. "God, now my back hurts. Suck."

I stood. "I think we need to try and get you to the nurse's office."

"Screw that, I'm not going out there!"

"But that . . . bite. We've got to clean it out."

"Look, we go out there, we're both getting a lot worse than bitten."

He had a point there. But I couldn't stay in here with him, either. I had to decide whether or not tell him what I'd read.

"Cody? Listen."

Like a professional little brother, he huffed out a sigh and cocked out one hip as he looked at me.

"The web is down. Phones aren't working. 911 isn't even working anymore. Something really big and really bad is happening right now."

His little brother act dissolved. "You mean besides school?"

"Yeah. It might be the whole city. There's no telling when someone might be able to help us. Do you understand?"

"Uh, no?"

"Okay, well, it sounds like maybe people who get—"

My breath caught and I couldn't finish. Cody stared at me, waiting to finish. Then he finished it on his own. I watched his expression change from irritated to understanding to dread.

"Bit," he said. "That's what you were going to say, right? Bit? What? What happens? Aw, Christ, were you gonna say that I'm gonna… naw, no, no way."

I held up my hands. "That's why we have to get to the nurse's office. We've got to try and clean it out, it might help."

"Is that what it said?" Cody demanded. Even as he spoke, he rushed toward me. I stepped out of the way, but it wasn't me he was after. He went to his phone and began trying to get a site to respond. "Goddammit! Is that what it *said?* I'm gonna turn into one those things?"

"Not if we can kill the germs."

I hadn't actually read that online, but I'd read enough to know that human bites could be very dangerous no matter what. I figured—hoped, maybe—that if we could treat his wound fast, it might prevent or delay what people were saying on the social networks, because what they were saying was exactly what Cody guessed. Sooner or later, he'd become like those guys in the gym.

Cody cussed again and kicked at a desk, which slid a few feet and toppled. We both stood still a moment, both of us breathing hard.

"Okay," he said after a minute. "Okay. How? We can't just waltz down the sidewalk. If they see us, they'll come after us."

"It's not that far," I said. "Just admin. I mean, it's a one minute walk on a normal day. We could either run for it, or sneak from place to place, or start with sneaking and then run if we need to. I don't know."

"What do we do when we get there?"

"Peroxide. Bandages. Wrap it up good. Ice pack, if you want."

Cody chewed on his lips, nodding. "Man. I knew I shoulda ditched the assembly."

I thought of Brian. Of Chad. Jack, Hollis, Cammy—everyone. I wondered where they were. Most of the guys had ditched class until after lunch. Jack had been with them, so they were probably on campus. Everyone except Hollis, who Cammy said stayed home sick. Now I couldn't help wondering just what *kind* of sick.

"Listen," I said. "I'm really scared. Okay? I am. But I'm a lot more scared of what'll happen if we don't get you some help."

Cody glared at me. "You think I'll come after you."

"I didn't say that."

"Didn't have to. Jesus."

"Are you going or not?"

Cody flinched a little at the tone in my voice. I could barely believe I'd said it myself. Where had *that* girl been my whole life?

"Yeah, okay," Cody said. "Just, lemme smoke first."

He pulled a pack of cigarettes out of his hip pocket, lit one, and shut his eyes. He looked even younger as he did it; not just too young to be smoking, but too young for us to be having a life or death conversation. He looked so thin, and so pale against his all-black clothes.

I checked the window again, and didn't see anything. Maybe the cops were already here, containing the situation. During a lockdown, like in case there was a shooting, we were supposed to stay in our classrooms with the lights off and the door locked. This was nothing at all like a shooting, though. Maybe if Cody hadn't been bitten we could stay put, which was exactly what my body wanted to do.

But I couldn't risk it. Cody would get sick too, he was getting sicker even as we sat here.

Cody stomped his foot on the end of his cigarette. "Okay. Let's go."

We got next to the teacher's desk and were just about to lift it together when the PA system popped to life, scaring me almost into a coma.

"Uh... This is . . . this is Vice Principal Brandis. We have, uh . . . a slight . . . *situation* . . ."

Cody and I traded looks. Mr. Brandis, a slender man with an easy smile, always came off to me as very calm. Even when something crazy happened, like the riot, Mr. Brandis had looked upset but not worried. Or scared.

He sounded scared now.

"Students are re-re-requested to go to their classrooms and remain there until . . . until we, uh—"

Suddenly a crash sounded on his end of the line, like a microphone being dropped, and it made me jump. Over the speaker, I heard something like a snarl, as if from a mountain lion. Then a growl, as if from a grizzly bear.

Then silence.

Cody and I looked at each other again.

"Maybe we should stay here," he whispered.

I nodded. "Thirty minutes?"

"Maybe like an hour. Or two. Maybe tomorrow."

I didn't answer. From what I'd read, two hours might be more time than he had. Still. After that announcement, I started thinking maybe waiting would be a lot safer.

For the moment, anyway.

I sat under the white board with my back against the wall and my knees hugged to my chest. Cody paced nervously at the other end of the room, smoking cigarette after cigarette. I watched him go back and forth like a ping pong ball, flicking his cigarette every three seconds or so. He spit, too. Into the carpet. Normally it would have grossed me out. Normally the smell of smoke would have irritated me. Not today.

Maybe my mind was elsewhere.

It wasn't like the movies. Not at all. Sitting there, I'd somehow imagined us talking to fill the silence. Sharing stuff with each other and all that. In the movies, that's what would happen. We'd sit and talk, tell each other our deepest secrets. Probably cry about some mean thing one of us had said to our mom that morning, the morning that we hadn't realized would be our last.

None of that happened. Other than Cody asking once if the smoke bothered me and me shaking my head, that was all the communication we had. We didn't talk at all.

So I watched the clock. And I watched Cody.

I didn't know what exactly to look for, but thirty minutes into our wait, I thought I could see changes. They were small, but there. I don't think Cody noticed them.

At first it was just how fast he walked back and forth while he smoked. When I'd noticed he'd slowed down, I chalked it up to just running out of steam, or maybe his lungs getting clogged up with smoke. But it wasn't either of those things.

Had I not been watching, I might've missed it. But as the clock ticked off the minutes on the wall above him, Cody began to lean his torso forward, his shoulders rolling in. He also began absently rubbing the base of his spine.

"Cody?" I said as the clock marked off one full hour.

He lifted a fresh cigarette to his mouth and cupped his hands around a silver lighter. But he hesitated, too.

"It's been an hour," I said. "What do you think?"

Cody didn't move. He seemed to be staring at something. He finished lighting the cigarette, and dropped his left hand. His right hand he kept up near his face, the lighter glittering in his palm.

"Um," he said, his voice muffled by the cigarette between his lips. "Maybe we should go."

I stood up, my knees popping. "Why?"

He didn't answer, and didn't come over. So I walked to him.

And sucked in a breath when I saw his hand. The knuckles had crusted over with yellow, translucent scabs.

"Does it hurt?" I said.

Cody made a fist, wincing and grunting. "Yep. Fuck. Yeah." He took a quick puff of his cigarette and then stomped it out. "God damn, it feels like I'm being *stabbed*. Shoulda listened to you about the nurse."

"Do you want to——?"

"Fuck it. Let's go."

We moved the teacher's heavy desk again together, one of us on each short side. Immediately, I felt naked and exposed with the door unblocked. I wanted my pills so badly.

But I forced myself to the door, and put a hand around the knob. "Me first?"

Cody nodded, looking even paler than he had an hour ago. The smell of cigarette smoke hung heavy around him.

I listened at the door, and heard nothing. I twisted the handle, expecting it to get ripped out of my hands by one of those creature-students from the gym. Instead the knob turned easily and the latch unclicked.

I pulled the door open slowly, trying to split my attention between listening and keeping my heart in my chest instead of letting it thump out of my mouth entirely, which it sure seemed like it was trying to do. Apart from that, I didn't hear anything.

"Okay," I whispered. "We'll go slow. If we have to run, try to run back here."

"Why."

"Because at least we know we're safe in here."

Cody snorted, but didn't say anything. Maybe it wasn't the best plan, but taking some kind of action felt good. Our friend Chad had this thing he liked to say: The best plans in the world go out the window when the first shot is fired. He was going straight into the Marines after he graduated this year, so maybe he knew something I didn't.

Still. For as terrified as I was, I wasn't just sitting around, either. Maybe people who've never been truly frightened day in and day out wouldn't understand that. People like Chad, for instance, who wasn't afraid of anyone or anything. For me, on the other hand, anything other than crouching in a corner was an improvement.

"What're you waiting for?" Cody rasped.

I blinked. Maybe I wasn't being as brave as I'd thought.

I opened the door and stepped onto the sidewalk. The campus seemed dead, for lack of a better term. I didn't hear anything at all. Maybe everyone had been evacuated.

Cody and I slid across the covered concrete sidewalk to the top of the stairs. I peeked over the railing of the sidewalk down to the first floor, and saw a body. From up here on the second floor, I could see the motionless form of the girl with the broken ankle. The girl I'd left behind. The top half of her body lay in a gelatinous puddle of blood, her arms splayed wide, her knees cocked over to one side as if doing some kind of permanent yoga pose.

I wondered what her name was.

Whatever sad semblance of bravery I'd imagined having drained out of me. I could practically feel it rushing out my feet and through the soles of my purple Vans and spilling down the steps as surely as that girl's blood had spilled from her neck. My breath shallowed, and I couldn't lift my hands off the stair railing.

"What?" Cody said.

"Can't," I whispered, my eyes refusing to blink or leave the shape of the dead girl's body. "Can't do it. I can't."

Because here it came, roaring into me like a train—the panic, the terror, the sensation of suffocating in the open air. I had to get back inside the classroom, had to go *now*, had to *go*—

"Fine," Cody barked, and took a tentative step down on the stairs, wincing. "I'll fuckin' go myself."

He took another step, and another, moving awkward and slow as if his knees wouldn't bend.

Clenching my eyes shut, I said, "Wait."

I could not let this happen again. Not after the girl. I had to help Cody, had to try. I opened my eyes and forced myself down the stairs past Cody.

"Sorry," I said. "I'll go first. I'm okay."

Total lie. But it felt good to say.

Together now, we took cautious steps down the staircase until we reached the bottom floor. I felt as if we'd moved onto a tightrope stretched across the Grand Canyon, where one wrong move would kill us both. I guess that wasn't so far from the truth.

Now that we were on the ground, I could see more bodies. At the far end of the east C buildings, I saw a few people lying on the concrete.

Smears of blood stained the sidewalks all around us. But I didn't see any of the crazy athletes.

We shifted over to the nearest classroom door on the first floor, pressing ourselves flat against it.

"Should we check the classrooms?" Cody said.

It wasn't a bad idea. Having more than two of us making a break for the nurse's office might improve our odds. I definitely wouldn't be opposed to the help.

But another thought crossed my mind at the same time. "Problem is they might not want to let you to go one we got inside," I said. "Or they… might not want us in with them at all."

Something like hopelessness passed over Cody's pale features.

"Either way, I think we might be better on our own right now," I said.

Cody nodded, slightly, like there was no point in anything. Maybe there wasn't. Maybe he already knew that.

We followed the wall to the corner and peeked around, first to the north. In that direction stood the D buildings and gym. The doors to the gymnasium were closed, and other than several bodies, we saw nothing.

Turning to look the other way, south down the main sidewalk, we saw them.

"Ah, *shit*," Cody whispered.

I counted six students for sure, but they kept moving, sliding dumbly across the concrete of the breezeway, making it hard to keep track. They weren't all football players, for one thing. For another—they were monsters.

All of them moved on their hands and feet, reminding me again of giant jungle gorillas. A few wore short sleeves, and I could see clustered crystalline formations on their forearms and hands. Their faces had that hideous melted look I'd seen earlier, the red of their lower eyelids visible even from a distance, their mouths deformed and lips jutting down to expose their lower teeth. All of them had bloodstains on their skin or clothes.

They wandered aimlessly near the B buildings, only four or five car lengths away. Beyond them sat the A buildings, then the cafeteria and administration, which lay across the breezeway from one another. The nurse's office was inside admin, so that meant getting past those monstrous kids.

"Go around?" Cody whispered.

I nodded. We scurried—slowly and quietly—back the way we had come. Each of the lettered buildings stood alone, surrounded by a concrete sidewalk; only the central sidewalk was covered by a blue awning. We headed west to the opposite end of our C building and checked around the corner.

More of them. A lot more of them. Ten, at least. Guys, girls, athletes—it seemed like one example from every clique and style was represented. Whatever was going on, it was spreading. Fast.

I didn't see my friends among the group of them, though. Not Brian or Kenzie, not Chad. Not Cammy or Jack or Hollis. Maybe they were alive. Maybe I could find them.

"*Shit!*" Cody said again. "Now what?"

I bit my lips, mind spinning. How could we get past them? Run? No. I didn't like those odds.

Distract them?

Yes. Maybe. Yes.

How?

"You have your phone?" I whispered.

Cody pulled it out and tapped on the screen. "You said the phones weren't working. And I don't think I got time for someone to come get me anyway, know what I'm sayin'?"

I took the phone from him. "We'll set the alarm, slide it toward them here. Maybe when it goes off, it'll distract the ones in the breezeway. Then we can run to the nurse."

"That's a pretty big fuckin' maybe."

"It's all I got. You have any ideas?"

Cody grunted softly as he switched positions. Already I could see the scabs on his hands had spread.

"Okay, no. Do it. Jesus this hurts."

I felt the urge to touch his shoulder, to reassure him. But I didn't. Because I also didn't want to come into contact him.

I set his alarm for two minutes, then waited, peering around the corner, hoping like hell none of them would wander this way. They didn't, and when their collective backs were to me, I tapped the start button and slid the phone on its back toward them.

I spun to Cody. "Go!"

We rushed to the other end of the building, and kept an eye on the monsters in the breezeway. Then Cody's alarm went off.

The speed with which those kids in the breezeway sprinted toward the noise took my breath away. They'd appeared to be in so much pain, the way they moved slowly, but it was like they disregarded that pain as soon as they thought someone might be nearby.

So *fast*.

But now the breezeway was clear, all the way to administration.

"Come on!" I said, and together, Cody and I ran for the building.

Or, rather, that was the plan.

All the plans in the world go out the window when the first shot is fired. Our first shot was not realizing how bad off Cody already was.

He took one big step with me as we started our run. I must've gotten five or six yards away from him, focused exclusively on getting into the safety of admin, when he screamed as though being stabbed.

I skid to a halt and looked back. Cody's eyes widened in agony as he held both hands to his back.

"Go, go!" he said through clenched teeth. He took a shambling step forward, and another, biting back wails with each movement.

They'd hear him. I knew it. They'd hear him and come after us. We had to move.

I raced back and grabbed his arm, bringing another cry from him that he couldn't contain. His skin felt hot and brittle.

"Run or die," I said.

He twisted his head to look west, down the length of the C building. And one of the monsters spun around the corner, roared, and galloped toward us.

Without a word, Cody leaned forward and began to run. I held on to him and followed suit, my breath scorching and my heart shooting warning flares in my chest.

It's coming, my mind chanted as we tried to run. *That kid is coming, more will be coming, they'll take us down and that will be it—*

We passed the intersection between B and C, and saw several of the monsters just coming around the corners, spotting us, and giving chase.

Keep going, keep going, c'mon Cody, keep going . . .

We passed the B buildings, then A. Behind us, dozens of whatever those kids had become fell into a wave of snarling, feral hunger, intent on taking us both to the ground. They were maybe twenty yards away.

We reached the admin building, and only dimly did an alarm go off inside me when I saw the windows facing the breezeway had been broken out. Some kind of fight had happened here.

No time to assess. As Cody cried out from the agony in his body, I flipped open the admin doors and yanked him inside after me.

Of course, locking the doors behind us was another story. School administration doors didn't come with giant oak beams to drop across

95

them to keep student monsters from chasing you.

So we rushed for the nurse's office without even trying to block the doors in any way. We did get a short break when the doors latched; opening them required a thumb button to be pressed, and it took the monsters a second to figure that out, it seemed, which bought Cody and me just enough time to make it into the hall that led to Nurse Garrett's office.

Nurse Garrett herself showed up in the doorway of another room between us and her office. She wore her dark blue scrubs as usual.

And streaks of blood. On one of her forearms, through a bloody tear in her sleeve, I saw a mouth-sized gash had recently congealed.

I almost said her name. I almost felt relief. A teacher, a nurse, someone who would know what to do.

But Nurse Garrett wasn't Nurse Garrett anymore.

With an inhuman screech, teeth bared, she leaped at us.

Nurse Garrett's arms had already sprouted the disgusting yellowish crystals, and her eyes had become jaundiced. With another feral yell, she came at us, fingers outstretched, seeking our flesh.

Cody had ended up in front of me in the narrow hallway. The nurse jumped, grabbed his shoulders—

And threw him aside.

Cody stumbled past her, collapsing into her office with a shout. Nurse Garrett lunged for me, and took me to the hard tile floor in one jarring crunch.

We hit the floor, with her on top of me, pinning my shoulders down and snapping for my throat.

4:31 p.m.

It's a strange thing to die. For one thing, I wouldn't have expected to have the clarity of mind to think something like, *It's a strange thing to die.*

Time slowed down as she killed me. I thought of the songs I'd never hear again. *I Got You, Babe,* by Sonny and Cher, which my parents sang to each other in the kitchen sometimes and laughed. Boy-band love songs

96

I pretended I didn't listen to after age twelve but still secretly danced to when no one was around. Kenzie's beloved Green Day songs.

I thought about the food I'd never eat again. Mom made this Italian meatloaf that I always asked for as my birthday dinner. Or Dad's cookies baked from scratch. Peanut butter only. It was the only thing he knew how to cook, or so he claimed, and they were really, really good.

I'd never know what sex was like. Brian and I hadn't done it. Partly, I felt bad that we hadn't, but I also felt kind of proud. Either way, it would have been nice to at least know. And it would have been nice if it had been Brian.

It didn't matter anymore, because any second here, any moment now, this woman was going to tear my throat out with her teeth the way the girl with the broken ankle had had her throat torn out while I watched. I suppose I deserved it. I'd feel Nurse Garrett's teeth puncture my skin and cartilage, pulling, tearing, the way a tooth feels when your dad has to use string to yank it out, only so much worse.

So much more blood, so much more pain, and no more music and no more Dad's cookies and—

"*No!*"

The scream came out of me with such force that for a second, I thought Nurse Garrett really had torn my throat apart. From somewhere inside me, a burst of crazed adrenalin exploded, and I managed to shove the monster off my shoulders.

She was still on top of me, but I used the short break to scrunch my body to one side, which put my shoulders against the wall. It gave me the leverage I needed to push again, and put a little space between me and her.

As Nurse Garrett shifted to spring at me again, I kicked as hard as I could at one crystalline arm. The scabs broke and the nurse pierced the walls with her scream. I shuffled to my feet and sprang for her office, slamming the door shut and falling with my back against it.

That's when, at last, I cried.

With fear, with relief, with gratitude to be alive just one more minute. How much was a minute worth now, what could I buy with just sixty more seconds of breath? I hoped to find out someday.

I don't know how long I sat there. I only know that no one—nothing—came banging at the door after us. I didn't want to think about why.

When I stopped crying, it slowly dawned on me that Cody was crouched in the far corner of Nurse Garrett's office. It was a small room, with white-painted cinderblock walls, a low vinyl-upholstered couch with a roll of paper spread across the top, a small desk, phone, and some cabinets. The paper on the couch was rumpled and smeared red. Cody huddled beside the desk, arms wrapped around his legs, his forehead on his raised knees.

Still breathing hard, I stared at him.

"She didn't come after you," I said, the words ragged.

Cody lifted his head. The whites of his eyes had become almost completely yellow, a hideous, cancerous jaundice that gave him a canine appearance.

"I think you better go," he said.

I slid to my feet, shaking. I went to one of the cabinets and opened it up. "We'll get some peroxide or something, clean out the bite, she's got to have—"

"Laura."

I froze, but did not turn to look at him. His voice was demonic, as if a lifetime of his smoking habit had caught up with his vocal cords all at once.

"You have to go."

I slammed the cabinet door. "Yeah? How? Huh? Where am I supposed to go? They're out there, just waiting for us."

Cody stood, very slowly, like an old man climbing out of bed. He reached for one of two crutches leaning against the wall near Nurse Garrett's desk.

"No," he said. "They're waiting for you. They don't want me anymore."

I couldn't answer.

"We'll try the doors to the parking lot," he went on through clenched teeth. There was a small guest parking lot right outside admin, and the school fence didn't go around it. If those doors were open, I could get off campus. Not sure what good that would necessarily do, though. Off campus and into what kind of nightmare waiting beyond?

"The lock down," I said. "They're probably locked."

"Still gotta try," Cody said. "If they are locked, we'll clear a path down the breezeway if we have to. Best we can. Get back to the classroom, like you said. At least it's open and you'll be safe there."

"I can't move the desk by myself."

"I think . . . we'd better . . . hurry."

There was no time to come up with a better plan. So I nodded, and Cody limped toward me. I got out of his way, then stood behind him as he put a hand on the door knob.

He hesitated. "Hey. Thanks for trying."

"Sure."

"Maybe there's a cure, huh? It's not like I'm gonna die, right? Those guys out there, they're not dyin', right?"

"Right," I said. And thought, *No, not dying. Just killing.*

"Okay. Cool. Here we go."

He opened the door.

4:35 p.m.

The hall outside Nurse Garrett's office was empty. Cody shuffled along the tile floor, holding the crutch in both hands like a lance. We both froze as a rustling sound crept around the corner toward us.

Cody motioned for me to stay put. So I did. He went forward with the crutch, peeked around the corner, then stepped out of the hall into the lobby. He was looking toward the admin doors leading to the parking lot, which is exactly where I wanted to go. Forget staying on campus, never mind the supposed safety of the classroom, and I didn't care what might be waiting outside. I wanted out of this place. Now.

The thought made my heart race harder, and I realized then how thirsty I was. I'd had nothing to drink since lunch time.

"Come closer," Cody whispered, sort of out of one corner of his mouth as he kept his eyes fixed on the doors. "But don't run till I tell you."

I slid along the wall, leaving clammy handprints on the white paint.

"What is it?" I whispered, still in the hall and unable to see whatever he was looking at.

"Four of them," Cody said in a low voice. "Even if the doors are unlocked, you won't make it to the parking lot. Try for the classroom."

I carefully moved to the opposite wall so I could see more clearly out the broken admin windows. It was a narrow view, and I saw nothing from this vantage. That didn't mean much—there could be a school full of monsters on either side of the admin windows and I'd never know it until I went out there. Then… well, then that would be that.

A flat run toward the C buildings would require pure and simple luck. That was it.

"What about you?" I whispered.

"I'll follow best I can. Keep your back clear. You ready? When I say go, you gotta go."

"Okay."

I crouched a little and braced a foot against the wall like I was on the school track. I didn't consider myself out of shape, exactly, but I also didn't go to the gym or anything. On the one hand, years of just staying home scared hadn't exactly built up my muscles or endurance. On the other hand, if I didn't run fast enough, well . . . I'd just have to. It wasn't a question of—

"*Go!*"

I sprinted toward the admin doors, not looking back. They couldn't have been more than twenty feet away, and the creatures behind me roared just as my hands landed on the crash-bar door handle.

I smashed through the doors and took off madly down the breezeway as I heard Cody shouting in the lobby. I risked a glance backward, and saw him swinging the crutch at the four monsters, buying me time.

But further behind me in the breezeway, down toward the performing arts building at the south end of campus, a group of the creatures saw me running and gave chase.

I had a good head start, though. So long as I didn't fall and didn't run into any more of them between here and the C buildings, then maybe—*maybe…*

From near the gym, more monsters wandered onto the breezeway. I stopped—stupidly—as I hoped somehow they wouldn't see me.

No luck. One immediately howled and took off down the sidewalk at me.

"Shit!" I wheezed, and turned left between the B and C buildings, remembering there hadn't been as many of the creatures on that side, and hoping maybe there weren't now. Again I'd have luck and nothing more to get me through this.

Then I slid on dust and hit the ground as I rounded the corner between the B and C buildings. My hip cracked against the concrete, sending pain riffling down my leg. I bit back a scream and pulled myself to my feet. My spill had let the monsters close the distance.

Barely able to breathe now, I skidded around the far west side of the

C building. No monsters. I swung myself against the wall to catch my breath, chest aching horribly, and peeked around the corner the way I had come.

The monsters—six, I think, maybe more—tumbled into the intersection where I'd slipped and began looking around, trying to figure out where I'd gone.

Good. They didn't have super-senses or anything like that. They'd have to find me the old fashioned way, by looking and listening.

I clutched at my throat, trying to force my breathing to slow, but terror kept my muscles tight. The staircase up to my classroom refuge was only around the corner and halfway again down the building, but who knew how many of the monsters might be there by now? All it would take is one of them to be hanging around the base of the staircase, and that would be it. I'd have nowhere to go. I'd have to run, and just keep running, and I could not do that, not forever. They wouldn't tire, they wouldn't stop. They'd come at me like cheetahs bearing down on prey in the savannah.

I'd run from C to admin, then basically got in a fight with a some diseased creature-nurse, then run again from admin back to here… my legs felt like plastic sacks of jelly and my heart seemed to have swollen up and pushed my lungs to the side.

The staircase wasn't more than forty yards or so from my position at the side of the building, and I *could not make it.*

My heart skipped one beat. Then another.

It's a disconcerting feeling, like the muscle is doing somersaults and predicting a heart attack. Now, in addition to being out of breath and weak from the exertion, panic started racing up my spinal nerves and electrifying my limbs.

Outta luck, Laura, outta luck, you got away with it this long but now time's up and they've got you.

"Please," I whispered. "*Please.*"

The powerlessness of my legs suddenly didn't matter anymore, because fear rooted me in place. This goddamn panic, this useless *fucking* panic—

The monsters in the breezeway shuffled away, banging accidentally into each other like mute fish in a tank. Others joined them from the area of the gym. Some I recognized as athletes from the initial attack.

They'd lost me, and were wandering now. No longer a group. I knew if just one of them saw me and bellowed, the others would come charging, but until then, they'd given up on me.

Okay. Okay. Breathe, Laura. Breathe. You've got a minute, here. You got a minute. Slow down. Take it easy. You might even be able to walk to the stairs if there aren't any of those things on that side of C, so take easy. Calm down. Calm—

An alarm went off.

The creatures on the breezeway looked up at the same time, then down the length of the sidewalk to where I stood still peeking around at them.

I gasped and pulled myself back from the corner, hoping but not believing that they hadn't seen me. I looked down and to my right, trying through my fear to figure out what sound had tipped them off... and saw Cody's cell phone.

One of the monsters must have picked it up or somehow unintentionally tapped the snooze key on the phone's screen after the alarm went off before, when we'd used it to distract them. Now it blared to life again, beckoning every creature within earshot, and thus every other creature who saw their new brothers and sisters shouting and running for fresh meat.

A helpless squeal squeaked out of me, and I tried to run for the opposite corner toward the staircase and classroom. I only managed a weak shuffle. I checked around the corner to examine the stairs, and saw creatures racing down the breezeway, but not headed this direction. Not yet. The coast was as clear as it was going to get.

I swept Cody's phone into my hands and smashed a numb finger against the screen, silencing the phone before turning the corner. Again I tried running, but still couldn't do it. The panic in my veins wouldn't let me. It wanted me to give up, to lay down, to die.

No!

I pushed hard against the cement, fighting the pain and fear with each step toward the stairs. *Just make it that far,* I thought, *just make it that far.*

And then, at the east end of the building, he came around the corner.

My limbs locked in place just feet from the bottom step of the staircase as Cody turned the corner and glared at me. Even from that distance, I could see the yellow in his eyes, or maybe I just imagined I could. His skin had already begun to fall and slide from his skull, and he was almost bent in half at the waist.

He made no sound as he broke into a ravenous run.

I rushed for the stairs. I had a huge head start, all I had to do was get up them, into the classroom—

And then what? I couldn't move the desk myself. I couldn't block the door.

My body paid no attention to these random thoughts. All I could do, all *it* could do, was move and take each second as it came.

With each one of those seconds, Cody got nearer. I couldn't believe how fast he moved now, as if whatever pain he was in was so severe the only way to alleviate it was to run. He wasn't on his hands and knees yet like some of the others, but his fingers hung only a few inches from the concrete as he charged, his diseased arms swinging numbly from side to side.

I reached the steps and grabbed the hand railing. The certainty that Cody would reach me stiffened each of my joints, making them hard to move.

I pulled myself along. One step up, then the next, and the next. I couldn't tell the last time I'd taken a breath.

Then his hands were on the hem of my hoodie. I felt the jacket being pulled away from me. The sensation tripped something inside me; I screamed and my joints unfroze. I kicked backward, connected with some part of him, and he let go of my hoodie.

I rushed up the stairs, not using the rails anymore. Cody growled and followed. I imagined feeling his breath on my legs as I climbed.

Reaching the second floor sidewalk, I lunged for the classroom door and got one hand on the knob before he crashed into me, sending me flat against the door and the knob drilling into the same hip I'd landed on earlier. Any breath I had left inside coughed out.

His teeth buried into my right shoulder.

I pushed against the door, sending us both toppling backward across the sidewalk. He rammed into the railing and barked out a howl, releasing me. Screaming, I spun to face him, then charged forward with both hands out. I caught Cody in the chest, and for one sickening moment I felt the thick, sharp crystal formations on his chest through his black T-shirt.

Then he flipped backward over the railing.

Cody didn't have time to make a sound. I just heard the awful thunk of his body landing below.

I peered over the railing. Cody lay on the ground, one foot twisted in a terrible direction, not moving. I'd killed him.

No—

He got up.

He got up and shook his head, now hunched completely over like the others, his hands on the ground, knees bent a little, back hunched. He twisted one shoulder upward to look up at me. I watched as he clambered toward the steps . . . paused . . .

And then he wandered off, making obscene chuffing sounds like an angry dog. He limped a little, but otherwise seemed either unhurt or uncaring that he was hurt. Just a skinny, pale kid dressed in black looking for a victim.

I went into the classroom.

Once I'd closed the door, I tried to push the teacher's desk against it, but like I'd expected, I couldn't move it on my own. So instead I made a pile of desks, a tangle of blue plastic chairs and wooden armrests in front of the door. I didn't think it would necessarily keep anything from getting in, but it would slow them down.

When I'd finished, I checked my shoulder. There were damp marks on the fleece where Cody had bit me, but all he'd gotten was a mouthful of my hoodie. He hadn't even bruised my skin. A lucky break.

Lucky. Could anything in this day really be called that?

What I wanted next was to sleep, but I didn't know that I could. Plus I needed one more thing. I searched but couldn't find quite what I was looking for until I spotted the American flag in one corner.

I grabbed it and yanked the flag off. Weren't you supposed to not let it touch the ground or something? I tossed it onto the teacher's desk. Like the pile of desks, it wasn't much, but the pole felt stout and heavy in my hands. It was the best weapon I could find.

Finally I sat down cross-legged at the far side of the room, holding the flagpole under my arm like a lance—like Cody had done with the crutch. As I sat, I felt Cody's phone in my pocket, and pulled it out.

I tried every number I could remember, and got no responses. The internet didn't work, either, but all the apps native to the phone worked fine.

Fighting thirst, I decided I'd leave a record in case it would be helpful later. A record, or maybe an elegy.

Wishing for just one drink of water, I tapped the phone's audio recording button and began to speak.

7:57 p.m.

And that's it. That's everything that happened. I've been in here ever since, waiting, too nervous to sleep. I'm hungry. I'm so thirsty. I don't know when—

Wait.

. . . I heard something. Outside.

Oh, God.

Something's coming. They found me.

Okay. Okay. Shit. Okay.

Mom? Dad? If anyone finds this, I love you, I love you so much.

This… oh, my God, this might really be my last moment on earth.

…Fine.

Fine. I'm not going to die on my knees. So help me God, I will fight whatever comes through that door. Mom, Dad, I love you. If you ever get this, I love you and I want you to know I beat it. I beat this. No matter what.

And Brian and Kenzie, I hope you're okay. Cammy, Hollis, Chad, all you guys, I hope you're all right. I hope I see you again. You were such good fr—

. . . It's here.

It's coming toward the door.

I have to go. I love you.

I love you.

I'm sorry.

But I'm not afraid.

. . . Bye.

THE STORY OF A DEAD GIRL

By Joe McKinney

https://joemckinney.wordpress.com

This is dedicated to Ted Conover,
for bravery in journalism.

A cold February wind fingered its way through the gaps in the walls. The little shack in which we'd taken shelter had been cobbled together from cinder blocks and castoff lumber, the roof a rusting sheet of corrugated tin held down by baling wire. Rotting sheets of plywood covered the windows, thin protection from the zombies massing outside. The place smelled of stale beer and sweat, mildew and rot, and the dim morning light revealed ice-encrusted trash on the floor. The broken beer bottles, tin cans, a scattering of cigarette butts and the occasional spent shell casing were sad markers of those like Jessica and I, who had taken refuge here.

Jessica hunkered down in the corner to get out of the seething wind. She had a tattered bath towel wrapped around her shoulders, but it was too threadbare to warm her, withered as she was from starvation. She scanned the garbage, her breath pluming in the cold. I figured she was looking for something she could use. Deprivation had made her keen that way. She never missed anything.

"Looks like we're not the first to hide out here," she said.

I looked around. It was hard to believe this was luck, but she was right. We were lucky to find the shack when we did. The surrounding countryside was empty grassland, nothing but an occasional mesquite thicket to break up the soul-sucking emptiness of it. There were few places to hide from the zombies. I tried to imagine all the others who had come this way before us, how every bit of garbage on the floor was a marker representing anxious days and nights waiting for the zombies to move on down the road. There was a faded blood stain on the wall above Jessica's head, spatter as though from a gunshot. As I stared at it, I felt overwhelmed by the emotional sediment of desperation and exhaustion that permeated the small space. I never really believed, even as a little girl, that a place could be haunted. But if ever a place had a right to be, it was that shack.

Jessica went to the wall and stared out through a crack. I joined her, noticing as I did the gap in the lumber was smeared with dried blood left behind by fingers that had tried to claw their way inside.

There were two other shacks that we could see, both about the size of ours, and both surrounded by thick knots of the infected. We could hear a man screaming from one of the shacks. He was one of the people we'd been traveling with when the zombies found us. Jessica had said she didn't trust him, that he seemed unstable, and from the way he was shrieking I believed it. But crazy or not, his screaming was driving the infected mad. He'd yell and they'd beat on the walls with renewed fervor, answering his fear with an ululating chorus of moans.

We didn't know who was in the other shack, but every once in a while one of them jabbed a sharpened stick through the walls at the crowd.

"They're idiots," Jessica said in a whisper.

They were idiots. She was right about that. But I was too scared to talk. As disgusting as the shack was, we were safe. I didn't want to say anything or do anything that would change that. I didn't want those things out there to hear us talking. I just wanted to shrivel up into a little ball and wait for the horrors to pass us by.

Be the reporter, I told myself. Watch, observe, soak it all in. Don't get involved. That was why I was here, after all, to report on living conditions in the Zone.

I almost laughed at that.

Like it or not, I was involved. I was involved up to my ears.

Just outside the door, a young female zombie had her face buried in the abdomen of a corpse. It was one of the men we'd been traveling with who hadn't made it inside quickly enough. A lot of meat had been torn from his bones, and what was left of the body jerked and twitched as the zombie tore bits of the remaining flesh away. We probably could have slipped by her, but she would have sent up a moan to bring the rest of the zombies after us.

"Why in the world would they bring attention to themselves like that?" Jessica said, still whispering. "They should know better."

I shrugged, silently praying that she'd stop talking.

"It's okay," she said, like she could read my mind. "Just whisper. They won't hear us."

"How do you know?"

I looked through the crack in the wall again. Most of the zombies were too intent on beating against the other two shacks, and those few that weren't with the main group were busy feeding off our dead companions. But still, scared as I was, I didn't want to chance it.

"They don't hear so well," she said. "They'll pick up on our movement, though, so try not to make any sudden moves."

She was right, of course. Moving would cause the light coming through the walls to flicker on our clothes, and that would be as good as jumping up and down and waving a flag. Though I'd only known Jessica for three days at that point, I found myself amazed yet again at her common sense and her grasp of survival tactics. She was like a soldier or a hardcore beat cop. Living in the quarantine zone had sharpened her survival instincts far beyond my own.

"I bet you're sorry you came, aren't you?" she asked.

I was scared like I'd never been in my life, but I wasn't sorry. Not a bit. I would have been dead without her, and when you get to the point that you can say that about another person, can you really be sorry about it? Doesn't that create a sense of loyalty that's worth a world of hardships?

Before I could answer she put a hand on my shoulder.

"Look there," she said.

I put my face up to the crack again. Something was happening over at one of the shacks. The building trembled. As we watched, a section of the wall caved in, and the zombies poured in through the breach, tearing the two men inside to pieces.

"Oh my God," Jessica said. There was no shock in her voice, just sadness.

"They were brothers, weren't they?" I asked.

"Yes."

The commotion caused even the female zombie in front of our door to join the swarm. My pulse quickened. Looking off to the right of the shack where the crazy man shrieked, I saw the field beyond was absolutely empty. If we were quiet, we just might be able to get enough of a head start to leave this crowd of zombies behind us.

Before I could say anything to Jessica, the crazy man burst out of his shack and tried to make a break for it. Several of the zombies lunged for him, causing him to swerve. But he was too scared to control his footing on the muddy ground and fell face-first into a puddle of water. He was up and running, still screaming, before any of the zombies could get to him. Jessica and I watched him go, shocked to see most of the zombies shambling after him.

"Wow," she said.

I agreed. I was impressed, despite the man's lunacy. "Lucky for us."

"Yeah."

We waited about two minutes, neither of us speaking. Only a few zombies remained in and around the shacks, and those were busy feeding on the fresh corpses of the two brothers. It looked clear to me, and I reached for the brace on the door.

Jessica grabbed my wrist.

I started to speak, but the look on her face stopped me.

With a glance, she gestured toward the gaps in the wall. A moment later, a male zombie stepped into view. It stopped and slowly turned its head toward us. The thing's hair was a stringy mess, matted with dried blood. Its beard was filthy, and its mouth swarmed with flies. What clothes it had left were little more than soiled rags hanging from its emaciated frame. The wind shifted. It was cold enough to cut us to the bone, and though it carried the zombie's stench with it, I didn't dare shiver or gag. Reacting would get us killed.

After a moment it went on its way, leaving us alone again.

I let out the breath I'd been holding. "That was close," I said. "Thanks."

"Tell me about it." Jessica pointed to the door. "It should be clear now."

***

My first night in the Zone I got caught in a sudden, hard rain that left me cold and miserable. I wandered into an abandoned bus depot looking for someplace warm to sleep. Jessica and the rest of her group were huddled in the back, barely visible in the darkness.

They watched me, alarmed because they didn't know me, but intrigued because I didn't look like they did. At that point my clothes were still fresh. My skin wasn't sun-burnt. I wasn't starving. For a long, uncomfortable moment we stared at one another, nobody speaking, nobody moving.

Then this woman separated from the crowd and walked toward me. She almost looked like a zombie herself, emaciated, filthy, face sunken and haunted-looking.

Only her eyes were different. They were bright, full of life.

And, when she got closer, I could see they were curious, even friendly. There was warmth there that reassured me.

"What in the world were you doing out in the rain?" she asked.

"I..." It was hard to speak, I was trembling so badly.

"Didn't you see the clouds forming?"

I shook my head.

"You couldn't smell the storm coming?"

"I'm cold," I said. My tone demanded mercy, not questions.

"I wouldn't doubt it. A storm like that, even the zombies have enough sense to get indoors."

"Can I stay here?" I asked. "Just for the night?"

"That depends." She looked me up and down. "Are you hurt? You bit anywhere?"

"No. Just cold."

She paused for a long moment, studying me. Her face was an honest one, and I felt like I could actually see her in silent discussion with her conscience.

Then, out of the blue: "I'm Jessica."

"Samantha," I said.

"Samantha, or Sam?"

I tried to smile, but my lips were turning blue from the cold. "Sam," I said.

"Sam it is. Come on, let's try to get you warmed up."

Jessica led me to a corner away from the door and showed me where I could sleep.

And that was how I spent my first night in the Zone.

***

When I woke the next morning, she was nudging me in the shoulder. I looked around, disoriented, and it took me a second to realize we were the only two people left in the depot. The others were outside on the road, set to leave.

"If you want to come with us we have to leave now."

"Where are you going?" I asked.

"East of here. We're gonna cross the wall into Free America."

I think my mouth must have fallen open. "Are you serious?"

"Of course I'm serious. You want to come or not? We have to leave now."

I couldn't believe my luck. My publisher had commissioned me to sneak into the Quarantine Zone, make a circuit of South Texas, and get back out again. I was to report on the conditions of the people there and come up with something to challenge the government's claims that the necrosis filovirus was so widespread as to make reclaiming the Zone a suicide mission. I knew going into it that it would be a dangerous assignment, but I figured it would be no less dangerous than being an embedded reporter in Afghanistan or Iraq. It wasn't a necessary risk by any means, but it was a risk I was willing to take, especially when the whispers of a Pulitzer started to reach my ears.

My publisher hired one of their other authors, an ex-Navy SEAL, to sneak me through the Coast Guard blockade on the Texas coast. He got me onto a weed-choked beach near Port Lavaca in the middle of the night. I still remember the sour look on his face when the wind carried the sounds of moaning in our direction. "You sure you want to do this?" he said. "I can get you out right now."

"No," I said. "I want to do this. I'll be okay."

"Where's your weapon?"

I hooked a thumb toward my backpack. I had a .40 Glock in my bag, plus three loaded magazines, for a total of 46 rounds - 46 more than I figured I'd need. "I have it in there where I can get it."

The wind carried more moans our way.

"If I were you, I'd have it out and ready."

"I'll be okay. I know what I'm doing."

I don't think he believed that for a second. All he was supposed to do was drop me off on the beach, and yet he had our Zodiac boat loaded down with night vision goggles and machine guns and a box of something that looked a lot like grenades to me. He kept asking me if I was sure I wanted to do this, and it was starting to get old.

"I'll be fine," I said. Our plan was for me to meet him on the same beach three weeks later. I had a cell phone with which to signal him. It was my first experience as an embedded reporter, but I had done my homework. I knew the lay of the land. I had studied up on the infected. I knew how to evade them, and how to deal with them when I couldn't evade them. In my mind, it was all going to be quite simple. "I'll call you," I said.

He shrugged and quietly slipped back out to sea.

But then came that night in the rain, and my chance meeting with Jessica. When she asked me to join them, I jumped at the chance. Busting the wall – something the government assured us was impossible, but that pretty much everybody believed was happening on a regular basis – was just too much of a story to pass up.

In my eagerness, I got up too fast and upset my backpack, spilling the contents on the floor between us.

Jessica reached down to help me pick up my stuff, but paused when she saw what I was carrying. She moved my pens and notebooks out of the way, uncovering the iPhone and a battery powered charger. I saw her mind racing.

Dark clouds of suspicion gathered in her face.

"Who are you?" she asked, her brow furrowed.

I'd been advised to keep my identity a secret for my own protection, but something told me I could trust Jessica. She had been the first to extend any sort of welcome, and she had come back for me while the others were ready to leave me sleeping in that bus depot.

"I'm a writer," I admitted. "I'm down here to write a story on life inside the Zone."

She stared at me for a long moment in frank, slack-jawed amazement. She must have thought I was out of my mind. And then she laughed.

"Hey Jessica," one of the men called from the road. "You coming or what?"

She waved to the man, then turned back to me. She studied me, my clothes, my shoes, shaking her head the whole time. "Well," she finally said, "we're leaving. You want to see life in the Zone, I guess now's your chance."

So I left with them.

We walked a long while, and the whole time I was thinking of the quarantine wall, and what it would mean for these people to get into Free America.

The idea of a wall to protect one society from another is an old one. Ancient China tried it. The Communists tried it. The U.S. tried it along the Mexican border. But none of those historical precedents were entirely effective. They all came with a great cost in human life and a lot of insane politics. Political borders, after all, rarely coincide with societal borders. To think otherwise is just plain stupid. Fences may make good neighbors, but walls do not keep countries safe.

That is, until the zombies rose from the flooded ruins of Houston. The military was able to contain the outbreak by constructing a wall that stretches from Gulfport, Mississippi to Brownsville, Texas. Imagine the scope of that project. That's 1,100 miles of cement, chain link fencing and endless spools of concertina wire, all of it constructed in the span of a month and a half. Many have claimed it is one of the modern wonders of the world, while critics maintain it's a wonder it doesn't have more holes in it than a fish net. But according to the government, and several independent quality control groups and news outlets, it doesn't. The wall is sound. It's the truth Free America entrusts its safety to and its impermeability is, to most Americans anyway, a lock-step guarantee.

But Jessica and her group didn't believe it. Lots of people break through every month, she assured me. And I could tell she honestly believed it.

Yet when I pressed her, she didn't seem to have much of a plan.

"We want to get across somewhere between Flatonia and Weimar," she said.

I waited for more. But after a moment, I realized there wasn't more.

"That's it? You don't know where? I mean, exactly? That seems like an important detail to me."

"How can I know something like that? That's up to the coyotes, isn't it?"

"I guess so," I said doubtfully. It seemed like an awful lot to take on faith, though. After all, to trust your life like that to a total stranger seemed crazy. But I answered myself with the same mental breath: Wasn't that exactly what I was doing here with Jessica?

"How much do they charge?" I asked.

She shrugged. "Nobody in the Zone has any money."

"Well, how then?"

She glanced around to make sure no one was looking, then showed me a handful of jewelry. They were nice, but nothing special, a few necklaces and charm bracelets, probably worth a couple hundred dollars at most.

"Is that how most people pay, with jewelry?"

"Mostly, yeah. It's the easiest way. But I've heard people paying with all kinds of stuff. Gas they've siphoned off old cars. Drugs they found in pharmacies. Liquor. Anything people want you can usually trade with."

This was insane, I thought. I guess it showed on my face.

"What?" she said. She was amused by my distress, I could tell. She was almost laughing.

"I just don't see how you can be so blasé about it. Where exactly you're gonna cross, how much it's gonna cost - those things seem like a big deal to me. I mean, you see that, right? They're important. It scares me you're not more worried about it."

The bemused smile left her face, replaced by a bitter seriousness.

"There's always a way for a woman to pay her way," she said.

"Jessica, I..."

She didn't flinch. "I won't go on living this way. Not in the Zone like this." She gestured to the soiled rags that passed for her clothes, at her emaciated body that hardly hinted at a woman's natural curves any more. "Tell me, what would you do?"

"I don't know."

When I went on with my questions, I was more subdued. I'd been humbled.

"What do you plan to do when you get to Free America?" I asked.

"I taught fourth and fifth grade before the wall went up. I thought maybe I could do that again."

"What about friends, family? They could help you get back on your feet."

"Maybe. I hope so. I had a boyfriend, you know. His name was Robert. He did IT stuff for an oil company. Made pretty good money. He was smart. We were living in an apartment together down in Corpus, but he left for a job in Oklahoma about a month before Mardell hit." She ran her left hand down the length of her right arm, fingers touching the cuts and scars and fresh bruises there. "I guess there probably isn't much chance of picking that up again."

"You never know," I said, in what I hoped was an encouraging tone.

She gave me a weak smile. "I won't kid myself. That old life is gone. It'd be like that Tom Hanks movie. Remember the one, he's on that island..."

"*Joe vs. the Volcano*?"

She grinned. "The other one. The deserted island one. Remember? His plane crashes?"

"*Castaway.*"

"That's the one. I was thinking of the end, after he gets rescued. Remember that? He goes home and his wife...what's her name?"

"Helen Hunt."

"Helen Hunt, that's it. Remember what happens when he tries to go home? Helen Hunt's character has remarried and they have that awkward moment on the doorstep. Life has passed him by, and there's nothing he can do about it."

I nodded. "You can't go home again."

"I remember hearing that. Was that from the movie?"

"No," I said. "Thomas Wolfe."

"Ah."

We talked about the movies. We liked a lot of the same shows - *French Kiss, Sleepless in Seattle, While You Were Sleeping,* anything starring Molly Ringwald - and that was nice. But it didn't last. It couldn't last. The movies are the movies, and real life is something else entirely. Jessica had changed too much. This world, this awful place, had changed her and we both knew it. Soon she grew sullen and morose again.

I couldn't blame her.

***

When we left the shack, we left the bodies of Jessica's friends where they lay. Nobody buries the dead in the Zone.

We walked the rest of the day, and around dusk we came upon a group of people headed toward a place off the main road. They said there was sort of a compound there, an old ranch house, and that we could get some fresh water there and probably something to eat, too.

It was dark by the time we arrived and they were all out of food. There wasn't any room left inside the house, either, so we couldn't even sleep where it was warm. It's easy to forget, while you're walking all day in the Texas sun, how cold the desert gets at night. The best we could do was to huddle beneath a vent that carried some of the hot air from inside. We spent the rest of the night in each other's arms, trying to stay warm.

The next morning we woke to gunshots.

"What was that?" I asked.

We had both flinched awake and stared around in panic. Jessica said nothing. Then we heard some men talking. Jessica and I traded a look. The men didn't seem excited at all, just talking.

"What's going on?" I whispered. Guns weren't all that common in the Zone. There were still a few around, of course, but not that many. That seemed odd to me, at first. This used to be Texas, after all. In Texas, even the liberals loved guns. I had expected there to be guns everywhere. When I asked Jessica about it she said most had been confiscated by homegrown militias in the early days of the Outbreak. Where those guns had gone to, she didn't know.

"Jessica, what do we do?"

"Let's go see what they're doing."

"Let's go...?" I didn't get a chance to finish. She was already moving.

I followed her around to the front of the house and got my first look at the place in daylight. It was dilapidated, of course, but still large and impressive, and I could see that it must have been something rather special before the wall went up. There were several large, fenced off areas that looked like they had once been horse pastures but were now being used for crops. Enormous Spanish Oaks, rising like green skyscrapers over the flat, grassy landscape, dotted the countryside. Until the shooting started again, it was quite beautiful.

The men we'd heard talking were standing in the middle of a wide circular drive. Beyond it was a long, straight driveway that led out to the county road. A large hurricane fence, topped with razor wire, surrounded the property, and a wrought iron gate that I didn't remember seeing the night before stood boldly at the entrance.

The shooting came from a pair of men in camouflage hunting outfits up in a deer blind near the gate. Their target was a knot of zombies that had gathered just outside the fence. They didn't seem to be in a hurry to do much killing though, only taking their shots when it suited them, and one of the men standing nearby remarked on that.

"Don't matter," one of the other men said. "They got three good ones."

"No fast ones, though." The man sounded sullen, like a pouting kid.

"They're good enough for the likes of Barry."

The men turned away from the drive and walked around to the east side of the house.

"What was that all about?" I asked.

"No idea."

A crowd had gathered around the east side of the house, so we went that way.

One of the horse pastures was sectioned off with hurricane fencing. In the middle of the small enclosure sat a man chained to a metal pole. He had his back against the pole and his knees pulled up to his chest, refusing to look at the people who had gathered around the fence. A few of them were chatting, but most seemed to be just milling around, waiting.

We weren't there long when the two men in camouflage who had been shooting from the deer blind trotted over to a horse trailer attached to the fence. One of them got up on top of the trailer and used a broom handle to pry open the door latch. Nothing happened. The door stayed close.

"Hit it," somebody yelled.

"Yeah, yeah," the man on top of the trailer said. He slapped the door with the broom handle and the door swung open. Three zombies piled out, staggering into the sunlight. They looked confused and lost. But then they saw the man chained to the pole, and as soon as that happened, the zombies staggered toward him, hands raised and clutching at the air.

"They're gonna kill him."

Jessica gestured for me to be quiet.

I watched the man chained to the pole, and I thought for sure I was going to throw up.

The man climbed to his feet, backing away to the furthest length the chain clasped to his neck would allow. He watched the zombies advancing on him, his eyes bulged in panic, lips trembling. He looked pathetic tugging on the chain.

But he didn't lose all self-control. When the lead zombie got in close he made his move. Holding the chain out in front of him, the captive sprinted to one side, catching the zombie just under the knees and sweeping it off its feet. The zombie pitched over, landing face-first in the dirt, then slowly climbed to its feet again.

I kept waiting for a bunch of redneck hooting and hollering from the assembled crowd, but hardly anybody spoke, much less yelled. One man, drunk already, though the day had hardly started, made a feeble attempt to stoke the crowd by yelling at the condemned man. Everybody ignored him and eventually he too fell into a sort of sullen, bored silence.

It was ennui, I realized then, that was the root cause of misery in the Zone. There were no prospects, no way to improve one's life, except through savagery and the debasement of others. Whatever the man had done wasn't enough to overcome the feelings of emptiness and bootless rage that afflicted these people. They watched him scramble around that enclosure, and even when he made a narrow escape, it wasn't enough to change the exhausted listlessness in their expressions. It was like all the life had bled from them.

Then, he got lucky. One of the zombies was a man in the remnants of an orange t-shirt and jeans. The zombie slipped and went down to one knee. The chained man got behind him, looped the chain around his neck, pushed him face down in the dirt, and stood on the back of his neck. I saw the zombie's expression change as he struggled against the weight holding him down. I don't know if it was muscle memory or some atavistic fear surfacing in its ruined mind, but I swear, for a moment, I thought I saw fear in its eyes.

The crowd grew interested too. They murmured. One man even chuckled. Most just leaned forward, hoping for something to break the boredom.

Meanwhile, the chained man was pivoting around, making sure to keep the other two in sight. They were closing on him, but he didn't seem willing to quit with the zombie in the orange shirt until he was dead.

One of the zombies reached for him, but the chained man was faster and kicked the zombie's legs out from under it. More and more people were getting interested now. The man who had chuckled just a few moments before was nodding now. He shucked his shoulders from side to side, the way my dad used to when he watched the fights on TV.

The zombie in the orange shirt and jeans stopped fighting. It looked dead to me. It wasn't even twitching. The chained man tugged on his shackles, pulling the zombie away from the other two, and started to unravel the chain from the dead man's neck.

He'd almost freed himself when the zombie reached out and grabbed the hem of his pants. The chained flinched as the prisoner kicked the zombie in the face, but he wouldn't let go. Unable to pull himself free, the man lost his footing, and the other two fell on him. The man screamed horribly, but his cries were choked off soon enough, and just like that it was over.

The zombies began to feed, and people started wandering off in groups of two or three, nobody speaking, their expressions inscrutable.

As we walked away, one of the men in charge of the place asked us if we were hungry and we told him we were. He said we could have a can of pork and beans to split if we were willing to clean some clothes first. Jessica and I said that'd be alright. He showed us where we'd be working and we got busy on three big piles of laundry, chatting about nothing in particular as we cleaned.

We were finished by midday and collected our food, then went out back to cook it over a fire pit they had there.

I took a few bites of my pork and beans and gave the rest to Jessica.

"You don't have to do that," she said.

"I know."

She pushed it back at me. "No, I mean you really don't have to do that. I've been hungry before. I don't need charity."

I felt a flush of embarrassment rise in my cheeks. "It's not charity," I said. "I can't eat. Not after what we just saw. Please take it."

She nodded and took it.

"Why would they do that to that man?"

"Who knows?" she said through a mouthful of beans. "He probably stole something. That's about the only thing that gets people upset enough to put a man to death that way."

Most of the work had stopped for the midday meal, and people milled about in the grass with paper plates topped with whatever they could scrounge. If it weren't for the rags they wore, their unkempt hair and the sour smell of unwashed bodies you could almost make yourself believe it was an old fashioned backyard barbeque. Almost.

I found it hard to marry the sight of so many people enjoying such a commonplace thing with the realization that we'd all just watched a man die.

"I guess a lot of people stay in places like these," I said, nodding toward a group of men lounging in the grass.

"They won't be staying here," she said. "This is just a quick meal. Most of them will probably be trying to get to Free America sometime tomorrow."

"Are we that close to the wall? I didn't realize."

She nodded. "Twenty or thirty miles."

"And these men" – for they were almost entirely men – "they all want to cross?"

She nodded again. "See the way they're dressed? The extra shirts, multiple pairs of pants? They don't dress that way because it's cold. That's everything they own."

She was right, of course. These men were hard-looking fellows with weathered faces and starvation in their eyes. A few had improvised sacks with them, but most had nothing but the clothes on their backs and heavy sticks to use against any zombies they happened to encounter.

"This worries me, Jessica. With all these men trying to cross, aren't we drawing a lot of unwanted attention to ourselves?"

"I doubt it. There's a lot of land out here. There are many

places to -"

She broke off mid-sentence as a large man in a red Coca-Cola t-shirt sat down next to us. He leered at us both, exposing a mouth full of black teeth and a tongue that wouldn't stop moving, like he was chewing on it.

"Where are you ladies headed?" he asked, and when he spoke, I could smell the booze on his breath.

"Nowhere," Jessica said.

He turned my way and looked me up and down, eye-fucking me like I was some whore he'd already bought and paid for.

"Well," he said, "if you're gonna be hanging around here for a couple of days, let me know if you meet anyone interested in getting across to Free America. Me and my buddies know how to get them there. It's what we do."

My pulse quickened. Jessica had told me that it would probably happen like this, a quick, unexpected encounter, and while I wanted to catch every nuance of this exchange, I still found it hard to believe that this man was a coyote. In my mind I had formed a picture of what such a man was supposed to look like. He'd be shifty, mean-looking, the kind of man men fear. But above all, the man I pictured in my imagination would actually look like he could do the job. This man, this boozy, greasy, black-toothed redneck, looked like a caricature of himself.

Jessica didn't shrink away like I did, but I did see her gaze sink to the grass. I didn't know it at the time, but Jessica was trying to save us both from looking too eager. This man was a coyote, true, and he seemed sure enough of himself that he could get us into Free America, but there was a certain etiquette to these things of which I was wholly unaware. Men like our thoroughly stewed companion in the red Coca-Cola shirt were, above all else, dangerous. They were opportunists. No doubt they provided the service they claimed, but appearing too eager, jumping right into the conversation, meant that you had something valuable to barter, and for that you were practically begging to get robbed. Or worse.

"I know a good place to cross. Quiet. The patrols pass through there, but they don't hardly ever stop."

"Why not?" I asked. Despite my better instincts, this guy had me curious. He was so sure of himself, like he knew the Quarantine Authority's business better than they did.

"Nothing around there. No towns, no nothing. Just open countryside."

"Well they have helicopters, right? Robot drones and stuff, too?"

His smile faded then, and I got the feeling that he was reevaluating his first opinion of me. He looked suspicious now, the wheels turning behind his eyes as he took in my clothes, which were dirty, but still holding together, my sturdy shoes, my skin, sun-burnt, but still healthy looking. I was different, and that was making him uncomfortable.

I happened to catch a sharp, warning look from Jessica just then. *Careful*, it said.

"Where are you from?" he asked.

I lowered my gaze. I'd just done a very dumb thing and put us in a bad spot by doing so.

"All over," I said.

I could feel him staring at me, but I kept looking at my hands in my lap. When I didn't offer anything more, he went on.

"The Quarantine Authority is no trouble. How much money do you have?"

"I don't have anything," Jessica said.

"Gold? Any diamonds? A wedding ring, maybe?"

Jessica shook her head.

He looked at me. "How about you? I know you've got something."

I shook my head.

The man went silent again. After a long moment, he got up to leave. "My friends and I are gonna be here till tomorrow. Let me know if you find something you can pay me with." Then he walked away without waiting for us to say goodbye.

"I hope we never see that man again," I said.

Jessica watched him go, frowning, but said nothing. I should have wondered then if she knew something I didn't.

***

After lunch, we walked away from the main house so we could talk.

"We should get moving," she said. "It's not smart to stay in

126

places like this longer than you have to."

"Okay," I said. "Where?"

"We should keep going east, toward Weimar."

"We can find somebody there to help us cross?"

She nodded.

"You're sure?"

"Pretty sure, yeah."

"Jessica, look. I gotta say, this is scaring the hell out of me."

"Me too."

"No," I said. I was fumbling for my words. I swept my hand in a vague arc, trying to make a point about everything we'd been through together. "I don't mean all this other stuff we've been dealing with."

"What then?"

I was frustrated with her, angry in fact, and it crept into my tone. "We don't have a plan," I said. "Doesn't that bother you? Even a little bit?"

"If you want to change your mind," she said, "I won't be offended. I can make it from here on my own."

"Jesus, Jessica." I threw up my hands.

"Why are you so upset?"

"Why am I so...?" I stopped there and huffed at her. "Jessica, don't you see? We could die doing this. This isn't some kind of game. The Quarantine Authority, those guys are for real."

"I'm very much aware of what's real," she said. She sounded injured, not haughty. "And for people like me, this was never a game. I hope you remember that when you write your story."

He words floored me.

"Jessica, no. I didn't mean it like that."

"It's okay."

"No, it's not. That was cruel of me."

"No, really," she said. "It's okay. You're sweet. I know you mean well, but we're living in different worlds, you and I."

I felt so ashamed. I didn't want to look at her.

But the shame made it easy to make up my mind, and when she got up to go, I did too.

"You're sure?" she asked.

I nodded. No words.

We set out on a County Road with a little water, but no food. Luckily there was no wind, and even though it was cold, the sky was a bright cobalt blue and the sunlight felt good.

After a few hours we came to one of those little towns that used to dot the Texas landscape, a mill or a cotton processing plant surrounded by rundown buildings. This town was little more than a stop sign and a handful of moldering doublewides, but it was enough to put us on guard.

"I lost a friend in a place like this," Jessica said.

I hadn't heard her talk about people she'd lost before, and so she caught my attention. "Someone you knew before the wall was built?"

She shook her head. "Just a girl I traveled with. We stopped in a little place like this to try to find some water. We were standing behind a counter and a crawler came up behind her and bit her on the leg before either of us knew it was there."

"I guess you have to be prepared all the time, don't you?"

"Yep." She scanned the town, taking it in with one slow stare. "See! Look right there!" she said, pointing toward a dilapidated gas station. "See it?"

I did. Stumbling through the waist high weeds that had grown up around the gas pumps was a female zombie. Its hands hung limply down by its sides, its hair a stringy, blood-encrusted curtain hanging over its face.

"The place looks deserted, but there are probably more around here," Jessica said. "Usually they can't survive if it's just one of them."

I watched the zombie for a moment, and was about to look away, when a shot suddenly rang out.

The female zombie collapsed.

Startled, Jessica and I spun around. We hadn't heard the truck coming up behind us, and for a moment, I couldn't believe what I was seeing. I knew there were a few vehicles still working in the zone, like the truck that had pulled that horse trailer full of zombies back at the ranch, but I hadn't seen any actually driving around.

And then it hit me. Oh shit, the truck from the ranch!

"Run!" Jessica said, grabbing my shoulder and pulling me toward one of the trailers.

As I ran I pulled off my backpack and struggled to get the zipper open. I started to fall behind. Jessica turned and yelled at me to hurry up, but I was too busy trying to get my Glock out of the special compartment I'd stitched into the interior.

I slowed down even more. It wasn't there.

Jessica looked back over her shoulder. "What are doing? Come

128

on."

I was frantic now. With the flaps open, my stuff was spilling out of the backpack, going everywhere. I lost my iPhone, my charger, my notebooks, a change of clothes.

But no pistol. Where was it?

"Hurry!" Jessica yelled.

But it was too late. The truck overtook us, swung around wide, and skidded to a stop, kicking up a wave of dust that covered us. I dropped down to one knee and groped for the knife I'd stashed there.

Again, I was too slow.

Two men in camouflage jumped out, and I recognized them immediately as the men who had been shooting zombies from atop the deer blind back at the ranch.

A third man got out of the truck's back seat.

It was our friend, the booze-soaked coyote with the black teeth and the dancing tongue.

His eyes narrowed on us. It was a sinister gesture, full of menace. "That one right there," he said. "In the black top." He motioned to one of the other two men, who promptly searched me, confiscated my knife, and the pulled my shirt up to my chin.

"Holy shit!" he yelled. "Hey, Jake, you were right. This one ain't no Zoner. Look at this; she's got a brand new bra on."

***

They put us in the backseat and drove east. The two guys in the camouflage hunting outfits looked enough alike that they could have been brothers. They sure acted like it, both of them stinking of beer and sweat and singing along with an Iron Maiden CD they'd plugged into the truck's stereo. The older man they called Jake sat in the back with us, a pistol across his lap. Jessica seemed to have slipped into a morose silence. She didn't react to anything the men said, just stared silently out the window at the empty countryside. Riding between them, listening to the two idiots in the front seat, all I wanted to do was become invisible.

Eventually I saw a sign for a town called Harmony Springs, population 1,405. Harmony Springs was bigger than the little town where we'd been abducted, and it had obviously been hit hard since the Outbreak. Most of the buildings were burned, or so thoroughly looted that they looked like little more than empty shells. But there were zombies here. A crowd of them heard our truck coming and stopped, turning their heads to follow our progress.

We pulled into a small motel. From the parking lot, I could see zombies out on the road, shambling toward us.

"Why did we stop?" I asked.

The man in the driver's seat found me in the rearview mirror. "Girl, if you gotta ask, this is gonna be more fun than I thought it was gonna be."

His brother guffawed and slapped him on the arm. "Hey, that was a good one."

The one they referred to as Jake kicked the back of the passenger seat. "Shut up, Tommy. Go and get the collars out of the back."

The laugh died in Tommy's throat. "Sure thing, Jake," he said, and climbed out.

I heard him rummaging around in the bed of the pickup. He came back to Jessica's side and pulled her door open.

"Get out," Jake said. He glanced over his shoulder at the zombies. They were still a few hundred feet away, but close enough to worry about. "Come on. Hurry up, girl."

Jessica climbed out.

"You too," Jake said, and nudged me in the back with his pistol.

I climbed out and stood next to Jessica, my eyes squinting against the sudden brightness of the sun. The man named Tommy had two blood-stained leather collars in one hand and two dog leashes in the other. My heart sank. These men were clearly no strangers to this kind of thing. Whatever sick abuse they had planned for us, they knew how to go about it.

Jake and the other man climbed out of the truck.

"Do it," Jake said. "Hurry up, so we can get inside."

"Yeah," the third man said. "Oh, yeah." Only then, when I saw the way his hands were shaking and the wild look in his eyes did I realize he was amped up on something, probably meth.

I was crying when Tommy put the collar around my neck. His breath smelled foul, and when he ran his dirty fingertips across the outside of my bra, pausing long enough to give me a hard squeeze, I began to shake. Tommy handed the leash to his brother and a terrible sort of acceptance washed over me. I was going to die, and worse, I was powerless to stop it.

Then he went for Jessica.

I was only half watching what happened. He put his hands on her. She flinched, backed away, swatted at his hands. He closed his arms around her, laughing, despite the zombies who were getting closer every

130

second.

"Hey," he said, "what you got there?"

I saw him take a step back. He looked amused as he reached for her belt buckle. She pushed his hands away. Her clothes were so loose she had no trouble sticking her hand down the front of her pants, from which she produced a small pistol.

My pistol! The one missing from my pack!

Jessica's face looked utterly blank.

Tommy stood less than an arm's length away, and he took the bullet in the left side of his chest, just under his arm. He didn't fall down, though. He staggered away, his hands hanging limply at his side, and bounced off the side of the pickup, leaving a smear of blood there. His face was deathly white. He stared about, confused by the pain and the sudden crazy turn of events, and eventually found his way over to one of the concrete curbs at the edge of the parking lot, where he collapsed.

Jessica didn't stop shooting. As soon as Tommy stepped out of her way she turned her pistol on his brother and shot him once in the chest. The man fell back onto the pavement, rolled over onto his side with a sickening groan, and died.

That left only Jake, the coyote.

He was reaching for his own holstered pistol when Jessica stepped right in front of him and deliberately lowered her pistol to his groin before firing.

The man collapsed to his knees, his face stricken, mouth open in a scream that never quite left his throat.

It took me a moment to recover. Jessica stood over Jake, watching him writhe in agony. The two brothers were dead or dying. And the zombies were closing in.

"Jessica," I said, snapping back into the moment. "Get in the truck."

She didn't answer me. She looked back over her shoulder to where the zombies were already entering the parking lot. They were seconds away now.

"You bastard," she muttered to Jake.

I watched as she scooped up the dog collar from the pavement and clamped it around Jake's neck. He tried to push her away, but he was in too much pain to do anything beyond a few feeble gestures. Next she took one of the leashes and clipped it onto Jake's collar, pulled the free end over to a light pole, and tied it off.

Jake groaned, trying to regain his feet. The zombies were close.

131

Jessica turned away from him without another word and motioned for me to get in the truck.

"Will you drive?" she said. "I don't know if I remember how."

I didn't need to be told twice. I jumped behind the wheel, slammed my door, and rolled up the window.

Jessica got in beside me.

I turned the ignition and the sounds of a big block V8 roared to life just as Jake let out a terrified scream. I looked in the rearview mirror and saw him wrestling with the collar around his neck, his fingers shaking too badly to work the clasp. The next moment, half a dozen zombies fell upon him and his screams of fear were choked off.

"Go!"

"Where?" I asked. "They're all around us."

"Run them down. Hurry!"

I dropped the truck into reverse and punched it. We took off with a lurch, tires barking on pavement. Several zombies were right behind us, and the truck shuddered as we ran them down. I kept my foot on the gas as we bounced over the curb and spun out in the middle of the road.

We paused there for a moment. The zombies in the parking lot were confused by our rapid escape. Some were getting up from the three dead bodies of our abductors and starting after us.

I looked from them to Jessica.

"When did you take my gun?" I asked.

She kept her gaze forward, eyes hard flints of rage. "I've been raped before," she said. "I made myself a promise no one would ever rape me again."

I wasn't mad. Maybe I should have been, but I wasn't.

She took a deep breath, then put the Glock on the seat between us. "I'm sorry," she said. "Stealing from someone is the most serious crime we've got out here."

I left the gun where it was. "I'm lucky you were there."

"Thanks," she said. She pointed east. "Weimar's that way."

***

Before the Outbreak, Weimar was a town of some 2000 people. It had a Wal-Mart, a movie theater, a couple of motels, and a string of fast food restaurants clustered around an exit ramp off IH-10. Its survival depended on the traffic flowing between San Antonio and Houston, and so the town had grown up in pretty much equal measure on both sides of the highway.

"You don't think it's strange, crossing here?"

"No. Why?"

"Well, I'd kind of thought we'd cross somewhere... I don't know... a little less developed. Why do you suppose this is the place?"

"I don't know," she admitted.

"I've asked you that already, haven't I?"

"Yeah."

I looked around, trying to see what made this place such a favorite crossing spot. But I still didn't get it. I didn't see anything that popped out at me. We'd made the trip to Weimar in no time in our newly acquired pickup, and we'd even managed to find a good campsite that afforded a view of the town and the wall. I saw a blasted war zone on our side, with at least a hundred zombies wandering the streets, and on the other side of the wall, a gently decaying abandoned ghost town. The difference between the two parts of the town was striking to say the least.

"You done eating?" Jessica asked.

She sat by our camp fire, picking the meat off a rabbit's leg bone.

We had figured out how to use the assault rifle our former abductors had left us, and a small, but quite delicious spit-roasted rabbit was the result. I stood there, watching her eat the first good meal we'd had in days, examining the town, and for a second it was easy to trust her. She had gotten me this far, after all.

But the feeling we were in way over our heads just wouldn't go away. "You can have it," I said, and went back to examining the town.

In the few hours since we'd made camp, I'd seen dozens of Quarantine Authority trucks racing up and down the length of the wall. I even saw a few helicopters wheeling overhead. Now, with dusk settling around us, the trucks were playing zombie moans over loudspeakers, and it was driving the zombies crazy.

"Why do they keep playing those sounds?" I asked.

"Augment their numbers, I guess."

"What do you mean?"

"What's the term, a force-multiplier? With the zombies wandering around, it's a lot harder for people to cross."

I thought about that. "So that means they must know about this place? Do you think that's true?"

"How should I know?" she asked.

"I can't believe I haven't heard anything about this. I mean, I researched the Quarantine Authority for months before coming on this trip."

"I'm sure they don't want to make it public knowledge."

"I should think not."

Jessica went back to her rabbit. She wasn't letting any of it go to waste. I watched her work the meat from the bone with a thoroughness that only someone long acquainted with hunger could manage. By contrast, my own small pile of bones on the flat rock by my feet contained a fortune of meat. Not for the first time I realized that I was a long way from walking a mile in her shoes.

"Hey, I've got to pee," I said.

"There's a good place over there by the fence." She pointed to the remnants of a white split-rail fence that ran along the ridgeline where we'd camped. "Better take the pistol, though. Rattlesnakes are apt to come out at night."

"Oh," I said. "Okay."

I didn't see any rattlesnakes, which is good, because I don't do well with snakes. Even still, I took my time doing my business, my butt down in the tall grass, my head full of at least a million reasons why crossing the wall in this place was a bad idea. But despite all my studying and knowledge of the technology the Quarantine Authority had at its disposal, something about Jessica's simple faith in crossing at Weimar kept quieting my fears. She seemed so sure of herself. Maybe this was doable, I thought. Maybe all the people Jessica had heard of actually did find a way to the other side, and maybe all the rumors back in Free America were true. Maybe we really could do this.

By the time I was ready to start back, I'd made up my mind to follow her the whole way.

I rounded the old live oak that sheltered our campsite and was about to step into the circle of fading firelight when I heard voices. Jessica's and someone else's. A man's voice.

I froze, my hand dropping to the pistol tucked into the front of my jeans.

I could only make out snippets of their conversation, but from the little I could hear I realized that I'd made a mistake. That wasn't a man's voice. It was a boy's. A teenager. He sounded like he was fifteen or sixteen, a kid, but still close enough to a man to be dangerous. I had my hand on the pistol when I heard something behind me.

I spun around to see an older man and a dog staring at me.

"There's no need for your gun, miss," the man said. "I'm sure you ladies have seen your fair share, but my grandson and I are harmless.

We're not armed."

"That doesn't seem very smart."

"Why in the world would I need a gun?"

The question caught me by surprise. I didn't quite know what to say. I looked from him to the dog and back to the old man. I had nothing.

"What's your dog's name?" I finally said.

"Guthrie," he said.

"Named for Arlo or Woodie?" It was the first thing that came to mind, but evidently it was the right thing, for his smile grew wide.

"Both, actually. Nice to meet somebody who remembers the joys of good music."

"My Dad," I said. "He was kind of an old hippie."

"Sounds like someone I would have liked," the man said. "My name is Frank. That's my grandson over there talking to your friend. His name is Will."

I nodded. I was starting to like this man, though my hand hadn't gone far from the pistol tucked into my pants. It didn't matter how nice his smile was. And certainly not after what had happened earlier.

"You mind if we go over to the campfire there?" he asked. "I'm a bit chilly."

"Sure," I said, turning to allow him a path to the fire. "Lead the way."

We entered the campsite and I took up a position next to Jessica. I could tell from her body language that this was a good thing, that she wasn't afraid of these men. It wasn't like before, when she spent long stretches of silence trying to shrink into herself, contemplating whatever lay beyond her death. This was different. There actually seemed to be mirth in her eyes as she listened to the old man tell of what had led them here.

They were coyotes. That they admitted from the start. In fact, they told us they had just come from a successful trip across the wall, for they knew of a good spot to cross.

Frank liked to talk, and as he was the first coyote I'd met who wasn't a drunken rapist with bad teeth, I started asking him questions. I was worried he'd be offended, but I think he was actually kind of amused by the whole interview process.

"Wasn't much of a stretch for us," he said. "Will here was living with me on my ranch about twenty miles from here. I've had a flag flying off my doorstep since I came back from Vietnam, and when the government started building the wall, Will and I, we did our part. We even helped those sons a bitches put up some of it. The way I saw it, it was my patriotic duty.

"Course then everything went to hell. I figured even an officer coulda told we wasn't infected, but they locked us up anyway. I couldn't believe it. I stood there on the Zone side of the wall and carried on a twenty minute conversation with a major, and all I got was fucked."

He looked at us then and actually blushed.

"Er, I'm sorry about my language, ladies. I don't usually talk that way in front of women. But it gets a fella awful mad thinking about it."

After what Jessica and I had just been through, I wanted to laugh.

But instead I said, "So you two became coyotes. How many people have you helped across?"

"I don't know." He looked at his grandson, as if he might know, but the boy just shrugged. "I guess we've taken, what, a couple hundred?"

"A couple hundred?" I said. "No."

"About that," Frank agreed. "We don't work cheap, though." He said it almost as an afterthought. "We're in this for the greater good and all, but we still gotta live, you know?"

"How about a truck?" Jessica said.

The directness of her offer surprised me. I gave her a questioning look, but she didn't acknowledge it. She was looking right at Frank.

"We have a Ford pickup, with a quarter tank of gas. Get us across and it's yours."

Frank seemed as stunned as I was. "I don't know," he said slowly. He looked to his grandson, then back to Jessica. "Where is this pickup of yours?"

"About a hundred yards down the rise there, behind a clump of hackberry."

Frank smiled. He didn't believe us. "That might be okay. You mind if we see it?"

* * *

Frank's expression changed as we pulled the vegetation away from the truck. He recognized it. That much was obvious right from the start.

"Where did you get this?" he said. The good natured friendliness was gone from his voice now. He was suddenly alert, scanning the dark

136

landscape all around us for signs of trouble.

"They won't come looking for it," Jessica said. She reached inside the cab and pulled out one of the assault rifles Tommy and Jake had left behind. "I can guarantee you that."

"You took this from them?" Frank asked.

"Like I said, they won't come looking for it," Jessica said.

She let that one sit for a moment. The two men looked uncertain, maybe even a little frightened. Clearly the men Jessica had dealt with so handily had been men with reputations. But eventually their uncertainty was replaced by a grudgingly offered respect and renewed curiosity. We had changed in their eyes.

"You'll give us this?" Frank said.

"You'll get us across?" Jessica countered.

Frank paused for a long moment, then smiled. "We can do that," he said

"Then the truck is yours."

"Okay then." He nodded at his grandson. "I guess we have a deal."

***

I got frightened by how quickly things happened after that.

I've always been the kind who plans ahead. When I go on trips, I have a schedule laid out. I've done my research. I know what to see and how to get there and how much I'm supposed to pay.

But now, as Will explained to us how this was going to work, I felt panicky. My heart raced. Where were the details? I had tons of questions and none of them were getting answered.

Jessica, meanwhile, seemed to take it all in stride. She listened to Will with a detached air I found unnerving. I couldn't believe she was so calm about it, like we were discussing plans for dinner or something.

I finally found my voice when he started putting bells on the dog.

"Why are you doing that?" I asked.

"This?" he asked. He had taken a harness, a lot like the kind they put on service animals for blind people, and strung bells down its length. He slid the harness into place and scratched Guthrie behind the ears. The dog seemed to love the attention. He wagged his tail eagerly, sending a wave of music through the bells lining his flanks. "Guthrie here runs diversion for us."

A few minutes later I saw what he meant.

Weimar had a greenbelt that ran north to south through town, running underneath the highway. Judging from the old growth vegetation that formed around its banks I figured it must have also doubled as some sort of drainage system. It was the kind of thing a small town that relied on thru-traffic for its livelihood would have kept hidden behind a screen of tall trees.

This was apparently Will and Frank's secret, for Will led us down to a cross street very close to the greenbelt. It was dark and the streets were lit only by starlight. I could see very little, but I could hear the zombies moaning, and they were getting closer every minute.

Will leaned down and whispered into Guthrie's ear.

For the dog this was clearly some kind of game. It began to bark and spin around in a circle, like it was chasing its own tail, sending the music of bells into the night.

The bells were answered by a chorus of moans that seemed to come from all around us at once.

"What in the world are you - "

But I didn't get to finish my objection. Will put up a hand and motioned at the dog. Guthrie sprinted forty yards or so down the street, right into the face of a growing crowd of zombies, and began to bark.

"What's he -?"

"Shhh," Will said. "Don't make a sound."

Zombies poured out of the buildings, so many in fact that for a moment I lost sight of Guthrie. But then he reappeared, still barking furiously, the bells on his harness like Christmas music in the cold night air, and he sprinted away.

My pulse quickened. The zombies were actually following him. This just might work.

But then he stopped. He turned and watched the zombies, almost like he was waiting for them to catch up.

"Go," I whispered. "Come on you stupid dog. Run!"

"No," Will said. He turned his palm toward me without moving his arms. "No sudden movements. They key on movement and noise. Just wait. Guthrie knows what to do."

And he was right.

The dog was good at what he did, and I began to see why Weimar had the reputation that it did. Within a few minutes, Guthrie had managed to lead all the zombies away from our position with an air of practiced efficiency that would have been the envy of any Border collie.

I heard him barking in the distance, apparently happy as a clam.

"He'll be okay?" I asked.

"He's a dog," Will said. "Why wouldn't he be?"

I couldn't deny the sense in that.

When the zombies were gone, Will led us down to the bottom of the greenbelt and began pulling away vegetation. I looked over at Jessica, hoping maybe to catch a glimpse of what was going through her mind. She had grown quiet since we left the campsite, and that bothered me. But she neither returned my glance nor gave any indication that she was anxiously waiting on Will's next move. She just stood there, patient as a saint, a strange, almost vacant acceptance on her face. She seemed to have gone robotic, much as she had been in the truck with Jake and the two brothers.

"This is it," Will said. He stepped back to reveal an open standpipe, a gigantic open maw, like the opening to a cave. "Go through here. When you come up on the other side, you'll be in Free America."

"Just like that?" I asked.

"Yep. Pretty much."

Again I looked at Jessica. I wanted some indication that she was okay with this, but all I got was a blank stare. She turned away from me, ducked her head, and slipped into the standpipe.

"Jessica, wait," I said.

Only then did she turn to look at me.

"What?"

"You're okay with this?"

She shrugged. I'll never forget that. There was no expression, just a vacant shrug. She turned into the darkness of the tunnel and started walking. Will gave me an encouraging nod, and the next instant I walked into the tunnel, trying to catch Jessica.

The crossing itself was anticlimactic.

We entered a pipe about five feet in diameter, so I had to duck slightly to move through it, and began to feel our way forward.

There was about an inch of standing water in the bottom of the pipe, and every step made a splash that echoed down the length of the tube. It was dark, too. Even though Jessica was only an arm's length ahead of me, I couldn't see her.

It would have been the perfect setting for something scary. Every sound sent reverberations away from us in both directions, but the truth is, I felt completely safe the whole way.

The crossing itself was a piece of cake.

I don't know how long we walked. A couple of minutes, maybe. But eventually we came up on the other side. I saw some shrubs, a patch of starlit sky, and then we were out, standing on the grass.

We had arrived in Free America.

But it was not the joyful homecoming I'd expected. I looked around. Something was wrong. The hairs were standing up on the back of my neck. But what was the problem? What was wrong?

There was a street off to our left and abandoned buildings, shop fronts mostly, on the other side of that. A cold breeze blew dust across the pavement. I heard moans in the distance, and even though all else seemed quiet, my gut told me we were in real trouble.

Jessica stepped into the street, looking back toward the quarantine wall.

A Quarantine Authority truck rolled down IH-10, moving slowly.

It came to a stop.

"Oh no," Jessica said.

"What's going on?" The truck was maybe a hundred yards away, which was close, but in the dark, I thought there was a chance they hadn't seen us.

The truck started to pull away, and I thought: Good! Yes. Keep going.

"Jessica," I said, "they're leaving!"

She turned to me and shook her head. "We have to get out of here," she said.

"But they're driving off."

It was true. The truck was accelerating away. It went down the highway a few hundred yards, and then suddenly its brake lights came on and it veered off the main lanes and back towards our position.

I couldn't believe what I was seeing.

The truck bounced over the median, crossed a parking lot, and then accelerated down a surface street that would carry it around behind us.

"How did they...?" I asked.

"Hurry," Jessica said. "Across the street."

"Where?"

"Those buildings." She pointed to the shop fronts across the street. "Hurry."

I ran.

I made it all the way across before I realized Jessica was still standing in the middle of the street.

"Jessica?"

"You need to go," she said. "Get out of sight."

"What are you doing?"

"I can't go with you."

The truck was getting closer. I could hear its engine pulling hard. And something else. Voices, the sound of boots on the pavement. Men running. Someone shouted orders.

"Like hell. Come on, Jessica."

"No, I can't."

"What do you mean you can't?"

She looked utterly deflated, miserable. "I can't go with you."

I could make out individual voices now and the clatter of equipment and guns. The soldiers were seconds away.

"But Jessica...?"

"That world doesn't exist for me anymore. It's all changed. I've changed. You can't go home again. Isn't that what you said?"

"Jessica, I —"

"Don't," she said. "There isn't time. I can't go with you, and I can't go back. But you need to hide. Now!"

The truck came roaring around a corner halfway down the block. I was out of time. I had to act. There was a narrow alleyway between two buildings a few steps away. I backed into it, into the shadows.

Out in the street, Jessica stood her ground.

From my research on the Quarantine Authority I knew they'd have helicopters over the area in just a few minutes. They'd have heat sensing cameras and all sorts of sophisticated people-hunting equipment to bring into play, which meant I had only seconds to get away.

But I couldn't look away from Jessica. Quarantine Authority troopers bore down on her, yelling for her to get down on her knees, while the truck skidded to a stop on the other side of her and hit her with a super-intensity floodlight.

I anticipated the gun shot, but when it came, I flinched just the same. I turned and ran, tears streaming down my face. And as I slipped away into the night I realized the woman had given her life for my escape, and I never even knew her last name.

DEAD HUNGER: TONY MALLETTE'S STORY

By Eric A. Shelman

A CHRONICLE IN THE DEAD HUNGER SERIES

http://www.ericshelman.com

$\mathbf{M}$y name is Anthony Mallette. My friends call me Tony. If I stand up really straight, I'm probably 5'9" tall. I'd put on a lot of weight after my accident, but since what I'm about to tell you happened, I've lost a lot of it. I'm only around 175 pounds these days.

I have a full, salt and pepper beard and kind of crazy, Elvis-like hair. Folks even used to call me Elvis when I was a kid. Huh. I just remembered that. It's funny how a world gone crazy can block out everything that happened before, both good and bad.

That just made me smile for the first time in a long while. Fuckin' Elvis.

If you're reading this now – and I'm not sure why you would be – I'm probably dead. I can't really see this little journal of mine being put to use by anyone else, so that would probably keep me from passing it along. If you *are* reading it, you probably got it from Serena Casteneda or another friend of mine, like Flex or Gem. Maybe Hemp. Sounds like something he'd do.

Anyway, for the moment, I'm living in a pretty strange world. I almost wrote that it's a world dominated by zombies, but that would seem to dismiss the fact that our group dominates them every time we run into them. So they don't so much dominate as they do occupy space and threaten.

They *always* threaten.

You might be asking yourself if maybe I'm modest, and that's why I think you wouldn't have any interest in reading my history. I wish I could say that was it. It's not.

It's that if I'm being honest – and I pretty much am, with everyone – I'm not that quick-thinking, at least not anymore. There was a time that I was, but that was before the accident. Now it takes me a few seconds to develop a plan on the fly. That can be rough in a world like this one, but I gotta give myself more credit that I give the rotters.

When I was in my mid-twenties I was a tough and crazy longhair, I loved to ride my Harley everywhere, and I was married to my childhood sweetheart, Linda. I put a quick end to all that. Well, not all of it. Most of it.

The accident I'm talking about happened in New York. I was a site foreman for a construction company in Brooklyn. One day, as I was leaving one job to get a work crew set up on another, I remembered we'd need a couple of pieces of plywood for some temporary barriers. I figured since we were heading over, we could just throw them on the truck. I walked through the site and saw the plywood leaning against a temporary fence.

All but one piece. It was laying on the ground in front of the fence. I figured it had blown over, so I bent down and curled my fingers underneath it on the eight-foot side and lifted it, walking forward as I stood it back up.

When I took my second step, there was nothing there. Open space. Next thing I knew, I was plummeting straight down in the dark. It felt like I'd never hit bottom.

On the way down, my head slammed into something; I don't know what it was to this day. I'm told I landed in a sitting position.

I had fallen forty-three feet straight down an open manhole into a sewer. There was water at the bottom, but only a couple of inches. I shattered my body; broke both my legs and fractured my spine.

I didn't know it at the time, but an older worker saw me drop. He ran over and climbed down the ladder built into the wall of the sewer access tunnel. When he got about twenty-five feet down, the ladder pulled from the wall and he fell another fifteen feet, landing on top of me.

Two men down.

I was fucking lucky to be alive and I know it now, but I didn't know anything then. I was in the hospital for three months. When I got out, I was still in a wheelchair. I went from there to a walker, then to a cane, and then finally… I walked on my own. It took me more than a year to do that.

I might have once known what happened to the other guy, but I've forgotten now.

Like I said, I'm not sure what my head slammed into on the way down. It might have been a rung of the ladder, maybe just the wall. I'm probably lucky it dazed me so I didn't have to worry about my continued trip south at high speed.

From that day on, I knew I wasn't quite right in the head anymore. Just formulating thoughts took me longer, and figuring out how to do something wasn't instinctive anymore. I had to really struggle to learn things, and still, when people talk to me, sometimes my mind wanders.

I never went back to my job after that, and I wasn't much fun to be around anymore. Linda left me and I felt like everything – everything I had and everything I loved – was done and over with.

I left New York before another year passed. I couldn't stop think-ing about a little town in Vermont called Shelburne. We'd vacationed in the area when I was a kid, and I remembered it as a small community with good people. I figured I could maybe get some kind of job in a sporting goods store or a gas station, or somewhere else to pass the time, and I figured getting away from the city might help me put all the bad stuff in my past.

I *needed* something.

It wasn't bad, either. I started calling Linda every couple of weeks, then every week. After that, she started to call me. Soon, we were talking a couple times a week, then every day.

Eventually, I went to get her and brought her back to live with me in Shelburne. I ended up with a job at a place in town called Davillo's Discount Guns and Tackle, just up Shelburne Road in South Burlington. I was pretty much an aficionado of guns, so it was a perfect fit for me. I worked part time just to get through my days.

Linda and I got married again. My life was different, but I sure as hell felt grateful for what I still had… and what I got back.

Linda's about 5'6" tall with dark brown hair and eyes. She's soft and pretty, and I was lucky to get her back. She was all I'd ever wanted since I was too young to know the difference. Call it luck, but every other rela-tionship I'd ever had was just filler; biding time.

But I had my Linda back.

Then June 19, 2011 hit and everything changed.

Linda got migraines once in a while – more in recent years. I was used to it. So I didn't think a whole lot of the headache she got the eve-ning of June 18th. It kept her up most of the night, and when she wasn't awake, she was thrashing and screaming.

I was awake most of that night, too. It was her growls that kept my eyes open and on her. They did not sound right *or* normal. They sounded savage and animalistic, and my girl had *never* made noises like that before.

She'd settle down occasionally, and I'd slow my breathing and relax, only for it to begin again. Thrashing. Tossing and turning.

Growling.

I was about to get up and call 911. It was time. Then, she was calm again. I lay there and watched her in the soft glow of the nightlight she insisted on for her nightly trips to the bathroom. Finally I fell asleep again, satisfied she was at least asleep.

It was around 3:45 in the morning when it all came to a head. It was pure luck that caused me to open my eyes as she stood over me, the table lamp in her hands, bloody mucus running down her chin and her eyes blank but mad.

She lunged at me, swinging the lamp toward my head, but I reacted fast enough to roll off the opposite edge of our bed.

"Linda! Babe, what the hell are you doing?"

Snarls. Growls.

I felt chills ripple down my spine as I made the decision to stay on the floor, out of her sight for the moment. I saw my jeans on the floor, so I reached for them. I was buck naked, for Christ's sake. I rolled onto my back and pulled my jeans on, zipping and buttoning the Levis. No shirt, as I'd taken that off earlier and dumped it in the dirty clothes hamper.

I rolled back onto my stomach and scooted underneath the bed, following my instincts. The king-sized frame sat on 10" risers, plus the added five inches or so of the bed frame's legs, so there was plenty of room under there. I lay still watching her planted feet. They were somehow more gray than flesh-toned. Easing my breath in and out of my lungs as quietly as I could, I watched her in the gloom.

She hadn't moved since I had dropped off the bed. I could still see her feet, planted on the other side. She let out another frightening screech, and I decided then that I *needed* to subdue her long enough to call 911 and get her help. I just had to make sure she wouldn't hurt herself or me in the process.

I seriously thought she had gone insane. I knew nothing about mental illness or how fast it could set in, but right about then, the woman I loved was scaring the hell out of me. I felt the tears running down my cheeks before I realized I was crying.

I hesitated as one foot moved toward the rear of the bed.

She was coming around! I had to stop her. I didn't know how aware she actually was, but I wasn't willing to take the chance that she'd figure out where I was and resume her attack at floor level. I scooted forward and threw my hands out, grabbed her ankles and jerked them toward me as hard as I could. Her feet slid out from under her on the hardwood floor, and she flopped onto her back, her head slamming into the floor with a powerful *thump*!

That impact would have knocked me out – there's no doubt. It would have knocked anyone out. Not Linda. Her growls and guttural cries never stopped. I was freaking out. I scrambled out from under the bed before she got her feet back under her, and bolted for the kitchen where my cell phone was charging. Her arm reached for me as I passed, but her clutching fingers just missed taking me down.

I got the phone in my hand and just ran. The cord pulled from it as I entered the hallway and ran into the bathroom. I called 911.

The operator answered. "911, what is your emergency?"

"My wife!" I said, my heart pounding so loud in my ears I felt as though I were yelling over the sound of a freight train. "She's... she's... having an episode or something. She's like... gone crazy."

"Is she trying to harm you sir?"

A pounding came at the bathroom door. I lowered my voice. "Yes," I whispered. "She tried to hit me with a lamp, and now she's pounding on the door. Hold on."

"Linda, are you okay, baby? Lin? I want you to go to bed, okay? Just get back in bed."

The scratching grew more frantic, and her growls increased in pitch until she was shrieking like a wild animal."

"Is that her?" the incredulous voice came into my ear.

"Yes."

"Wow. The boards are lighting up here."

"What?"

"We're getting inundated with calls."

"Hurry, okay? She's really sick, like she's gone insane!"

"Are you on a mobile phone?" said the operator, sounding distracted now.

The pounding now turned to a scratching-clawing. It sounded as though she were trying to shred the wood with her fingernails.

"Y-yeah," I stammered, my eyes on the door.

"What is your address so we can dispatch police officers and an ambulance to your location?"

The operator sure sounded a hell of a lot calmer than I felt.

"3025 Hinesburg Road, in Charlotte," I said. "Hurry, please. Tell the guys to put their sirens on and hurry!"

"I've dispatched them," she said. "Look, I'd ordinarily stay on the line, but I have to take these other calls. We're lit up light a Christmas tree here."

I hit the END button and put the phone back in my pocket.

The clawing was relentless. "Linda!" I shouted. "Linda, baby, it's me in here, okay? You're gonna be fine in a bit, Lin. They're sending police and paramedics, and they'll find out what's wrong with you. Please, just get back in bed."

The clawing didn't stop. It grew more frantic with each passing second. It began to sound like she was actually making headway. My eyes fell to the floor.

The gap beneath the door was about three quarters of an inch. I struggled to kneel on my once-shattered legs, my joints arguing with pops and cracks. When I got down, I ran my finger over the wood floor. It was covered with slivers of wood. I felt something on my fingers, and rubbed them together. It was slick. I squinted at it, and smelled it.

Blood. She was really ripping her fingernails off.

"Lin, stop it! Please, baby! You're gonna hurt yourself, honey!"

I heard the sirens in the distance, and started to cry. One way or another, it was going to come to an end. I wanted her sedated and in an ambulance. I had no doubt that when she awoke, she would be back to the woman I'd loved since I was a kid.

The siren's wail grew louder and louder, finally cutting out. Next thing I heard was a pounding on the front door. "Help! In here! Come in, please!" I screamed the words at the top of my lungs. I looked at my watch. I'd been in there for twenty minutes.

I'm not in Shelburne proper; Lin and I couldn't afford to rent there. Neighboring Charlotte was more spread out and cheaper, especially for homes like ours that were way out on Hinesburg Road. If we'd lived in Shelburne, the ambulance would've been there in three minutes max.

The scratching stopped. I eased toward the bathroom door and put my ear to it. Suddenly the sound of glass shattering rang out, and I heard men screaming. Their cries were followed by three gunshots, and then by even more men screaming.

"Hey!" I shouted. "Hey, help!"

The next sound I heard was an entire magazine emptying, shot after shot. There were at least fourteen rounds expended. I pulled out my phone again and hit 911 again.

We're sorry. All circuits are busy. Please try your call again later. If this is an emergency, please hang up and dial 911.

"Shit!" I screamed. I ran toward the bathroom door and started pounding on it from my side. "Help! Help me! Is anyone there?"

Silence filled the space behind the door now, and somehow, it felt louder than the scratching.

I don't know how long I waited. I was shaking worse than when I was a little kid and I disobeyed my parents by watching a horror movie before going to bed.

This time I looked at my watch and set my mind to remembering what time it said. 5:19 AM. , been dealing with this craziness for one hour and thirty-four minutes, but it felt like a lifetime. I remembered what time

I woke up. I sure remembered that. It was 3:45.

I decided I'd stay there until six o'clock. If I didn't hear anything by then, I'd bolt out of there, get to my bedroom to get my gun from my nightstand, and handle shit myself.

What are you gonna do, tough guy? Shoot Linda? The girl you first kissed when you were eight years old and she was six? Not gonna happen.

No. I knew it wasn't. I turned behind me. The window.

It was small, but I figured if I could get my ass up to it, I could crawl through it. The toilet would help me, and the rest would be up to my agility, which wasn't quite up to par.

What happened next made my decision for me.

Out of the blue, the door rocked in its frame. Then again.

"Hello? Who's there?" I called out.

A savage growl came from the other side of the door. As I stared, a reddish-pink mist began pouring in through the edges of the door. Curious, I moved toward it, and took a deep breath.

* * *

I woke up with my head thick with confusion. The lights were out. I sat up and rubbed the back of my head and instantly felt a knot. Whatever that crap was that I inhaled, it had taken me down and out.

The scratching had stopped. There was no longer any of the red-pink mist coming in, either. I pulled out my phone and looked at the time in the upper corner.

4:00 PM.

I stared at the time. I held the phone up to my watch. It turned 4:01 as I watched it.

I'd been out for almost eleven hours.

I got to my feet with much difficulty. My body was already battered, and falling from a standing position wasn't doing me any good. I held my cell phone up to act as my guiding light, and stepped onto the toilet. I flipped the lock on the bathroom window and slid it up. It left me with around fourteen inches to squeeze through. The width would accommodate my shoulders, but just barely.

I fed my arms through and positioned my head dead center with the hole.

Behind me the scratching began again. I was glad I couldn't see; it sounded like the fingers were ready to break clean through the hollow-core door slab, and I didn't want to be in there when that happened.

I pushed off, scrambling for a grip. Outside the window, my right hand found a conduit pipe and I wrapped my fingers around it, pulling with everything in me.

A splintering sound came from behind me. Adrenaline surged through me and I kicked my legs with reckless abandon and let go of the pipe, trying with everything in me to swim my way through mid-air to get through that window. My body halfway through, I pushed off the exterior wall with both hands and launched myself out, just as I heard a primal growling from behind me. It didn't sound anything like my Lin.

I toppled down onto the dead grass below, and rolled. When I looked back up at the window I saw a gray hand with tattered, bloody fingers and no sign of fingernails left, clutching at the window ledge above me.

I got to my feet and ran toward the back of the house.

I needed to get to my guns. What I had heard and seen was not the Linda Mallette I knew anymore.

* * *

I rounded the rear corner of the house and stopped, breathing hard. I checked myself out to make sure I hadn't broken something during my fall out of the window and my adrenaline was just blocking the pain.

I was alright. I closed my eyes for a second and tried to gather my more-than-usual scattered thoughts. What the hell had knocked me out for eleven hours? I couldn't sleep for eleven hours in a row if someone smashed me in the head with a mallet.

Yet somehow, I had.

Just then I heard similar growls and what sounded like a yelp coming from behind my rear fence. I checked behind me and ran across the lawn. The window blinds were closed on our bedroom, so if Linda had wandered back there she wouldn't see me. I reached the fence and peered between the old, weathered boards.

Bill Frederick, a single guy who lived behind us, was crouched over his dog. It was a golden retriever named Sam, and at first, I wasn't sure what I was seeing.

Bill, who'd had us over for his 56th birthday party a couple of weeks before, was a bald, pot-bellied man who couldn't top 5'2" tall. He was quick with a wave and didn't have an enemy in the world that I knew of.

"Bill, what the hell are you doing?" I yelled. "What's wrong with Sam?"

At first he didn't raise his head. I squinted. I didn't have my glasses on, but my first impression that I was witnessing the embrace of an injured dog by its owner was shattered in the next second.

Bill raised his head toward me. Trailing from his teeth were the dog's dripping entrails, and Bill's mouth chewed relentlessly as he stared at me, as though trying to figure out what I was. My eyes fell to his hands, which continued to claw into the dogs insides. He stared for another moment before dropping his head again. He burrowed his face deeper into the dog's shredded abdomen and feasted.

I doubled over and threw up.

I staggered back from the fence and stood there, my heart racing wildly. After another few seconds of indecision, I spun around and ran back toward the house. I didn't know what the hell to do.

My wife had attacked me and was incoherent. Bill was... what? *Rabid?*

I realized I still had my phone with me, so I stood there, my back against the exterior of our bedroom wall, and dialed 911 again.

This time I got no automated message. It went straight to a fast busy signal.

I stuffed the phone back in my pocket. It had charged all night, so was at 96% battery remaining. That was good, in case the emergency lines opened back up eventually.

How many people like them were out there? Was this an illness?

The questions ripped through my foggy mind. I needed to protect myself.

I had a nice Benelli M4 12-gauge shotgun and a nickel-finished Sig Sauer 1911, along with plenty of boxes of .45 rounds and 12 gauge shells. I kept the shotgun in the back left corner of my bedroom closet and the Sig in my nightstand. When I ran out of the bedroom, I guess I was a little freaked out, so I didn't think to grab my gun.

Why the hell would I? Was I going to shoot my wife?

A little freaked out. Hell. Under-fucking statement of the year.

Anyway, the ammo was in a lingerie chest. The bottom drawer was granted to me by Linda for that purpose. I moved to the window. Linda often opened it in the night to let circulation flow through the house, and on more than one occasion she'd left it unlocked. I leaned down and curled my fingers beneath the window and pulled.

Locked.

"Damnit!" I shouted. A split-second later, the glass before me shattered outward, and I staggered backward. Linda's body fell through it and landed atop me, even as I swung wildly in my surprise.

153

My fist connected with her face, knocking her back and off of me. I felt warm blood leaking over my chest, neck and face, and I again rolled over and sprung up from the ground like a sprinter. Once I got on my feet I ran into the yard and spun around.

Linda was just getting back to her feet, and my eyes moved from her to the window, then to the back porch. My push broom was there. I charged for it.

My wife staggered now; I wondered if she had hurt her leg or another part of her body as she had either fought with the police or fallen through the window. She wore only a thin nightgown that was soaked through with blood. Parts of her gown appeared to be shredded.

I had no idea what had happened to the paramedics and police. There's no way my Linda – my little, unimposing Lin - had done anything to harm them. They must have encountered something outside of our house or been called to another, more serious situation in progress.

But what about all the gunshots? I should have heard more sirens approaching, but I didn't.

I got the broom in my hands, and turned to see Linda five feet away, a strange, pink glow in her eyes. I held up the broom and ran toward her, hoping she would veer away.

She didn't. The bristle end of the broom hit her chest and I pushed outward, hard. She staggered away, but let out this crazy shriek and came right back toward me.

As she drew near, the pink mist reappeared and this time I could see the source: it poured from her eyes. I remembered what happened last time I got near that crap in the bathroom. I didn't want to think what she would do to me if she had her way. In response, my brain answered the question.

She'd do to you what Bill was doing to Sam. She'd tear you open and eat you.

I jumped back and ran around her in a wide arc. I made a dash toward the bedroom window, fully aware that broken glass fragments littered the grass in front of it. About six feet from the house, I dove for the opening, flying over the shrapnel that would have shredded my bare feet.

It was all I could do to make that jump. I felt the pain in every part of my fucked up legs, and when I landed, I did what I could to roll onto my shoulder and get back on my feet fast.

Well it didn't work out nearly as well in reality as it did in my head. Instead, I landed on my chest and slid head-first into the base of the lingerie chest, stopping like a bus hitting a brick wall.

The pain reverberated through my body, but I was more afraid of

154

what would happen if I didn't act quickly. I pushed through it, rolled over to a sitting position and leaned forward to pull open the bottom drawer of the chest.

I scooted back and yanked the entire drawer out, spun on my ass and got to my trashed knees to drop it on our bed with a grunt. Then I struggled to my feet and ran to the closet on shaking legs. Sliding the door open, I leaned in and grabbed the shotgun.

Back at the bed in seconds, I jammed my hand in the drawer and came out with a box of shells. I opened it and had time to get five shells loaded before Linda was at the window again, trying to push her way in.

Rather than shoot her – I wasn't there yet – I used the barrel of the Benelli to push her back. I heard her bare feet crunching through the glass just yards away from me, but she didn't seem to notice.

I yanked the nightstand drawer open and pulled out my Sig Sauer, stuffing that in the front of my pants. It was already loaded with a round chambered, like I always kept it.

Linda was back. She fell through the window this time, the pink mist pumping out of her. I held my breath and kicked at her, trying to lift her head enough to kick her back through the window. I felt my foot slip and drag across her teeth, and jerked it back. The second my foot was clear, her teeth clamped together, and I watched as half of her tongue dropped to the floor at my feet.

"Oh, God!" I shouted, my heart pounding as I jumped away. I raised the shotgun again and rushed her, using it to push her back outside. She toppled away and I turned and ran toward the closet. I yanked a tee shirt from the top shelf and threw it on, then pulled a small duffle bag from the closet floor, ran back and threw it on the bed, upending the lingerie chest drawer full of ammo into it and zipping it closed.

A second later, Lin flew through the window, sending the clinging glass shards into the room and landing, along with her body, between me and the dresser. I threw the shotgun's strap across my shoulder, grabbed the duffle bag and leapt over her reaching hands as I ran for the front door. By the smashed bathroom door, I saw my boots – another thing I dropped where they came off when I got home from work – and leaned down to grab them on my way to the front door.

I skidded to a stop. A cop stood there blocking the doorway. The door hung on one hinge, having clearly been kicked in by the responding officers. The middle-aged cop was staring at me, his neck ripped open and blood running down his uniformed chest. His eyes held the strange illumination, too. Behind me I heard a snarl and whirled around.

I sidestepped into the living room; both Linda and the cop now staggered toward me; the cop's gun was on the floor by the door. I raised the shotgun. "Stop," I commanded, my voice shaky and weak.

He didn't.

"Stop!" I croaked again.

Linda moved from my left. The cop moved straight for me. I fired, blowing him back into the doorframe. I followed my shot, not wanting to confront my sick wife, and I ran into the brightness of the day once more. I glanced at my watch and saw it was now approaching 5:00 PM.

"Hey!" shouted someone as I ran. I turned to see a young cop sitting in his police cruiser, the window partially down. I couldn't understand why he hadn't come out to help.

I ran to him. "Why didn't you help me?"

"My partner tried to attack me. I emptied all my magazines at both of them! I shot my own partner at least nine times, and I shot that lady in there seven times. Nothing. No difference. Something's really fucked up, man!"

"You shot my wife?" I asked. "The woman in there?"

"Yeah, I'm sorry, man. I told you, I shot my partner, too! He was the same as her! But man… it didn't *kill* them! It barely even slowed them down!"

I stared at him, but in my peripheral vision, I saw bodies emerging from my house. The cop was in front. I'd shot him in the chest with the shotgun. Dead hit in center mass. Gore hung in strands from the gushing wound.

"Look!" shouted the cop, pointing from the car. "He's still fucking alive. He's got the keys to the car!"

It made sense. I could tell he wouldn't have sat out there passing the time for almost half a day if he had the keys.

I raised the shotgun again, and this time I aimed for the deranged officer's face. He charged toward me in what appeared to be a drunken stagger. I fired, and his head disintegrated into a mist of red.

As he fell, Linda charged out behind him. She tripped over him and fell to the ground, her face smashing into the concrete walkway, her arm twisting beneath her and snapping like a tree branch. I felt sick to my stomach again when she got up and stared through me, her pink eyes glazed and lost in madness.

She gnashed her teeth and every time she opened her mouth I could see her half-bitten tongue.

"Shoot her!" shouted the young, frightened cop. "Kill it!"

Kill it. *He called her an It.*

She *was* an It now I supposed. She wasn't acting human anymore. I raised my shotgun and pointed it at her head.

She stared, gnashed and snarled. I said a very quick prayer, quickly touched the St. Christopher medal that hung around my neck since the day I left the hospital so many years ago, and fired with my eyes closed and turned away so that I'd never have to see. When I opened my eyes, I saw the neighbor from two houses down – Byron Drake – staggering down the middle of the road. His eyes appeared to be locked onto me.

"Get the goddamned car keys!" the cop screamed, and I charged back to where the officer lay still, bent down and unclipped the ring on his belt. I returned to the car, opened the door and heaved my duffle bag to the young officer. I fed my shotgun in and he rested it between his legs as I jumped into the driver's seat, breathing hard.

Drake was staggering toward me. He was now half a lawn away. My body ached. I hadn't put myself through physical stuff like that since before the accident. I knew I wouldn't be able to move at all once the adrenaline receded.

"Drive to the station," he said, relief on his face. "Please. Just drive us there."

"What the hell is that smell?" I asked.

"Sorry," said the young cop. "I… pissed my pants. I was in here for hours and I was freaked out. My partner was up against the car and like I said, I ran out of ammo."

I understood. I guessed I was just glad he hadn't pissed in the driver's seat. I put the key in the ignition and fired the engine. A moment later I floored the accelerator and got the car onto the street.

* * *

I was in a daze. My mind was spinning over what had just happened, and now here I was, driving a cop to the police station in his patrol car, a .45 stuck in my pants and the officer holding my shotgun.

People – or things, because I had no idea what they had really, truly become yet – wandered into the streets, and I saw individuals and groups of them move toward our car as we passed. Lots of people were running and screaming, but the cop beside me just kept yelling, "Go around them! Go! Just drive!"

I couldn't put it together. None of it made any sense. I wondered how the other cop drove the car there if he was like Linda. He had to have

157

changed *after* he arrived at our house, but how? Was it that fast? Linda had showed signs of whatever it was for hours before she changed. The cop that attacked me inside our house had bite marks on his body, but Linda wasn't focused on him at all by the time I faced both of them. She only cared about getting to me, just like the cop. They both wanted to get to me.

It took me back to the old Sesame Street show. *One of these things is not like the others…* I was the one thing. Tony Mallette *wasn't* like them.

There were a thousand more questions than answers, and I didn't have the mental capacity to take them all on. I swerved and dodged, and even ran a few of the things down as they staggered in front of the patrol car and were knocked to the ground by the heavy steel tube guard that had been mounted there.

The streets were like some crazy nightmare all the way there. People were running and screaming all over the place. I moved to grab my .45 several times, but every time, the cop yelled, "No, just keep driving!"

As a kid, I was trained to listen to cops, even if they looked like they were about to shit their pants. I glanced over at the guy in the passenger seat every now and then to see if he was about to give me some instruction, but he was freaked the hell out and seemed to only be competent at telling me what not to do.

Yeah. If I was scared, this guy was petrified. I could see it in his eyes, his brain was squirming like an earthworm just dug out of the dirt.

* * *

We got to the police station on Shelburne Road to find the same thing we'd found everywhere else: madness. The minute we pulled up, the staggering men and women things came at us from all directions. Just like in Bill Frederick's back yard, many of the people, clearly so sick they didn't have any idea what they were doing, crouched over fallen bodies, ripping into them like children tearing into a piñata stuffed with candy.

I thought of poor Sam again. Bill loved the dog. Treated him like his kid. He had to be really fucked up to eat him. My mind began to work. I turned to the cop.

"What are you gonna do?" I asked.

He stared through the windshield. "Drive," he said.

"Look, I'm not your fuckin' chauffeur. If I drive, I'm goin' to my wife's best friend's house. Erica Swanson."

He stared blankly for a moment before answering. It was as though he'd settled on a solution. "Go."

I dropped the car into gear and drove. I checked my watch and saw that it was 5:35 PM. I turned to the cop. "What's your name, man?"

The guy looked down at his name tag that said T. Wiggenhauser. "Uh... Tom," he said.

"Look, Tom. I don't wanna be out in this crap after nightfall. There's this mist stuff... it comes out of their eyes. I got caught in the crap through my bathroom door and I went out like a light in seconds and didn't wake up for eleven hours."

He stared at me.

"Did you hear me?"

He nodded. "You got knocked out for eleven hours? That's why you didn't come out of the house sooner?"

At least he heard me. "Yeah. That knockout stuff might be how they're taking these people down. Surprising them around a corner or something. They don't look very fast. I don't know if they can suddenly pour on the steam or anything, but I haven't seen it yet. My wife didn't do it."

His eyes went wide. "That was your wife that you... shot... at your house?"

I almost nodded, but stopped myself. "No," I said. "It wasn't. She was, but not by that time. It wasn't her. What worries me is what she became, and why." I felt myself ready to crumble, and bit the inside of my cheek. I wiped the emerging tear from my face, and no more followed. For the moment.

"Maybe they're just sick," he said. "Maybe it'll go away. Like a 24-hour thing."

In my head I hoped he was right, but I hoped he was wrong, too. I'd just shot my rabid wife in the head and killed a cop. If everyone started recovering in a day, I'd never be able to live with myself.

I shook my head. "Worst fuckin' 24-hour flu in the history of bugs," I said. "I guess we got about eleven hours to go 'til we see."

* * *

I turned the wheel, directing the cruiser around a car that had slammed into a telephone pole and erupted into a burning blaze. I could see a body inside, engulfed in licking flames. There's no way the person should still have been moving, but he was. Even without this hell going on I wouldn't have tried to save him. It would be hell on earth, living with

159

burns like that.

I fishtailed the rear end onto Webster, and hung a quick right on Acorn Lane. Erica's house was down on the right side, hidden in the trees. I pulled out my phone as I cranked the wheel and pulled into her driveway. When I skidded to a stop I found her name in my directory and dialed Erica's number.

Erica was a tall, exotic-looking black woman who I think was from Kingston, Jamaica. I'd been to her house a couple of times just briefly. She'd lived with her father until he died. Just the two of them came to America, so I wasn't sure what the story was with the rest of her family. Her dad had died of cancer about a year before. Of course, Linda and I were at the funeral.

What I did know for sure was that Erica was Lin's best friend and if I could help her, I would.

A man was on her porch, pounding at the door. I watched him as I held the phone, but the damned busy circuit message came on again and I disconnected and jammed the phone back in my pocket.

At the sound of my sliding tires, the man turned and started staggering toward us. I said, "Shotgun," and held out my hand. Officer Tom lifted the gun and I took it as I opened the door.

Just as I stepped out, the front door opened and Erica called, "Tony! Be careful! He's insane or something. He's been on my porch for hours. I tried 911 –"

"911's out, Erica," I called, not taking my eyes from the advancing man-thing. "There's people like him everywhere. This is an epidemic."

The guy kept moving toward me and I eyed Tom, who again stayed safely in his cruiser, watching. He was clearly a rookie and he was scared shitless.

I walked sideways, easing my way toward the house, but with each maneuver I made, the crazed, pink-eyed man changed his jerky direction toward me.

"Tony?" called Erica.

"Yeah, Erica?"

"You're not going to shoot him are you?"

I looked at her, then at the thing. I stopped. It moved toward me. Pink mist began pouring from its eyes. "Erica, turn away!" I shouted.

"Tony, no!" she called.

"Turn away!" I said, insistent. In my peripheral vision, I saw her go back inside the house. I raised the gun and said, "Stop."

The mist pumped from its eyes. I took a step back. Once more.

"Stop!"

It did. Its dead eyes seemed to be looking at the gun. *Recognition? Something?*

I lowered the gun. It resumed its stumbling trek toward me. I raised the gun and fired in one motion, blowing its head off. The body crumpled to the ground.

I heard Erica's scream from inside the house before I saw her face in the window.

* * *

Officer Tom and I made our way into the house, where he sat down on a sofa in the front room. I didn't get the chance to sit down before Erica lit into me.

"What did you do?" she screamed. "You shot him!"

"Have you been out there today?" I shot back. "Erica, I don't know how to say this any other way…"

I stopped talking. Now wasn't the time. Linda was her best friend.

"What, Tony?" she asked. "Why is that cop with you?"

I turned. Officer Tom sat on the sofa, fiddling with his cell phone.

"Because I don't think he knows where to go either."

"What?" asked Erica.

"Erica, where have you been?"

"I work the night shift. I got off at 4:00, and I slept most of the day and read the rest. Tony, what's going on?"

"When did that guy I shot show up?"

"I don't know, two hours ago. I've tried to call 911, but I can't get through. I tried both you and Linda, too, but the circuits were busy. What's going on?"

"I know this sounds like some shit from TV, but you're gonna need to sit down."

"Tony," she pleaded. When I didn't answer, she ran to where the officer sat and leaned down to push him on the shoulder, hard.

He looked up with frightened eyes. He wasn't upset about the contact, which surprised me. A New York cop would've clocked her. He said, very solemnly, "This is everywhere."

"What?" Erica responded.

"There's an outbreak of some kind. It's everywhere. All over North America at least."

"Where did you see that?" asked Erica.

161

"Yahoo News."

"What the hell is it?" I asked. "Where did it come from?"

"CDC doesn't know yet," he mumbled. "I have to get to my mom. I can't call anywhere. Ma'am, do you have a land line?"

"Yes, right there," she said, pointing at a cradled phone.

Tom grabbed it and dialed. A moment later he put it on the couch beside him. "Same thing. All circuits busy."

"Go on then," I said. "Erica's got a car if we need to leave."

"I'd suggest you stay here," said Tom. "This is bad. If this is everywhere, I have no idea what can be done to stop it."

"Tony," said Erica. "Where's Linda?"

"She's dead, ma'am," said Tom, standing. "She changed into… what that man at your door was. She basically went insane."

Erica looked at me. "Tony?"

I nodded, tears already rolling down my face. Then I broke down into sobs. "I killed her, Erica! She attacked me a bunch of times and I didn't have a choice. I shot his partner, too. A cop. He was the same. They have this mist —"

"You *shot* her?" she said. "You fucking shot Linda?" She rushed me, her fists pounding my chest. I gave her that release for a few seconds before grabbing her wrists and pulling her in close to me for a tight, controlling hug.

"He had to do it," said Officer Tom. "Don't you think I'd have arrested him if he didn't? He shot both of them in front of me."

"No," whimpered Erica. "Not Linda."

"Yeah," I said. "My Linda. You know how much I love her."

I felt her nod. She said nothing. I felt more explanation was necessary.

"When they turn like this, they don't talk and they don't understand, Erica," I whispered. "They growl, they claw, they grind their teeth together and they attack."

I held Erica to me against her struggles, tightening my grip on her even more. "I loved her, Erica. You know that. After my accident, I fought to get her back." Her tension relaxed and became shudders under my embrace.

"He didn't have a choice, ma'am," said the officer.

"Stop calling me ma'am!" she said, pushing away from me. "Stop talking!"

"I'm going," he said. "I recommend you stay here until the military gets things under control. Has to happen eventually. Got food and water?"

Erica didn't answer. I nodded at Tom.

"Alright, then," he said. "I'll come back and check on you if I get the chance. Depends on what I find at my mom's."

I nodded again and he left.

I walked Erica to the sofa and we sat. I waited for her to be ready to talk.

* * *

Erica said nothing when she finally got up and walked to the window. She stood there, the curtains pulled back, staring out at the street. "That's Lila Webb out there," she finally said. She suddenly jerked away and let the curtain fall closed.

She hurried to the door and opened it. "Lila! Lila, come here!"

"What are you doing?" I asked, jumping to my feet.

"I told you it's Lila!" said Erica.

I watched her as she turned and moved toward the house. She wasn't normal. I knew it. I pulled Erica by the shoulders off the porch and into the house, closing and locking the door behind her.

"I'm 99% sure she's one of those things," I said.

"She's not like that man was," she said, desperation in her eyes.

"She's walking funny, like that other man who was here, but not as jerky."

A thump sounded on the wooden porch slats. I moved back to the window and eased back the curtain. The woman's face was right outside the window, inches from mine. I staggered backward, my heart slamming in my chest. "Shit!" I said, trying to control the level of my voice.

"What?" Erica whispered.

"She's right there!" I whispered back.

"How did... she was in the street. How did she get here so fast?"

"I haven't seen them move like that. None of them. She's different, too. Her hair isn't all messed up. It's like... straight."

"That's weird," said Erica. "Lila has really curly hair. Maybe she straightened it."

"Shh." I put my ear close to the window. A second later I heard footsteps moving away from the house. I eased back the curtain again and saw her moving away. "She's leaving. Her hair is really straight. Hey, is she wearing a maternity top?"

"Yes, she's about six months pregnant," said Erica. "With a boy."

163

I looked at her. "How the hell does she know?"

"Know what?"

"If it's a boy or a girl?"

"Are you serious right now?"

I stared at her. "Yeah, I'm serious."

Erica shook her head. "Have you ever watched *any* television? Seen a medical show?"

"She knows from watching *television?*"

"Tony, she *knows* because the doctors told her. You ever heard of an ultrasound?"

"I don't watch TV, and I thought… well, never mind. I never had any kids, so I didn't know. Anyway, when she looked at me her eyes were blood red and her skin was like a pale gray."

"Her eyes were bleeding?"

"No," I said. "Not bleeding. Just solid red. Like a real bad case of pink eye."

"I hope she's alright," said Erica.

"I don't think she's alright," I said, pulling the curtain aside again and looking out. Lila was still standing on the porch about eight feet from the door, facing the street. A moment later another figure emerged from around the corner. It was followed by yet another. Then, within another five minutes, three more came.

"We've got a party going here," I said. "Erica, do you have any weapons?"

"Tony, they could be my neighbors. Maybe they need help."

"Not this gang, Erica. These guys are like the cop, like Linda, and that guy at your door earlier. If they hang around, we're going to need fight our way out of here."

"There's no reason to go anywhere, Tony," said Erica. "I have food and water. This will have to blow over in a day or two. Let's just wait."

A sound came at the front door. Scratching and scraping. I eased over to the window again and peeled back the curtain. The woman called Lila stood there again, her face inches from mine. She drew back her lips to expose teeth with bits of meaty gore caught between them. Her hand came up quickly to hit the glass, which cracked in a spider web with a loud pop.

I jumped back again, spinning toward Erica. "Jesus! Did you see that? I don't know what they can do, but if these things learn, she might just break a few more window panes."

"Where are the rest of them?" she asked, moving toward the door.

She looked through the peep hole and let out an abrupt scream and jerked toward me. "Tony, they're on the porch!"

I ran over and nudged Erica aside. When I put my eye to the peep hole, I saw distorted faces and eyes, gore-smeared teeth and the sounds of their desperation came right through the door and into my ears.

A ghost jumped onto my spine and slid all the way down. I shuddered involuntarily and moved to a different window where I might not be met with a face. Near the far corner of the house, I peered out.

More were coming. I craned my neck to inspect the porch that ran across the front of the plantation style home, and there were about seven or eight of them. Five or six more turned in from the street.

"Erica, can you get to the garage from inside the house?"

"Yes," she said, her eyes wide. "Why?"

"Do you have any plywood or lumber?"

"Why?"

"To put up over this window," I said. "Erica, if they–"

The harrowing sound of glass breaking met our ears again. This time an entire arm reached through the broken pane, clawing at the curtains.

Instinctively, I reached for the hand to shove it back outside, but caught myself. I didn't want to touch them.

I turned and ran into the kitchen and straight for the butcher block. There was a meat cleaver there – not as big as I would have liked – but it would give me some weight and leverage. I ran back to the door. If these things learned lessons, maybe a severed arm would teach them a thing or two about reaching into somebody's window.

The cleaver raised high, I ran back to the window where there were now two arms, both with long, black-red cuts dripping from wrist to elbow. I brought the cleaver down hard, hitting bone and feeling it snap. I didn't know it then, but I realized later that I'd been screaming as I hacked at the invading arms. I took aim, closed my eyes and hacked.

The limbs dropped onto the sofa, but the moment they fell, two more came through, and another glass shattered.

"Upstairs!" shouted Erica. "Tony, we can't do this!"

"Grab some food and water and get your ass up there," I said. "We don't know how long it'll be safe down here. Erica, *do you* have any plywood?"

"My dad practically had a woodshop in there when he was alive, but it's all covered in tarps, so I don't remember what's left. I don't go in there. C'mon."

She turned and ran and I followed. She pushed open the garage door and hit the light switch. The fluorescent lights hummed to life and I saw the shop immediately. There were several tarps. I analyzed the shapes and ran to one that looked promising. Grabbing the edge of one, I yanked it. Beneath the tarp were sheets of plywood.

"There!" I said. "It's only 3/8", but that's good. Not too heavy. Help me with it, would you?"

I leaned down, my bad knees and back protesting, and curled my fingers beneath the first piece. Erica took hold of the other end and we stood it upright.

"Nails," I said. "I'd prefer screws, but I don't think we have time."

She rushed to a drawer and pulled it open. There were several boxes of 3" construction nails, and three hammers hung on the pegboard over the workbench. We each grabbed a hammer and a box of nails.

I jammed the hammer into my waistband and we hoisted the plywood and threaded it back through the door inside the house. By the time we reached the front room again, there were seven arms reaching and pushing against the bank of window panes.

"Hold on!" I shouted. I grabbed the bloody cleaver from the coffee table and hacked at several of them. "They don't feel any pain!" I yelled. I was swinging and connecting with gray flesh that seemed to be indifferent to the damage I was doing. The only way I could even tell if it was having an effect was when the limb finally severed.

"Let's just jam the plywood against them and push them back out!" shouted Erica.

She was right. This was fucking Whack-A-Mole times ten and we weren't winning.

"Okay, go!" I shouted, lifting the piece. "You get the right side. Hurry!"

"Wait!" said Erica.

"What for?"

"It's Monica!"

I looked, and saw a woman running frantically toward the house. Suddenly she stopped short and stood there, shifting back and forth from foot to foot, appearing unsure where to go.

Erica hammered her open palm on one of the intact pieces of glass. "Monica!" she shouted, her voice loud and piercing.

Either Monica heard her hand or her call, because she ran toward the house again, angling away from the many changed humans on the front porch. I eyed the one with straight hair, and she moved quickly toward the

166

left side of the porch. I watched as Monica ran around the side, pointing toward the back of the house.

"I'm going to the back to let her in!" said Erica, scooting her knees off the couch and running.

She left me holding the full weight of the plywood, so I rested it on the couch and leaned it against the window, hoping they didn't break through while we were helping Erica's friend.

I knew Monica, but not very well. She had come over with Erica once or twice to pick up Linda for a girl's night out. I'd never really talked to her.

When I reached the back door, Monica was already inside. I saw the freak with the straight hair round the rear corner of the house, but I ran along the back wall closing all the blinds until it was basically dark in the kitchen and dining area. "We need to finish the window, Erica. Now."

"You're bleeding," said Erica, holding Monica's arm. "Come here," she said, leading her over to the counter where a roll of paper towels sat. Monica was shivering like it was twenty degrees inside. Erica pulled a length from the roll and quickly wrapped it around her bleeding arm. "Hold this. We'll take care of you better when we're done boarding the front window. Sit down at the table."

We ran back into the living room and quickly lifted the plywood. "Okay, raise it high, until the base is just above the level of the back of the couch," I said.

Erica raised her end. "Good?"

I looked at what had to be ten arms reaching through six broken panes. "Now's as good a time as any," I said. "On three, just push straight back and watch that they don't nick you."

"Okay. Count off," she said.

"One, two, three!" I said.

We both pushed hard forward, and the protruding arms either bent down, up or sideways. "Back it off!" I shouted, "Then push right back, hard!"

We did. This time, only one arm remained to block us from mounting the board flush. "It's on my side. Leave yours where it is," I said, struggling with the plywood sheet that felt heavier with each passing second.

I drew my end back and slammed it repeatedly into the window and heard another pane break. "Shit!" I shouted.

"Tony?" asked Erica. "Can you get it?"

"One more try," I said. "I'm getting tired. Try to start one nail, okay?"

Erica had filled her pocket with the long nails. Her face strained, she held the plywood against the wall with one hand and got a nail, popping it between her lips. She then put the nail tip against the plywood near the top of the board and pulled the hammer from her waistband. She drew the head back and tapped twice hard.

"Got it started," she said. Now she put her left palm against the plywood and slammed the nail home.

"Okay," I said. "I need to get that cleaver. Hold this for a sec, okay?"

"Hurry," she said. "My arms are wasted."

I ran over and grabbed the cleaver I'd used earlier from the coffee table. When I got back to the window I said, "Okay, I think there's only one. When I get into position, I'll tell you to go. I want you to pivot it up like a foot. The nail should act like a hinge."

"Okay, hurry."

I stood there, the meat cleaver in my right hand. I held it so tight and I had so much adrenaline pumping through me I think I could have cut through a tree trunk. "Go!" I shouted.

Erica pivoted the board upward and I took aim at the protruding arm that had just realized it was free. I slammed the cleaver in a direct hit. The black-red blood sprayed onto the couch as I dropped the cleaver and took the bottom corner of the plywood. It slammed home flush against the window.

Using the hammer and nails I had taken, I secured the board to the wall, catching studs every time. From there, Erica and I stood on the sofa and hammered in nails every six inches.

When we were done, she stared down at the mess of body parts on her sofa. "Oh, my God," she whispered, moving closer to it.

It looked to me like she was fighting her gag reflex, even as she forced herself to inspect one of the severed limbs more closely. "That's a Stanley Cup ring. That's Scott DeAndrea's arm."

"Who?"

"He's the only ex-hockey player who retired to Shelburne, Tony," she said. "He played with the Tampa Bay Lightning when they won the cup in 2004. It was his last year and he moved here."

"Shit. Did you know him?"

"Yes," said Erica. "He was a really nice guy. He volunteered with Seth and Bill coaching the soccer games for Shelburne High."

"I feel bad enough already," I said. "Don't tell me any more."

I figured if the guy got cured, he'd probably consider five for fighting to be a worthwhile penalty to take in return for me hacking off his arm.

"What happens if they move to the other windows?" asked Erica.

"You don't have an endless supply of plywood," I said. "But we could use two-by-fours to at least make it so they can't squeeze through."

"Erica?" came Monica's voice from the other room. It sounded strained. We both hurried in.

"Hey, Monica," she said, kneeling down beside her friend. Monica stared at her, her eyes bloodshot. She held her head in her hands.

"Terrible headache," she said. "I mean, like my brain's about to explode."

Erica looked at me, worry in her eyes. "Let's get you upstairs. You need to lie down."

Monica nodded and stood. As Erica walked her up, I called, "I'm grabbing more wood, Erica. I'll get as many of the windows locked down as best I can. Hopefully the government will mobilize somebody over this way eventually."

"I haven't even heard a siren," she said, shaking her head. I watched as she disappeared upstairs.

She was right. I hadn't realized it. No noise came from outside the house except for the animalistic growls coming from what used to be people we once shopped and pumped gas with.

I got to work.

* * *

I used every piece of wood I could find in the garage. I tried to block off all the most vulnerable windows but there wasn't enough wood, so I muscled larger pieces of furniture in front of them; china cabinets, curios. By the time I was done, I watched dozens more of the mindless creatures surround the house.

Exhausted, I fell into an overstuffed armchair for a good twenty minutes before finally dragging my ass upstairs.

As I rounded the corner, I saw an open bedroom door on my left. Monica was lying on her back in the middle of the bed, and Erica sat beside her. Monica's head was covered with what looked like a wet washcloth.

Erica turned as I walked in and nodded to me. "Hey. Got it all secured down there?"

"I kinda trashed your house. Broke some china."

Erica smiled. "It's okay. I don't have much need for it anyway. Thanks for all the hard work. I feel safer."

"Me, too. There's a lot of them out there now. How is she?" I asked.

169

"I'm not good," said Monica, answering for her friend.

"I'm sorry," I said. "Did you take any aspirin or anything?"

Monica nodded her head. "Yeah, but it still hurts. It's throbbing."

"I put some antibiotic ointment on it, but she might need some actual antibiotics, which I'm fresh out of."

"Let's let her rest," I said. "I need to eat something, then I think we should try to get some rest ourselves."

Erica nodded. "Okay. Monica, we're going to let you try to sleep. Need anything else?"

"Got any horse tranquilizers?" she asked, trying to force a smile.

"Xanax, maybe. Let me know if you think it'd help."

She nodded and we left the room, closing the door behind us.

"I think we're better off upstairs," I said. "Those things make me really nervous." I pulled the gun from my waistband and popped the magazine. "There's one chambered and six left in the magazine. You got any weapons?"

"Two 12-gauge shotguns," she said. "And we have tons of shells."

"Where are they?" I asked.

"In a cabinet in the study. You've got that gun for now. We'll eat and get them checked and loaded," said Erica.

She made some ham and cheese sandwiches and I ate two of them. She plated an extra one that she wrapped and put in the fridge.

As we were about to get up, we heard distant gunfire.

"What the hell? Is the cavalry finally coming?" I asked, standing and moving to the peep hole.

The sound grew louder, but I couldn't see anything as far away as the street. There didn't look to be as many of the infected people near the front door though, so I had some view in that general direction. "They're moving, whoever they are."

"God, let them round these sick people up," said Erica. "I don't like being afraid."

A vehicle came into view. It was hard to tell because the sun was down, with just the residual light filtering through the trees. It appeared to be a Jeep Wrangler with two guys in the front and one in the back. The sound of gunfire erupted again, and several holes appeared in the door just above my head, chunks of door blowing inward as I dropped to the floor and covered.

"Down! Down!" I shouted, but as the words left my lips, I heard Erica cry out in pain. She didn't so much drop as spin around and fall.

"Erica, are you alright?" She had fallen in front of the couch, which blocked me from seeing her.

"I don't... think so," she moaned.

I crawled around the sofa and stopped beside her. The automatic gunfire peppered the front of the house with ear-shattering efficiency. Chunks of plywood and plaster flew over our heads, some raining down on top of us. Thumping sounds came from the front porch – probably from the people falling when they took rounds.

Erica was on her back, and her shoulder was pouring blood. I pressed my hand to it and held it, even as she winced under my touch. "Can you move your arm?" I asked.

She pivoted her left arm and I breathed a sigh of relief. "Good. Good," I said. "Did it pop or anything?"

"My arm?"

"Bones. Anything feel dislocated or broken?"

"No, but it stung bad when it hit me. Now it's kind of numb."

"It'll probably hurt again later," I said. "I shot myself in the foot once, so I know." I peeled back her blouse, exposing her wound. It wasn't swelling, so it looked like an in-and-out shot that missed the bone.

"Stay flat," I whispered. I pressed my ear to the floor, also keeping as low as possible. In another thirty seconds, the engine of the Jeep revved, and the gunfire stopped. We listened to the sound of the engine recede to silence before I sat up and helped Erica into a sitting position. From there I got her to her feet.

"You're bleeding pretty good," I said. "Let's make more use of that first aid kit of yours. Upstairs."

"Tony, go see what's happening out there. Check through a crack first, but if we can get out of here, maybe we should."

I shook my head. "Erica, I don't know who that was just now, but they're not military. It's not like them to just fire at homes without knowing the potential for collateral damage. Like us."

"Maybe this is serious enough that they expect collateral damage."

"It's serious," I said. "Still, the military would probably use a loudspeaker to make announcements before firing into a private residence. Did you hear anything?"

She shook her head with a wince.

"Okay. Upstairs. I'll come down and check the status of the porch later."

It was well after dark now. I helped her upstairs, got her into bed and cleaned her wound. Again, I thought of Linda beside me in that hospital room, all those months. I shook it off.

171

Locating the exit wound, I was relieved there would be no need to search for the bullet. When I finished I taped both holes and wrapped it.

She looked like a goddamned football player on her left side. I'm not much for bandages, but it would do the trick.

"Rest. I'll go outside and see what they left behind. You good?"

"No," she said, and the tears came. I watched them roll down her face and a moment later felt my own face getting wet. I wiped them away. I thought of Linda and the young cop who left us. I wondered if he was still alive.

"Maybe this will be a short nightmare," she whispered.

"I hope so."

* * *

I grabbed an LED flashlight from a kitchen drawer and moved to the front door, my Sig Sauer in my hand. I looked at the gun in my hand for a moment, then tucked it into my waistband and retrieved my Benelli from the wall beside the front door. I checked it over. I'd forgotten to lower it to the floor when the rounds were shredding the front of the house, but it wasn't damaged.

I made sure a shell was chambered and checked the peephole.

It was clear. I opened the door and turned on the flashlight.

At my feet were torn bodies. I heard a sound coming from my right and pointed my light in the general direction. The beam fell on a woman's head. It was connected to the neck still, but only by a thick flap of skin. It rested at a ninety-degree angle to her shoulders.

Her eyes were locked on me; they were still glowing pink, but no vapor or mist or whatever it was came from them. Her teeth continued to grind and the guttural moans were constant. I tried to accept what I was seeing.

The head was alive. I knew that nothing from the body had anything to do with it, it simply continued to go on.

I felt the sandwiches coming up, but it was out of my control. I threw up on the mass of wrecked bodies and wiped my mouth on my sleeve. Too soon. I puked again, and again. When I was pretty certain I was finished, I stood up straight.

Black spots invaded my vision. The world started spinning around me and I realized I was falling. My mind was intact enough to suddenly grasp that I would be landing atop the nasty, shredded meat that once made up Erica's neighbors, so I threw my arm out and caught the doorframe with my hand. I remained vertical for the moment.

I don't know how long I stood there steadying myself on that wall, staring at the carnage.

I couldn't see all the way to the street, so there might have been others out there. I pulled out my Sig and pointed it at the twitching head. I fired, and the explosion rang out, echoing through the silent neighborhood. Black goo sprayed my leather boots.

The mere action of firing the gun brought me a slight surge of adrenaline. My mind clicked once or twice, allowing me a thought.

In Shelburne, Vermont, that sound should bring police in a flash. Firing guns within city limits was easy to hear a long way off, and it would always get the attention of the town's citizens.

I raised the gun and emptied the remainder of the magazine into the air. I wanted someone to come.

Just not *these* things.

I looked down again. The head was dead.

* * *

I went back inside. I needed to get some rest, because despite my extended nap in the middle of the day, I was beginning to see double. I was dead tired.

The gunfire had tattered and weakened the plywood. I didn't trust it completely anymore. I needed a different plan to alert us if anything got in.

Then I remembered a video that Linda had showed me on YouTube once. This kid played a trick on his buddy by putting all the pots and pans from his kitchen cupboards on the floor by his bed, and when he got up, he stumbled through them, making a racket.

I went to the kitchen and got what I needed. I started by carrying them all to the top of the stairs, then put two or three of them on every step. I had to use some glasses, too. When I was done, I knew that none of those stumbling sickos would be able to sneak anywhere near us without us knowing about it.

Monica's door was closed when I walked by. I put my hand on the knob, but stopped. If she was finally sleeping, there was no sense in disturbing her. Let her get a good night's sleep.

I heard Erica's soft snores, so I found the last empty bedroom, which was probably another guest room. Before stretching out on the bed, I walked to the window. It faced toward the side of the yard, so there wasn't anything to see, as there was a distinct absence of light. The darkness out there somehow numbed my thoughts and gave me a sense of doom that I couldn't explain.

The power was still on, which I guess was a good sign. I shuffled back to the bed and saw the television remote on the nightstand. I picked it up and hit the power button.

For some reason, with everything being so hectic, I hadn't even thought about it. Linda and I hardly ever watched TV at home, so it wasn't second nature to turn it on. There wasn't even a television in Erica's living room, so I guessed she was pretty much the same.

The screen lit up and Channel 3 was broadcasting. I knew they were a local channel out of Burlington, Vermont.

The man onscreen wasn't one of the regular anchors, at least not the ones I'd seen on billboards for WCAX. The first thing I noticed about him was that he was holding a microphone rather than using a clip-on, and his face was red. He had clearly been crying like I was earlier.

I caught his broadcast in the middle of his sentence:

"... mom, tell her I love her and to stay inside. We haven't gotten any word that the government is putting together a plan, but nobody's communicated with us for quite a while. If you are just tuning in, I'm Larry Peale. I'm only broadcasting now because I arrived at work about three o'clock this morning. Some of the staff got sick and went home, so it looked like they wouldn't have enough people for the morning news broadcast at 6:00. If you're watching this then you know it was a Sunday, so our staff was smaller anyway. Later on we just show reruns."

He was rambling. I wanted to know what he knew; I needed to know what was going on out there and what this disease was.

"Anyway," he continued, his eyes bloodshot and drooping, his brown hair mussed. "Frank Stafford, one of the engineers, was in the equipment room growling or moaning or something. I didn't know at the time. Lisa Potter, our morning anchor, had been... I know I'm on TV now – or I think I'm still broadcasting – but she'd been ripped open and some guy I don't know was over her, his hands inside her. I screamed at him that he couldn't help her and that he needed to call 911. He turned toward me and I saw her insides hanging from his teeth, and her... intestines clutched in his fingers."

Larry Peale stopped for a long time. He broke down, his shoulders hunched, his entire body shuddering. "I'm so worried about my wife, Nancy, and our little girl, Tamara. I can't reach them and they haven't texted me or anything. I hope they're alright." He then raised his eyes.

"Nance, Tam, if you're home, please hide. Hide in a closet. These things aren't smart. They're like animals as far as I can tell. Hide and don't open the door for anyone. Someone will come to help us soon. They have to."

I knew it was more a wish than a sure thing. We all figured help would come. It always had before.

He waited until he could continue and said, "I started to run out, but Frank stepped into the hallway in front of me, blocking my way out. I turned to get to the fire exit, but Patti Foster was there, and she was the same as Frank. She let out some… I don't know, this fog or something, from her face. It came from her face somehow! I don't know what it was, but she was stumbling toward me, Frank was behind me, and I just ran in here, into the studio. I locked the door. That was at around 3:30 this morning."

I turned it off. I couldn't watch anymore. He didn't know any more than I did.

I lay back and my head hit the pillow.

My eyes slammed shut. They didn't open until I heard the clatter of pots, pans and breaking glass.

* * *

I sat up and grabbed my shotgun from the bed beside me. A scream broke the silence and I got to my feet and tried to shake the cobwebs from my brain as I bolted for the door. I had to pee and I could barely see. It was morning, but it was also a weird new world.

I yanked the door open to see a man standing at the top of the stairs. Erica's door was closed.

"Erica!" I yelled. "You okay?"

"Yes! I went out and saw the things on the stairs!"

"Things?"

I couldn't see the rest of the stairs, but a sudden clanging came from behind the strange human-like thing, and I tensed.

The man with gray skin and blank eyes did not turn at the noise; instead, he stared at me as he took jerky steps, advancing toward me. As he drew closer, the strange, pink gas beginning to pump from his eyes, I slapped my hand on the wall of Erica's room and yelled, "I'm going to fire!"

I pulled the trigger. The noise of the explosion overpowered the thing's moans as I watched it fly backward off its feet and down the stairs. The dozens of pellets peppered the intruder in the neck and chest, pulver-

175

izing him from my short range.

I ran forward and watched him toppling down the stairs, the pots and pans and three more of his sick friends caught by his tumbling body and taking a fast trip to the bottom.

A woman wearing a red and white polka-dotted dress broke through the railing and landed on one of the split rails. It punched through her midsection and came out her back as she came to rest with a heavy thud.

I raised the shotgun again as I heard the door open behind me. I pulled out my Sig and gave it to Erica. "You ever used one of these?"

"No," she said. "I've never fired a gun."

"Then point it at the floor. If anything gets by me, let it get close to you and point that end at its head and fire. Use both hands."

"Tony," she said. "Tony, they're coming!"

"I know, I know!" I said, keeping my eye on the other two thrashed men. At least the guy I'd shot with the Benelli wasn't moving.

I heard the door to my right open and saw Erica going into the room where Monica slept. Rattling pots drew my attention to another of the creatures that had now made it three quarters of the way up the stairs. "Fuck!" I shouted, taking aim again. I aimed for the head and fired.

The round blew his head into shreds and he did a backward somersault down the stairs. To my left I saw the woman with the piece of railing protruding from her belly stand up and stare at me.

Her teeth gnashed and she growled. She should be dead. So dead. But she wasn't.

That was when I reached into my brain and said the word for the first time, if only to myself.

Zombies. She was dead; nobody could live with that giant piece of wood running all the way through them. Nobody. It had to have snapped her spinal cord, so she wouldn't be able to move.

I knew a lot about what the human body could take from my own fall. I *really* had luck on my side when I landed. I should have been dead.

So should the woman downstairs, now making her way – stair rail and all – toward the steps again.

I walked to the stairs and hurried down to the midway point, careful not to trip on anything along the way. She was now on the second step. I raised my gun and fired.

Her facial features dissolved into raw meat as she flew backward, her arms flailing wildly. When she landed on her back, one arm bent behind her and snapped. Just the realization of what the sound was made me nauseous.

The railing that had run through her middle pushed outward as her back slammed into the floor, tilting to the side and coming to rest against another dead crazy.

The scream from behind me almost caused me to lose my footing. I recovered and grabbed the remaining rail, pulling my self up. "Erica!" I shouted as I reached the top of the stairs, grabbed the inside of the door frame and practically slingshotted myself into the bedroom.

Everything seemed to move in slow motion. Erica held the gun as Monica advanced on her. As she backed away from her changed friend, moving toward the window too fast, I opened my mouth to yell at her to stop, but I had seen the peril too late.

She crashed through the window, the many small panes shattering as the French window gave way.

Monica turned toward me. Her face was shredded, as though she had been ravaged by one of the creatures that had come into the house, but when I looked at her fingers, I saw her fingernails were covered in blood and pieces of hanging flesh.

She had done it to herself. She went for the window and I fired, blowing her against the wall before she reached it.

I ran toward her. I'd hit her in the chest and she was turning over, trying to get her feet back under her. Instinctively, I ran toward her and kicked her in the face, just as her own version of the knockout mist began pumping out, and I raised the shotgun again, blowing her face into a disgusting stain on the wall.

Acutely aware that there could be more of the monsters coming up the stairs, I spun around and slammed the door shut, then turned toward the window and looked out.

"Tony!" shouted Erica. The pitch of the roof was steep; she had a handhold on a vent pipe that looked strong. I turned and looked at the bed. It was queen sized. "Hold on, Erica! I'll get you in a second, okay? You okay?"

"I can hold on," she grunted. "Hurry!"

I spun around and threw the comforter off the bed, then tore the sheets off. With surging adrenaline coursing through my veins, I ripped the sheet in half and tied the ends together. I repeated that process with the fitted sheet. When I was done I had a good length of makeshift rope.

I tied one end to the heavy bedpost and pulled the other end to the window.

It was a good thing I'd slept in my boots. I kicked out the rest of the broken glass; the last thing I needed was my rescue rope to slice through in

177

the middle of my rescue operation.

Sounds came from outside the bedroom door.

Moans, sounds of hunger. Growls; animalistic. Not human.

I stepped through the window, holding onto my sheet as I made my way the nine feet or so from the gable window to where Erica clung. I had the sheet under me and fed it out like I'd seen people do when they rappelled in movies. It got me to where she was.

"Can you pull yourself up by this? Got enough strength?"

"I can," said Erica, her grateful, brown eyes staring at me. "But what about you?"

"Let's get you in. I'll swap you for the vent pipe, and you just tie a knot on the end and throw it back down to me when you get inside."

"Okay."

"Ready?"

"Yes, I think so."

I held the vent with one hand above hers and felt it give, just a little. It was almost imperceptible. I didn't say anything. With my left hand, I reached down and got a good grip on the waistband of her jeans. "Okay, take the sheet. I got you."

She let go of the vent pipe, got the sheet, and pulled herself up the angled roof shingles. I pulled with my left hand, helping her along. In thirty seconds she was above the vent pipe, and put her foot on it, taking a short break.

I felt it give again. I still didn't say anything except, "Hurry, Erica. They're outside the bedroom already."

She looked at me, and I felt her sadness. "Is Monica... dead?"

"I think she was already, Erica. I'm sorry. Now go, okay? Don't look down to the left when you get in."

She nodded and continued pulling herself up the sheet. She had removed her foot from the pipe and I was glad. I said a prayer. If I could have touched my St. Christopher medallion, I would have.

As she stepped over the windowsill, I took hold of the sheet and released my grip on the vent pipe. I pulled myself, despite my screaming back, up the sheet and into the bedroom. When I was inside, I pulled the sheet up and spread it open, laying it over Monica's body.

"Thanks for that," said Erica. "Tony, what's happening?"

She burst into tears. I fought doing the same.

I shook my head. "This is serious. I know you know that, but it's scary serious, Erica. These things. They're dead. Before I shoot them. They're dead."

"Like… like zombies?" she asked though her tears.

"I don't know what else to call them."

Erica's tee shirt was ripped at the shoulder, but still served to cover her. Aside from that and her blue jeans, she had a pair of canvas Vans on her feet, which looked good for any running we might need to be doing. I was glad to have taken my boots when I left my house because I needed something I could move fast in when necessary. I'd been wearing work boots my whole life, so they were like a part of me.

"Where's the gun?" I asked.

"It went off the edge when I fell out the window," she said. "I'm sorry. It's probably in the back yard in the bushes."

"Don't worry about it," I said. "Where are your car keys?"

"In my room. In my purse."

"You hear that out there?"

"The… things? In the hall?"

"Yeah."

"We need to get out of here. That's the only way, and we have to get to your car, too."

"We don't know how many are out there, Tony," she said.

"I know. I'm gonna hold this shotgun at the ready and you need to pull that door open. I'll take care of any of them, but we *need* to move our asses. They've obviously gotten past our window blockades."

"Wait!" she said. She went to the closet and pulled the door open. She leaned in and a moment later she emerged with what looked to me like a pretty high quality croquet mallet. "Will this help?"

"You okay with bashing your neighbors in the head with that thing?"

"If they come at me, I think so."

"They will, I'm pretty sure," I said. "That's what they seem to do."

She nodded. "Let's hurry before more come." She put her hand on the knob. "Ready?"

"No," I said. "Open it."

She pulled it wide open and stepped back, gripping the wooden mallet with both hands.

Luckily, in the hall, just three more of the creatures waited. When the door opened, they poured in like flowing water following the path of least resistance.

The first one tripped on something and fell to the floor as the woman-creature behind it trounced on his back.

Erica raised the mallet and brought it down in a swinging arc, slamming into the back of the thing's skull.

179

The monster behind her was blowing the pink mist as she fell in, and I staggered back. Erica was not as prepared, and it engulfed her head. She moved to wave it away, but her eyes fluttered back and she collapsed beside the creature she'd pummeled.

I knew she'd be out a while. I raised the shotgun and fired again, blowing back the next creature, sending it into Erica's room where it lay still.

There was no more rattling of pots from the stairs. I took another glance at the zombies near Erica, made sure none were moving, and charged in to grab her purse off the nightstand.

Jogging back to the bedroom where Erica lay, I rested the shotgun on the floor and knelt beside her. Slapping her face lightly, I put my other hand beneath her head and lifted it up. Her eyes fluttered, but did not open.

Fuck it. I needed to prepare. With my messed up body I would not be able to carry her, but with more time maybe I could get her awake.

I checked the dead zombies beside her once more to be sure, before digging through her bag to find her car keys. Next, I grabbed my shotgun and ran into the hall, pulling the door closed behind me.

I charged down the steps, barely paying attention to the kitchen obstacles I'd put there, and ran into the kitchen. I'd left my bag of ammo there. Slinging it over my shoulder, I saw another of the creatures slipping through the window on the west side of the house. I fired, blowing his left leg into hamburger. He was down enough for me.

Erica drove a Cadillac Escalade. Bad on gas, but big and tough. I'd take number two for now. I pulled the door open and jumped inside. Searching the interior, I saw a button on the ceiling. I pushed it and immediately heard the garage door begin to open.

I pushed it again and it stopped. Once more and it dropped again. Good. We had power, a vehicle and one gun.

We needed more in a world like this one. I again wondered who the men in the Jeep had been. Were they good guys or bad guys? They sure didn't seem to care about harming innocent people, so I'd guess they weren't model citizens. There were a few bad apples in Shelburne before all this went down, and they were just the types to take advantage of widespread chaos.

I put the key in the ignition and turned it. She had a full tank. Good. Perfect.

I reloaded the shotgun to capacity again before tucking the ammo bag in the back seat along with Erica's purse. Then I ran back inside the house and up the stairs, gun in hand.

The door was still closed, so I opened it and went inside, kneeling down beside Erica again. I put my Benelli aside and lifted her head with my left palm, lightly slapping her cheeks with my right. Her eyelids fluttered and opened.

She was awake. "Tony?" she croaked. "What... happened?"

"Can you get up? We have to go."

"Help me," she said, holding out her hands. I stood and pulled her to her feet.

"Feel alright?" I asked. "You got doused by that pink mist stuff that comes out of their eyes."

"How do you know about it?"

"Same thing happened to me. Linda was putting the stuff out. I got sprayed and went out for double-digit hours. I'm glad you woke up at all."

"Wow," she said, staggering. I caught her arm. "We're between attacks for now, but we gotta move. Steady yourself on the wall on the way downstairs. Anything else you need to get before we make a run for it?"

"Your gun, Tony. It's in the bushes still, right?"

"I won't need it," I said. "We're going to my work."

"Where's that?" she asked.

I realized she didn't know. "I've been working at Davillo's Guns in South Burlington. Anyway, Nick DeSante and his son run the place, and there should be plenty of guns," I said. "I just hope they're still alive."

"I don't need anything else," she said. "Let's just get out of here."

We got downstairs with minimal hassle, but as we passed a photograph of Erica and her parents, obviously taken some years earlier based on Erica's appearance at the time, she snagged the entire frame.

I didn't say anything. I knew why she took it. In a crazy world, memories of a time when things were normal and good could get you through.

* * *

"Damned roads are barely drivable," I mumbled as I cranked the wheel around yet another crashed car. "And what the hell is with all the shot-up cars?"

"Police?" said Erica.

"But why? Just because of this outbreak? Cops just start shooting at houses and cars with people in them?"

I got onto Shelburne Road and headed north toward Davillo's. It was only five miles, and we'd driven three of them when I saw a vehicle coming up fast behind us. I couldn't tell much about it except that it was a pickup truck of some kind.

"Somebody's behind us," I said.

Erica turned to look. "They're coming up on us fast."

"I don't know why I'm nervous," I said, pushing my foot on the gas pedal just a bit harder. "Probably from what happened at your place."

"They're still gaining," said Erica, tension in her voice.

The rear window of the Escalade exploded in a blast of shattered glass that flew all the way into the front seat.

"Drive!" shouted Erica, dropping low in her seat. I did the same, cranking the wheel hard right onto a side street, then making another quick left as I straightened back up in the seat. I made my next right and turned left into an alley.

"Where are you going?" asked Erica.

"Not sure. Just want enough turns between us that they don't know where the hell we are."

I saw what looked like an RV repair yard to my left, the fence chained. "I think I can run through that chain link," I said. "Sorry in advance for your paint job."

Erica didn't respond to my misplaced joke, but I turned the wheel and floored it. The front of the Cadillac smashed into the fence. Rather than breaking it, the poles bent forward and the entire fence fell flat to the ground. We rolled over it, cleared it and I spun the wheel hard to the right to slide the SUV behind an old Forest River fifth wheel.

I looked behind me and prayed for the dust to settle fast. With a turn of the key, the engine shut off. I rolled down both windows and we listened.

"I hear the motor," said Erica.

"I don't hear shit," I said. "Bad ears."

"I know," said Erica. "Linda told me."

"At least it's legit," I said. "Not selective hearing."

The sounds of an engine grew louder, and we even heard some tires squealing as the chase vehicle apparently rounded a nearby corner. I was just hoping they hadn't yet been in this part of town and seen the fence intact.

The noise eventually faded and disappeared completely.

"What is this place?" asked Erica.

"I thought it was a repair place, but now I'm thinking it's a storage yard."

"Think we can go now?"

"After that, I'm afraid to travel during the daytime at all," I said. "We're pretty vulnerable."

"Maybe, but I don't like the idea of doing anything at night with those things out there," said Erica, pulling her long, black hair back into a pony tail and securing it with a band she took from her purse.

"Let's give it an hour or so," I suggested. "Then we'll see if we can take side roads to Davillo's."

She nodded.

Only two of the strange new humans wandered into the yard while we waited there. The lot had been closed as it was a Sunday, and the fence was secure before we arrived.

We waited.

* * *

I drove slowly out of the parking lot and made a left, then a right. I went as far as I could, zoomed out on the GPS screen to see the best route, and then zigzagged the Escalade through the outskirts of South Burlington until I was on a dirt road running through tall, green trees. I knew the turns pretty well from that point, and soon I was in a massive grass field behind the small gun store/gas station/bait shop. There was a shooting range back there, but currently, nobody was honing his or her skills.

I parked close to the building out of view of the street. Just for the hell of it, I pulled out my cell phone and tried Nick's cell. It went to a fast busy signal. Not even a recording, and definitely not helpful. "I'm gonna have to go knock," I said. "Back door, though."

"Maybe you should go around front first to see what's what," said Erica.

"Yeah," I said. "Probably a good idea. Make sure it's not smashed in and looted. Will you be okay here until I get back?"

"Hurry," she said, nodding. "And be safe, okay?"

"I will."

I got out. "Lock it," I said before closing my door.

I heard the clunk of the locking mechanism as I walked away, my Benelli held in front of me. I hugged the building's south side and moved along the windowless wall until reaching the corner. I eyed the street, didn't see anybody, and slapped my hand on the intact, glass window in front.

Then I knew why it wasn't broken; it was airplane glass. I remembered when they'd put it in their display cases and in the front windows. It was almost impenetrable.

I looked toward the street again just to be sure, and stood. This time I walked in front of the store and slapped my hand on the glass again. I heard something from my left, turned, and saw the door fling open. "Tony!" shouted Nick.

I ran to him. "Nick! You're alive!"

"Yeah," he said. Nick was maybe 5' tall and no more than 85 pounds soaking wet. His head was as bald as a cue ball, and he told a lot of jokes I didn't understand. I'd always laugh anyway and never let on. He seemed to really enjoy the telling, so who was I to mess up his fun by acting confused at his comic timing and delivery.

I threw my arms around him and squeezed him hard. "Is Jason here?" I asked.

"He is," said Nick. "He made it fine."

Something changed in his eyes. Sadness.

"What about Gaetane?" She was his petite wife, originally from Montreal, Canada. She was, if it was possible, even shorter than Nick, and as soft-spoken and sweet as any woman had ever been. I really liked her.

Nick shook his head. "Gaetane wasn't as lucky," he said. "She turned into one of those... things. It went from a bad, bad headache to her gurgling something about being hungry, to complete stillness."

"She what? Passed out?" I asked, reaching out to squeeze his shoulder.

"Come on in first," he said. "I've been hearing gunfire out there, and those things are everywhere."

I went inside and he closed the door behind us. His son Jason, a nineteen-year-old of approximately Nick's height but with a few more pounds on him and shoulder-length dark brown hair, walked out from the back storage room. "Hey, Tony," said Jason. "Glad you're okay."

"Hey, Jase," I said. I walked to him and hugged him. We shook afterward. "How you holding up?" I asked.

"I've been better," he said. He did not smile.

"Anyway," said Nick, turning to his son. "I was telling him about what happened with your mom yesterday. Sure you want to stick around?"

Jason shrugged. "I was there. I know what happened." He shrugged again.

Nick nodded. "Gaetane wasn't passed out. She died. She was dead. I know because I tried to do CPR on her while Jason called 911. It never worked, and he just kept getting those circuits are busy recordings. We never got hold of anyone.

"I kept trying to call them. I was obsessed with getting through. Next thing I knew, Jason came running in, telling me that mom was awake. I ran after him and by the time I got to the room, she was growling and grinding her teeth and trying to grab Jason. I ran in there just in time to keep her from injuring him. She came at me instead."

"She wouldn't have hurt me, dad," said Jason, his eyes dark and brooding.

"Hell she wouldn't have. She wasn't herself."

"What did you do?" I asked the question, but realized immediately that I shouldn't have. He didn't need to go through it for me. I'd been through my own hell and I didn't need to drag him through his own again.

"Initially I pushed her away and tried to calm her. When I saw her eyes – all pink and clouded, and when I figured out she couldn't understand me, I just thought she was delirious from the sickness or something. She kept snapping her teeth at me and trying to claw at me. I got worried it was rabies or something, maybe from a rabid bat. I don't really want to talk about the rest if you don't mind."

"You shared enough," I said. "Sorry. I'm really sorry." I told him what happened with Linda, and about the pink mist that knocked me out.

He listened. "Think it's some kind of mutated strain of rabies, Tony?"

I shrugged. "I thought that was pretty much under control. I don't know. If it's rabies, it's the worst outbreak in history, I guess," I said. "Linda turned, and so did lots of Erica's neighbors and a ton of other people in town, too. I was at the police station. It was crazy there, too. Lots of cops changed."

"At least we have guns," said Jason. "Lots of them. Plus ammo."

"I need to go out back," I said. "Linda's friend Erica is out there in her SUV."

"She okay?" Nick asked. "Not hurt?"

"Physically, yeah, but she lost her best friend," I said. "I did, too. No, I think it's safe to say it'll be a while before any of us are okay again."

They nodded. Before we reached the back door, gunfire shattered the silence of the dead town.

I burst out the back door to see a blue pickup truck with what looked like two guys in the cab and one in the back. The man in the passenger seat held a rifle of some kind and he was firing at the Cadillac. One man crouched in the bed firing what I recognized as an AK-47 at the Escalade.

All of the windows of the Cadillac had been blown out and I didn't see Erica anywhere. I hoped to God she'd gotten out and run.

185

I ran toward the pickup, firing as I went. My first shot put a spray of holes in the side of the truck bed, so I raised the weapon to correct, still in a full run. The driver tapped the horn twice and the guy in the back of the truck held on as he spun it around toward us. I adjusted my angle in the opposite direction to try and stay out of their line of fire. The guy in the bed couldn't fire at all while he held on, so I raised my shotgun, now just fifteen yards from the sliding truck.

My blast looked like it hit right into the midsection of the man standing in back of the bed.

He flew over the opposite bed rail as the truck's rear end fishtailed once more and the driver floored it.

I heard another report and turned to see Nick holding a long-barreled .45 – which I recognized as his favorite gun, a stainless steel Colt Python revolver.

As the pickup was just a split second from being around the corner, the rear window exploded behind the men. Then it was gone.

I ran for the Cadillac while Nick and Jason ran after the truck to see if our last shot had taken out the driver.

I reached the Cadillac and looked inside.

Erica's body lay limp and sopping wet with blood, every inch of her form riddled with bullet holes.

"No, God no!" I shouted, and slammed my fists on the hood of the SUV, heat rising into my face. "Fuck!" I screamed at the sky, feeling the tears on my face even as my anger surged.

From the corner of my eye I saw movement. The man I'd shot had rolled over. I turned and ran toward him. I reached him and dropped on top of him. I dropped my shotgun and took him by the shoulders, slamming his head into the ground.

His eyes rolled back and I pulled him back up and slammed his head into the earth again. It wasn't hard enough to kill him – the grass was hard from a lack of rain, but it wasn't enough to fatally wound him.

His hand reached downward and I snatched his wrist and twisted it until I heard a snap. He screamed, "Goddamnit! You fucking broke my wrist!"

"Get the fuck up you son of a bitch! You killed my friend! You goddamned killed my friend! She was unarmed, you asshole! An unarmed woman!"

"Tony," said Nick from behind me, his voice soft and steady though his short breaths. "C'mon. Let's get him inside and have him explain who he and those other guys are."

I stared at the guy on the ground, his eyes wide with fear. I drew my arm back and punched him in the face, hard. My balled fist connected with his cheekbone, catching the side of his nose, which erupted in blood.

"Tony!" shouted Nick now. "C'mon."

I got off of him and walked slowly back to the Cadillac, looking inside at Erica. Her face had been spared, save for two bullet holes, almost perfectly centered above each eye. The two streams of blood ran down her face and dripped from her chin to her shirt.

My tears flowed. One by one, everyone I knew, whether intimately or casually, was dying. As hard as I tried to keep control, I felt myself racked with shuddering sobs as my weak fingers slipped from the SUV and I sank into the grass. I lay there staring at the blood dripping from the SUV, and I wished everything would just go away.

* * *

"Do you know what the hell's going on?" Nick asked the man. They'd taken the flak vest off of him and saw his chest was angry and red. The ballistic vest had saved his life. I wasn't happy about that. I wanted him dead for what he did to Erica.

"All we know is what Carville told us."

"Carville?" asked Nick. "Ryan Carville?"

Ryan Carville. A billionaire real estate magnate who lived in a mansion on Shelburne Bay. He made all his money in New York real estate, among other ventures. He'd gone broke a few times but had managed, like a phoenix from the ashes, to rise up and become more powerful than before.

The worst of his problems had ended fifteen years earlier. The last few years had been nothing but success for Carville, and his empire was bigger than ever.

Carville's compound on the bay had fenced grounds, security guards and means. It was rumored that he had food, water and fuel stockpiles for years to come.

"I work for Ryan Carville," continued the stranger. "Or I did. I was his driver for years. Looks like he plans to hole up at his place until his guys clear the town, though. I guess. I don't have any idea what he's got planned, and I don't know where all his thugs came from so fast, like out of the blue."

"You're taking orders directly from him?" I asked.

"No," he said, shaking his head. "I haven't seen him since a week or so before this shit started. All I know is I was going to be allowed into the compound after we went out on a clearing run. Those *things* out there were attacking everyone and Carville's guys had guns and a plan. I didn't see as I had a choice."

His brown eyes darted back and forth between me and Nick. Jason sat behind the counter, a .22 rifle in his hands, watching out the front window of the store. The glass was covered in thick, steel bars because of the age of the building and the stock inside; had they not fortified the old building, it probably would have been broken into dozens of times.

From what I knew, they'd never had a break-in.

"What about Carville?" I asked. "And you'd better start spillin' it, or I'll cut off your nuts with one of those hunting knives. Who are you, to start?"

"Paul Germaine. Like I said, I worked for Mr. Carville."

"So he's got his guys out... what? Killing people during a crisis?" I asked. "I thought he was supposed to be a good guy! Giving to charities and shit like that! Why is he sending you dicks out in the middle of this crap to hurt people?"

"He's not! He didn't say to do this. I don't know why Pete and Rory started shooting everyone. At first it was just the things, you know? The zombies or whatever they are?"

Jason said, "Zombies, dad."

"They're not zombies," said Nick. "They're just delirious. Crazed to the point they don't know what they're doing."

"Like hell they don't know what they're doing," said Paul. "They know *exactly* what they're doing. We just saw a whole house full of people, all practically in stacks. Those things were in the middle of the rows of people, dragging them through the house and stacking them. We shot the ones outside, but when we got in the house, it was horrible."

"What was going on?" asked Jason, mesmerized.

Paul shook his head. "Those things were just... just..."

"Eating them?" I finished.

Paul looked at me, his eyes teeming with fear and uncertainty. "Yeah," he whispered. "They were eating them."

"What did *you* do then?" I asked.

"They made me go look inside the house after they killed the ones outside. I didn't want to go, but Rory said he'd shoot me if I didn't. So I ran up there to the open door and looked inside. When I saw that shit going on, I had to act like I wasn't scared shitless."

"I asked you what you *did*," I said.

The guy threw his hands out. "What do you mean, what did I do? I saw those... those things eating those people. Like goddamned zombies or something, just tearing them open and burying their faces in their meat!"

"Did you kill them?" asked Nick, rubbing his bald head with one hand.

Paul shook his head. "I just looked for a second or two, tried to act calm and turned around and walked back to the truck. I wanted to run at full speed."

"What'd you tell them?" asked Nick.

"That the house was clear. I just wanted to go back to Carville's. I don't like these things. I don't like looking at them much less chasing them down and killing them. They don't die easy."

"You sure didn't have a problem killing Erica," I said.

"Maybe you didn't see him, but Rory was holding a pistol on me through the sliding rear window. I told 'em I didn't want to do this anymore and they fucking threatened to kill me. Plus, I thought the person in the truck was one of those things. She was moving back and forth inside the cab and I never really saw her. I sincerely believed she was one of those—"

"She wasn't!" I shouted. "Not by a goddamned long shot!" I was back at him with both hands clutched around his neck in seconds.

I squeezed, watching his face turn as red as blood.

"Hey!" shouted Nick, putting his gun down and yanking me off him. His little frame was wiry, but he was a strong little dude when he got an adrenaline rush. I didn't fight him.

"Don't be a fucking idiot, Tony!" shouted Nick. "This guy knows stuff we need to know, so mellow the fuck out!"

I dropped into a folding metal chair with terrible padding. "So, what's next?"

"Go on, and you'd better talk fast," Nick said to Paul. Jason stared from behind the counter. His mouth hung open as he tucked his long, dark hair behind one ear.

"Look. I haven't seen Carville and I'm not even sure what they're telling me is true. All I know is I wanted to be safe, and his compound seemed like the best bet. If I had to work a bit to make that happen, that's what I would do."

"Did they tell you anything about why Carville's doing this?" I asked.

"I heard his daughter and his twin brother turned into those things. He's got 'em locked in a cage."

"A cage?" asked Jason, looking mesmerized. "Where did he get a cage?"

Paul shook his head and swiped his hair away from his eyes. "It's like a see-through plastic cage. Acrylic or something," he said. "He had some secrets, I guess you could say. Had some private parties that I heard got a little weird. The cages are three stories below ground, in what was like a playroom."

He shifted in his seat and stretched his neck, cracking it. "So now he keeps his twin brother and his daughter in there. They turned into those things night before last. The minute he saw it was happening all over on TV and stuff, he sent Rory and Pete out and they recruited like thirty guys and some chicks in no time."

"What for?"

"Gathering supplies and weapons, anything. He told them it was important for all of our survival."

"But he didn't say to kill anyone," I said.

"It's not like the guy I know," said Paul. "Like I told you, Pete and Rory have been running things from the start, at least outside. You know Carville's not leaving that place. He doesn't have to. Pete and Rory told us we were dead if we tell Carville what we're doing out here."

"I'll fucking kill them," I said. "I should kill you."

I wasn't a killer. I was blowing smoke. It still felt good to threaten him; he didn't know me.

"I don't want to tell him. If he boots us, we're screwed. He said he'd trade what we bring him for security and shelter."

"Yet here you are out in the trenches," said Nick. "Real secure. Then you come for our guns when you fucking well know we need them to survive."

"I'm being honest with you guys. You should be real careful around the guys they've got patrolling the streets. Most of 'em are jumpy," said Paul. "They're petty crooks, not killers. Their switches are either on full kill mode or off. Their philosophy is better you than them."

"Where is this house?" I asked.

"Which house?" asked Paul.

"The goddamned house with the people stacked in it. We can't leave them there."

"It's about half a mile from here. Over on Hillier Street."

I looked at Nick. "We need to go help those people. They're probably just knocked out like I was."

"Help them?"

"Yeah," I said. "If it was us, we'd want someone to come, right?"

Nick nodded. "When?" asked Nick.

I looked at Paul. "Are the patrols organized already? This fast?"

"Not really. It's pretty late. They won't be going out again tonight."

Occasionally, Paul grew reluctant to share more information. When he stopped talking I toyed with a Boker combat knife. I'm not a violent man, but the stakes had changed.

His eyes fell to the knife in my hands.

The words kept coming.

* * *

"Help!" The voice penetrated the twilight. "Somebody, help me!" The faint sound of running footsteps came to us.

Over the previous hours, we had transferred as many guns and as much ammunition into Nick's Dodge pickup truck as we could. Even the beefy suspension was showing signs of its capacity to bear weight.

"What's that?" asked Jason, running to the window. "Sounds like a girl's voice."

We ran to join him. A woman ran down the middle of the street, jerking her head back and forth, obviously looking for help.

"Move," I said, nudging Jason aside. I turned the triple deadbolts and slid off the steel bar that slid into position by way of a key from the outside. Pushing through the door, I yelled, "Here! Come here!"

The woman staggered to a stop and looked at me for a moment before turning to check the progress of her pursuers.

She made her decision and turned toward me. I moved back inside and held the door. Once she was inside, I pulled the door shut and reset all the locks.

"Thank you," she huffed. "Thank you so much."

Jason slid over a chair and she dropped down into it. He followed up by handing her a bottle of water. "Here."

She looked up at him for a moment before taking the bottle and nodding her thanks. She was of Hispanic descent. Her hair was dark and long, and her large eyes were almond shaped and brown. She was tall; I'd put her around six feet, give or take a couple of inches.

Our captive, Paul, cleared his throat. He was zip-tied to a chair by his wrists and ankles.

The woman's face changed. She dropped the water bottle and stood, backing up against a rack of fishing tackle.

"Please, don't worry," I said. "But that guy right there tried to kill all of us. He killed my friend Erica."

She stared at Paul for a moment and he finally nodded and said, "It's true. I did. But I didn't want to. I'm trying to explain that —"

"Shut up," I interrupted, before turning back to the woman. "I'm Tony Mallette," I said. "This is Nick DeSante and his kid, Jason. The asshole in the chair is named Paul, if he's telling the truth."

"I am," he mumbled. We ignored him.

She nodded again, still catching her breath. "I'm Serena Casteneda," she said, her accent strong but her English perfect. "I saw some others hiding away while I was out there, but nobody came out to help."

"They may not have been what you thought," I said. "I lost my wife and her best friend to those things, plus a couple of others. I guess your story isn't much better."

"My husband and son changed," said Serena. "And my... my mother. I've lost everyone."

Her tears flowed then. I guessed she hadn't had much time to really grieve. It's tough when things are trying to kill you.

"Take all the time you need," I said. "We're trying to devise a plan. Some guys are rolling around town shooting everyone — even the ones who aren't sick, like us. This dick was with them." I motioned to Paul.

He nodded.

"Why do you keep him alive?" she asked.

I liked her more already.

"Because he said he was at a house earlier where a bunch of people are trapped by these things, and I think I know how. Have you noticed the pink mist stuff that pours from their eyes?"

Serena's face brightened. "Yes! They start pushing it out when they get close to you. What is it?"

"Near as I can figure, some sort of chloroform stuff. Knocks you out, but lasts way longer. Not that I'm an expert on chloroform or anything, I mean, I've only seen it used in the movies."

"So they use it to subdue people?"

"Long enough to eat them," said Jason. He smiled slightly before working to wipe it away.

Everyone deals with the impossible in their own way. It's like laughing at a funeral. People are devastated. It's inappropriate. It's a method of dealing and it's not usually in your control.

"We're going to try to save them. With those loons out there, we need safety in numbers. You know of any other survivors?" asked Nick.

192

Serena shook her head. "No. I had enough on my plate just trying to stay ahead of them. They're everywhere. It's almost everyone, right?"

"I have no idea," said Nick. "We went out for a bit, but we attracted the things like burlap sacks stuffed with salmon in a world populated by Grizzly bears. We figured out pretty quick it was safer here."

"So what changed your mind?" asked Serena.

"Paul here, and his buddies – what, Rory and Pete? Killing Erica and shooting up her SUV. They'll be back. They probably came because they know we sell guns."

"I don't know how to shoot a gun," said Serena.

"You'll need to learn," said Nick. "I'm a trainer. We've got a selection of silencers, too. Once we get where we're going I can work with you safely."

"It's dark," said Jason.

"Yeah, we need to go," I said. "I lost my Sig at the house. You got something that'll fit one of your silencers?"

Nick nodded. "I got a few Walther P99s all set up. Let's travel light, but we'll need to take my box van and swing back by here to get the pickup. I'll pull it into my garage while we're gone."

"Your box van didn't get shot up?" I asked.

"Nah," said Nick. "I had it parked on the other side of the building. It's got a big dual cab, room for everyone."

I held up a hand and got everyone's attention. "Look, guys. I'm not the sharpest knife in the drawer anymore, but I've figured out a few things. One's the mist. Stay out of it. I mean out. If you get in it, one breath and you're done. Out like a light."

I waited, and everyone nodded. "Okay," I said. "Next, don't get bitten. Monica, a friend of Erica's, showed up at her house yesterday. She had a bite, but we didn't think anything other than she needed medical attention. She turned that night. We just got lucky enough to avoid being attacked. That's about all I know."

"Can I stay with you?" asked Serena, her eyes filled with hope.

"I thought we'd already determined we need numbers," I said. "You're in."

Nick and Jason didn't object. Neither did Paul. If he had, I'd have just shot him right there.

* * *

With the headlights out, we drove along the dirt backroads of South

Burlington. Every couple of streets we spotted clusters of the stumbling stiff creatures, and every single one of them turned to watch the truck roll by. I counted four of them that we hit at slow speed. It broke their bodies as they were crushed beneath our wheels, but none of them cried out in pain.

It was eerie.

Nobody spoke until Jason broke the silence. "Where do we go when we're done?" he asked. "You said we can't go back to the store, right?"

"We have to get the pickup with all our stuff, and Paul said Carville's guys wouldn't likely be going out again tonight," said Nick. "After that, I have an idea we can work on in Shelburne. We'll just find a house or two there to hole up in until it comes together."

Nick looked like a little kid behind the wheel of the big truck, his 5' tall frame barely allowing him to see over the steering wheel, even with the pillow underneath him.

"This is the street," I said. "Hillier. Where's the house?"

"You should turn on the street behind it," said Paul. "The front of the house was crawling with those things."

"Where is it on Hillier?" I asked.

"At the end on the right," said Paul. "Would you guys consider letting me help?"

"Wanna do it without a weapon?" I asked.

Paul shook his head.

"Then no. But feel free to change your mind."

* * *

We parked the truck, reversing it to stop between two houses that backed up to Hillier Street. There was no room to get around either side of the truck, so we ducked underneath just in front of the rear tires and crawled, emerging from the back. Paul was strapped to the handle above the door and wasn't going anywhere. We zip-tied his ankle to the base of the driver's seat.

"Everyone loaded and silenced," said Nick, ever the tactician. "Just shoot them as they notice you, but don't shoot the people."

"How will we know who they are?" asked Jason.

"You'll know," I said. "They'll be asleep. If they're not, their eyes aren't pink and their skin isn't gray or mucked up like those things."

I had longer legs than Nick, so I ran to the front. I had my shotgun and the Walther. The shotgun was just in case. It would work well to bash heads in if I needed to. Otherwise, it was just strapped on my back.

I felt the knob turn underneath my grip as I glanced up at the moon, which shone pretty bright. It would be enough light without flashlights.

"Ready?" I whispered. Everyone answered in the affirmative but Serena, who said nothing. I realized she wasn't even looking at me. She was nervously scanning the yard behind us.

"Hold on," I said, turning to her. "Serena, you can go back to the truck if you want, if you're not ready for this."

"I'm not," she said. "But I have to be. If you don't mind, I'll stay in the back."

"Don't shoot us," I said, smiling.

"I'll try not to."

"Ready, guys?" I asked.

"Go," said Nick, his gun held in two hands, pointed at the floor and ready to fire. Jason and I were in similar positions, only Nick's kid had two P99s in his hands. Nick had given Serena a high-capacity .22 caliber pistol and told her to aim for the head at close range.

We went in. Quietly.

* * *

As we moved into the rear hall, there was a laundry room on the left. It was empty. Next, a bathroom on the right.

A figure emerged into the hallway ahead of us. I raised my P99 and fired.

The thing's head flew backward and it dropped like a stone.

The dull thump the gun made when it fired was so vague it was almost impossible to tell the origin of the shot. The house was cool. I noticed it. It was downright cold compared to outside.

I eased sideways, having not yet reached the body of the thing I'd put down. Reaching another door, I turned to look inside.

I jerked back and caught my breath. The room was filled with crouched, feeding things. Bodies lay torn open beneath them. I choked down vomit.

"Oh, God," whispered Jason, turning away from the open door.

I stepped out of view of the doorway and looked at my friend. "The... things. They're eating," I said.

"Yeah, it seems that's all they do," said Nick, leaning inside to look.

"Oh, my God," he said. "Too late. Way too late for them." Without another word, he walked into the room.

195

"Nick!" I whisper-shouted, but it was too late. Nick fired away, blasting the creatures one by one. I moved in and assisted, taking out the last three.

Nothing could be done for the people they were feasting upon.

Noise came from the front of the house.

"You gotta shoot them in the head,' I said. "Otherwise they don't die." I didn't remember if I'd said anything, or if they'd already figured it out.

"It's instinct for me," said Nick. "I've never been a center mass kinda guy. The ones in the back room won't be getting up anymore."

We moved toward the front of the house and startled one creature who was busily dragging a body inside the house through the open front door. I immediately scanned the living room and saw bodies everywhere. Motionless. It was too dark to determine if they were breathing or not.

I fired at the one in the doorway and the female went down in a pile of nasty flesh covered in the gore of its own brains. I saw the pink light in its eyes go dark.

Several more of the creatures emerged from dark corners, and our efficient murder team took them out one by one.

I felt like I was in a video game that I never would have played in the real world.

"Watch the door," said Nick, speaking to his son.

"Let's see if we can wake these guys," I said. "It only depends on how long it's been since they were doused with the mist."

We moved around the room. Eyes fluttered open. Groans broke the silence. We told each of them to file into the hallway. We had closed the doors on both sides to set their minds at ease.

Jason, still at the front door, fired outside. The shot was followed by a thump on the porch. Seconds later there was another low, muffled shot, followed by a louder thump.

"Hurry up guys," said Jason. "It's getting busy out here."

I was leaning over a woman whose eyes opened to reveal pink. She opened her mouth and a black tongue covered in horrid sores wagged at me. I put the Walther against her head and blew her brains out.

A man behind her screamed. His cry triggered similar screams from the others we'd awakened.

"Shut up!" said Nick. "Please, you've got to be quiet or those things will come! We'll get you out!"

After we got them quieted, one young woman pointed again to the creature I'd just shot and said, "She got scratched. I was right beside her.

The thing went to grab her and it just missed and scratched her. Then it blew out this gas stuff and I don't remember anything else until I saw you."

"But she was scratched?" I asked.

"On her left arm."

I knelt down and lifted her arm. The scratch wasn't more than an inch long. I searched for other marks and didn't see anything.

It was the first time I figured out just how little it took to change. Erica's friend had been bitten.

I looked at the young, blonde woman. "She got scratched, then she was put to sleep?"

"Yeah."

"So she changed in her sleep?"

"I guess," the woman nodded. "Get us out of here, please?"

I wiped the sweat from my forehead. "We will. I think we're done here. C'mon."

She took my hand and I pulled her up.

We pushed our way through the crowd. Some of the men and women were in nightgowns and pajamas, a few wore only blue jeans. Others still, were entirely naked. Obviously, they were the ones that slept in the buff.

We stood at the front of the compacted group of survivors, ready to turn the doorknob. "Jason, bring up the rear, son!" shouted Nick now, with the house clear of zombies.

"Go!" said Jason.

We hadn't turned back toward the door for a split second when a rumble came from the front of the house. We turned to see a new horde of monsters filling the front porch and pushing in the door.

Jason spun around and unloaded with both Walthers, firing one, then the next, with amazing accuracy. I guess it pays off to teach your kid to shoot when he's four.

Jason backed down the hall as he fired. "Go, go!" he shouted.

Once Nick saw his son would be okay, he opened the door. In the back yard were at least six of the world's newest killing machines, all putting out guttural sounds that chilled my soul. Their moans sounded like demons embedded in my brain.

With several more accurate shots from our Walthers, we took them down in short order. Waving everyone forward, we rushed across the yards to the box van.

The ramp was down. "Inside, and hurry."

One man stopped. "How do we know you're not going to take us somewhere and sell us or something?"

"Buddy," I said. "Take a chance. We just saved you from the worst death I can think of. That was because we need people, not cash."

It was enough. "Thank you," he said as he mounted the ramp.

When they were in, we closed the door almost all the way and pushed in the aluminum ramp.

Back in the cab, Nick drove again. "Let's go back to Davillo's and get the pickup with our supplies," he said. "Then we'll take back roads to Shelburne. I got some good buddies there. If they're alive, they'll help us figure out how to keep all these other folks breathing."

* * *

That night we got to Shelburne, and Nick went straight to his friend's house. Jim wasn't home, but another guy Nick knew, Bill Richards, was waiting at his house for him. He told Nick that Jim was alive and well and out scouting for supplies.

Bill was a round-faced man in his early thirties with pale skin and freckles. His medium length, ginger hair was wispy and thin, and he had a fuzzy little billy-goat beard on his chin.

He told us they had already avoided Carville's guys twice, and there were more than just two vehicles patrolling the streets, too.

The men were out on kill missions, and it didn't seem to matter if you were a zombie or alive. If you moved, they didn't ask questions; they just fired at you.

Jim had an idea to black out the windows on his house and seal up the cracks around the garage door. Within five hours of their second encounter with Carville's men, they closed all the bedroom doors and painted all the front facing windows black.

We took all of our new people into the garage and inspected each one under a fluorescent light. There were twenty-two people. Nine women, six boys and girls, and seven men.

Of these, one boy, one girl and a woman had scratches that looked like they had been inflicted by fingernails. Since there was no way to be sure if it was from the zombies or humans, and we knew now what happened to people with scratches, we fed them, apologized to them and walked them to an interior room. Bill assisted.

Of the three, the boy named Adam, who said he was seven, and the woman named Crystal, who claimed to be twenty-seven but looked thirty-eight, both had headaches. The girl, Eve, who was twelve, did not.

I insisted on speaking with them before we locked them in the bedroom.

"Look," I said. "This isn't what we do. It's not what we want to do. But my wife changed into one of these things. She got a bad headache first. Really bad, just like what you got. It might be nothing, but it might be a symptom."

"When will you know if we're alright?" asked Crystal, tears pouring down her washed-out cheeks.

I shrugged. "When you turn. Or maybe by tomorrow if you don't."

"Is someone staying in here with us?" she asked.

The children said nothing. They looked exhausted and numb. I don't think they heard much. I felt like a reluctant Nazi prison camp guard.

"No," I said. "We'll check on you every hour. If anyone turns, we'll take them outside. Stay away from one another, please. If you get in that pink mist stuff, you're not going to be able to protect yourselves."

"Why am I here?" asked Paul.

"You're not a zombie but we know you're a problem," said Bill. "We can't afford to let you go tell them where we are."

"I won't!" he said. "I want to stay here anyway!"

"I saw you kill an unarmed girl sitting in her car," I said.

Crystal gasped.

"It would take a lot for me to let you stay anywhere with me. But letting you go isn't in the cards."

"You know," said Bill. "We'd better strap these guys to opposite corners. One to a bed post, the other to the opposite one. If any one of them gets to the others, it could be a mess."

"Don't treat us like animals!"

"Crystal," I said. "One day. By tomorrow morning we should know. Please, just try to sleep."

Her tears flowed.

We secured everyone and closed the door.

I went in for the 6:00 AM check. Everyone was fine except for Adam. The boy had turned in the previous hour. His pink eyes pumped knockout mist into the air as he gnashed his teeth and struggled against his restraints, surely frightening the others tremendously until we came.

We got everyone else out of the room, threw a blanket over him and shot him in the head.

The rest of us mourned the boy that nobody claimed to know.

Then we started to make a plan.

A survival plan.

Just about a month after the beginning of the end of the world, something else began to awaken.

Rats.

We didn't know why. The rats initially appeared to have clustered into huge groups where they died. We'd seen several warehouses and empty, dark spaces where the piles of rat bodies lay.

We never touched them. We never noticed they weren't rotting.

When they flooded the streets, it created a whole new terror, and we lost a lot of people. There was no escaping them. They were as ravenous as the infected humans, but they could get in almost anywhere.

Sealing up our buildings became really important. The rats were still somewhat nocturnal; that gave us the daylight hours to fortify against them.

No vapor blew from their eyes. That was a relief.

As for Carville's marauding killers, they made the streets more dangerous than the zombies or the rats did. Jim Cole and Bill refused to leave because this was their home and they wouldn't run. If order was not to be restored to Shelburne by the government, they would continue to fight until they either won or died.

For the moment, there was strength in or numbers. Before long, we had organized and conducted regular training sessions in hand-to-hand fighting techniques as well as firearm training. No age group was excluded. Anyone new who joined us was evaluated and trained. We had them complete questionnaires about their skills and what they liked to do.

Our little underground community began to thrive in the shadows. We got good at it.

I enjoyed working with the kids and teaching them how to fight. This was a world where that kind of knowledge could save you. I instilled empathy and an attitude that insisted you never turned your back on someone in need.

There would be strangers, friends and even family whose injuries would eliminate any hope of saving them. I wanted to make sure all the kids – and the adults – recognized that when they saw it; it would keep them alive.

Carville owned two helicopters, and his men began air raids as well. The first winter was hard. The power had gone out months before, and when we lit fires to keep warm, the smoke was a beacon to those seeking us out.

We never learned the reasons why they came after us all. Paul believed it was because of limited food and water. He said Carville never planned to leave his compound, so he relied on those men to keep supplying him.

In turn, Ryan Carville would provide them with a safe place to live. I wondered if Carville knew what they were doing to the people of the town he claimed to love.

Bastards. All of them. I swore one day I would be the one to kill him.

Ultimately, we located, cleared and secured several houses throughout Shelburne. We called these homes *Zombie Free Zones* and gave them numbers so that we could map and identify who was in which house.

I ended up running ZFZ-4. Serena, Matt, Jason and some others moved in. The only limitation was the size and location of the particular home. Each was stocked with firearms, ammo, food and water, and we began monitoring Carville's men almost as much as they searched for us. We killed them when possible, but there always seemed to be more.

I really just wanted to share my beginning with you and tell you how we came to be in that little house off the main drag with boarded up windows and gun turrets cut through the plywood, made to look like knotholes.

I also want to add one last thing to this record before I put it away.

* * *

I sat with Serena one evening, about four months into this new apocalypse that we soon learned was worldwide. The previous night had been busy, with multiple parties out gathering supplies to stock our safe zones. Water, food, batteries, radios: everything we needed required ingenuity and some travel. Carville's people were clearing out supplies for miles around with their air capabilities.

That particular night, everyone else had gone to bed. Serena and I were on watch duty.

Without a word, she began lighting candles and placing them along the edges of the room, completely surrounding us.

We sat in two soft, but worn chairs, and she took my hand.

"Tony," she said, "Have you grieved for your wife?"

"Everyday," I said.

"Have you spoken about her to anyone? Really talked about her?"

I thought about it. "No," I said. "Not really, just people telling me they're sorry when they hear. Kind of surface stuff. Like stuff they have to say and stuff I'm supposed to say back when they do."

"Tell me about her."

I looked at her, the candles flickering in her sad eyes, and knew she needed it too.

"She loved me beyond what even made sense. I told you what happened to me. Linda sat by me in that hospital bed for three months, and stuck with me when I got out, too. I wasn't near ready to leave, but they just didn't have enough beds to let me stay there anymore. Anyway, I was having a tough recovery and I was angry and pretty much hated the world."

"Did you take it out on her?" asked Serena.

I nodded. "Yeah, and even then I knew what I was doing. I wasn't walking yet. Every day seemed like a setback. I didn't want her with a man who couldn't be what she deserved. She was smart. After my brain injury, I felt like I dumbed her down."

"You're smart," said Serena. "Smarter than you know."

I shrugged. "It's tough. I struggle with every problem. Takes me time to understand them."

"But you take the time you know you need," said Serena. "I never see you rush into a decision, Tony, and when you make a choice, it always feels like it was the right one. At least to me. I think everyone else here feels the same."

"Linda made me better than I was, even before the accident. When that happened, in my mind I didn't deserve her at all. In the end, we couldn't be apart. We lived a simple life together, but I loved her and she loved me. We showed each other every day."

I paused for a second, the thing that had been bothering me finally bubbling to the surface.

"Beyond missing the hell out of her, my biggest fear is that I'll become what I would've been without her."

The tears came unexpectedly. I really believed I had gotten past the sadness at losing her.

Serena gave me the time before speaking.

"Anthony, you are a good man. You've only grown to be a better man in the time I've known you. You're a leader and someone that all of these people rely on. Linda lives on in your heart and in who you are."

I looked up at her. "Thanks, Serena. If this was supposed to be a therapy session for both of us, I guess I've stolen all the time."

Serena checked her watch. I saw it was 3:00 in the morning. She looked up and her eyes met mine.

"My husband betrayed me more than once. With other women. I had my twelve-year-old son, David. I won't say any more other than to tell you that when I left, my son had become one of those things out there. So had my mother. What happened to Enrique is not important."

I stared at her in the candle light. "We can go there, you know. Put an end to it."

Serena's tears flowed. "No. It would be too hard. When I put my son into the bathroom, he was already one of those things. I think he still looked mostly normal then, except for his hunger. I couldn't see him again. Not the way he would look now."

"Remember him as your loving boy," I said. "Your mom, too. Remember the time you shared with her. The good stuff."

Serena sighed. "I do that every day, Tony. I find myself smiling, and I know there are many more memories to come, all of which will draw those smiles. Maybe when I need them the most."

I leaned over and put my arms around Serena, and she hugged me back.

This is what we needed, to share our pain and grief. It would help us cope enough to get us through another day, then another and another. Eventually, we could maybe start to build new, good memories.

It *would* happen. I already have proof of it, even as I write this.

I lost Linda. The order of the world collapsed, utterly and completely. You can guess that I never – not in a billion years – believed I'd laugh and sing and enjoy life ever again.

Within that same year, I made the best friends I've ever had in my life. We care for one another and there isn't one of them I wouldn't put my life on the line for – and they'd do the same for me. I don't have even the tiniest doubt.

I love all of them.

* * *

If you want to know what happens from here, I can tell you that my story wasn't the beginning of this post-apocalyptic saga, and it isn't the end, either. It's just one chronicle jammed in the middle of a set that continues to grow as others in our group share what they went through and continue telling their little chunk of history.

Flex and Gem have always encouraged everyone who joins their group to put their stories on paper. They say it's cathartic – which I guess means it'll keep you from going nuts – and that it could be helpful to others having a tough time living with the experience of losing almost everyone they knew and loved. Not just losing them, but doing it in the most horrible of ways.

Flex and Gem are keeping these volumes safe, which is why I'd recommend you try to find my group. We were all in Whitmire, South Carolina the last time I knew. We were prepared to stay there for the long term; trying to build our new little America.

There's Flex, Gem, Hemp and Charlie. Doc Scofield, Dave Gammon. Too many good people to mention.

Flex Sheridan wrote the first chronicle. He eventually named it Dead Hunger. Most of our group took turns writing them, so we've put together a really great record of what happened and what we did in response.

I still think it sucks that I'm dead. I know it's the only reason you've got your hands on this. If you ever run into the person who let this chronicle out, I'm not sure if I want you to punch them for me or tell them I love them.

Thanks for reading this. I hope it helped you in some way.

I know I feel better.

~ Anthony Mallette

RILEY V RESURRECTION: THE FINAL PATH HOME

by Mark Tufo

Discover other titles by Mark Tufo
at marktufo.com and http://zombiefallout.blogspot.com

ONE

For those unfamiliar with me, my name is Riley and this is my story, I am a dog, specifically an American Bulldog according to the two-leggers, yet the heart of my wolf ancestors still beats loudly within my chest. The fact I am a ninety pound female and a mere three summer seasons old should in no way dissuade you from how tough I am. Unlike what some misinformed scientists have claimed, I *am* self-aware. I love my pack of humans, I enjoy television, although for the most part, unless a cat is falling off of something I find it boring. I can see colors and I thoroughly enjoy human food more than the cardboard kibbles they place in my dish. I just have the good grace to not beg at every opportunity like Ben-Ben, yet if he gets something I will make my presence known. The night the world changed, the only ones of us who survived were myself, Jess the teenaged girl who is easily my favorite, her infant brother Zachary, and Ben-Ben the Yorkshire Terrier who I have been learning to tolerate. I hadn't gotten a decent night's rest since they brought him back from the animal dumping facility, or to you humans, the pound. And last, and *definitely* least, the last sole survivor was the cat, Patches. I'd promised that one day I was going to catch that little fleabag and...well, let's just say it wouldn't have been pretty. Yet she proved herself alongside Ben-Ben numerous times as we escaped various hardships on our quest cross-country to reunite Jess with her old boyfriend Justin Talbot.

I guess I'll start at the beginning because two-leggers tend to be so busy they forget things, including taking their dog out on a proper walk. The day the alphas brought Ben home, I was mourning the passing of my friend George the English Bulldog, who was perhaps the most majestic animal I'd ever known. Yes, the new guy was originally known as Ben but he would get in so much trouble the humans would have to say his name twice to get his attention, and so it stuck as Ben-Ben.

"Ben." Normal conversational tone. Then a much louder, "BEN! Get out of the trash!"

"Ben. BEN! Stop eating your crap!"

"Ben. BEN! Stop tearing the couch up!" You get the point; eventually it was just easier to say Ben-Ben.

I don't know what the two-leggers were thinking if they thought this thing could ever replace the irreplaceable. Then the zombies came and that little crazy dog stood paw to paw with me on the top of the stairs as we defended our home. I'd thought we'd lost him. He somehow found his way out of the pile of zombies and so began our trip. The five of us were heading to a place called Colorado, to Jess' old boyfriend, someone she'd had to leave behind after the great move.

The trip was more difficult than we could have thought, Patches only got along with herself and even then I don't think that was always the case. Water and food were scarce and Zachary was sick and getting sicker. We had to seek out two-legger help. I was warned by Patches and Ben-Ben that not all two-leggers were like our alphas. I'd had a hard time believing it back then, but not anymore. We did find two good people, Winke and Faye, and they took us in. Ben-Ben was convinced Winke was Santa, the bringer of bacon to good dogs everywhere. They helped Zach to get better and made us feel as if their home was ours. It's possible we would have stayed there if not for Christmas Eve when Winke made an ill-advised trip to get a present for his wife. He was bit by a zombie and it was all we could do to escape before we were eaten as well. Oh yeah, the cat made it out too.

We were back on the hard-packed ground, heading through a place called Nevada when things went from bad to worse. Zachary had been improving at Faye's but he had not gotten completely well and was now getting sick again, rapidly. I watched as the cub died and then came back. The joy I felt was somewhat muzzled when the cub began to speak. Not aloud but rather in our heads, everyone except for Jess, which was strange. The one good part of the whole thing was watching the cat as all these things happened; she couldn't stand it. For that reason alone I thought it was the best thing ever. Zach said his mother had given him the ability when he saw her, said he would need it to survive. Ben-Ben wouldn't stop licking his face, I guess because he was happy the cub was alive, but I think more for the fact he thought the baby would be able to get him bacon now.

It was the first good news we'd had in a while, then we got to Las Vegas. It had gotten bad real fast. Jess was taken to see the leader of their community, a madman known as Icely. Ben-Ben was taken by one of our captors as was I, though I ended up in a small cage alongside a bunch of other dogs. The cat, well, she slunk away like cats are apt to do. I was forced to fight another dog to the death. Thorn was a huge Rottweiler, I tried to talk to him about the craziness of what we were doing but he believed completely in what the two-leggers told him to do. I beat him, I thought it was the most disdainful thing I'd ever been through and it was, at least, for half a day then the cat came back and rescued me, that was worse. I found that I had to start appreciating what she did, that was worse.

We escaped the kennels and went to find Ben-Ben who seemed to be living the high-life in his new home. We almost left him behind; again, I was wrong on the motives of my pack mates. He was doing what was necessary to survive, much like we all had been. Our next stop was to get Jess and Zach who just so happened to be at Icely's home. We were able to get them out with the help of another female two-legger named Mia. Leaving Las Vegas was not nearly as easy as getting there but finally we managed. We all thought we were safe, only Mia knew the depths of Icely's insanity; he would never let his prizes go. We weren't too far out of the two-legger habitat and the hunt was on.

We encountered wheeler problems and deader problems. We'd had to retreat into the home of another two-legger: his name was Koala, and his ancient dog Jumper. Funny name for a dog who could barely lift his head off the couch cushion. They took us in and we were thankful, they even fought next to us when Icely's hunters found us. It was a narrow escape once they burned the house down. Koala, Jumper and Mia paid the ultimate price to secure our freedom, and the cat made it as well. Icely would not stop his relentless pursuit even though we bled his hunters. In the final showdown I took him down like the rabid two-legger that he was. We were all exhausted, although, hope did begin to rise as we got closer to where Justin lived. Then that same hope was crushed as we saw the community had been in the middle of a small and savage war. Not much remained of the buildings.

Jess had broken down and cried uncontrollably. We waited and offered the comfort we could, except the cat. When she realized there were others involved she finally got herself under control and began to explore our surroundings. We found what she called the clubhouse and it was a large building. What was even more impressive about it was the amount of food stored inside of it. We had a comfortable living for a season or two, enjoying each other's company and just living life. Jess' sadness pervaded. It wasn't anything she displayed outwards but it could always be felt when one got close to her. She missed her alphas and the boy and just two-leggers in general. I thought maybe getting rid of the cat would make her happier but Zach told me that wouldn't be a good idea. He's a cub though, what does he know?

It wasn't home, but at the same time it was, and I don't think we would have gone anywhere new for a long time to come if not for the two-legger named Alex. He had lived in this community before and had come back after losing his family, said he wanted to die where it all began. He would have too if not for us. He'd found someone he could help, and he said he knew where Justin had gone and would help us to get there. The cat was reluctant to go and one would think I would have tried to convince her that her path was correct; instead, I fought for her to come with us. We weren't completely over our differences but she was part of the pack and that was all that mattered. So back onto the hard-packed ground we went. The vast majority of travelling across the country went without so much as a hitch until we got to the state of Maine. Alex had died saving Jess and so had I, if I'm being honest. This continues my fifth and final installment in my story; I just hope it is a happy ending as I have grown so tired.

* * *

The biting from the zombie was an unimaginable pain. I thought the sting of losing Alpha and his mate, of losing Ben-Ben's Santa, of losing Mia, I thought this might have been inexpressible. The heart-wrenching pain of watching Jess, Zachary, Ben-Ben and even the cat, Patches, as they drove away was equally as bad, and I thought that was the most I could ever suffer. I was wrong. The zombie tearing into my flesh in an effort to get at my pack was so much worse. I saw my beloved George in what I figured to be my final moments alive. Oh, how I missed the majestic George, the English Bulldog that taught me everything he knew. It was so good to be next to him, to smell him to be able to lick his face again. I could be happy here, and there was not a cat in sight!

George and I had been walking for a while, he didn't say much, he usually never did. Ours was an easy-going relationship, the mere fact of proximity was generally enough. I loved sharing in his company. The walking part was a bit strange, George wasn't much for any extended activity.

"Where are we going?" I'd asked him after a time.

"Nowhere really. I just like to walk now that I can. No pain in my joints and I don't get winded, I love it here."

"Will I always be able to stay with you?" I asked him hopefully.

He stopped. He didn't actually look at me, he was looking at something far ahead of us. "One day."

"But not this day?" I had some alarm in my voice.

"No." Now he did turn. "Your suffering is not yet complete. I had hoped to take you away from as much of it as I could."

"I want to stay, George. I miss you so much it aches inside."

"You have always been a faithful friend Riley and I have missed you as well. Fear not. In the end, all will be as it was meant to."

"Does that include Ben-Ben?"

"Of course."

I gulped. "What about the cat?"

"What do you think?"

"That's not really an answer."

"Tell ThornGrip I said hello."

"Who is ThornGrip?" And with that I retreated, no, I was *pulled* back from the warmth and love of George and the place we were in, back to the cold and the pain of whence I'd come.   The numerous places I'd been bitten burned as if fire had been placed on them. I knew the pain of fire, once while camping with Alpha and his male offspring as a puppy I had stepped in the small stone ringed enclosure. The pain had been immense. George could only shake his head, he was smiling as he told me to go put my hurt paw in the small stream we were next to.

"Thank you, thank you, thank you!" I'd told him repeatedly before licking the side of his face.

"Can I get some sleep now?"

"Of course." I'd licked his face four or five times more, maybe as many as eight times although I can't count much higher than seven with any degree of accuracy.

I was snapped back to the present, the fire-wounds momentarily forgotten as I looked up into the face of a monster. The animal was immense, and if the savage snarl and drool were any indication, it was as angry as I'd ever seen anything could be. A paw easily the size of my head swept over me and into the zombie that had been biting me. The zombie had been removed from atop of me, a gaping wound opened in its chest. The large animal walked over me, I was enormously happy that it had missed stepping on me. If by design or happenstance, I don't know, I was grateful either way. I rolled off my back and onto my side just as the beast before me pounced on the zombie. Claws larger than my teeth burst though the zombie's chest and thighs, pockets of black blood flew into the air.

The zombie bit wildly at the large animal but could not get through its thick fur and hide. I managed to shakily get to my legs; I whined as I did so. The bear, for that was what it was, wrapped its mammoth jaws around the head of the zombie. It did not crush but rather pulled the head free from the body with a slight shake of its head. I could not even begin to imagine the immeasurable strength the animal had. I was transfixed by the death it had just dealt. So much so I did not think to make a hasty retreat, although I do not believe I would have been able to do so. She then spun and raked her huge front paw across the mid-section of the next nearest zombie, the white of spine shone through for a moment before the zombie collapsed in on itself, not dead but out of the fight. The bear took out three more zombies in similar fashion, two she laid completely open, diseased and grayed internal organs fell wetly to the ground. The last she snapped the neck of, the sound loud enough to hurt my ears.

"Can you move dog?" The bear swiveled her head to me. There was a wild look to her eyes, she took no great pleasure in the kill and something told me she was afraid to be this close to the dead ones.

"Some."

"We don't have time for some, there are too many of them." I thought it was the end. I couldn't figure out why George would send me back just for this. The bear wrapped her maw around the scruff of my neck and picked me up. We were the right size I suppose for her to treat me as a pup, that didn't mean I didn't feel a little indignity in it. I think it would have hurt less to run on my own than being in her mouth but how does one tell a bear something.

When we stopped, she gently let me go before collapsing herself. Her tongue lolled out as she took in mighty breaths. Neither of us said anything. I watched her warily, wondering if she were to fall asleep should I just quietly leave?

"I will not harm you," she finally said.

"Are bears trustworthy?"

"I am not a mountain lion." She scoffed. "My name is Thorn-Grip."

"You know George?" was all I could think to ask. She only stared blankly. "My name is Riley. Thank you for saving me. Why though?"

"Is that how you often express gratitude?" She yawned.

"No, not at all, this just seems like it came from a very unusual source."

"Do not bears help dogs where you come from?"

"I do not believe so," I answered truthfully.

"I need to sleep now. I may tell you the reasons upon awakening. For now you should wash your wounds out. There is a river just over there." She pointed with her snout. "Do not go in too far. The current is swift and you are small. If you are taken I will not be able to save you again."

"Thank you," I said, but it fell upon deaf ears, she was breathing deeply and was soundly asleep. The water was cool and greatly soothed my bites. I was also able to slake my thirst, something I did not think I was going to be able to do when I first started lapping the water up. When I was done I moved back to the shore, I found a small clearing illuminated by the warmth of the sun and laid down. I was fearful for Jess and the rest, but right now the best thing I could do for them was to regain my strength. I would seek them out when I could.

My mind pictures were untroubled, most revolved around lying with my head on Alpha's lap as he absently stroked my fur, sometimes behind my ear, sometimes on my chest. It mattered little where the contact was made, just that there was some.

I don't know how long I slept. When I woke, the burning disc was hanging low in the sky and my wounds, although they still throbbed, were not at the forefront of my thoughts. What was more important was the hunger now gnawing at my stomach. I stood up, thankful the wobble in my legs was not nearly as pronounced as it had been earlier. I stumbled as something hit me in the side of the face and fell to the ground, flapping.

"You like fish?" ThornGrip asked. She was in the middle of the stream looking at me. I took note that there were four good sized fish all flopping around me.

I wanted to tell her not really, that the only time I ate fish was when I was stealing it from Patches, the cat. Instead, I stepped on one with my paw, trying to keep it from finding the water. I watched as ThornGrip grabbed another clean out of the water and ate it. She ripped the head off and then peeled the meat from the inside. I copied her moves as best I could, although I could not grab the fish like she had, I used the ground and my two front paws to achieve the same effect. It wasn't my favorite thing to eat but it beat air. There was only one fish left by the time I was full. I ate that one too. I felt my belly swaying; I thought for sure it was going to start dragging on the ground.

ThornGrip had come up to join me on shore. Her size was impressive and if I'm being truthful, terrifying as well. She would not need to do much more than tap me with that paw, and I would be done.

"Did you enjoy your dinner?" she asked as she sat on her hindquarters, so she could lick her front paws.

"I did." I paused. "I do not normally enjoy the creature but this time I could barely eat enough of it."

"How could you not like fish?" She was done with her paws although she stayed in that strange sitting position. She looked much like a two-legger the way she was posed. "I saw the human vehicle leave before I came over. Did they hurt you?"

"What?" I was confused. "No, no, they were pack-mates. I believe they thought I had gone over."

"You had," she said matter-of-factly.

"Huh?"

"You *were* dead. I could smell it from in the woods."

"Why did you help then? Why risk injury?"

"My destruction of the infected humans was not to save you but rather to kill them. If you had not somehow revived I would have kept doing so. But since you were alive I thought it better to keep it that way. You looked like a newborn foal standing there all gangly-legged, I had to get you away from there."

"Thank you, I am not fond of zombies."

"Zombies?"

"That is what the two-leggers call them."

ThornGrip sniffed in derision. "I have not much use for the un-infected either," she said stiffly.

"They are not all bad. Some, yes." I was thinking back to Icely and even of the people Ben-Ben had been 'rescued' from. Not all people were bad but neither were all people good.

"Unlike you, Riley, I cannot wait to see on which side of that line a person stands. Have you ever heard of hunting season?"

I shook my head in negation.

"For that, alone, consider yourself lucky. It is when men, and sometimes women, use pointed projectiles or their long reaching weapons to kill us."

"Fire-sticks? They use fire-sticks to kill you? Are they feeling threatened? They do strange things when they feel like they are at risk."

"This is not a matter of us showing up at their homes, they come out here to where we live and they lie in wait, and like cowards, they strike out with weapons we cannot fight back against."

"That's horrible," I told her, and I meant it. The fire-sticks were a mighty weapon and maybe the only way a two-legger could win a fight against a bear, but that didn't make it right in my mind.

"That is the way of the world in which I live. It is all I can do to survive and raise my cubs."

"Where are they?" I asked, looking around thinking they might bound out at any time.

"My first died two seasons of spring ago. He had injured his paw on an old machine of man, before succumbing to illness. My second was doing well, I did all that I could to keep him away from the world of men. It was the infected, zombies, that took him. Man has suffered greatly from the sickness let loose and now that they do not number as many, the zombies turn to other food sources."

"I am so sorry," I told her.

"We ran for days to get away from them, but they would never stop. TinyPad could not sustain. I fought until I could fight no more. I suffered a great many wounds and still they took him. I laid waste to over forty of them before it was over, but by then TinyPad was no longer of this life."

ThornGrip was looking off into the distance. I had no words for her, what could I say that would alleviate the sharp pain of loss she was feeling? We sat for a while longer.

"Where are you trying to go Riley?" She turned to me. "Home?"

"We have no home any longer. The zombies took it. My pack was heading to a friend's home."

"A human dwelling?"

"Yes."

"Do you know how to get there?"

"No."

"What will you do now?"

"I... I do not know. I have just traveled back from beyond. I do not think I was supposed to still be alive."

"That must mean that you have something to finish here before you can move on."

"Is that how it works?"

She shrugged her massive shoulders. "I do not know the answer to this little one, but it appears that perhaps I saved you for some reason you do not understand yet."

"I am grateful for all of your help ThornGrip, yet I will need help from the very beings you despise if I am to complete what I think needs to be done."

The bear said nothing.

"My wounds need tending to, there are humans with small sharp objects. Sometimes they hurt but they mean well, and oftentimes they make us feel better when we are not well."

"Your wounds are indeed grievous, there is a chance you would succumb like my BerryDancer."

217

"That is a beautiful name."

"He was a beautiful cub."

"I must seek out one that could maybe help me. You have already done so much for me I cannot ask that you do more. That you have given me a second chance on life is a debt I may never be able to repay."

"Yes, I have restored a forfeited life. Perhaps I would like to stay with you a while longer to see what it is I saved you for. If you would have me."

"I would very much like that ThornGrip."

We rested that day, ThornGrip hovered over me like a doting mother. I was not sick, not yet, but my joints began to subtly throb. Whatever was inside of me was building up its strength to work its devastation upon me. Tomorrow we would have to leave and seek out that which she hated the most. If I was going to make the most of what had been given to me that was the only way I knew how. I woke up once during the middle of the night, a chill wind had swept over me, and the howling of a wolf off in the distance had drifted in with it. ThornGrip was close enough I felt her fur bristle.

The next morning my head was cloudy, thoughts were more difficult to come across. I felt something like that one time when my alpha male had dropped his drink from his hand and had fallen asleep in his chair. Alpha female had been mad at him that I had got ahold of what she called his beer. He had laughed when he saw me stagger away, I had just felt funny, and slept most of that day.

"Are you alright Riley?" ThornGrip had asked. "You should take in some water before we begin."

She was right. I waded off into the water, the idea of bending my head over and in from the shore did not sound like a good idea. My head was already swimming.

"How far?" I asked when I had got my fill. I felt better for it.

"Darkness will be approaching before we are there."

"We should get going." I started walking. ThornGrip was not following.

"You are going the wrong way," she told me, waiting for me to turn around and catch up.

"You could have told me sooner."

"I could have." She did not show it but I believe her to have been smiling.

As the day wore on my thoughts drifted. ThornGrip was a silent travel companion, she had told me that she lived the majority of her life alone except for when she was raising her cubs. I could not wrap my mind around that notion at all. It was so strange, such a cat way of life. The pack was everything. How did one survive without others helping? My respect and my sadness for her increased.

"Do you get lonely?" I asked after we walked an indeterminable amount of time.

"I miss my cubs if that is what you mean. Other than that, I do not often think of other bears. I look for food and water. I eat, I drink. I find someplace warm and safe to sleep and come the next day I do the same thing."

I could see the benefit to this lifestyle, I could. How many times had I wished Ben-Ben the incorrigible incessant Yorkie away? That does not even take into account the cat, whom I could not for the life of me understand what spell she had over alpha male and female that they allowed her to stay in that house with us. The selfish, self-centered ingrate was about as much a pack animal as the hulking bear next to me and even scarier. The burning disc had crested high overhead and was now heading down. My throat was parched and sore, my joints which had merely ached earlier were now inflamed, my pace had slowed. I tried to keep up with the easy gait of the bear, but it became impossible, I was thankful when she slowed to stay with me.

"You do not smell well Riley."

"I do not feel well ThornGrip."

"We still have much forest to travel before we come out across a human clearing."

I almost told her to go on without me, then I realized that the only reason she was going at all was because of me, and I laughed.

"There is humor in that?" she asked with concern.

"No not that." I wanted to explain, I just didn't have the energy to do so. She was probably thinking to herself why she enjoyed the solitary life so much right about now. It's not always easy dealing with the emotions, thoughts and motives of another. You can trust yourself and your own instincts and that's about it.

The traveling became slower as I began to walk almost as much side to side as I did forward.

"I know this is not your preferred method of travel but I fear that if we do not move quicker you will not make it into the night."

Protesting was out of the question. I was not even absolutely sure where I was or who she was. Fever had taken root, and all rational thought was being reduced with each step taken. I felt pressure around my neck, then my legs were lifted effortlessly off the ground. I sagged like a wet puppy, the strength running out of me like the previously mentioned water. ThornGrip's pace picked up. I think she was running though I am not entirely sure, I lapsed in and out of consciousness. It was dark when we stopped. ThornGrip placed me down tenderly.

"Where are we?" I whined.

"We are where the humans grow their food and keep their livestock."

"We are at a farm?" I knew what those were. One of Zachary's favorite bedtime stories revolved around Sunnyvale Farms and the nice farmer, his wife, their chickens, cows and horses. They were smart two-leggers who had four dogs, yet they also lacked something as they had barn cats as well. Maybe what I told ThornGrip earlier needed to be amended. Even good people might have some bad parts. Perhaps now was not the time. Even through my haze of pain and discomfort I could feel waves of nervousness sheeting off of her. She wanted to go no closer.

"Can you walk?" She was not looking at me but rather at the large domicile in front.

"Yes." That was a lie, I could barely pant.

"Go then," she urged.

"Okay." She turned and I heard her go into the woods a few steps away.

"You are not moving, dog."

"I'm working on it."

Neither of us did anything for many beats of our hearts. I rolled over, yelping as I did so. I got my legs underneath me and pushed up, the first step I took ending up being my last as I pitched to the side.

"I fear humans," ThornGrip said as she once again wrapped her massive jaws around my neck. I thought there might be a chance she would just end my suffering there and then and that way she would not be exposed to the inherent danger the two-leggers posed.

She tentatively brought me to the bottom step of the porch leading into a large home.

"Bark," she urged. "Make some noise."

I would have liked to comply but my throat was closing, I was having difficulty just swallowing.

"You insufferable dog, you are going to get me killed." Her fear had her eyes wide in the moonlight. The words were harsh, the tone was not. She lifted up her head and let a roar go that shook my body and sent

220

ripples up my spine. If I could have gotten up and run away I would have done so. She stayed over my body. I heard a door open up behind me...

"Oh my." It was a female voice. "Harold! Bring the shotgun!"

"Dagnabbit woman I've told you not to answer the damn door anymore. Well jumping jehovites!"

I heard the metallic clicking of a fire-stick being prepared.

"Run!" I was able to hoarsely get out for ThornGrip.

Instead she tenderly picked me up.

"What's...what's the bear have?"

"I don't know Mabel, stay in the house, I've got to kill this thing!"

There was more fumbling around and then I heard a bunch of the metalbees strike the wood and roll to various points around the porch. "Dagnabbit!"

"No swearing Harold, we're good Christians."

"We're about to die, I'll apologize when I get there."

"You'll do no such thing. Put the rifle down." Mabel was more scared than ThornGrip, who had ascended the steps. My head was lolling to the side, I was looking directly at Harold who had been leaning over to get his bees.

I stuck my tongue out and licked the side of his face.

"What is going on here?" Harold put the rifle down, ThornGrip placed me on the porch gently.

"I think the dog is hurt."

"I can see that Mabel, but why was that giant bear holding him in his mouth and why are they on our porch?"

ThornGrip was nudging my body towards Harold.

"What am I supposed to do?" Harold was looking back towards the door and wondering if it could withstand a bear attack.

"I think you should help."

"Easy for you to say back there. I'm going to pick up the dog big fella, don't eat me." Harold's hands were shaking as he placed one under my neck and the other on my back hips. He lifted me up. "I need to get the dog under some light so I can see what's going on. I'm going in. Is that alright big fella?"

Harold backed up. I could tell he was hesitant to turn his back on an animal that outweighed him nearly three times over.

"I've got the kitchen table cleaned off, bring her in here!" Mabel shouted. There were candles lit up all around the room. Mabel gasped as Harold put me down on the wooden table.

"What?"

She pointed. ThornGrip had forced her way through the door opening. She'd come in through the living room and had come up into the kitchen. Her large nose taking in all the scents of the home before she settled and sat next to me.

"Thank you," I told her.

A large tongue came out and licked the side of my face. I wasn't used to that, I was normally the one giving those.

"They're friends?" Harold said. "I'll take care of the pup, big fella."

ThornGrip growled.

Mabel had a small smile. "I think the big fella is a husky woman."

"My pardons!" Harold said sincerely, meaning every word. "Mabel, gonna need my vet bag. I'm going to boil some water and could you maybe get something for our... umm... guest to eat so that I look less appetizing?"

"You're all skin and bones, Harold, she wouldn't want you."

"You seem to be taking this rather well."

"If she wanted us dead, dear, that tour group would have already left. She's looking out for her friend."

"Well, if you feel so safe go over and give her a hug of sympathy."

"Just because I say my prayers every night and ask to be delivered from evil does not mean that I would flaunt that in front of the devil. Hurry up and boil the water."

That was the last thing I remember before I lost consciousness. When I awoke the burning disc was up and streaming through the viewer. ThornGrip was next to me, empty boxes of cereal all around her.

"These are fabulous!" she said happily holding up a box with a drawn two-legger on the cover wearing a funny head piece. "I think the human woman said something about a crunchy Captain. I don't normally like meat but I'll eat more Crunchy Captains." She put the box on the floor and shredded it open, licking the inside contents for any pieces she may have missed.

A small cough came over to my side. "May I?" Harold asked ThornGrip, the man was pointing to me. ThornGrip gave a little acquiescing grunt as she looked for more cereal.

Harold sat on the couch with me. "It was touch and go that first night, pooch. Didn't think you were going to make it."

"That first night? How long have I been asleep?"

"Three nights." ThornGrip grunted, tearing open another box.

Harold jumped.

"You're making a mess!" Mabel had her hands on her hips and was berating ThornGrip. The bear looked forlorn. "Get over here, I found you another box." ThornGrip almost looked giddy as she bounded the two steps, sliding on the slippery floor in the kitchen before she came to a forced stop running into the far wall. Mabel laughed. "Not very graceful." She opened the box up and handed it over. "SLOW!" she said as ThornGrip grasped it in her hands and tilted the box up into her muzzle, sending flakes spiraling down into her mouth and floor.

"Ummm… so good," ThornGrip grunted.

"Between you and me pup, that bear could be here for ten years and she would still scare the hell out of me. But my Mabel, she's not afraid of anything, those two, they took together like they're old friends reuniting. I've got a feeling you can understand me because I swear that bear knows everything we're saying. I only wish it worked the other way around because I'm thinking you have a hell of a story to tell." I licked his hand.

"Are you sure your friend isn't going to eat us once she realizes we're out of cereal?"

I gave him a small bark to let him know I figured they'd be alright.

"Alright I'll take your word for it. I have to change some of these bandages. This is going to hurt some. I am sorry for that." He began to work, I tried to stay as still as possible. "You had over a dozen bites on you, more than a few had taken flesh with them. I don't know how you survived."

Just then ThornGrip bellowed when she realized the box was empty.

"I guess maybe I do know." Harold smiled.

"Well if you stopped to breathe while you were eating them maybe they would have lasted a little longer!" Mabel was yelling at Thorn-Grip. "Get out of here while I clean up your mess, pesky bear." Thorn-Grip howled as Mabel playfully hit her in the rear with the floor cleaner.

"I would not suffer the mortification if not for her wonderful boxed treats." ThornGrip huffed down, sitting next to Harold making sure she was touching him.

"That frightens him," I told her.

"I know." ThornGrip pulled her paw to her face and began to lick the cereal stuck there off her pads. When she was done she swiveled her massive head so that her nose was less than a snout length from Harold's ear. She began to needlessly lick her chops.

"Well!" Harold said with a high-pitched voice, "it appears you are doing much better pup. I'm, ah, I'm going to get you some aspirin to take some of the pain away." He left quickly.

"ThornGrip, why are you tormenting the two-legger?"

"He pointed one of your fire-sticks at me, Riley."

"He didn't know any better, now he does."

"Perhaps. He is just lucky I enjoy the female so much. She made something called cookies yesterday and they had peanut butter in them. I don't know if I've ever had anything better Riley. I feel bad I ate them all. I couldn't stop myself. She was hitting me with some material she called a dish towel, didn't matter I couldn't stop. I'd do it again, even though she kicked me out of the food room for the rest of the day."

"She kept you out of there?"

"She said she wouldn't give me anything else if I didn't listen to her. How could I ignore her?"

"Peanut butter is pretty good. Alpha would often make toast and coat it with peanut butter. Many times he would give me half his piece as he left our home in the morning."

A scream brought us out of reverence for the creamy goodness.

"Mabel?" Harold called out, coming from down the long thin room. He first looked over to us, I think making sure ThornGrip wasn't somehow involved.

"They're back."

"Zombies. I'll get my gun."

"You be careful," she warned him.

Harold was heading for the door. ThornGrip bumped him out of the way and pawed at the door, although when she did it, wood shavings curled up and fell away from the stout wood.

"Don't you dare let her out!" Mabel warned.

"Okay honey, I'll tell the nice little bear she can't go out, or would you rather I let her break the damn thing down?" Harold scooted past ThornGrip and opened the door then reached past to open the second viewer door as well. I could see outside from my vantage point, a group of zombies coming, there were more than seven. I could not see Thorn-Grip's eyes but the rest of her body, the tension, the slight movements, the increased breathing, all let me know just how incensed she was becoming. She went out the door and was standing next to Harold.

"Help her!" Mabel admonished Harold.

"Help her. That's hilarious, who is going to help me?" Even so

Harold stepped outside. ThornGrip did not flinch as Harold raised the fire-stick to his shoulder and fired a metal-bee. A zombie fell away, most of its head dissipating in a cloud of bone and blood. The next shot seemed to be all ThornGrip needed to launch her own attack. She stood on her two back legs, dwarfing Harold. She bellowed a roar loudly, the force of it could be seen projecting out from her. If zombies had any awareness or need for self-preservation they would have left as quickly as they'd come. ThornGrip dropped down and charged at them as they were coming to meet her.

The collision was devastating for the much smaller framed zombies. They were broken and battered as she rammed into them. Her claws ripped out, savagely laying multiple zombies open, their bodies pooling on the ground before her feet. Harold was still shooting. ThornGrip was taking care of the majority of the zombies, but once they'd caught sight of their favorite meal, more than a few peeled off from the fight and were running for the front porch.

"My God there's too many of them."

"Harold get in the house!"

"I will not let that bear fight them herself!" he shouted.

I rolled off the couch slowly, trying to get a grasp on how I was feeling. Not bad, throat was still a little raw and I was not yet at full strength, but I was not as weak as a lamb anymore. I moved quickly to the front door. I'd had enough experience I knew what to do from here. I jumped up, my front paw resting on the small black release. The door swung open and I dropped to the ground.

"Harold, the dog is out!"

I was standing next to him, my fur bristled, a low mean growl issuing forth from my belly.

"Go girl, go back." Harold shot again, the closest zombie that had been coming up the stairs was halted as the left side of its face flapped back from the impact, its jaw line and teeth exposed, along with the bottom part of its brain before it collapsed into a heap. The next time he tried to fire I only heard a dry click, no metal-bee came forward.

He turned his fire-stick back and forth looking for the problem. A female zombie, although I do not think gender plays a part in their packs, was halfway up the stairs when she launched herself at Harold. I pushed him out of the way as I intercepted her progress, her teeth coming within a paw-span of biting into his mid-section. I tore through her ratty fake skins and into the tainted flesh of her breast, ripping her corpulent meat away. She did not pause to inspect the damage, she did not try to push me away, she did not yell out in pain, she just kept try-ing to get at Harold, who had fallen over and was back-peddling with his legs to make more room for himself as he looked in his pockets for more metal-bees.

She was chomping away, like those fake plastic teeth Zachary's brother used to tease Ben-Ben with. The zombie was on her hands and knees after I dragged her down. I ripped at her hamstring, pulling the long ropy muscle free from her leg in an attempt to get her to stop her progress. She was steadily making her way past Harold's ankles and was heading straight for his reproductive organs.

"Goddamnit!" he shouted.

Every time I grabbed a piece of the zombie it came away in my mouth, yet that did little to stop her. My energy level was already begin-ning to wane, I had to end this now. I rammed my head into the zombie's hindquarters, spinning her slightly. She finally turned to look at me and I took this opportunity to wrap my teeth around her neck, I bit down until I cut through her veins and muscles, and then heard the satisfying crunch of her windpipe underneath. I then shook my head back and forth as vigorously as I could, hearing more audible crunches until I was finally able to pull the head free from the rest of the body. Harold was gagging, Mabel was screaming.

"Look out!" she cried.

Too late, we'd been joined on the porch with three more zom-bies. I was already having a difficult time standing, I would not be able to do much more than watch as we were eaten. Still I would do my best to display my fierceness. I spun to face the threat, teeth bared. This was when the entire porch jumped. I was launched into the air. ThornGrip had stormed back and had cleared the stairs to land directly on the back of one of the zombies. His form was crumpled much like I'd seen Alpha do to a can. Her claws raked out and severed the head of the second one. The third she reached down and grabbed by the mid-section, bisecting the small zombie as she shook her head back and forth much like I had.

We were all breathing heavy, except for Harold, he was hitching heavily. I looked past ThornGrip's shoulder, the immediate threat had been removed.

"They...they saved me," Harold said aloud.

"They wouldn't have had to if your damned fool self hadn't gone out there and almost got yourself killed! Oh, Harold." She was crying as she came out the door.

"They're dead. Are you okay?" I asked ThornGrip.

"I am, and you?"

"Fine but tired."

"The human?"

"He is fine as well."

"You fought bravely Riley."

"Could not have done it without you, ThornGrip."

"Come let's see if the woman has more cereal."

Mabel kissed Harold tenderly on the lips before she bopped him on the side of the head. "What do you think you're doing? And where do you think you're going?" She turned to look at ThornGrip and me. "You're both filthy! To the tub with you both!"

"Oh no!" I whined.

"Is that bad?" ThornGrip asked me.

"It is. It is a large container of water where we are forced to bathe. It's almost torture!"

"Sounds wonderful, lead the way."

"Be gentle with her stitches." Harold was sitting on what the two-leggers called the throne. He was absently stroking ThornGrip's back as he watched Mabel clean me off.

"This is what you are so afraid of?" ThornGrip laughed.

We were stuffed in that small room yet none of us seemed in too much of a rush to be alone.

"This isn't the first injured animal I've dealt with Harold James." I could tell by her tone she was still angry with him for his reckless act.

She treated me tenderly, even more so than when Alpha was made to clean me. Even the toweling off was a breeze in comparison. This isn't saying that I enjoyed the experience, just that it was more tolerable than normal. ThornGrip could barely contain herself, nearly shoving me out of the way in her rush to get into the tub, when I was done. I could not help but laugh, she looked like she was going to get stuck in there as she wriggled her butt around trying to force it down into the tub.

"This is divine!" she said as warm water began to touch her.

"You look like a hippopotamus in a teacup." Mabel laughed as she filled a jug so she could pour water over and onto ThornGrip. We were in that small room for a long time by the time Mabel finished with the bear. I believe there was more water on the floor than in the tub. I do not believe that she cared. She used many fake skins to help ThornGrip dry off, then when she was done she hugged the large animal fiercely. She came to me and did the same, although not quite as hard as I was still in pain.

"Thank you, thank you both," she said as she pinched our cheeks. "Now get out of here, I have to clean up. That means all of you, even you Harold James."

"Yes ma'am."

"And get these two something to eat, they must be starving after saving your behind."

"Yes ma'am."

"It is funny to me watching the smaller female boss the larger male around."

"Is it not the same way with you bears?"

ThornGrip paused to think. "I guess it is."

"I suppose you'll want these." Harold was holding two boxes of cereal for ThornGrip.

ThornGrip began to shake, first very slightly at the back of her legs, and then as it traveled down the length of her spine, it intensified, sending sheets of water all over Harold and the room the two-leggers called the kitchen. When she was done shuddering herself dry, she tenderly gripped the boxes out of his hand and came into the room the two-leggers lived in.

Harold was sopping wet, his hand still outstretched as he came to terms with being bathed in bear water.

"What have you done!?" Mabel yelled at him as she came out of the refuse room.

ThornGrip was busy munching down cereal. "This really is the best stuff ever." Her mouth was full and flakes were falling to the floor.

"Asked you to do one thing Harold James, get out of here with your wet clothes, now I have to clean up in here."

"It... it was the bear," he entreated.

"Oh blame it on the bear, she can't defend herself."

Harold left with his head hanging low. "This isn't over bear," he told ThornGrip as he passed. She snorted. I laughed.

Mabel put a loaf of meat into a bowl, she broke it into small pieces and then brought it over to the couch, which she helped me onto.

"The dog is eating on the couch? You don't even let me eat on the couch."

"Please. She's neater than you."

ThornGrip snorted again.

"These damn animals understand everything we say Mabel, don't you find that strange?"

"No. I really don't." She started back up before he could question her. "This may sound like heresy given my religious upbringing. Or maybe it doesn't." She paused with her hand on her chin, her gaze faced upwards. "Remember when we were talking about how many people we thought were left?"

"I do but I don't know what that has to do with..."

"Hush! I'm trying to make a point, and I'm not sure if I can."

He dutifully did so.

"We thought perhaps after the infection and the zombies that three billion people were still alive. What if it's far less?"

"Okay." I could see the confusion on his face but I also knew he was smart enough to stay quiet.

"What if there is far less? What if there are way more zombies than we thought and far fewer people? Say around a hundred million."

"Worldwide?" Harold gasped.

"That would be roughly the same number of people when Jesus was born."

"Mabel?"

"I told you hush. That was the age of miracles, waters parting, curing of diseases, walking on water to name just a few. What if that was because there was an energy in the earth? A life force, maybe. Don't look at me that way, I'm not quite ready for the loony bin. So there's this finite life force and the inhabitants of the planet are tapping into it. Then the world population explodes, you have that same column of energy, only now seven billion people are using it. It would get pretty diluted don't you think?"

"I... I don't think I understand Mabel. This doesn't sound like you at all."

"I know how it sounds, I've just always wondered why we've never seen the miracles today that seemed so prevalent just a couple of thousands of years ago. Maybe there's a reason why."

"What would Father Hickens say?"

"Relax Harold, I'm not saying the Catholic church doesn't exist, I'm suggesting that perhaps Jesus was a great man who had the potential to tap into a much vaster well than we've had, at least up until now."

"So somehow you're saying that because there aren't that many people left, animals can understand us?"

"I guess sort of I am, I wouldn't doubt in a few more months we'd be able to understand them."

I was tempted to tell Mabel that as far as I knew, animals could always understand two-leggers, it was only recently that they began to notice.

"I don't like that at all Mabel."

"Why?"

"Because that will mean there will be even less people and less of a chance for things to return to normal." Harold looked dejected.

"You feel it, I know you do. We're more in tune with nature than we've ever been, and we're already pretty close, considering we once ran a farm."

Harold said nothing for a few moments. "I don't know if I want to believe you or not. What do you think pup, has my wife lost her marbles?"

My ears perked up at the question.

ThornGrip growled. Mabel laughed. "The bear doesn't think so."

"Why should she? You feed her. You on my side pup?"

I shook my head. Mabel again laughed, this time Harold joined in with her. Harold walked around the room peering through the viewers, when he was confident nothing was coming he sat back down on the couch with me. "Alright girl, we're going to figure out your name."

I was curious as to how he was going to do this, and so was Mabel, if the way she was leaning forward was any indication.

"Don't suppose you can spell?" he asked me, holding up a pen. "Do you know your alphabet?"

I knew the letters made words; that was about the extent of my knowledge.

"I'm guessing probably not, but we can still do this, going to try the phonetics route."

I had no idea what he was talking about but I wasn't going anywhere anytime soon, and I was happy to be the center of his attention. He spent a few moments drawing one large character on each page until he said he was done.

"Alright, we might as well start at the beginning. This is the letter A," he said, holding up a piece of paper with a symbol that I guess was the two-legger version of that letter. I wasn't sure. "Okay, this can be said either the long way 'ay' or the short 'ah'. Does your name start with either of those sounds?"

I yawned.

"Are you sure?" he asked.

"I think she told you exactly what she meant, move to the next Harold," Mabel admonished him.

"This is the letter B, pronounced either be or bah." He was looking at me rather intently.

I stared back at him.

"What is he doing?" ThornGrip asked, leaning over to me.

"I don't know but he looks funny," I told her.

Harold was through most of the sheets of paper, and he seemed to be losing confidence that his test was going to work, that was, until he got to the letter he called an R.

"This is an R, pronounced ar or rah."

My ears perked, and I barked at that second part.

"Alright." Harold seemed excited. "I think it has to be a vowel next. Back to the A, does your name start Rah or Ray?" I didn't say anything. "Alright, on to E, how about Ree or Reh."

Blank stare from me.

"How about I, does your name start with Rye...?"

I barked and stood on the couch cushion.

"So we're getting somewhere! Good girl." He scratched behind my ear.

"Think he'll figure it out?" ThornGrip asked as she laid down.

"I hope so, I don't like the name pup."

"Wake me if he gets it." And with that ThornGrip slid quickly and easily into a deep sleep.

I almost missed the L sound when he finally got to that letter. He had been giving so many name choices along the way I was starting to get confused. Riban, Richael, Ridell, Rifle, and on and on. So when he got to the L and said the el or lah sound, I didn't hear anything that sounded right, at least until he gave an example of a name.

"Rilead?"

I barked.

"Rilead? That's your name?" I just stared at him.

"What kind of name is Rilead, Harold? Try shortening it," Mabel told him.

"Rilea?"

I was still looking at him.

"Rilee?" I jumped over and licked his face, my tail moving back and forth. Here was a two-legger that knew my name. That meant something. If felt good, made this place feel more like a home away from home.

"I think you got it!" Mabel said coming over to give me a hug. "Riley, you are such a good girl." She buried her face in mine.

"Well, Riley, I've got to imagine someone somewhere is missing you pretty badly," Harold said, looking at my face.

"She lives here now," Mabel said quickly and defensively, "they both do."

"How long are we going to be able to keep that bear happy with cereal, Mabel? At some point she's going to need to go outside and forage for food, that's what she does, that's what she's done her entire life."

"You don't know that she could be a circus bear! Maybe she doesn't know how to get food on her own."

"Do you think we're going to be able to get enough for her? Mabel, I love them both as well, but they're not ours to keep."

"What are you going to do Harold, read every name in the white pages until she lets you know that's the right one?"

"I'd... I'd never even thought of that. That's a great idea."

Mabel threw her hands up in the air and walked out.

"Lucky for you girl, the Maine phone book isn't all that big. We're going to take a break though, my throat is a little hoarse and you look tired. Let me get you a cookie or something and then you need to get some sleep." He scratched behind my ears before he got up.

I agreed with Harold, my eyes were indeed getting heavy but I was happy he knew my name. The excitement of the day had begun to wear off, and I was more tired now than I'd been in a long while. That didn't mean I was going to fall asleep before he came back with the promised cookie though. I wished I'd just gone to sleep so that I would not have to hear the pain in Mabel's voice as she talked to her husband in the kitchen.

"They belong here now," she said in hushed tones.

"Someone is missing that dog something fierce Mabel. And the bear is not some circus animal; that is a wild animal. I don't know if I'll ever figure out why she just hasn't mauled us to death and taken our food. I don't know. My guess is it has something to do with Riley. That's a special dog, and she has a powerful influence on those around her."

"She has to stay here, Harold. If she was so important to someone, why did they leave her behind?" she nearly shrieked.

"You of all people know how things are now, Mabel. They must have got split up during an attack, and with those wounds, they may have thought she was dead."

"And she would be if not for us!"

"Just because we helped her, Mabel, doesn't mean we own her."

"If she goes out there she'll die Harold!" With that Mabel left the room.

"I think I'm in the doghouse Riley." He watched her go.

I'd heard about two-legger doghouses but I'd yet to see one. I hoped he would show me his.

I ate the cookie and dozed off, it was a long and restful sleep. When I awoke Harold was sitting on the couch looking over at me.

"You ready Riley?" I got the feeling he hadn't moved. "Good thing Maine isn't too big," he said as he reached into a drawer and pulled out a book. "This has all the names of the people in Maine, well at least the ones with phones. Do you know your owner's name?"

"Of course I do," I barked. "And she doesn't own me, we're a pack."

"Sorry, sorry not own, the name of the person you live with," he clarified when he saw he'd upset me.

I didn't know how this was going to work, Jess wasn't from here, neither was Justin or Justin's sire. What had Alex said? Michael was heading to his pack-mate's home. They would have the same last name of Talbot. I did not know their first names though. Would it be enough? We started the long process of going through the letters. ThornGrip had just awakened for dinner in time to hear our success at finding what Harold called the familial name, however, this joy was short-lived when he told me there were a hundred Talbots in the state. I don't know how many that is, but by Harold's face I thought it was more than seven.

"So how about a first name?" Harold was looking at me.

My head sagged.

"If that gesture means the same in dog as it does in human I'm thinking you don't know it. It's alright girl, you tried. We'll think of something different. In the meantime, I better get something for Tiny over here before she gets upset."

"I'll show him upset." ThornGrip pulled her lips back to expose her wicked teeth."

Harold left the room in a hurry.

"What are you going to do now?" ThornGrip asked.

"I don't know, nothing's changed other than he knows my name and the last name of the family where my Jess has gone. I'm no closer to knowing where they went."

"Are you sure?"

"Do you know something I don't?"

"No, but I bet you do."

"You're starting to sound like the cat."

"Take that back."

233

I did, and quickly, one did not poke a bear lightly.

"I hate to be the one to tell you this bear, but we are down to five boxes of cereal and I'm not so sure I want to be the one that tells you when the fifth is gone."

ThornGrip deftly grabbed the box from Harold's hand.

"I am never going to get used to this," Harold said, looking at his paw, probably to make sure all his fingers were still there. "Mabel, I am going to have to make a supply run soon or our rather large friend is going to become disgruntled with her current living arrangements. Should I make a list?" he asked.

I almost rolled off the couch when he pulled out a small piece of paper and grabbed the tool that made the letters. I barked wildly, Mabel came running in.

"What are you doing to her?" she asked.

"Nothing. I was getting ready to write a list of things we need."

"What's going on Riley?" ThornGrip was getting up.

"On a piece of paper. On a piece of paper!" I shouted excitedly.

"You're making no sense which makes *you* the one that sounds like a cat."

"Sorry, sorry. The male two-legger we were traveling with had the location in a small piece of paper just like Harold has."

"Riley, the zombies ate him."

"They don't eat the fake skins."

"Yes but they chew through them."

"It's a chance I have to take."

"The human letters make no sense to you."

"No not to me, but to him they do."

"Oh. When do we leave?"

"Tomorrow, when the burning disc first comes out."

"Do you think they will give me all the cereal before we leave?"

"I cannot imagine anyone not giving you exactly what you want, ThornGrip."

"This is true."

TWO

"**W**hat has happened to my sister?" Zach wailed.

Ron Talbot had blown a hole the size of a fist through the zombie woman's back but the damage was done. Jess had been bitten several times, and was beginning to choke on her own blood as her lungs filled with the fluid.

"Has the baby been bitten?" Ron shouted to his sister Lyn as he kept his gun trained on the non-moving zombie.

Jess struggled to lean over, she stroked the side of her brother's face and whispered something softly in his ear.

Lyn skirted around the bed and quickly scooped the baby up and away from his sister who fell back on to the bed. After a brief but thorough check she told her brother the blood was not the baby's.

"Get him out of here." Ron flipped the zombie over with the barrel of his gun. Jess's eyes were large as she looked at Ron, her chest rapidly heaving as she fought to breathe in precious oxygen. "I'm so sorry," he told her.

Patches jumped on Jess's stomach and hissed at Ron as he approached.

Ben-Ben was next to the girl, looking from her wounds to her face. "Is she dying Patches?" he asked.

"She will," the cat told him.

"That can't be," he said, licking the girl's arm.

Ron reached out to move Patches away and do what needed to be done before she joined the ranks of the undead. Patches swatted at him, claws extended.

"I understand girl, I do, but it's too late for her. I'll be helping her not to suffer any more."

Patches hissed. A coughing fit tore through Jess, racking her entire body. Globules of blood were forcibly expelled from her mouth and into the air to land heavily on her chest. Her eyes were wide in terror and shock.

Ben-Ben moved up and licked the side of her face, whining softly as he did so. "I love you," he told her before he jumped off the bed and walked out of the room, tail tucked behind and underneath him.

"Where are you going?" Patches caterwauled.

Ben-Ben turned in the doorway. "The sickness is moving through her quickly, she is now more one of them than she is the two-legger we knew."

"What? How can you tell?"

"I can smell death."

Patches looked to Jess's face, which had taken on a serene quality as if the girl had passed over and been reunited with those she loved. Patches knew enough to realize that once those eyes opened back up, there would be no humanity in them whatsoever, and Patches herself would be close enough to become the zombie's next meal.

"You were a brave human and I will miss you, but I am no one's meal." Patches slowly moved off Jess's stomach. She hissed once at Ron then leapt off the bed and joined Ben-Ben.

Ron closed the door, and a few moments later another loud shot tore through the house.

The next day the family stood around the small grave site. Lyn was holding an inconsolable Zach. Ben-Ben circled the woman's feet hoping that he could help comfort the infant. Patches had climbed a tree and was watching the proceedings from a safe distance. Later that day Patches had walked into the room where Lyn was holding the baby; it seemed that neither was in a rush to let the other go.

"How are you doing, baby-that-should-not-talk?"

"My head and my stomach hurt from crying so much. But it is the pain in my heart that is the worst. I miss my sister, I miss my parents, I miss my brother."

Patches' ears perked up at the obvious slight. "And what of the dog?"

"Riley? I miss her but in a different way. She's still alive."

Patches was taken aback. "That's impossible. I watched her die."

"My sister said differently right before she died. I need her back here. We need her back here. We've suffered enough already."

"We don't need her here." She almost added that they were doing fine, but that wasn't the truth, not by a long shot.

"Riley's alive?" Ben-Ben's head was tilted, he was in the doorway.

"Oh no, now the village idiot knows. I'll never hear the end of it," Patches lamented.

"Where is she?" Ben-Ben's tongue was lolling out as he did three

three-sixties in an attempt to locate his friend. "I don't see her and now my stomach doesn't feel so good," he said as he stumbled into the wall.

"She's not here." Zach smiled slightly.

For once Patches was happy for the goofiness of the dog.

"Where then? Is she getting some bacon?" Ben-Ben had finally pulled away from the wall.

"I don't know for sure but I think where we left her would be the best place to look."

"That is a long and dangerous trip, baby. How can you be sure she's alive?"

"Jess told me before she died."

"I loved that human like no other, but she was in pain and shock and on the verge of dying, can you trust anything she may have told you?"

Zach's eyebrows furrowed in anger. "I expected resistance from you. Ben-Ben, can you help Riley find her way home?"

Patches scoffed. "Ben-Ben? Really? That dog couldn't find his own tail."

"It's right here." Ben-Ben began twisting around again. "There it is." He was moving faster. "There it is again." One more time around. "There it is again!"

"Splendid," Patches told him.

"Ben-Ben, can you find the way back to where Riley was?" Zach ignored Patches.

"YES!" he answered quickly. "Just tell me where she is again."

"Oh great cats of all cats, please help me." Patches touched her paw to her forehead in a very human gesture. "I will help Ben-Ben look for Riley, although we both know it will be I who will be doing all the finding while Ben-Ben runs around in circles looking for hidden stores of bacon."

"People hide bacon?" Ben-Ben thought on this for a minute. "I could see why they would do this." He thought on it some more. "No... no, I can't. Why wouldn't they just eat it?"

"Can I leave him here?" Patches asked Zach.

"You need him more than you will admit," Zach replied, sage for his years.

"Only because he runs slower and the zombies will get to him first."

"Zombies?" Ben-Ben looked around, while Zach's eyes brimmed with tears.

"That... that was rude of me," Patches said. "We will leave tomorrow at first light." She strode out of the room.

"Where are we going again?" Ben-Ben asked Zach.

* * *

The sun had just peaked up over a small hill in the distance, brilliant ranges of red burst into a golden halo as Ron's wife Nancy stepped outside to take her guard duty shift. Patches silently slid by, the woman none the wiser for the cat's passing. Ben-Ben nearly sent her sprawling as he ran into Nancy's right leg, knocking it out from under her. If she hadn't grabbed the doorframe, she would have unceremoniously ended up on her buttocks. "Don't let me get in your way Ben-Ben!" Nancy shouted out at the dog. "Hey, where are you going?" she asked as the dog and the cat ran down the steps. The animals ran underneath the very same gap in the fencing that the zombie that had killed Jess had used to get in.

"Do you know what we're doing?" Ben-Ben asked after they'd been walking for a while. "I'm really kind of hungry. I should have eaten more before we left. Whoa, was that a mouse? Do you think we'll find a bacon store? I sure could go for some water."

"Are you going to shut up any time soon?" Patches had turned and was looking at the dog.

"I wasn't planning on it."

"That's what I figured." Patches resumed walking.

"Do you remember that one time I found floor fries in the Alphas' wheeler? Or how about that time I tore the trash open and there was that smelly meat? Oh that was so delicious."

"If I remember correctly you had a stomachache for almost a week."

"I don't know what a week is but eating it was great."

"You kept vomiting all over the floor. I thought the female human was going to send you back to the pound."

"NO!" Ben-Ben had stopped walking, his ears were pulled back and his eyes wide. "No, no, no, I won't go back!"

"No one is sending you back to the pound, dumb-dumb, I'm telling you that the alpha female was so upset she wanted to."

"NO! NO! I won't go back! It's horrible there," he said much more quietly.

"Ok, forget I brought it up."

"I'll try but it won't be easy."

"Bacon."

"Oooh bacon. I love the deliciousness, the chewiness mixed with the crunch of bacon-y goodness."

Patches smiled. 'Dogs are so stupid,' she thought.

Ben-Ben had chattered incessantly for most of the morning and into the afternoon. As the sun began to wane, so did his voice. "Are we going back now?" Ben-Ben was looking to the horizon and the setting sun.

"No, but we're going to have to find a safe place to sleep for the night."

"We had a safe place to sleep the night," Ben-Ben told her.

"We're going to find Riley, remember?"

"I kind of wish she was here now."

"If only so she could make you talk less, then so do I." They walked a little further, the light now beginning to diminish. "This will do." Patches had left the road and was now moving up the overgrown driveway to a house, the front door standing askew within the frame.

"In... in there? But it's dark inside."

"That's good, I'll be able to see them before they can see me."

"Exactly who will you be seeing first before they can see you?"

"Come on Ben-Ben, I need to sleep and so do you. Then we can look for food. I bet there's something in there we can eat."

That was all the persuasion the little dog needed. He passed the cat by and gingerly went up the steps and through the door without so much as looking in either direction.

"The best he can offer me is an early detection system as he gets himself killed." Patches followed him in. There was a smell of death in the house; it was old but it lingered in the shadows like a malignant growth.

"Perhaps upstairs," Patches told Ben-Ben, who had not moved from the center of the room. He seemed to sense the same thing she had. He followed her without saying a word.

The first room they encountered had its door shut, the next was partially open. Patches cautiously peered inside. "It was a girl's room," she said.

Ben-Ben pushed the door the rest of the way open with his nose. The pink shade of the walls looked more like the deep purple of severe bruising in the dying light. "Look at all the stuffed animals she has! Do you think they can still talk?"

"Still talk? They never could."

"I remember Daniel talking to his."

"Probably giving the poor thing its last rites before he pulled its head off."

Ben-Ben gulped. "The bed looks comfortable, do you think they'll mind? Sometimes the two-leggers get mad about me getting on their stuff."

"I don't think these people will mind, and maybe if you hadn't gone outside and stepped around in your own offal and then brought it inside and jumped up on her white couch, she wouldn't have gotten so mad at you."

"Do you think that was why she was so upset?" Ben-Ben got a running start and jumped up onto the bed. "Made it!" he said proudly, looking back down at the cat. "You coming up?" he asked. Every time she moved to a side to jump up, he would move with her, looking down. "Are you? There's plenty of room."

"I would if you'd get out of the way."

Ben-Ben tilted his head at her, in a 'What are you talking about?' pose. "I wish Jess were here," Ben-Ben said after they settled down and got comfortable. Patches said nothing, though she agreed. She was tired and did not wish to start a conversation where the small dog would quickly get around to talking about bacon and Santa. Ben-Ben had rolled onto his back, his four paws sticking straight up, snores making his lips puff out with each breath.

"If I weren't so tired I'd stick a claw in those gums of yours, you slob," Patches said right as she slid into a peaceful sleep. She awoke a couple of hours later, Ben-Ben's nose was touching her head, his hot expelled breath blowing in her ear and down her neck. She was on the verge of telling him off, but when he spoke first, his words nearly froze her.

"Someone's in the house."

Patches was immediately awake, her small heart beating quickly. She listened intently. She may have better reflexes, be more agile and see better at night, but the stupid dog could hear and smell better than she could. She hated to have to rely on him but she could hear nothing, she would have to take his word on it. She could just make out the fur on Ben-Ben's back beginning to bristle.

"Human?" Patches asked.

"No," he answered coldly.

"Animal?"

"No."

"Do they know I'm... we're here?"

"Not yet."

"We need to leave." Patches hopped down off the bed and winced as Ben-Ben followed - not nearly as graceful and twice as loud. "Next time see if you can knock something over."

"Why would I do that?"

"Shh." She went out of the room and to the top of the stairs. She could hear something moving around down there but from where she was she could not see anything. The smell that wafted up was almost a physical entity, something strong enough to strike her down. She had a strange momentary pang of pain for the dog who was experiencing the pungent odor more than herself. She turned back around to check on his status. Ben-Ben was standing at the doorway to the room. "Come on!" she told him.

He shook his head. "I don't want to go down there."

"They'll come up here eventually."

"Maybe if we're real quiet they won't notice."

"And if not, we'll be trapped. Come on Ben-Ben."

He reluctantly walked over to her. Patches turned back and looked down the stairs. A zombie was staring back at her.

"Too late!" she yelled, and sprang back down the hallway leaving a dumbfounded Ben-Ben to wonder what was going on. It only took the first footfall on stairs for him to realize what she was talking about.

Ben-Ben came into the room. "Patches!"

"Under the bed, hurry up!"

The zombie was rapidly climbing the stairs as Ben-Ben tried to shove his head between the bed frame and floor. "I ron't rit," he said with his muzzle squished.

Patches pushed his face away, partly because he was going to give her away but partly because the dog would keep trying to get under and he obviously wasn't going to fit. By the time he figured that out, the zombie would have chewed through his hindquarters.

Ben-Ben got the hint when Patches stuck him with one claw in his sensitive snout.

"Ow, Patches that hurt."

"Go hide!" she hissed.

The bed moved slightly as she realized Ben-Ben had jumped up onto the bed. She was going to tell him to look for someplace better when she saw the feet of the zombie at the doorway. She thought she would be able to get away while the zombie was busy eating the dog. The zombie was not moving, wasn't doing much of anything actually, and then she heard him sniffing. He was sampling the air. He knew something was here, and he would not leave until he found it. One foot shuffled in closer, Patches inched backwards. The zombie moved all the way in. His feet were now halfway under the bed.

'How can he not see the dog?' she thought. The bed moved violently as the zombie tossed things around. She crawled to the edge. She would make a run for it the moment Ben-Ben squealed in pain. That was her plan right up until another set of feet appeared at the doorway. She moved back again. The other zombie came in, apparently to see what his travel buddy was up to and to make sure he wasn't eating anything by himself and not sharing.

Patches stopped moving when she heard the muffled barking of Ben-Ben who must have been under the covers. Both sets of zombie feet were now in front of her; they shuffled back and forth as they tried to get the food that was maddeningly scurrying around. Patches was startled as Ben-Ben landed to the side of her.

"That was fun!" he said as he looked around. When he saw Patches he told her, "Hi, watch this!" He then ran around to the back of the zombies. His mouth opened up in a savage grimace and he sank his teeth deep into the back of the zombie's leg, below the calf and above the back of the foot. He shook his head vigorously and then dug his paws into the rug as he pulled back. A wet popping sound was immediately followed by Ben-Ben falling over, a small piece of white flesh in his mouth. He quickly spat it out and darted out of the way. The zombie he had bitten was now falling over. Its head landed with a heavy thunk as it collided with the floor. It seemed relatively uninjured, and now that it saw new prey, it reached its hands under the bed in an effort to get to Patches.

"Come on cat, the other one hasn't figured out what's going on!" Ben-Ben yipped. Patches was afraid to move, those cold eyes were upon her. If he caught her there would be no mild beating like the humans sometimes did, but rather a slow and torturous death by consumption. "Patches! The other one is wearing heavy fake feet, I don't think I'll be able to do the same thing - we have to go!" Ben-Ben entreated.

"Go!" Patches hissed.

"Not without you. I am not leaving anyone else behind, EVER! Come on!"

Patches low-crawled past the outstretched fingers of the zombie, who watched her as she moved out from under his following eyes.

The other zombie was getting on his knees in an attempt to see what the other was trying to get. Patches and Ben-Ben were halfway down the stairs when they heard the groans of frustration.

"That was close," Ben-Ben said when they got out of the house and had made a run for it. They were now a safe distance away, looking back.

"Th-thank you," Patches said, the words not coming easily. She thought it a victory she'd been able to get them out at all. "What did you do?"

"Something Riley showed me. She said zombies already have a hard time walking because they only have two legs. Remove a small piece from the back of their leg and they fall over!"

"Who knew you were going to be useful? We should get going." Patches had mustered all the gratitude she could for one evening. It was easier to keep moving rather than keep talking.

THREE

ThornGrip had taken matters into her own hands the next morning. She knew exactly where Mabel stored the cereal and she had deftly opened the small food room door to get at it. She'd finished three boxes before Mabel had awoken and come in to the sound of her heavy crunching.

"Oh, so now you're just helping yourself? Get out of my pantry!" she berated her.

"Does she not realize that I am nearly four times her size? I am the ruler of the woods!" ThornGrip roared.

Mabel hit her with a straw ended stick. "Get out! You're making a mess!"

ThornGrip retreated, I laughed at her. "Apparently this isn't the woods."

"I guess not," ThornGrip snuffed, trying to regain her pride. "Are you ready to go? I fear I will unleash my wrath upon the human if we do not leave soon."

"Yes, I do believe you were getting the better of her."

"She is an unnatural being." ThornGrip stepped back as Mabel shook her stick her way.

"You two want out?" Harold asked, going to the front door. This was our ritual in the morning, at least after I told ThornGrip that eliminating her waste inside was frowned upon. The male two-legger had nearly vomited three times, having to pick up the amazing specimen. I'm not entirely sure but it looked roughly the size of Ben-Ben. I missed the little dog but that didn't make me want to get any closer to ThornGrip's waste.

Harold stood on the porch and watched like he was wont to do. I hid behind a bush and took care of what needed to be taken care of. ThornGrip was right in the front, in a clearing. She cared not that every-one could see, in fact, I think she was proud of it.

"I have left a little something for them to remember me by."

"We're coming back."

"We will see which way the river winds Riley," she said, as she looked off into the distance.

I turned and barked 'thanks' to Harold for all he had done for us. I wish I could tell him what we were up to. He would most likely think we were leaving for good, and if by chance ThornGrip's river did unwind away from here, he would never know the reason why we left.

"Hey wait!" Harold called. "Where are you going? Stop. Riley, please, where are you going?"

"To find a way home." Maybe he understood, maybe he didn't, but he stopped halfway across the yard and looked at us.

"Good luck." He waved.

Now it was Mabel's turn. She'd heard her husband yelling and came out to see what was going on. "Wait! Harold where are they going? Stop them!" she pleaded.

"I'm not sure how you expect me to do that," he told her.

"Bear, I'm sorry! You can have all the cereal I promise!" she wailed. "Harold is even going to get more, aren't you Harold?"

"I don't think that is what this is about," he told her.

"Tell them!" She reared on him.

"Fine, I'm going to get more cereal should you come back!"

ThornGrip bellowed her approval back.

"She said thank you." Harold seemed to be questioning himself.

"How do you know? You don't even know when I'm hinting for an anniversary gift and now all of a sudden you're the bear-whisperer?"

"It's the 'calm' you were talking about, I... I think they're going to try and find Riley's home."

"Oh you know that do you? Stop them, they'll get hurt out there!"

"I think they'll be fine, Mabel. Who is going to bother that bear? Good luck!" he shouted.

We were almost out of sight when I turned around. Harold had put a paw around Mabel and was leading her back into the house, her head was upon his shoulder.

"I will miss cereal," ThornGrip told me. "Maybe I'll go back when this is all over."

"Back to the unnatural monster female?"

"Exactly."

"I think she would like that very much."

"Of course she would, I am a pleasure to be around."

247

"Are you sure there is not a little bit of cat somewhere in your bloodline?"

"I could go back now."

"Sorry," I told her as we plunged on. My injuries still ached but it still felt good to be out and walking. To be moving closer to my pack, I had to hope that there was enough of the brave two-legger Alex left that I could bring his small cowhide holder back to Harold, it would have the location to where I needed to go. The next question would be if Mabel would let him do it.

The walking was easy enough, as was the conversation, when it happened. ThornGrip didn't have much to say as we moved, probably wasn't used to it, having mostly been on her own. Her thoughts she kept to herself.

"Smell that?" She pulled up, and I nearly walked into her rump.

"I mostly smell bear," I told her as I backed up. I waited for a moment and took a sampling smell. "Meat, prepared meat."

"Humans."

My mouth salivated, I knew the smell well enough, the two-leggers called it salami and Alpha had shared it with me often when he ate it. I didn't beg but I always made sure I was in his line of sight while he was preparing a sandwich.

ThornGrip's head was swiveling back and forth as she looked for the two-legger. I was just happy it was not zombies, this I knew because they would have no need for salami.

"I do not see him, they are usually as noisy as bear cubs in a pile of fallen leaves." ThornGrip was worried, so much so her rear quarters were shaking.

I'd been around enough two-leggers to share in her distress, although unlike her, I still trusted them for the most part.

"We need to leave here."

"I agree," I told her. "But we need to figure out where they are before we do so." Neither of us moved as we kept scanning. It was me who saw him first. I nudged ThornGrip and told her to look up. The man was sitting in a chair about the height of ThornGrip when she stood on her hind legs, up in a tree. We both could clearly see the fire-stick in his lap. He was looking off to the other side, which was good for us.

"Hunter," ThornGrip said.

"For zombies?"

"Food." She did not take her gaze from him.

"Do two-leggers eat bears?"

"Yes." Her unwavering stare was unnerving.

"Let's go around now that we know where he is."

"Okay," she said, finally turning away. ThornGrip took one step as she twisted, this was followed by the loud crack of a stick as she broke it in two. We froze as the hunter's head turned towards us. We were partially concealed and two-leggers don't have the best eyesight, but hiding ThornGrip behind a tree was like me hiding behind a few blades of grass.

I started barking profusely and moving away from ThornGrip.

"What are you doing you stupid dog?"

"I am taking his attention away from you. He will not use a metal-bee on me."

"Two-leggers are worse than animals, they will eat anything!"

"Even dog?"

"Even dog."

I watched as the hunter raised his fire-stick. I took off just as I heard the loud report of a metal-bee being launched. I darted quickly in and out of trees, metal-bees flew past me and into trees next to me. It was the unearthly roar that made me turn my head. While I was running to get away, ThornGrip had been racing towards the man. She'd stood and swatted her arm out hitting the man and his seat. One of the straps that attached him to the tree had broken and he now hung suspended upside down, the fire-stick lay on the ground out of his reach. He had a wound on his side that did not appear life threatening but certainly painful.

ThornGrip stayed on her back legs for a moment longer then dropped down to all fours, she was now face to face with the man. He was shaking uncontrollably, with the large bear not more than a muzzle length away from him. Her roar tore through the woods, coating the man's face in a thick layer of saliva. Fear-urine poured from him and dropped to the ground.

"What are you going to do?" I asked her, coming back.

"He would have killed you."

"I know that."

"He would have killed me."

"I know that too."

"What would you have me do with him?" she asked.

The man was looking wildly back and forth to me and Thorn-Grip.

"When he gets his fire-stick back he will use it on us," I told her.

The bear reared up and with her massive front paws came down on the weapon repeatedly until, much like the earlier stick, this one snapped in half.

"Now he will not," she said triumphantly. She roared one more time into his face, just to make sure that he got the message. She could have killed him but spared his life instead.

We could hear the man crying as we left.

"That will be a lesson he will not soon forget," ThornGrip said.

"He will forget that lesson, and he was not worthy of receiving it," I replied. The man had undone the one remaining strap and was now on the ground next to his broken fire-stick. He took something from his side. A pang of alarm ran through me as I realized it was a small fire-stick that he was now aiming in our direction. His arm was shaking heavily as he held out the device towards us.

"Fucking turn around!" he screamed. "Who has the power now!" He laughed maniacally.

"Perhaps it is I that should have learned the lesson. Never trust man." ThornGrip turned.

"I'm going to blow both of your fucking heads off." He was wiping away the fluids that poured from his nose and eyes as he cried, the fire-stick still dancing around wildly.

"Do you mean to shoot us or drown us?" ThornGrip asked.

His first shot was nowhere close, I could not tell the path of the bee. The second was much closer. He would not get a third. Zombies had been attracted by all the noise, the first bite tore through his ear and ripped it free from his head. He screamed and turned, attempting to shoot the zombie that was now chewing and swallowing his flesh down. ThornGrip was already walking away, I watched as two more zombies joined in the feeding. The man's cries pierced the silence, and were soon replaced with the smacking of wet meat being pulled from bones and the gnashing of teeth as he was consumed. His eyes settled on mine in an accusatory stare before fading into death.

"It would have been kinder if I had killed him," ThornGrip said after we had safely removed ourselves from the area.

"Do you wish you had?"

"Part of me does, another part is happy that he died slowly and painfully."

"We will have to push on further than normal tonight, the zombies have seen us and once they are done they will come looking for us."

"Perhaps we should have killed them."

I hadn't even thought of that. My first concern had been to get away from there. "That would have been a better idea." Night comes dark and fast in the thick of trees. I could see okay in the dark, nothing like the cat and apparently nothing like a bear. She seemed completely unaffected as we kept going, I stayed right in behind her as she deftly avoided all manner of obstacle. And if for some reason she could not avoid it she just went through it.

"There is a small human dwelling up ahead, do you wish to stop for the night?"

"Are there two-leggers there?" I winced, I was tired and my body was beginning to ache all over. I'm sure ThornGrip would have given me a ride if I'd asked. If we went much further I would have to let my pride go and do just that. To be honest, I do not even think she would have felt me upon her back. I would have been able to bury myself in her thick fur and get a decent nap while she plodded on indifferently.

"Not usually. It is far from everything, I believe it to only be used during times of great need."

"Would now not be considered a time of great need?"

"It is more when the weather turns cold and snow falls. Humans do not seem to like that."

"Neither do I," I answered truthfully.

A few minutes later, ThornGrip half-grunted, half-laughed. "Nor do I."

By the way that ThornGrip was talking I had thought that we would be upon the small home soon. That was not the case, her idea of 'close-by' was much different than mine. Close-by to me meant the edge of Alpha's yard where the infuriating man in the light blue uniform would come almost every day and then cowardly leave things in a small box before scuttling away. I would bark at him savagely, telling him to stop coming by our house without announcing himself. Yes, our 'close-bys' were different, I think I'd fallen asleep more than once as I trailed behind.

I awoke to ThornGrip staring at me. I barked in fright. "Sorry."

"We will have to keep moving," she told me.

"Is it near?" I hoped the change of words would get a better answer out of her.

"It is, but we cannot stay. There are zombies surrounding the structure and humans inside."

I felt bad for those who were trapped, but there was no way to tell if they were even worthy of saving. There was as much a possibility they were good people as there was that they would shoot us once the other threat was over. We could not chance it; unknown two-leggers were just too unpredictable. I had a cramp in my chest wondering if they were anything like my Jess, and if they were I would mourn their loss.

I stopped. "I cannot go any further," I said.

"We will rest soon, I promise."

"That is not it."

"Then what?" she asked, turning to look at me.

"Those two-leggers."

"You want to help them? After everything we both know to be true about two-leggers, you want to help them?"

"What if it were Mabel and Harold?"

"It is not them, they are at their home where they should be."

"Can you be certain that Mabel did not try to follow and is now stuck in that house?"

"It is not them, and I see what you are doing, Riley."

"But it could be someone like them, and that is the problem."

"This is why bears are solitary creatures, we don't have others to help us get into trouble."

"Does this mean you are coming back with me?"

She sighed in resignation. We crept closer to the small home, more than seven zombies surrounded the hut and were banging on the viewers and walls. "I smell something." My nose was lifted to the air.

"How could you not?"

"No, something familiar."

"Zombies would be a familiar smell I am sad to say."

"No beyond that."

"You can smell something beyond that?"

"Sort of. What is your plan?"

Some of the zombies turned as ThornGrip walked towards them. She stood like she had with the hunter, her massive arms swinging back and forth, tearing jaws free from faces, tearing skulls from necks, arms from bodies. It was carnage, here was a beast who had no rival, and not for the first time, I was thankful we were on the same side.

"Join in whenever you wish!" ThornGrip told me, she was a blur of savagery but I could also hear the weariness in her voice. I did what I could while also making sure to stay completely away from her. The problem was that her size was drawing all of the zombies her way. I hobbled those that I could, and when the zombies had left the viewers I barked at the two-leggers inside to let them know that help had come and maybe they should give us aid as well. The male came to the window.

He looked down at me, I do not know which of our eyes grew wider. I now knew why I recognized the smell. It was Icely's man Ned, an enemy whose throat I swore I would tear out if I ever confronted it again. His bitch came to the window as well when he cried out. She paled in an instant.

"Let's go!" I cried to ThornGrip. "There is no one here worth saving."

"Now you tell me," she said as she swatted a zombie, cracking its neck so violently that the head was now resting on its shoulder.

"Wait please!" Ned begged to our retreating forms. Some of the zombies returned back to the window at the sound of his voice. "My daughters are here!"

My first thought was 'good' get rid of the entire pack bloodline.

"Why are you stopping?" ThornGrip asked.

"He has cubs."

"Are they worth saving?"

"Perhaps."

"Riley, I am only doing this because of you. I care little for the affairs of man. We stay and kill the zombies or we leave. Tell me now."

"Cookies!" It was the best expletive word I could think to use. I turned back and chewed through the thigh of the nearest zombie, as he fell over I gripped the side of his head in my jaws and crushed his skull, stilling him instantly.

"That could not taste good." ThornGrip was back and clearing a path to the hut. It was not long before we had taken care of all the zombies in the area. The ground was littered with their parts. I rubbed my muzzle on the ground to remove most of the detritus. I tensed as I heard the hut door open, the barrel of a fire-stick poked through. First it was aimed in the direction of ThornGrip, she was looking the other way at a zombie that was still crawling.

I barked savagely. "You are a treacherous two-legger." I lunged for the door, I hit the plank at nearly full speed pushing it open and Ned to the floor. I came to a rest, my front paws on his chest, my bared teeth inches from his throat, the fire-stick had fallen away. A deep grumble rumbled in my chest, long lines of drool found their way onto his face.

"Oh my God!" Dianna, Ned's mate shrieked. The light behind me had nearly been blocked out. ThornGrip had found her way to the doorway. I looked up to see the female clutching two small females to her breast. They were both crying as well.

"No bullets, no bullets!" Ned begged. "I was going to come out and help, I swear it on my soul!"

"You have no soul!" I placed my teeth against his neck. He at first tensed and then relaxed.

"Do it if you must, just please let my family live, they are all I care about."

"What are you doing?" ThornGrip came up next to me. She growled when she watched the female look over to a wooden bench and a small fire-stick. The woman cried out a little and Ned began to shake.

"This man and his mate worked for another named Icely that imprisoned us and then chased us across the land. He swore that he would leave us alone. I promised him if I ever saw him again that I would rip his throat out."

"Do it then so we can get moving. I do not like the smell of this place. And what of the cubs?"

"They are innocent in all of this."

"They will die if you fulfill your promise."

"What are you doing here?" I pulled away and was now barking into his face, he turned away.

"We're...we're sorry." It was the female that spoke, she let one of her cubs go to put her hand out in front of her. "Please don't hurt him. We're done with Icely, we haven't seen him in months, I swear it. We went back to Vegas and picked up our kids and left. We've been looking for a safe group to join or a safe place to live. We've been moving around ever since. We found this place by chance and thought what safer place could there be. That was until Ned shot a deer a few days ago. That attracted all these zombies, we fought them until we ran out of ammunition. We're starving, my kids are starving, we are dehydrated, we're barely hanging on. Please do not kill him, he dies, and we all will," she pleaded.

"Do you believe her?"

"You understand lying? I thought that was a two-legger trait."

"You should hear male bears during mating season." She laughed.

"I do believe that they will die, I do not know why they are here. It is too close, we were very far from here when we parted ways."

"It would be more merciful to kill them all now than to let them starve or be eaten."

I took a moment to look around the small cabin. There were some cub toys, some blocks and dolls. Things I'd seen Jess and Daniel play with when they were younger. There were also large fake skins the two-leggers used to keep warm. The place had the smell of them throughout. They had been here, I was not sure for how long, but enough that the place was clean and lived in.

"This is the second time I could have killed you," I told Ned as I stepped off his chest. He sat up slowly.

"Thank... thank you. You've saved me and more importantly you saved my family. You didn't need to do that. May I stand?" His hands were out in front of him.

ThornGrip knock the small fire-stick to the floor.

She moved closer to the woman and cubs. She gripped them so tightly they were in danger of being crushed. ThornGrip put her paw up and dug deep grooves into the wood as she pulled the fire-stick down. Ned watched it carefully, it was not more than a stretch away from him to get.

"What will you do?" I asked him as he looked to the stick, then to me and then to ThornGrip.

"I am frightened, maybe more scared then I have ever been in my entire life. But I am telling you I mean you no harm. I will not go for the pistol." He pushed himself up. I moved closer, ready to tear into any part of him necessary to bring him down. He backed up and got closer to his family, stepping in front of them to potentially protect them.

ThornGrip moved in closer and began to sniff him. "Watch this," she told me. "This really scares them." She lowered her head so she was sniffing around his genitalia. Ned didn't look like he could be any more uncomfortable.

"Do you have much opportunity to smell two-legger crotches?" I asked her.

"Do not make me regret helping you." She turned, she was still smiling though.

"Let's go. I would like to find Alex's remains. I just want to be done with this, with all of this."

ThornGrip was now peering into Ned's eyes. She harrumphed and turned. Ned did not move until she was out the door and then he dived for the gun. I was standing by the open door when he grabbed it.

"Ned!" Dianna shouted at him. "How dare you!"

He looked over to her and me, confusion clearly etched in his features.

"That dog just saved your family, does that mean so little to you?" The gun shook in his hand as his mate spoke.

"I'm an idiot," he cried. He put the fire-stick down and slowly approached me. He got down on his knees in front of me. "I owe you dog. I owe you everything. I don't know why I've seen you again. And I'll

255

never be able to repay you properly. I know that. But I promise you that you have a friend for life in all of us. Please forgive me for everything we've done to you." His head bowed down.

I took a step closer and licked the side of his face. "I will accept your promise two-legger. I sense truth in your words and perhaps kindness." And with that I turned and left.

"That was interesting," ThornGrip said once we got back on the path.

"I liked it better when the most interesting thing of the day was when we went to the dog visiting area or when I snuck up on the couch to sleep. I'd even take having to deal with Patches over this constant fighting for survival."

"This is the way of my world. The zombies are a new wrinkle in the grand design but every day is a quest for survival, to find fresh water, to find food, to not be shot. I do like being with Harold and Mabel, it offers an opportunity to take a respite from the rigors of life. Perhaps you dogs have it right."

"The wolves don't see it that way."

"They are elitist jerks who believe themselves to be better than everyone and everything else."

"Oh, I see you have had run-ins with them as well."

"On a few occasions, I have had to let them know that they are not as superior as they wish themselves to be."

"I am sure glad I met you."

"Likewise Riley, besides my young, I did not think that I would like to travel with another."

"I think that you could probably keep going. But I was exhausted before we fought the zombies."

"This is as good a place as any." ThornGrip backed up to a small row of trees, and dropped down. I was mistaken, she was obviously more tired than I assumed as she was fast asleep before I could even begin my spin routine as I looked for the perfect place to lay. It just so happened that the place was right up against ThornGrip's side. I slept peacefully that night. Who wouldn't with a bodyguard that big?

"Comfortable?" she asked as she looked over at me.

"Actually, very," I replied with a big stretch and yawn.

"We are very close to where I found you."

The excitement began to build in me, I was one step closer to reuniting with my pack.

"Let's go!" I jumped up.

"Wrong way," she said as I trotted off into the woods.

The burning disc had not even reached its highest spot when we came out onto the road and to where I had fallen. The zombies that ThornGrip had destroyed were still there, looking worse for the wear.

"Alex was right back there," I said as I bounded back into the woods.

"Be careful." ThornGrip followed after a moment.

I had at first been racing back and forth across the area looking for any trace of Alex, then I slowed and really began to smell around trying to find his scent. It was faint and what little of it there was, was seeping into the ground.

"Anything?" ThornGrip was watching as I began to feel my elation slipping into despair.

"I do not even see any of his fake skins."

"Zombies will eat anything with the scent of meat on it."

"I need his cowhide pouch, ThornGrip! I cannot get back to those I love without it!" I was close to crying.

"Would staying with Harold and Mabel be so bad? And me, of course."

"They are nice two-leggers, and I appreciate their help, but they are not my pack. As for you my giant friend, I was hoping you would join me with the rest of my pack when I got to them. I...I don't know what I'm going to do now."

"I will help you look. I don't know how you could find anything with that small nose anyway."

We spent almost the entire day looking for something, anything that would help us get back to Jess. Besides some torn remnants of the fake skins there was nothing. I was as sad as if my entire pack had died, for I would never see Jess, Zach, Ben-Ben or even the cat again. And even the last one struck a chord of hurt in me.

I was too busy whining, it was ThornGrip that heard it first. She spun to face the new threat.

I bristled and spun with her. Not yet realizing what she'd heard, but by her stance I knew the threat was real and it was dangerous.

"Got some real trouble Riley." I looked over to ThornGrip, her ears were pulled back and her eyes were wide. Her fur bristled up, making her somehow look even bigger. Her lips pulled back revealing teeth nearly three times the size of mine.

"Zombies?" I asked quietly.

She shook her head.

"Is it Ned? I should have killed him when I had the chance."

She shook her head again.

"Hunters? Wolves?"

She just kept shaking her head. I had given up on asking and was just preparing myself the best I could for what was coming, and then I heard it. The meow of a cat but not just any cat. This was THE cat.

"Patches?" I barked.

The woods went deathly silent, this was quickly followed by the frenetic yipping of Ben-Ben. ThornGrip looked over to me as we heard the dog crashing through the woods, sounding like something easily seven times his size.

"Riley, Riley, Riley, Riley!" He would stop to catch his breath and start over. "Riley, Riley, Riley!"

"I take it you know him?" ThornGrip asked.

I nodded, but I was all grin. Ben-Ben came blazing out of the woods and pulled up short when he caught sight of ThornGrip. He looked over to me, unsure what to do although he kept repeating my name. He was now bouncing up and down in place, not yet moving forward.

Out of the side of his mouth, he asked, "Who's your friend Riley?"

"Ben-Ben, this is ThornGrip."

"You are the most beautiful dog I have ever seen!" Ben-Ben told the bear. I just let my head drop.

"I see that his is not the sharpest claw on the paw," ThornGrip said to me.

"No, that's safe to assume," I told her.

"Riley, Riley, Riley!" Ben-Ben decided it was safe enough to come and jump on me, or more possibly, he forgot about ThornGrip. "I missed you so much." He nuzzled my face and licked my jaw and chin.

"I missed you too little dog."

Ben-Ben whispered in my ear. "Soooo who's your friend? She's beautiful. We could make wonderful puppies together."

"I'd like to see you try Ben-Ben."

"Did he just call me a dog again? I am no dog!" ThornGrip roared.

Ben-Ben seemed transfixed. "Your beauty transcends your anger, but perhaps it has clouded your judgment. You have a long muzzle, four legs and a tail. Everything about you says dog."

"I might have to kill him," ThornGrip said.

"I'd understand," I told her.

Ben-Ben had circled around to get a better sniff at ThornGrip.

"You smell back there and I will eat you!" ThornGrip warned.

Ben-Ben reluctantly relented. He was going to wait for a better opportunity. I don't think any of us knew just how quickly he would get the chance.

Patches emerged from the woods. "A bear, Riley, really? Could you perhaps not find a sloth to accompany you?"

I knew part of me loathed the cat and all that she stood for, but a bigger part of me wanted to lick her entire face. Seeing her brought an entire range of emotions, but for the most part I was happy.

"You know this feline?" ThornGrip asked, she nearly spit the words out.

"ThornGrip, this is Patches."

"Patches? Well, that's a name that will strike fear into the hearts of your enemies."

Patches skirted the edge of the clearing. Constantly moving, I would imagine she was sizing up ThornGrip. Although how long one would need to do that before realizing ThornGrip was massive, I didn't know. Didn't seem to concern the cat much though.

"You do realize that the humans make little stuffed animals in your likeness to calm their children before sleep. That sounds fierce," Patches mocked.

"I knew cats were arrogant, I did not realize that stupidity was also one of their main traits."

"Stupid?" Patches hissed. "I will pluck your eyeballs out and leave them for the birds!"

"What? What is going on?" ThornGrip spun. Ben-Ben had circled behind her and was standing on a rock trying to get a better vantage point to smell her.

"You have a strange aroma like nothing I have ever smelled before," Ben-Ben yipped.

"Riley! These are your traveling companions? How did you possibly make it further than your Alpha's home yard? Get away from me dog or I am going to hit you so hard you will be embedded in the tree next to you!"

"She's a feisty one!" Ben-Ben yipped.

"Stop! Everyone stop for a second!" I barked.

"She started it, Riley." Patches was sitting down and making a grand display of licking her extended claws.

"Please," ThornGrip said, making sure that her massive curved claws were shown.

"ThornGrip, these are indeed friends of mine. Ben-Ben has proven more than once he has the heart of our ancestors the wolves without all the arrogance. And the cat has proved her trust and value on more times than I can count. Each and every time that I doubt her, she does more than I could ever hope for. She has been a brave ally and..." I paused. "And an even better friend."

"Touching, really," Patches said snidely.

"I am trying to prevent this situation from getting out of paw," I told her. "ThornGrip saved me when I was dying, if not for her I would have passed over."

"Passed over? Like everyone gets a cookie but you?" Ben-Ben asked.

"Something like that."

"I would have given you my cookie, Riley." Ben-Ben's tail was going fast enough that his back legs were swaying back and forth and he was losing balance. "But would I be able to get another?" He was thinking about missing out.

"I wouldn't take it, Ben-Ben."

"Oh thank goodness. I'm very hungry."

Then it occurred to me. "Why are you here?"

"Is that any way to talk to those who have come to rescue you?"

"Rescue? You seem to have a skewed version of the word, cat. Do we look like we're in trouble?" ThornGrip asked Patches.

"Any time a bear is involved, there's trouble," Patches said. "Always rooting through trash, stuck up in trees, stealing picnic baskets, all manner of malfeasance."

"Do I look like I climb trees?" ThornGrip grumbled.

"I guess you couldn't, the tree would never hold you."

ThornGrip thought it a compliment because it meant her size was immense, but the cat had said it with such derision I'd known she had not meant it as such.

"Jess is dead," Ben-Ben blurted out.

My legs nearly folded in on themselves. The world tilted at a violent angle as I tried to stay standing. "No!"

"The human girl is gone?" ThornGrip asked. Ben-Ben nodded his head. "I am so sorry, Riley."

"I AM more sorry!" Patches jumped in between ThornGrip and me, I suppose to offer some solace, although she must have been fright-

260

ened because the paw she used to soothe me with, her claws were extended and she ended up ripping through my fur and into my side.

"Could you be a little less comforting?" I moved away. "What happened?" I asked, when I finally felt like I could stand without the wobbling effect.

"A zombie snuck in, attacked while we were sleeping. It was horrible, Rileyyyyyyy," Ben-Ben whined. He turned and threw up what little it seemed he'd had for breakfast.

"How is Zach? Is it safe there?"

"The Talbot home is as safe as any place we've ever been, even more so. The zombie displayed a high level of intelligence and was able to get by their defensive barriers. I tried, we tried..." Patches started. "We tried to protect her, to save her. We let our guard down, we thought we were safe, we slept, when we awoke it was too late. The zombie struck."

Ben-Ben was still being sick, and I felt like joining him. His mouth hung open and he was breathing heavily, long strings of drool and bile hung from his teeth.

"Jess is dead. Everything we tried to save has been lost." I was mired in despair.

"The baby-that-should-not-talk is still alive. That is why we are here. He said you were still alive and that it was imperative we found you."

"Yeah, *imperfect* that we find you," Ben-Ben chimed in.

Patches shook her head.

"I have to see him," I said with a rising sense of alarm. He was alone now, his whole pack either dead or away.

"That's why we're here, Riley." It held a note of a condescending tone, but for the cat it was almost negligible.

"What of you ThornGrip?" Her main mission had always been to help gather the information and then go back to Harold and Mabel's.

"I will see you safely to your new home," she replied.

"You don't really need to do that. I'm here now," Patches said.

"Did something speak? I thought I heard a mouse." ThornGrip was looking around.

"I'm going to rip that gigantic nose off your face!" Patches spat.

"Yeah? I'm going to wipe you off the bottom of my paw as if I stepped in scat."

"ENOUGH!" It was Ben-Ben uncharacteristically taking control of the moment. "Jess is dead and Zach is alone. We need to get home," he huffed. "Plus, they have bacon."

261

"I am impressed," ThornGrip said to him.

"Does this mean we are dating?" he asked her.

"For the last time dog, I am not a dog."

"You just keeping telling yourself that." Ben-Ben sidled up to her.

"Lead on Patches," I said.

"As always," she mumbled.

I marveled at the circumstances that would bring such a strange group together. Maybe Mabel was on to something. Was there ever a time when a bear would have befriended a dog? Or even stranger, a dog befriending a cat? I don't care what Patches says, I still think she's lying about her and George being friends.

The mood was mostly somber as we walked. I was still trying to come to terms with the loss of Jess. Sometimes Ben-Ben was the luckiest of us, as he would completely forget and just start yapping like crazy, about bacon and floor fries, or floor anything. Then he would invariably round that off by professing his undying love for ThornGrip.

"Perhaps if you were ten times your size I would entertain the idea," ThornGrip finally relented.

"Don't tell him that," I told her. "Now he's just going to eat more."

"What is the difference from what he already does? Although there is the possibility he will attempt not to eliminate any more so as to conserve weight. This could be fun to watch." Patches was smiling.

"We will need to find shelter soon." ThornGrip was looking at the darkening sky. "I believe it is going to rain tonight."

"We could use you to shield us from the water. It will be a shame that you will get wet but the rest of us will remain dry. The sacrifice of the one for the good of the many."

"On the surface she makes sense, but I still would like to send her airborne," ThornGrip muttered to me when Patches turned back around.

"Why are you whispering?" I asked.

"Her tongue is sharper than my claws, I would not suffer her long if she were not your friend. I am afraid if she heard me she would continue speaking, and it wouldn't matter who knew her, I would just need to make the forest blissfully quiet again."

I knew explicitly what she meant, and I wondered if Patches realized just how close she had been to being wiped out of existence. Probably not, or maybe she did, it wouldn't stop her either way.

The rain that threatened, finally found its way to the ground. We were thoroughly soaked by the time we found a hill with a small outcropping of rocks that afforded us some shelter. Patches was incensed that she was wet, it made her prickly disposition even more caustic. I was afraid for her with us being in such a confined area. She was shaking, at first I thought rage, then I realized it was from the cold. The already small cat looked like a shadow of her former self with her fur clinging to her frame. I don't think I'd ever seen her look so small, diminished almost. Maybe that was why cats hated the water, it showed them for what they really were. A small set of bones with thin meat to hold it together, wrapped in a ball of fur. I knew why the zombies didn't try to eat her, it wouldn't be worth the effort for the meager amount of a meal she would supply.

"What are you smiling about?" she asked.

"Nothing... nothing. I'm just happy to see you guys."

"Yeah, me too. I'm thrilled we came out to get you. I could be in a warm bed right now."

"I love it here." Ben-Ben was completely outside the shelter, snuggled up as close to ThornGrip's belly as she would allow. She'd pushed him away several times and then apparently had just given up. He was a pest, that was for sure, and a persistent one at that.

I had moved close to Patches, not necessarily because I wanted to, I was just hoping to afford her some of my body heat. Much like ThornGrip she had resisted at first but I can be persistent as well, and she was a more willing partner, even if it was self-serving. She was a lot of things, dumb was not one of them.

The night grew darker and the storm more violent, crashes of light in the sky and sheets of rain making visibility near impossible. I more than expected Ben-Ben to come bounding under with me, then I realized he couldn't possibly be safer than where he already was. I fell into a fitful sleep, my head pictures were troubled with Jess screaming as she ran away from a dark blackened zombie. As I tried to run to her, my paws kept getting stuck in mud, the more I struggled the deeper I sank, never able to move faster than Zach's crawling. I barked in rage and impotence as I tried to help her. The zombie just kept chasing her and Jess kept running further and further away. I could only hope she had gotten away, and then I heard her distant screams that let me know she'd finally lost. I awakened with a start. Patches was right in front of me, her eyes shining in the black.

"Bad dream?" she asked.

"Ye...yes," I said, trying to pull away from the disturbing images. "How did you know?"

"You were crying in your sleep."

"I'm sorry."

"It's alright, I was up anyway."

"Bad head pictures too?"

"I have to eliminate."

"Oh."

"Sasquatch over there is in the way though. I wish the rain would stop, I've dried off." She said nothing else as she proceeded to walk over ThornGrip's body. I held my breath expecting the worst.

If ThornGrip noticed at all, she did nothing about it. "That cat is crazy," I said softly, remembering to not cross her... ever.

I nodded off back to sleep, I don't know for how long. I'd been keeping sort of awake, expecting the cat to come back and disturb me but that didn't seem to happen. At least not in the way I'd been thinking. I heard a far off distant mewling, it reminded me of Jess's distant screams as a zombie tore into her.

"Patches!" I shouted.

ThornGrip grunted.

"Something is wrong!" I nudged. "I can hear Patches."

"She get treed by some chipmunks?" ThornGrip asked.

"Maybe she found some bacon she wants to share!"

"If she found bacon she wouldn't share." Patches wasn't much the type to divvy something up.

"It sounds like she's screaming." Ben-Ben was picking up on the alarm.

"Let's find her. I just made a promise I would not lose anyone else in my pack. I should be able to least make it through the night."

I know ThornGrip had meant for me not to hear her mumbled words. "How bad would it be?" She didn't like the cat, but at least she came with me and Ben-Ben.

"Zombies." They were everywhere, if the smell was any indication, yet I could not see them in the inky blackness of the night. The crashing light lit the forest and the horror was shown for what it was. My sense of smell had not let me down, though I wish it had. Zombies flashed in front of me for a moment. ThornGrip grumbled and swung out, an arc of blood erupted from the zombie's side as its innards were spilled onto the ground. Ben-Ben yipped, I caught sight of him as another flash struck. He was alright, his paw had been stepped on, and even now he was paying back the transgressor by ripping into the back of its calf.

I cried out in surprise as a zombie's knee struck my side. Apparently, they were only going on their sense of smell as well, or the knee would have been replaced by a mouth and I would be receiving a bite. I moved to the side and bit, savagely ripping into the calf muscle of the zombie. Lightning crashed again, muscle slithered in my mouth as I pulled it back and away from its host body. Rain slaked down as I released the meat. The zombie fell, and I immediately tore into its skull, careful to stay away from the gnashing teeth.

I looked up when the zombie stilled, waiting for a light flare so that I could attack the next zombie. I could hear Ben-Ben engaged in combat and the deep growlings of ThornGrip as she fought furiously, yet I could see neither, though I had the feeling ThornGrip was closer.

"Behind you Riley!" Patches shouted.

I spun. I heard the clacking of teeth no more than a nose away from my ear. I tilted my head and grabbed the zombie on either side of its cheeks and sunk my teeth deep, my canines scraping against his as I tore through skin and muscle. I pulled him down to the ground so that I could get on his back and bite through the back of his head. With a satisfying crack I got off of the dead zombie.

"Patches where are you?" I was looking around. Another strike of light and I could see the nightmare around me. Five zombies were attacking ThornGrip. Ben-Ben had one zombie down and another was moving in.

"Ben-Ben needs help. I'm in the tree."

"Figures," ThornGrip grunted. "Just like a cat to start trouble and leave."

As I was moving towards Ben-Ben, I heard a sound I hope to never hear again, it was the painful cry of ThornGrip, she'd been bitten, and deeply, by the sound of her wail.

"Ben-Ben?!"

"I'm okay! Could use a bacon treat right now though!" He was panting heavily.

"Coming to help, ThornGrip." I wanted to make sure she didn't swat me away like a bug.

She was enraged, her wail changed to a howl as she struck out. Another crash of light showed her rearing up on her legs. Striking out wildly as zombies began to pile on her. Bodies were being broken against trees with the might of her swings, yet still they came. I started pulling on the backs of the ones on the outer edge of the circle. Tearing through leg and back muscles, not taking the time to kill them, just to remove them from the fray. I would step on and over them as I worked my way closer to my friend.

"Too many!" ThornGrip cried. Another crash of light and I could see the fear in her eyes. Her back was up against the tree and right above her head was Patches. Incredibly, the small animal was preparing to leap.

"What are you doing cat?" I asked, not loud enough for anyone else to hear. Patches could fight, I had no doubt about that. But there was just too much going on, too many ways for her to get hurt. The best place for her was to stay in that tree. What could she possibly do? After tonight I would never doubt her again. I ripped, rendered, tore and chewed, working my way to ThornGrip. When the light blazed I would look up to catch glimpses of Patches as she alit from one zombie head to another, clawing eyeballs out and sinking her sharp teeth into faces as a way to thwart zombies from attacking ThornGrip, and it seemed to be working.

ThornGrip once again had a small clear area in front of her where she could effectively fight back against the press of zombies. I cried out in fright when Ben-Ben came up next to me and barked in my ear.

"Don't worry I'm here now!" he said almost happily. "Miss me?"

I would have told him I had, if my mouth wasn't full of zombie. I tore through a thick thigh muscle, the zombie crashing over to the side. Light blazed again, hope finally found a small place in my heart. The zombies were succumbing to our efforts. The fear in ThornGrip's eyes had been replaced by pure rage, again, and not for the first time, I was thankful we fought on the same side. Patches had wisely once again got back up into the tree. She seemed as calm as if she were waiting for two-leggers to refill her food bowl. She was preening herself.

ThornGrip had got back down on all fours and was now raising her front half and bringing herself down on zombies that had been dropped but were not yet dead. As if the rain had portended the events of the evening, it stopped when the last of the zombies became still. Heavy breath came forth from my mouth, and I could see the smoke-like vapor as the burning disc began to reveal itself. Ben-Ben looked like he had once again knocked over the alpha female while she was preparing what she called tomato sauce. He was covered in a thick layer of red, all that showed cleanly of the dog were his teeth and eyes.

ThornGrip was bleeding from numerous wounds. None appeared fatal they did look painful though. She had her head bowed, blood dripped from her mouth as she also struggled to catch her breath.

"It's okay," Ben-Ben said coming up next to her and licking her face. "I'm here now."

Patches came down from her perch. "They were heading right for you. I tried to lead them as far away as I could before I had to climb for safety."

The more likely story was that Patches was out doing her business and got surrounded then climbed a tree, but I had no desire to call her out on the little lie. She was brave and that was all that mattered. She just does, and always will, look at the world with her own version of events no matter how far they are removed from the truth. To her it is the truth, and maybe that's all that matters.

"You fought valiantly," I told her.

"I know. If you will excuse me, I never got a chance to umm..."

"I understand." I watched her walk away wondering how something so small could be so lethal. I moved closer to ThornGrip and Ben-Ben, he was offering her words of encouragement and sympathy.

"Are you okay?" I asked.

"I'm fine!" Ben-Ben yipped. "I just kissed ThornGrip, we're in love now."

"I'm too tired to push him away," she told me. "I need to wash my wounds out. The pain is lessening but it still hurts."

"Come on, I will help you." Ben-Ben leaned into ThornGrip as if he were somehow going to be able to support her weight. If she collapsed, there would be nothing any or all of us could do to move her.

I swear though, the little guy was trying. He was straining as he pushed against her bulk. I think maybe ThornGrip liked the attention as well, maybe giving him just a tiny fraction of herself so he could feel like he was aiding her. The burning disc was bright, the clouds were moving away, the rain and the crashing noises had stopped. Once we moved away from the dead, the day felt right and full of promise. ThornGrip seemed to have an innate sense of where water was, or maybe she just knew the woods like the backyard that it was for her. She brought us to a small stream that had swelled from the rain. The bear winced and grimaced as she waded in. A small tidal pool of browns and reds swirled away from her heading downstream.

"Can you swim?" Ben-Ben jumped in, I suppose in an effort to save ThornGrip who wasn't going anywhere.

"I think I'll be alright," she told him.

It was a relief to see the real dog under all the remains he'd been bathed in. Ben-Ben swam out to ThornGrip and paddled next to her face. "I'll keep you safe."

"I bet you would," she said tenderly. "Now go back to shore, I will be fine. I would like to clean my wounds a little longer, and you look exhausted."

"Okay," he told her, yet he did not move, except for his paws which were paddling fast.

I took a few steps out into the strong current, only so far that I could dip my head and get my back and shoulders wet. I stayed staring upstream so I did not have to watch what washed away from me. The surprise of the day had to be when I noticed Patches off to my side, she had reluctantly gotten into the water with me.

"Strange day," I said as I looked at her.

"I had pieces of eyeball on me." That was all she said and I understood perfectly. She may have a deep hatred of all things water but no one wants pieces of eyeball on them. When I felt sufficiently clean I waded ashore, followed almost immediately by Patches, who began preening herself instantly, hoping to lick the water off of her. I think ThornGrip could have stayed in the water most of the morning but she knew Ben-Ben would not leave her unattended. He was beginning to flag although he wouldn't say so. He would just start drifting down the stream and then paddle furiously to get back by her face. ThornGrip kept nudging him towards shore as she came towards us. I was laying on my side enjoying the soft grass underneath me and the fact that we'd made it through the night.

"It's not far from here," Patches said not looking over at me.

"Will we make it while the burning disc is out?"

"If you get up I would imagine anything is possible."

Ben-Ben couldn't even make it out of the water without help. ThornGrip had tenderly gripped him around the torso with her mouth and lifted him to shore. He'd fallen asleep before she could place him down.

ThornGrip moved away to shake the excess water from herself before she came back and sat next to Ben-Ben. "He is pretty cute for a dog."

I shifted my eyes to Patches. I knew she had something to say, but for once she held her tongue. Probably the smartest thing she'd ever done in her life.

"Are you alright?" I asked. I hope she knew I meant because of her wounds and not because of her thoughts about Ben-Ben.

"I will be. Thank you Riley, thank you Patches." Patches bowed her head ever so slightly. "I heard Patches speaking. I would very much like to reach our destination before dark. I do not believe I could fight another battle like last night this soon."

"I've known Ben-Ben long enough to realize he's probably going to sleep all day and most of the night," I said.

"I'll carry him."

"You barely look as if you can carry yourself."

"This coming from the dog that cannot pull her head up long enough to look at me."

"You know the way back?" I asked Patches. "You're not going to have Ben-Ben's help."

"Please, that dog couldn't find his beloved bacon if there wasn't a grease trail."

"That's funny." I grunted as I stood.

ThornGrip flashed her extremely large teeth and picked Ben-Ben up. I shuddered thinking that he would be not much more than a snack if she decided to chew. He sighed contentedly yet did not stir, his back legs and head hanging low on either side of ThornGrip's mouth.

We were moving slower and slower as the day wore on, stopping occasionally so ThornGrip could swallow properly without a bundle of fur in her mouth. The burning disc had long since passed overhead and was beginning to hide atop the trees.

"We are close Riley," Patches told me when I looked over to her with a questioning stare.

We were on a two-legger path of hard packed ground, a red four-wheeler up ahead.

"That's Jess's wheeler!" I said excitedly. Until I realized she would never drive it again. I took comfort in the dog that had often times ridden in there with his two-legger friend, the one called Talbot.

ThornGrip pulled up short just as we passed the wheeler and had the two-legger home in sight. She placed Ben-Ben down, he finally awoke.

"Whew, I'm exhausted." He yawned. "Oh look we did it!" He exclaimed happily once he saw the house. "I was so tired I barely remember walking here, it must have been hard because I'm covered in sweat!"

"You don't remember because you slept the entire time. And dogs don't sweat," Patches told him as she swept her tail under her nose.

"Then why am I soaked? I smell good though."

"I will go no further," ThornGrip announced. She was looking up at the house with concern.

"Sure, come on. They have food and they're really nice. I'll share my bed with you," Ben-Ben told her.

"Riley, I know part of your pack is in there but you should retrieve him and leave this place. Something is not right here. I smell, I don't know, something old, something corrupt. It is not a smell that has a place in this world."

I could smell it too if I concentrated on it. I was convinced whatever had caused it was not here at the moment. I would have to take my chances, we could leave before it came back. Zach was most definitely part of my pack and I would do all that I could to protect him. And right now that meant staying with these two-leggers because we would not be able to do the job on our own out there in the wild.

"I...we have to stay," I told ThornGrip. "Zach is too young."

"When you do leave this place, please come find me."

"Where are you going?"

"I think you know. I will miss you Riley, and even you Patches, you are indeed a beast to be taken seriously."

Patches' chest seemed to puff out, although she did her best to pretend ThornGrip's words did not affect her. ThornGrip turned and began to walk down the path. Ben-Ben looked crestfallen.

"Oh." She turned. "One more thing. Ben-Ben, yes, perhaps we would have made beautiful puppies, perhaps a small lick to remember me by."

Ben-Ben yipped his way all the way to her. A tongue the size of a side of beef, swept along Ben-Ben's head and down his entire body.

"I love you," Ben-Ben told her.

"Stay well little one. Perhaps we will meet again."

"I would like that."

We all watched until ThornGrip was no longer in sight. Ben-Ben came back up to myself and Patches.

"Love hurts," he said.

"Sometimes," I replied.

I barked to get the attention of the two-leggers. A male came out on a deck and was looking down at us.

"That is Ron. He is the brother of the one called Michael and he is the uncle to Justin," Patches informed me.

"Oh, I just thought he was the food bearer," Ben-Ben said.

"Are you Riley?" Ron asked as we approached. He got down on one knee and held his hand out for me to smell. "Jess thought you were dead. It's good to have you here girl." He gently rubbed the side of my face and behind my ear, I let him. I liked the smell he gave off. There was sadness in the man but strength as well. "Missed you guys too, what were you thinking running off like that? Come on into the house. I have food and treats for all of you."

"Bacon, bacon, bacon." Ben-Ben zipped inside.

I cautiously walked in and sniffed around. Zach was sitting on the couch.

"That is Nancy, Ron's spouse, holding Zach."

I jumped up onto the couch, placing my head against Zach's. His fat paws gripped either side of my face. "Riley, I have missed you so. Jess is dead." He started crying into my fur. We stayed that way a good long time until he was all cried out.

* * *

ThornGrip took a few moments to decide what she was going to do when she left Riley at the Old One's home. It wasn't much of a debate. She walked through the night not wanting to let a feeling she'd never experienced before creep into her. Loneliness had never been a concern of hers, but the more she was around Riley and the humans, the more she found she liked being around them. She wasn't sure if she'd stay forever, but it would be nice to have a home to come back to. She was at the edge of the yard, standing next to a few trees watching as Harold chopped wood. He stood, his eyes grew wide, and then he placed the flat of his hand up to shield the sun.

"That you, bear?"

ThornGrip stepped out. "It is, but we are going to have to work on you getting my name correct, like you did with Riley."

"Mabel has been in a right sad mood since you two left. Where's Riley? Is she alright?"

ThornGrip snuffed what she hoped was a comforting gesture. It seemed that Harold understood.

"She got home? I'm happy to hear it. I didn't think I'd ever see you again. I told Mabel as much, didn't matter to her, she still made me get as much cereal as I could. Made four trips, got enough cereal to last me a lifetime, but maybe enough for a month with you."

ThornGrip moved closer to Harold.

"That blood? Come on girl, let's get you patched up. There's go-

271

ing to be someone mighty happy to see you."

Harold opened up the back door, Mabel was in the living room. "That was quick. Are you already done?"

"Mabel, you're going to want to come here."

"Did you hurt yourself again?" she asked as she was coming into the kitchen. "Oh, my God!" She dropped her knitting and rushed forward, hugging ThornGrip's head. "I missed you so much."

"I missed you too," ThornGrip told her.

"Riley made it home?"

ThornGrip grunted a contented "Yes."

TARA

...SIX YEARS LATER

By T.M. Williams

From
The Apocalypse: Undead Winter

www.theaccidentalwriter.com
www.theaccidentalwriterblog.com

Dedicated to: Veronica

ONE
Mallory

Washington D.C.

"A word," Christoph said.

"What?"

"It's just a word," he repeated, as if I didn't really hear him.

"What is?"

"Zombie."

I rolled my eyes. "Are you just coming to this conclusion?"

"What else is there to do now?" he asked, as his eyes darted back and forth over the overgrown green vines that had all but consumed the Washington Monument.

I ignored him, hoping he'd shut up.

"This was once all yours," he said, oblivious to my secret wishes. "Yours last."

"More now than ever."

He laughed. A sound I had become too familiar with. "You really think that, don't you?"

I leaned back on my elbows and crossed my feet at the ankles. "Why wouldn't I?"

I was met with silence. We would, or could, sit still for hours. There was nothing to do anymore. We were two of the few left.

"You know what I miss?" I asked Christoph. When he didn't answer, I continued anyway. "I miss being able to kill someone with a conscience."

Christoph rolled his head around his shoulders, stretching his neck.

"Like you," I added.

"You want to kill me?" he asked, his tone dry and his eyes continuing to dart around over the park – landing where the Sylvan Theater Stage once stood. His eyes narrowed and he sat up, his spine straight – alert.

"No. You don't have a conscience. That's my point. I'd like to kill you, but I wouldn't get anything out of it. Like I said, I miss being able to kill someone with a conscience."

"My point was far more interesting than yours."

I leaned my head back and closed my eyes. He was probably right. I couldn't even tell anymore. Everything had become so fucked up. "It's more than just a word," I decided.

"What?"

"Zombie," I said. "It's more than just a word."

"How so?"

"Because, it's what we are."

"Says who?" he asked incredulously.

I sighed. I hated when he became philosophical. He said it was part of him being a poet and I doubted he even knew what that meant anymore. We both knew that if it weren't for the lack of food or any other of the Undead we'd have killed each other long ago. It was each other or nothing, and nothing was much less appealing.

"We've been zombies for what? Six years? And you're just now questioning this?" I asked.

"What else is there to do?"

I grunted. Perhaps nothing *was* better than being with Christoph.

"I know what you're thinking," he said. "You're thinking of killing me."

"I'm always thinking of killing you."

He smiled. "We don't have much time," he said, his eyes still focused on foliage in the distance.

When he stood a moment later, I remained seated. He looked back at me, his eyes narrowed. "Are you just going to sit there?"

I shrugged – a battle of indifference and instinct warred inside me. The hair on my neck rose. "What is it?" I asked – my voice just above a whisper.

"I'm not sure," he said.

"What is it?" I asked again, unused to being on alert anymore. It was a strange feeling. Washington D.C. had become barren and old habits died hard. I didn't want to leave the city – or what was left of it. Besides, we had plenty of food supply in our own make shift *refrigerator*.

Christoph growled at me.

I rolled my eyes and stood up, walking alongside him as we headed toward the theater. The closer we got to the theater, the more alert we both became. Instinct kicked in.

"One of us?" he asked.

"Impossible," I said, though I didn't believe it.

"Not a human. Maybe a wild animal?"

In the distance, I heard a male laughing. I began to sprint toward the sound and felt Christoph on my heels. Because of our speed, we reached the area within seconds. We were fast, but that didn't mean our lungs and heart didn't work overtime. I could hear the blood gurgling in our lungs, a sick raspy sound that I never got used to. Our entire body was made of blood – even our lungs used it instead of air.

The sound of our gurgling breath filled the silence, but my ears could still hear the slight shuffling of feet against old wooden floors that hadn't been used in years. When I heard the laughing again, I turned to Christoph whose expression mirrored my thoughts.

"You've gotta be kidding me," he said.

Danny Ruiz looked about the same as I had seen him about six years prior. At the time, we thought we had witnessed the last of the human deaths. But over the years, I had found more hiding in bunkers. It became a hunt I greatly enjoyed and during one of those hunts I ran into Christoph.

It was more of a convenience to work with Christoph than anything else, but Danny Ruiz was someone neither of us had seen since that last day in the streets of Los Angeles. I just assumed he had been killed, and now seeing him, I sort of wish he had been.

"I thought I'd find you here," Danny said. "Figures you would still think you have some hold over D.C. You realize there's no Presidency anymore, don't you? You personally made sure of that." His red-filled eyes sparkled with mischief, reminding me exactly of what I didn't like about him. I growled instinctively in response.

Christoph folded his arms in front of him, appearing bored.

"What brings you here?" I asked. "You're obviously looking for me."

"Well, it seems you've forgotten one minor detail since this whole mess started."

"What's that?" I sneered.

"That you have a daughter."

There was a beat of silence and then Christoph's boisterous laughter cut into it like a chainsaw.

"Like she gives a shit!" Christoph explained. "Oh, you stupid fool. Are you that bored? Perhaps you have the first stage infection instead."

Danny glared at Christoph. The second infection was a cleverly designed disease that took us all by surprise. When our group had become infected, we thought there was only one epidemic that affected the frontal lobe of the brain, inhibiting any all moral inhibitions – respectfully making all of us act on raw and primal instincts. For some, this was more brutal than others.

However, it wasn't long into the annihilation of the human race that we soon learned two stages of the infection had developed. It was the second type that made the infected like Christoph, Danny, and myself. But the first type was more primal, and short-lived. They were the infected that killed each other maniacally, ripping off limbs, having absolutely no intellectual capacity for anything – except brute murder. It was interesting to watch.

They killed off most of the humans and also most of earth's population, leaving a very small population of the second infection; us plus a few thousand others like us. They call us zombies because the first infection had a similar effect as zombies in movies did -- haggard, dead-like (on the inside and out), as well as dumb.

"What's going on with you two?" Danny said, ignoring Christoph's bellowing. "You make a cute couple."

I narrowed my eyes at Danny and took a step closer to him, a growl forming deep in my chest. Maybe killing someone without a conscience could be fun as well. "My daughter was a human last I heard," I hissed. "And not really sure if any of that matters. Either she died or she became one of us."

"The latter," Danny said – his tone flat.

"And?"

"And," he smiled, his teeth somehow still white and shiny. "She's looking for you."

TWO
Mallory

Danny had just finished explaining how he had stumbled across my daughter. "She definitely takes after you," he said – and it nearly sounded like a compliment. But I knew better.

"How old is she now? Twelve? Thirteen?" Christoph ticked numbers off his fingers.

"She's thirteen," I whispered.

Danny quirked his head to the side, watching me. The thing with Danny was you always needed to be on your guard and I had nearly forgotten that after all these years with Christoph, who was indifferent to the world.

"Is that emotion?" Danny asked me. Christoph snapped around at me. I chuckled. Wouldn't that be something? "So she's creating an army? What for?" I asked.

"I guess she wants to rule the world."

"There's nothing to rule."

"There's you," Christoph said.

"She's holding a grudge. She turned young and is the only child I know of that turned to the second infection and survived."

"No, there's another," Christoph said, his eyes staring off into the distance as if at a distant memory. He shuddered and I realized it must have been a human memory. I didn't care to ask.

"So how does that explain the grudge?"

"Her human memories are few and only consist of you. I guess what she remembers isn't good."

"I was good to her."

"Didn't you murder her father in front of her?" Christoph reminded her.

"I had already turned and he deserved it. And she wasn't in the room anyway." I watched Danny, and still didn't really understand his reasons for telling me. "What's in this for you?"

"I'm bored."

That I could believe. "What else is in it for you?"

283

"She's a child and stupid. She's creating problems that'll completely wipe us off the face of the earth."

"Isn't that the point?"

Danny nodded. "Of the virus they created? Yeah, some biological martyr – the government decided self-sacrificing was the way to go."

"That doesn't make sense," I said.

"You read the journals that were left behind."

"Yeah, but why would they wipe out everyone?"

"Maybe this is our chance of finding out," Christoph remarked.

"So," Danny said, brushing off his pants. "Show me this fancy *refrigerator* of yours."

THREE
Tara McDowell

I had grown used to sleeping in a crouched position. It was really the only way I could sleep since they locked me in this dog cage that was too small for a dog, let alone me.

The guy next to me, whoever he was, had been chanting 'bitch' for what's probably been hours and finally stopped a few minutes ago. Maybe he was dead. Here's hoping.

Somehow, I had survived the worst of it. When all hell broke loose a small group of conspiracy theorists had helped me by giving me shelter in one of their underground bunkers. They were prepared. They had a year's worth of supplies and food for over a 100 people. There was only twenty-five of us – which meant we had four years' worth of food and supplies, not counting expiration dates. I didn't question it.

Don't get me wrong. Regardless of the fact that we were dealing with real-life zombies and an apocalyptic event, I still thought they were nuts. I mean really, what were the odds? They just lucked out – and well, I lucked out with them because I had survived.

By the time we came to the surface I had trained in enough combat and self-sufficiency that I felt ok enough to venture out into the world, whatever was left of it. Twenty-five of us had dwindled down to six. Why? Because humans suck, that's why. Stick a couple dozen of us in a hole in the ground and all hell breaks loose.

You would think being a woman meant I was more susceptible to being a victim being around a bunch of men who no longer had laws governing them. But I used it to my advantage and in the end, they feared me.

Out of the six of us, I had selected only two people to travel with; Heidi and Dick Jr. Not only were they the only competent ones, but they weren't bad company. Then Dick Jr. (that's really his name) lost his mind. Imagine that, he survives in a hell-hole for eighteen months and within two weeks of being on the surface, loses his mind.

That's when me and Heidi were caught by the zombies. They killed her instantly and it wasn't pretty. Apparently there weren't too many humans left and the ones that were became like rare caviar. As soon as they got their hands on her they ripped her from limb to limb – literally ripped her. There were four of them and I managed to kill three of them, completely ignoring the female.

That was my mistake. I assumed because she was the female with three males that she was the weak link. Turns out she just didn't want to get her hands dirty and the three males were merely her minions. That's when she told me she was taking me to her refrigerator.

Hell if I knew what that meant but I knew these creatures enough to know I was fucked. Well, here I am – in the refrigerator. I'd laugh if I weren't the one at the bottom of the food chain.

My neighbor's chanting woke me up from my thoughts, reminding me of the miserable place I was in. "Shut up!" I yelled, already knowing it would do no good.

I should've stayed in the hole.

"How long has he been like that?"

I heard the chocolate-smooth voice deep in the dark corners of this prison we were in. I didn't hear them bring in a new prisoner, so it must've happened while I was asleep.

"A long time," I said, my voice broken. I was thirsty. I never knew thirst before but they had an IV in me giving me just enough fluid to keep me alive. My mouth was burning dry and my throat felt like sandpaper. I could no longer make spit in my mouth to swallow, which would coat it. If I tried, I'd choke instead from the attempt, my mouth rejecting the motion without fluid. Sometimes I thought about chewing off my own wrist just so my mouth wouldn't be so dry. But that would make me like one of them.

"When did you get here?" I asked.

"Just now," he said.

The room was so dark that it felt like I was in a void. His voice at times sounded just inches from my ear and at other times came from the corner where I first heard him.

"How'd they catch you?"

Surprising me, he laughed. I was more startled by the ache I felt from not having heard laughter in years. It didn't matter that it was sinister coming from the stranger.

"Your name is Tara," he said, drawing out my name.

"How do you know my name?"

They never spoke to us to give us any information. The fact that he knew my name meant only one thing.

"You know why," he said, confirming my fear.

Instinctively, I cowered within myself. A true feat considering the tight space I was already in.

"What do you want from me?" I asked. "You guys have kept me locked in here longer than the others."

"Yes, I heard."

"You heard?" Was he new? Different from the others?

"Yes, I was just paying a visit and was told that Mallory kept you – crazy bitch that she is. I just thought it was strange that it happened to be you – makes things a bit easier for me."

"I don't know what you're talking about," I said, shifting slightly and attempting to move my weight as my hip cramped painfully. I hissed involuntarily in pain.

"You're in pain," the man said.

"Isn't that the point?" I didn't care if I angered him. I was tired.

"I suppose it is."

"What do you want from me?" My voice broke.

"You don't remember me, do you?" the stranger asked.

"I can't see you," I reminded him, getting irritated with each passing second.

He tsk'd. A split second later, the room was bathed in a blinding light. I cried out in pain as my eyes burned from the sudden brightness. I squeezed my eyes shut until the pain subsided, then slightly opened one eye until I adjusted to the light. Finally, I had both eyes open enough to see my surroundings for the first time. It was strange. I knew my eyes should water from the light but I was so dehydrated that no tears came, causing a continuous burning and itching.

Eventually, I looked up at the stranger. Underneath the scaly, copper-stained skin and black pools of eyes, I recognized the man, though I couldn't be sure from where. At one time, he had dark Latin features and as I studied them, realization dawned on me.

"I know you," I admitted.

His eyes were wild, shifting constantly. There wasn't a trace of humanity left in him. "Dr. McDowell," he said, reminding me of a name I haven't been called in years – lost forever because of the outbreak, because of people like him.

"I'm no doctor anymore, just like you aren't either, Danny."

He smiled, revealing pearly white teeth – a contrast to his darkness. I thought of all the flesh of innocent victims those teeth had torn into and shuddered.

"I'm a doctor in my own way," he said and I didn't want to know what he meant. Besides, I had a feeling I was going to find out regardless.

He approached my cage and I remained motionless, my eyes slowly beginning to adjust to the light.

"How long have I been here?" I asked.

He pursed his lips and took a deep breath. Instead of answering me, he closed his eyes, a slight smile spreading on his mouth. I was no threat to him. That's when the idea dawned on me. I never said it was a good idea, just an idea. Besides, what did I have to lose?

"I suppose you're a doctor in your own way," I said. "But, I'm sure you haven't accomplished much in your new form."

His eyes shot open, startling me. No matter how many times I had seen them, I never got used to the pools of blood in place of the iris and the whites of the eyes – a red so deep it was ebony unless you see them up close, like I was doing right now. Something, most people never lived through. In fact, I'm sure I was one of the few – though, at the time, I thought I was seconds away from dying. I had no idea then what would become of me and there was nothing that could've ever prepared me for my short future.

He laughed, though there was no humor. "Accomplished much?" he repeated. "You have no idea what I've accomplished."

"Oh, I'm sure I do. I know you pretty well, Danny. You were always the over-achiever – though not achieving anything, really. Poor, Mexican boy who made it all the way to the top – all – by – himself."

He growled. A low, guttural, liquid filled growl – reminding me just how little of a human body was left in these monsters.

"I mean, shit, you don't even know Spanish anymore. Do you?" I pressed on, seeing the anger visible in his features – nearly tasting it in the air.

A breath later I was hurtling through the air, still inside my cage. The room spun in a blur and I braced myself as best as I could, hoping the crash would kill me instantly. I felt the impact against the wall and it was worse than I had expected. Pain shot through me, taking my breath. I wasn't sure if I had the air knocked out of me or if I couldn't breathe because of the shockwaves of hurt I felt. My vision blackened and then turned blinding white as I lost all sense of my self. At that point, I didn't care what happened. I just wanted the agony to end.

I thought it couldn't get worse until I felt my flesh rip. I always assumed that when something that traumatic happens to our body that our brain does something blissful, like make us pass out. No, I didn't pass out. I felt my flesh tear. It was like being stuck with a branding iron but actually feeling the skin blister and singe. I'm sure I screamed. Mentally, I was begging for my world to end, to pass out, for anything to happen.

Through the haze I managed to catch a final glimpse of another cage being thrown at me, a man crouched inside. I couldn't tell if he was dead or alive, but I knew it was the end for me.

Finally, blissfully, darkness wrapped me like a warm blanket.

* * *

"Tara?"

My nose stung and eyes watered. There was a second, perhaps a second and a half where my brain had yet to catch up with the fire consuming me.

"Tara?"

I couldn't move. Even if I had the ability to move I couldn't. The pain encroached on every fiber of my being.

"I think you'll want this," he whispered, far too close to my ears.

I opened one crusted eye, the other too swollen to see through. Danny Ruiz spun a syringe between his fingers as if they were poker chips. I opened my mouth to respond but the taste of blood and the strange sensation inside my mouth stopped me.

"It's Morphine," he said. "A lot of it too. Not enough to kill you, of course. But enough to make you feel pretty damn good. You should see yourself."

He leaned in and I felt the cold steel of the needle against my arm. Stupidly, I wondered if he would at least swab my arm with alcohol. Within seconds, the drug spread through my body. He was right, I felt pretty damn good.

"Actually," he continued – as if I had responded to him before. "You look pretty shitty, but I don't think anything's broken. You're missing a part of your shoulder, but I'm sure it'll get better. I already bandaged you up. Aren't I nice?"

"No," I whispered, my voice sounding completely foreign to me.

"How do you feel?" he asked.

"Fantath-ic." I had a strange lisp.

"I was going to kill you."

"Tho, why didn't you?" I moved my tongue around in my mouth, wondering why it wasn't cooperating with my words.

"Curiosity got the best of me."

"I thought tho."

"That was your plan?" he asked.

My eyelids grew heavier and heavier as the Morphine dulled my pain and brought on a strange calm that made me feel euphoric. "Yeth."

"Well, it was a good plan," Danny said. "You have my attention."

FOUR
Mallory

"You fucked her up," I said. Not that it mattered.

Christoph rubbed his chin and then sighed.

"What's your problem?" I asked.

He shrugged.

"Are we boring you?" I pressed.

"A bit. What are we doing, anyway?"

Good question. I turned to Danny, who had been smiling for the last twenty minutes. After giving Tara a strong dose of morphine and a sedative, he had been on cloud nine.

"She has a point," he said. As if I knew what he was talking about.

"And that would be?"

"We've been able to recreate nearly every disease in history, except this one."

"What would be the point?" Christoph asked as he leaned against a table.

"A cure?"

Danny laughed. "No, nothing that stupid."

"Then?" I asked.

"Because the zombie virus was man-made. Of course, it was never meant to get this far. But since when is anything executed the way it's planned?" Danny asked.

I stared at him a long while. So did Christoph. We didn't speak after that. Not until Tara finally woke up. I wasn't sure what Danny was up to, and didn't really care. I wanted to find my daughter before she found me. I assumed she was pretty angry with me and my instincts kicked into high gear.

Eliminate her.

It's all I could think of.

"Where do you think your maternal instincts went?" Christoph asked as we waited on Danny and Tara to join us outside. Sometimes I wondered if our new form gave Christoph some mind reading abilities.

"Don't look at me like that," he said. "The second Danny told you about your daughter I could tell you went into hunting mode. I'm not a father and doubted I would've been a good one anyway." He smiled. "Not that you're a good mother," Christoph added. I didn't disagree with him.

"I don't know," I admitted. "I'm not sure I ever really had those instincts."

"What are you two talking about?" Danny asked, stepping out onto the top of the porch with Tara under his arm. It looked as if he was at a bar carrying a drunken girlfriend.

"What did you give her?" I asked.

"Apparently too much sedative. I think it had something to do with the fact that you guys haven't been feeding any of them."

"Now we leave?" I asked again.

Danny nodded, half-dragging Tara with him.

"This is going to be a long walk," Christoph said, reflecting my thoughts.

"I have a car."

FIVE
TARA

I was on the floor. It's strange how comfortable a floor can feel when you're on morphine and not bounded inside a cage. I could move, a little. When I did, I was surprised that I wasn't rocked with pain.

I love Morphine. I didn't realize I did until that moment, of course. If I ever managed to survive and this apocalypse managed to go away and zombies didn't run the earth anymore and I could have a kid, I would name it Morphine. That's how much I love Morphine.

Apparently, I loved it so much that I was chanting it over and over again. Danny Ruiz must've thought I needed more because he shot me up with another dose, sending me further into bliss.

I love Danny Ruiz.

Groaning interrupted my mental love confession and I momentarily believed it was my own sound -- until I realized with conviction that I didn't sound like a dude.

"Hello?" I asked.

No answer.

"To the dude who just groaned. Are you there?" I had a determination to figure out who was there, and in the midst of my search, I realized my recent lisp was also absent. I had bit into my tongue earlier after upsetting my new love crush, and my tongue now felt more like raw eggs in my mouth.

A sliver of light shone from underneath the door to the room, enough for me to make out dark shapes. There were six empty cages and one malformed one against the wall. The long, willowy figure of a man was

292

half sprawled outside the cage, the other half of his body still inside. It was then I remembered the cage and the man inside being used as a throwing weapon when Danny launched them at me earlier, sending me to what I was sure was my certain death.

I army-crawled to the figure, my body still not fully cooperating – whether it was from the drugs or damage inflicted, I wasn't sure. He groaned again when I was inches from him, a desperate sound, like that made when someone was unconscious. Good for him. He was unconscious and by the looks of it, on the brink of death. Each slow rise and fall of his chest seemed to be his last.

"Sorry, buddy," I said. "But it's probably better this way, anyway."

The light in the room switched on, but it didn't have the same blinding effect as before.

"Time to go," I heard Danny said.

"Yes, Dr. Ruiz."

I got to all fours when the room began to spin and then dropped down again.

"We're going to have to feed you if you're going to be any good to me." He lifted me with ease. "I'm surprised by you Tara."

"Dare I ask why?"

"What happened to the sweet veterinarian I knew?"

I ignored his jibe.

"The old you would've done everything in her power to help that man in there, even if that meant risking your own life. You were always stupid with your affection for animals."

"He's not an animal."

"No, but you were always the first to help others, to a fault. I never understood it."

"You're a doctor, how could you not understand it?" Every word I spoke was painful and I felt like I couldn't take a deep breath.

"I did it for the money and prestige."

"How nice."

"Hey, I gave you Morphine, when I didn't need to."

Danny dragged me out of the room and onto the front porch. The sun's rays felt like a blanket of happiness. I either was really high or we were in a car. It had been five or six years since I had seen a functioning car, let alone ride in one, but I was pretty sure that was what the rumbling was below me. But my eyelids grew too heavy for me to contemplate much longer and sleep took me once again.

When I woke it had felt like I had been sleeping for days and whatever relief I had felt from the Morphine was long gone. Every inch of my body ached and my ribs were tender to the touch.

"I'm guessing you have two broken ribs," Danny said.

"No shit." I could barely see out the dirty window, but what I could see was nothing new -- old buildings slowly being taken over by nature again. It was a relief, in a way, knowing that after we were long gone that nature would take its claim back on what we had stolen.

"It's inevitable," I said.

"What's that?" Danny sat in the backseat with me and the two strangers sat in the front. Neither gave any indication that they were interested in our conversation. How I had ended up in a car with three zombies was beyond me.

"You guys will die out."

"You don't think you will?" Danny said, without missing a beat.

I shrugged. "If we do, then you definitely do. If we don't, then it's because we outlasted you."

"Well I guess we'll need to change that, won't we?"

I didn't respond further. Why piss him off again? He expected me to help him. What choice did I have?

"Where are we going?" I said after a few minutes.

"Chicago," the man in the front said as Danny handed me a bag.

I looked inside and was surprised by the contents. "Take it slow," Danny said, "Or you'll vomit it all up and there's no more where that came from."

I started with the water. I tried to take it slow, but my body was desperate for more. The cool liquid coated my aching stomach, causing strange and painful contractions – as if my body never expected to feel that again and rejected the nourishment.

After drinking half of the large bottle I stopped, realization dawning on me that I might not get water again. There were two bags of potato chips and a can of soup with a pull back lid – cold, of course. I ate the first bag of chips and drank down every drop of the soup. Never had I tasted anything so wonderful. I was sure I'd be sick soon but I didn't care, it was worth it.

Like a drug, the food had made my eyes droop again. I knew it was mostly due to how weak I was, but I also knew that a large part of it was that I finally had some food and water in me.

My mouth ached from my torn tongue, but I didn't care. As I drifted off to sleep the taste of salt still lingered and all I could think was that no matter what happened now, I would die happy. My belly rumbled in a mix of pleasure and pain, confused by the sudden change and food it had craved for so long.

When I awoke hours later the weather had drastically changed with sideways rain pounding the roof and windows of our questionable car. Danny was in the front seat now, his eyes narrowed to thin slits as he struggled to see through the rain. Even his better vision couldn't help him on roads that hadn't been maintained in years.

The only other woman in the car sat to my left, looking bored. I realized then who she was -- the former First Lady of the United States. Or would she still consider herself the First Lady?

"How far are we?"

"Just a few hours," Danny said.

My stomach churned, hungry again. Mallory looked like she wanted to kill me for the bothersome sound. Fortunately, or unfortunately, depending on how one likes to see things, something hit our car and caused Danny to lose control. The road being covered in fallen leaves and debris from years of neglect didn't help much, giving us the effect of driving on an ice-skating rink instead of on a paved highway.

I held onto the back of Christoph's seat, gripping for dear life. I imagined my other three car-mates relaxed and cool as a cucumber. But, of course, I couldn't check since we were sliding sideways down the road, threatening to flip over. The inertia made my insides, especially my ribs, scream in pain.

Finally, miraculously, we came to a stop – still upright.

"What the fuck?" Mallory asked.

I wondered if she was always so eloquent or if the vernacular of a zombie was just more abrasive. But, then again, she was a politician – weren't they always zombies? I chuckled at my own lame joke, causing three pairs of blood-pooled eyes to look at me all at once.

Trying to avoid being the sole focus of any zombie, I quickly turned away and rubbed my arms.

"Someone hit us," Danny said.

I quickly turned until a sharp pain through my body reminded me that I had cracked ribs. "Who hit us?" I asked.

"We're about to find out," Christoph responded as he opened his door. Mallory was halfway out the door when she said loud enough for us to hear, "It's Katelyn."

"Who's Katelyn?" I asked.

"My stupid daughter."

I got out of the car. Not because I was interested in seeing a zombie battle, but because I realized that this might be the only opportunity I ever have for escape. Unfortunately, Danny was one step ahead of my thought process and was standing next to me, his cold hand wrapped around my aching arm.

"Don't do anything stupid," he said.

"Why would I do that?"

Fifty yards down the road, behind our long trail of skid-marks that reminded me of a Sidewinder snake, stood a young girl still in her teens, surrounded by about forty zombies. Fuck.

Normally, I would've taken solace in the fact that this young girl was still obviously human, except that the zombies surrounding her were standing like her own personal army. She might as well have been one of them. Besides, what chance did two humans have against this army of the Un-dead?

Surprisingly, Mallory walked toward her daughter completely at ease -- perhaps she couldn't see the look of death her daughter shot in her direction. Pushed along, I followed behind Christoph with Danny on my heels.

"Hello, Mama," Katelyn said.

"You don't want to kill us," Mallory responded.

Reflexively, I laughed. Remember what I said earlier about not wanting to be the center of focus of any zombie? I was now the center of focus of dozens plus Katelyn, who raised her eyebrows at me.

"Why did you bring another human?" she asked, ignoring her mother's bold statement.

"She's part of the reason you don't want to kill us," Mallory said, sounding like a politician. "You see, she's a doctor as well and so is Danny and they can find a cure."

It was Katelyn's turn to laugh. "What makes you think I care about a cure?"

"Don't you?" Mallory asked. "Isn't that what you want? For things to go back to normal?"

"Normal? You thought things were normal? You and dad were both fucking other people, literally, and the rest of the world, figuratively."

Even though Katelyn was still a young teenager, she had years on her. Some people would call her an old soul but it was more because she had survived the last six years and somehow formed an army of zombies ready to kill their own.

"We could also recreate the virus," Danny said.

Katelyn raised her eyebrows and in that instant, I saw her as the child I remembered from before the earth went to shit. She was a demure and timid child, always clutching onto her fathers hand when he wasn't speaking. In photographs and on television appearances she was with him, not her mother. One of the last photographs the media focused on before everything shifted to the zombies was Katelyn holding her new puppy in one hand with her other arm wrapped around her father, the President of the United States.

It was that fatherly figure that won him the presidency. No one cared about the First Lady until they had become comfortable in the White House. But in that last photograph, Mallory stood to the side with her arms crossed and all of a sudden the world woke up one day and realized that the First Lady had never been seen holding her own daughter or being affectionate. All at once, the world deemed Mallory a horrible mother.

No wonder Katelyn formed a zombie army to kill her mother. Rumor went around that Mallory had killed the President almost immediately, though it was just a rumor. But the look on Katelyn's face told me one thing; she knew that rumor to be the truth.

I saw that picture of Katelyn in my head, although today she was a few inches taller and her once perfect brunette bob now reached the middle of her back, wisps flying around her dirt stained face and bright eyes. She looked almost the same, except that she couldn't look any different. Since that photograph, Katelyn had lived several lives, surviving – somehow – each one.

"She's going to kill us," I whispered to Danny.

He seemed to have come to the same conclusion because he had taken a few steps back while I was reminiscing. How I had ended up in a position where I was taking refuge by being near a zombie was beyond me. But hey, one does what they need to.

"How can you recreate the virus?" Katelyn asked to both Danny and me. Not missing an opportunity, Danny responded. "The virus was formed in the frontal cortex of the brain, where we lose our inhibitions, essentially. But, as you can see by where you stand now, sometimes we don't need a virus to do that."

She crossed her arms and looked at me. "Is this true?"

"It's a plausible theory."

"What?" she asked, reminding me that even in all her street wisdom she had acquired, she was still a teenager – a teenager who hadn't gone to school since she was a child.

"It's possible," I said.

She pursed her lips together and took a deep breath. "So you need a lab and all that?"

"We would."

"Ok," was all she said.

SIX
TARA

"Are you going to kill her?" I asked Mallory.

She shrugged. We were following the troop of cars back to a lab and she was back in the driver's seat. Well, they were calling it a lab but it was an empty warehouse.

"I'll never understand it," I said to no one in particular.

Mallory glanced in the rearview mirror at me for a brief moment.

"She's always been a callous bitch," Danny said.

"And you? What's your excuse?" I turned in my seat to face him. Christoph remained silent in the passenger seat as always.

"My excuse?"

"This is all just some grand experiment? That's all you care about?"

"We don't have a conscience," Danny said.

"That's it? That's your explanation?"

"You're annoying me."

I turned back in my seat and faced forward, crossing my arms. We pulled up to the warehouse moments later.

To my relief, the zombie army didn't follow us inside the warehouse.

SEVEN
MALLORY

"A lioness will risk her life every time to protect her cubs. It's ingrained in her, an instinct," Danny said.

Christoph crossed his arms and stood in the furthest corner of the small room, tucked inside the eastern side of the warehouse. He kept a distance from all of us, including me, even though we had walked side by side for years as companions. It was clear that his concern had always been for himself, and with my life in jeopardy now, he was slowly distancing himself.

I winked at him when he caught me watching him. He smiled back before responding to Danny. "That instinct is missing in our First Lady," he said.

My daughter hopped up on a counter and Tara stood between Danny and her, as if unsure of who would protect her more. Before today, I would've laughed at the notion of a human having any power, but her ability to command a zombie army meant she had something that I lacked. My own daughter.

Tara leaned with her hand on her ribs and I was half-tempted to kick her just to see a reaction.

"Why do you think that is?" Danny asked, ever the doctor.

"A lioness protects her offspring because the instinct is to continue her line. Reproducing is our most core instinct," Christoph said, engaging in Danny's conversation. I half-listened, already knowing how fucked up I was before turning.

"And now, we're supposedly acting on our most primal instincts?" Danny asked as he paced.

"It seems you're trying to reproduce in a way," I pointed out. "With this whole dumb experiment."

"I'm just bored," Danny said and shrugged.

"I thought you were looking for the cure?" Katelyn said, her eyebrows knitting together.

Danny spoke slowly, as if Katelyn was five years old, "In order to find a cure, we need to find the cause."

"That's dumb," she said, and a flash of memory reminded me of when she was a child. When she didn't like something she'd say the exact same thing and it was usually followed by a temper tantrum that always got her stupid father to bend her way.

"Do you have a better idea?" Tara asked. "Because if you do, I'm all ears. We can't continue this way," she said and I wondered if she meant all of us, or them as humans.

Katelyn took a deep breath and exhaled slowly. She narrowed her eyes at Tara, as if noticing the girl for the first time. "Okay," she finally said.

In the blink of an eye, Danny had Katelyn pressed against a wall, her feet dangling inches above the floor. "Seal that door," he hissed. "Make sure none of those shits get in."

Katelyn turned an ugly shade of blue. I was so caught up in the realization that my daughter was dying before me and I had absolutely no feelings about it that it took Christoph yelling to bring me out. "Snap out of it Mallory!"

I still took my time walking to the door, mostly because now I wanted to kill Christoph for yelling at me. I turned the lock on the door, knowing it was fruitless in keeping an army of our kind out. But, it would give us enough time to escape if we needed it.

"What are you doing?" Tara asked.

"Keeping little miss bitch here quiet," Danny responded.

"I was wondering if you had gone soft," Christoph asked.

Danny let go and Katelyn crumbled to the floor in a heap, gasping for breath. A bruise was already forming around her neck.

"You really don't care, do you?" Tara asked me. She was brave for questioning me, I'll give her that.

I ignored her and watched as Katelyn slowly regained her composure.

"You know you guys will never get out of here alive now, don't you?"

"I'll worry about that later," Danny said. "Because I have an idea."

"Do tell," I said.

"Well, you my dear, are living proof that we were fucked up long before we became zombies. Some of us were just further from the cusp than others." Christoph laughed and for the time being I ignored him. "And I think that the drug the 'powers that be' created backfired for exactly that reason."

"What do you mean?" Tara asked.

Even though she was just a veterinarian, based on what I witnessed, she was capable of far more. Of course, she probably thought she was doing a noble job.

"Yeah, Dr. Ruiz, what *do* you mean?" I asked.

"I have a theory," he said. "That the apple doesn't fall far from tree."

"Okay, and?" I pressed on, getting annoyed.

"Well, there were certain diseases that individuals were predisposed to developing while others could carry the disease but it would never develop."

"Yeah, but those weren't man-made like this one," Tara said.

"Right. But even the man-made ones didn't develop the way they expected."

"Who is 'they,' anyway?" Christoph asked.

"You think I know?" Danny replied, growling through the words. "Who gives a shit who made it?"

I couldn't help but smile.

"But for your theory to make sense, we all need to have been implanted with the virus," Tara said and then her eyes widened. Whatever Danny was onto, Tara had clearly caught on. But by the looks of everyone else, we were all still in the dark.

"Care to bring us in on your little love affair?" I asked.

"Somehow, we were all given the virus. Some of us reacted just the way they wanted us to. Others went off the deep end and became your typical raging blood-thirsty lunatics. But they died off quickly because they were easy targets, by both our kind and whatever humans were left. Something must have activated that virus, and I think I know what it is," Danny said. He pointedly looked at Katelyn – who managed to get up to a sitting position and leaned against a wall. "What are you going to do?" she asked, sounding like a little girl.

"He's going to push you to the brink of insanity," Tara whispered. "to see if he can activate the dormant gene."

Katelyn laughed. "Fuck off," she whispered.

"It won't be that bad," Danny said and reached his hand in his pocket, pulling out a gun.

Tara's eyes widened at the sight. "Where'd you get that from?"

"I've had it this whole time."

There were many things I expected to happen next. What I didn't expect to happen was him handing the gun to Katelyn.

"Uh," Christoph muttered, taking a step back sideways toward the door.

"You wanted to kill your mother," Danny said. "Now's your chance."

"What's going on?" Tara said, her voice an octave higher than normal.

I crossed my arms in front of my chest. "This is stupid."

Katelyn took the gun from Danny's hand, gripping it tightly.

"Don't do this," Tara pleaded with Katelyn.

Katelyn raised the gun in her hand and pointed it at me. The look in her eyes was cold and calculated. My daughter. Other than the blood filled darkness that she lacked, she was one of us already.

"That's right," Danny said, encouraging her.

I was mesmerized. Never had a gun been pointed directly at me. For that matter, never had I imagined dying anytime soon. There were so few left on earth that I thought Christoph and I would have a stand-off from boredom first.

I was tempted to take my eyes off of Katelyn and her weapon to see what Christoph thought of all of this. "Funny," I whispered. "I thought I would've outlived Christoph."

He grunted in response, though I didn't know if it was an admission or disagreement.

"Katelyn, please," Tara pleaded when there was a crash against the door.

"Seems like my little army is growing bored," Katelyn said when a second crash hit the adjacent wall. They were on all sides and I knew that either I was dying at the hands of my daughter's gun or getting ripped to shreds by the restless zombie army outside the thin walls.

"Seems like you sealed your own fate as well, Danny," I reminded him as the restlessness outside grew so loud I had to yell at him to be heard.

"It'll be worth it," he said, smiling.

Tara began pacing. "Katelyn, please."

"You were supposed to find a cure," Katelyn said to her. "How's that going to happen now? Look at her," Katelyn waved at me with her free hand. "She's not curable."

I couldn't disagree with her. "She has a point," I said to Danny. "So perhaps we should end this experiment?"

"What makes you think we could even find a cure?" I asked Katelyn.

"Shut up!" she yelled back at me.

"You really think that someone like Danny Ruiz can find a cure? Were you really that stupid?"

"Why shouldn't he?" Tara asked. When I turned to face her, her eyes glistened with unshed tears. It was an emotion I hadn't had since the day I turned – the day I tasted blood for the first time so many years ago and yet, it still felt like yesterday. "Why shouldn't he?" she repeated. "Your kind is dying off as well. Returning to humanity is the only hope we have."

I laughed. "Hope?"

Katelyn chewed on the corner of her lip nervously and the gun began to shake in her hand - perhaps a little from the weight of it, but perhaps mostly from me. I smiled at her.

"You're a bitch," she said and I shrugged.

"One doesn't become First Lady without being a bitch, my dear."

"You're not the First Lady anymore," she said. "You're a no one. You're not even human."

In the distance somewhere, a window broke and then another. "It seems that our time here is up," I said. Katelyn placed her free hand on top of the other, steadying her gun and then pointed it right at my face.

EIGHT
TARA

$\mathbf{M}$y stomach churned and I pressed my eyes shut, willing
the image away. But I could still hear Danny laughing.

"Huh," Christoph said. "I didn't think the little bitch had it in her."

Katelyn raised the gun and pointed it at Christoph. "Tell me there's another bullet in here, Danny."

"There's another bullet in there," Danny responded.

The smell of gunfire was strong in the air. Or maybe I imagined it. When
I knew I wouldn't lose what little food was in my stomach I opened my
eyes, avoiding the far wall of the room. Yet, with my peripheral vision, I
could see the wall was coated in blackened bits of brain matter and skull.
In a strange twisted heap on the floor was what was left of Mallory, the
First Lady of the United States – or former First Lady according to her
daughter.

"You're no better than them," I said.

Katelyn spun on her heels. "And you are?"

"She was your mother."

Katelyn chuckled once. "She gave birth to me. But that was it. It takes a
lot more than giving birth to be a mother."

She looked back at Christoph and fired another shot, killing him instantly.
Surprisingly, Danny Ruiz didn't react once. It was as if he knew all along
what would happen.

"We can find a cure," I whispered to Katelyn. "It doesn't have to be this
way. We can figure something out."

The door crashed in and three zombies stood in the doorway, their eyes
filled with lust for human flesh. Whatever control Katelyn had over these
zombies was no longer there and I wondered what she even did to gain it
in the first place.

With a snarling growl of a response the tallest zombie in the front, his
shirt a copper red from blood stains spoke to her. "It is done," he said.

She fired a third shot at Danny Ruiz and by then I had grown used to the
gruesome scene – or maybe just numb. "No, now it's done," she said.

The zombie looked around at the bloody room, grunted, and stepped
back through the door. When I turned to face Katelyn, her arm hung

limply at her side, as if the gun carried the weight of the world. Her eyes welled with unshed tears.

"I don't understand," I said.

"We all do what we need to do to survive," she said barely above a whisper. The chaos outside the room had dulled to the sound of shuffling feet and grunts as the zombies departed the warehouse, leaving us in the bloody wake. "And sometimes that means bargaining the ones you love for your own life."

"Danny arranged this whole thing?" I asked.

She nodded and a tear fell. "He thought it was his way to lead an army. But I couldn't let him win. Not after the sacrifice he forced me to make."

"We all have choices," I said, more to myself than to her.

"And I made mine."

"So now what?"

"Now, we move on and try to survive."

"I'm not sure it's worth it anymore," I said and walked out of the room and the scene that would haunt whatever nightmare-filled nights I had left. We had all become more than savage. We were and always had been our own worst enemies. A man-made virus was just a catalyst, not a cause.

I wasn't sure where I would go from there, but a tiny flicker of what defined us as humans still buried itself deep in my gut. That flicker was called Hope. To us, it was more important than food and water. For now, it was so far buried I didn't know it still existed, and when it resurfaced I wouldn't know how it would affect me. But, for the sake of whatever humanity remained - if any – I could only hope it resurfaced in time for me to do something about it.

BIOGRAPHY

DANA FREDSTI
AUTHOR

Dana Fredsti is an ex B-movie actress with a background in theatrical combat (a skill she utilized in Army of Darkness as a sword-fighting Deadite and fight captain). Through seven plus years of volunteering at Exotic Feline Breeding Facility/Feline Conservation Center, Dana's had a full-grown leopard sit on her feet, kissed by tigers, held baby jaguars and had her thumb sucked by an ocelot with nursing issues. . Her other hobbies include surfing (badly), collecting beach glass (obsessively), and wine tasting (happily).She's addicted to bad movies and any book or film, good or bad, which include zombies.

She is the author of the Ashley Parker series, touted as Buffy meets the Walking Dead, as well as what might be the first example of zombie noir, A Man's Gotta Eat What a Man's Gotta Eat, first published in Mondo Zombie edited by John Skipp, and more recently published as an eBook by Titan books. She also wrote the cozy noir mystery Murder for Hire: the Peruvian Pigeon, and co-author of What Women Really Want in Bed. She guest blogs frequently and has made numerous podcast and radio appearances. She lives in San Francisco with her husband and fellow author David Fitzgerald, their dog Pogeen, and a small horde of felines.

TOM LEVEEN
AUTHOR

Tom was born and raised in Arizona, where he lives with his wife. From the first time his second-grade teacher asked him to read to the first graders a short story he'd written, he was hooked. Writing fiction has been a part of his life ever since.

Tom has more than twenty-two years of theatre experience as an actor and director. He is the former Artistic Director of two companies: Is What It Is Theatre, a community theatre company; and Chyro Arts Venue, a mixed-use venue hosting theatre, live music, visual art, spoken word, independent film, and other arts. Tom is currently writing young adult fiction full time.
"The best part of the job is the school visits," he says. "I love meeting teachers, librarians, and students, talking about writing, publishing, and life in general. I write YA because for all the drama and trauma I went through in high school my life. When you're a student, anything is possible. The best stories are found in that time of life."

Tom is the author of PARTY, a YA novel told from 11 different points of view.

JOE MCKINNEY
AUTHOR

Joe McKinney has been a patrol officer for the San Antonio Police Department, a homicide detective, a disaster mitigation specialist, a patrol commander, and a successful novelist. His books include the four part Dead World series, Quarantined, Inheritance, Lost Girl of the Lake, Crooked House and Dodging Bullets. His short fiction has been collected in The Red Empire and Other Stories and Dating in Dead World and Other Stories. In 2011 McKinney received the Horror Writers Association's Bram Stoker Award for Best Novel. For more information go to http://joemckinney.wordpress.com.

ERIC A. SHELMAN
AUTHOR

When Eric started his writing career, an outsider would never have guessed he would eventually write about witches, serial killers and zombies. His first actual book release was Out of the Darkness: The Story of Mary Ellen Wilson, co-authored by Dr. Stephen Lazoritz. It is about the first successful rescue of an abused child in America. Little Mary Ellen was a 9-year-old who was rescued in 1874 by the American Society for the Prevention of Cruelty to Animals. The ASPCA.

His writing career began in the late 1980s in a very low-key way; writing short horror story after short horror story with really no idea how to go about it. He had poor character development, minimal plot lines and probably every other bad habit of inexperienced authors.
Check him out on YouTube. Just punch in "Eric Shelman Brown Eyed Girl." That video is approaching 4,000,000 hits.

So check out his writing. Download a sample for Kindle if you like. He thinks you'll like his style, because he writes very conversationally - he's not interested in creating prose that dances around your head before dropping into your ears. He gets to the point, but does it with some skill.

Visit his web page at www.ericshelman.com. He'll keep you updated on his new releases! You can also email him if you want to order shirts or autographed books, at authorshelman@gmail.com. ALSO, look him up on Facebook - it's AuthorShelman there, too.

MARK TUFO
AUTHOR

Mark Tufo was born in Boston Massachusetts. He attended UMASS Amherst where he obtained a BA and later joined the US Marine Corp. He was stationed in Parris Island SC, Twenty Nine Palms CA and Kaneohe Bay Hawaii. After his tour he went into the Human Resources field with a worldwide financial institution and has gone back to college at CTU to complete his masters.

He has written the Indian Hill trilogy with the first Indian Hill - Encounters being published for the Amazon Kindle in July 2009. He has since written the Zombie Fallout series and is working on a new zombie book. Mark Tufo was born in Boston Massachusetts. He attended UMASS Amherst where he obtained a BA and later joined the US Marine Corp. He was stationed in Parris Island SC, Twenty Nine Palms CA and Kaneohe Bay Hawaii. After his tour he went into the Human Resources field with a worldwide financial institution and has gone back to college at CTU to complete his masters.

He lives in Maine with his wife, three kids and two English bulldogs. Visit him at marktufo.com or http://zombiefallout.blogspot.com/ or http://www.facebook.com/pages/Mark-Tufo/133954330009843 for news on his next two installments of the Indian Hill trilogy and upcoming installments of the Zombie Fallout series.

T.M. WILLIAMS
AUTHOR

T.M. Williams began her writing career by accident when a song inspired a story. Once she discovered the writing bug she couldn't stop, pegging her 'The Accidental Writer'. Since beginning her writing career early in 2013 she has gone on to publish a dozen plus novels.

She has been recognized by award-winning international film director, Biju Viswanath, and has contributed writing to Kids Need to Read. Her blog can be found at www.theaccidentalwriterblog.com and website www.theaccidentalwriter.com